THE
REBELLIOUS
Heart

BEPPIE HARRISON

CAMDEN HILL PRESS

The Rebellious Heart

Published by Camden Hill Press
ISBN 978-0-9916620-5-0

Cover design by Dar Albert at wickedsmartdesigns.com
Formatting by Author E.M.S.

Published in the United States of America

For

Our three daughters and our son,
born on four different continents,
and now Ashley as well, sharing North America
with her husband
You are the treasures of my heart.

I love you.

TABLE OF CONTENTS

Gloucestershire, England 1813

IT BEGAN IN THAT EARLY morning, private part of the day before breakfast.

Well, to be exact it had begun nineteen years before when Melissa Preston was born, as her mother loved to recall, with the most wonderful crop of hair. The fuzz on her head had been dark then, or so her mother told her. As she grew older, the color lightened and the hair curled. Masses and masses of curls, until finally Melissa worried she was becoming primarily a support for a heavy mane of reddish-gold hair that curled defiantly whatever she did to it. It certainly took any opportunity to tumble out of the complicated network of pins she used in the attempt to keep the bush where it belonged, on the top of her head.

That early morning she had had enough. In a fit of exasperation caused by her hair's stubborn resistance every single morning of every single day, Melissa seized the scissors and began to cut. At first it was worse than before, but as she went on cutting, she realized her face was no longer overwhelmed by a mass of wild hair. Her eyes were now much more obvious, and rather a nice brilliant blue. It was even possible to notice she had a small, neat chin. Before when she passed a looking glass all she could see was the undisciplined mass of hair, rising like yeasted bread dough.

She had finished the top and the sides, or as far as was visible to her, when she realized she would need help for the back. She looked around the room and eyed her maid who had been making her bed and was now staring at her in horror.

1

"Miss Melissa!" Her voice was a terrified whisper.

"I need you to cut the back of my hair," Melissa told her.

The maid immediately backed away until she bumped into the bedpost. "Oh, I couldn't, miss. Your mother—she would be so angry with me."

"I daresay she will be upset with me, but that will be my problem. The die is already cast, as you can see. I cannot go about with long hair down my back to my waist and short hair everywhere else. I would collect a crowd if I left the house."

"But Miss Melissa! She will turn me out of my position!"

"Horsefeathers." Melissa had heard a man say that once and had been waiting for an opportunity to say it herself. It was a most satisfactory retort. "My mother is the gentlest soul in the world, and everyone who works in the manor knows that. It is entirely my responsibility, so if anyone is to be turned out, it will be me."

"Oh, no, Miss Melissa. She would never do that."

"Exactly." Melissa handed her the scissors with a flourish and sat down on the stool by her dressing table. "It would be faster if the scissors were larger, but we must work with what we have."

The maid, daring to scowl a little, took the scissors and tentatively began to cut.

"You can cut faster than that," Melissa told her. "It doesn't have to be cut absolutely straight. The hair curls right up whatever you do."

The maid went on cutting slowly and Melissa went on instructing her, but in the end the last long strand fell on the floor and Melissa stood up, an emancipated young woman. Her head was so light she almost feared she would drift up toward the ceiling. Best of all, when she looked in the looking glass, she saw a headful of short curls, tumbling from the top of her head to lie around her face, a few falling on her forehead.

Beaming, she went downstairs for breakfast.

She had expected her mother might be cross, but she did truly not anticipate that her mother's reaction to what was admittedly an impulsive action would be quite so explosive.

They encountered each other first at the breakfast table. Penelope, Melissa's younger sister and the only other member of the family still at home, was not there yet and so missed their mother's appalled reaction to Melissa's hair, or, more accurately, to Melissa's lack of it.

For a moment Melissa truly feared her mother was going to have an apoplectic fit right there at the breakfast table, and what would they do then?

Fortunately the moment passed and her mother's breathing returned to something closer to normal.

"What possessed you to do that?" She was still slightly wild-eyed.

"I am not interested enough in my hair to devote hours every day to coping with it."

"Melissa! Your hair was your crowning glory! Whoever will be attracted to a girl with hair shorter than many men?"

"Men only like long hair because they don't have to deal with it on their own heads. Even so, if there were any sensible men, they wouldn't care."

Her mother clearly had calmed down somewhat, but she was continuing to lament rather than listen to anything Melissa said. "But there won't be time for your hair to grow out to a suitable length for the Season next spring!"

Melissa had taken a piece of toast and was spreading marmalade thinly but dropped it on the plate and stared at her mother, appalled.

The Season next spring? She had gone through all the horrors of the Season this year: the anxious wait for someone to ask her to dance, the ill-disguised competition between the young ladies as to who was more beautiful and had the more fashionable gown, the struggle to look elegant while dancing with some well-meaning young man (she would give them that) who had no sense of rhythm and no care as to whether he put his huge feet down next to hers or on top of them. Was her mother seriously proposing that she go through all that again?

"Mother. Do you think I am going back to London next year?" Melissa tried to keep her voice respectful although she would rather have had a temper tantrum as she did when too young to express herself in words. Unfortunately, with her mother words did not seem to make a great impression. Had it been different when her father had been alive? That was seven years ago. Then three years ago her brother Hugh had left Gloucestershire for Ireland to take up the title and estate he had inherited from their uncle there. Since then, only women lived at the manor house.

Did it take having men around to make women sensible? That would be a discouraging thought. Pondering it as a maid poured more tea into her cup, she realized her mother was speaking.

"…many girls do not marry their first Season, so there will be nothing unusual about you returning next year."

"Mother! I thought I only had to do that once! It was dreadful and such a waste of good money. Don't you remember how much all those gowns cost? Then there were shoes, and flowers, and shawls and scarfs and stockings. I know you were helping Aunt Marcella with all the expenses—and yes, it was very good of her to sponsor me, but Mother, that cost a fortune and you ought not do it again, I am sure."

"And if we do not, how are you to find yourself a husband? You have not shown any interest in any of the men around here." Her mother, who had risen to her feet in her agitation, sat down again and buttered her own toast.

"Nor have they shown much interest in me," Melissa commented. "Not that I grieve over that. They are old or fat or looking for a wife more attractive than they are or richer than I am, although I know Hugh has been very generous in providing my dowry. But is there any one of them here you wish I would consider?"

"That is exactly why you must return to London next Season." Having proved her point to her own satisfaction, Mrs. Preston poured herself another cup from the teapot. Then she looked back at her daughter, again overwhelmed by her missing hair. "But what good it may do when you look as silly as a sheared sheep, I do not know. Perhaps we should keep you home next year to give your hair a chance to grow."

"But cropped hair—even shorter than mine—is all the crack now, Mother. They call it à la victime, in tribute to those unfortunate French."

Mrs. Preston gave her daughter a hard look. "Is that why you cut it?"

Melissa sighed. "No, Mother. I cut it because it was heavy and bushy and I was so tired of stabbing pins into my scalp to hold it in place. Why is it so important that I get married in any case? You know Father left me some money of my own."

"You will not spend your life as a spinster, my girl. Don't you realize that would mean living on the edges of another woman's family?" Mrs. Preston lifted the cup to her lips, stopping halfway, clearly arrested by a thought. "That is what we will do. We will send you to Ireland to stay with your brother and his wife. It will give your hair time to grow back and give you a taste of living in someone else's home as a dependent relative. I'm sure that Anne will be grateful for help with the children— the babe was born only recently, and young Charles is not three yet." Self-satisfaction beaming from her face, she raised the cup the last bit and drank.

"Ireland?" Melissa gasped. "How will it get me married—if that is your dearest wish—to send me to Ireland?"

"Perhaps it will be more sensible to postpone your return to London to give you a chance to decide what sort of life you want for yourself."

Her mother looked thoughtful. "Yes, your father left you a reasonable sum of money, but not enough for you to set up a household independently, and in any case, you will not have access to it until you are 25 years old. You have been making it increasingly obvious you are dissatisfied with living here with Penelope and me. I think it equally obvious you should try living somewhere else."

What appalled Melissa the most was that her mother was no longer so visibly cross and indignant. She sounded very much as if she had made up her mind.

But Ireland!

Admittedly she had no desire to return to the whole matchmaking circus of the London Season. She was not well suited for constant sociability with people she did not know when she doubted they had little in common. She point blank refused to enter into the sly competition with the other girls making their debut. She'd had no intention of returning to the merry-go-round for a second or third year if unsuccessful the first time around. True, there had been two or three girls she had enjoyed. Still, there was so little time to develop any kind of friendship during the frenzy of the balls and dinners and evenings at the theater and concerts. Friendship mattered little when it was more important to be seen than to hear words or music.

The men she had met? Well, a few were boys with unfortunate complexions and not much skill at dancing. Most of them had formidable mamas. There were some dashing gentlemen, but few of that sort seemed to take much interest in her. Perhaps it was the mass of ungovernable hair? The older men, and there were some of those as well, made her uneasy and grateful her dowry was not substantial enough to capture their attention.

No. She would be considerably relieved not to be forced to return to London for more. But Ireland? What did she know about Ireland?

It was far away, across the Irish Sea. Her brother lived there. He had a wife now and two children. It was very odd to think of Hugh with two children. He had always been too old to be a playmate, but she remembered him best as a very young man who teased her and spent a lot of time working with the steward on the estate. From what her mother reported about his infrequent letters, he was doing well there in Ireland and was reportedly very happy. It seemed he spent a great deal of time improving conditions on the estate. What had their uncle, who was his predecessor, been doing?

Hugh's activities would undoubtedly have interested her more if she had been his mother. Certainly their mother was visibly cheered each time she received a letter. But the life the letters described was not exactly an inviting prospect for Melissa herself.

It sounded even more boring than Gloucestershire.

For the hundredth time, she wished she had been born male. Men had so many more possibilities. They could go off by themselves, and no one raised an eyebrow.

Her eyes widened at the thought. Of course!

"Mother," she said, taking care to sound neither difficult nor resentful, "how on earth can I go off to Ireland by myself? That is a very long journey, and would it not be unsuitable for me to travel alone?"

To her gratification, her mother looked thoughtful. "I shall have to give that some consideration. Perhaps I can take you as far as the port at Holyhead, which is no great distance, and Hugh could meet you in Dublin. I'll have to consult him."

Melissa's heart dropped. This was beginning to sound more and more inevitable. Surely her mother did not intend her to spend the foreseeable future in Ireland!

"But Mother, I don't want to go to Ireland." She tried to keep her tone reasonable, but it came out more like a mutter.

"I appreciate that fact," Mrs. Preston said. Her voice was firm. "The difficulty is you are becoming more and more unmanageable."

Melissa sat up straight, indignantly. "I am not! Is all this simply because I cut my hair?"

"Cut *off* your hair," her mother corrected. "Not precisely. It is simply the latest example of your unwillingness to behave in a way suitable for the daughter of a good family. You came back to Gloucestershire at the very first opportunity instead of pursuing your opportunities in London. Then you have excuses for why you cannot participate in social activity here. You have made it impossible to return to London next year. You are cross much of the time, which is an undesirable example for Penelope. Thank goodness she is still young enough so most of it does not concern her, but it most definitely concerns me. At the rate you are going you will end your days as a spinster, destined to spend your life on the edges of someone else's family."

"But I have not met anyone with whom I can imagine spending a week, never mind the rest of my life."

"Then perhaps you are looking for the wrong qualities."

"Someone I can talk to? Someone I can imagine liking?" Melissa jumped to her feet, embarrassed and angry that her voice caught, almost like a sob. She marched out of the room.

Mrs. Preston came along rapidly after her.

"Melissa, that is precisely what I am talking about. I do not understand how you have reached your present age with no comprehension of the role in society you were born to fill. Do you not want a home of your own someday? Do you expect to die childless? This is your time to make yourself attractive and obliging, not behave like a hedgehog with prickles in every direction."

Melissa stalked ahead of her mother. "I cannot say I appreciate being treated like a piece of fish that will go bad if left out too long."

The sound of her mother's footsteps still followed her. "I admit that is not the most attractive picture, but the analogy is not entirely misplaced. Your youth is a precious asset, and it does not last forever. I do not know how I can make it clearer to you the mistakes you are making. Perhaps some time in Ireland will clarify your thinking." The footsteps stopped. "I do wish your father were still alive. He would surely point out to you the folly of your arguments."

Melissa started to climb the stairs, and then turned to face her mother. "Perhaps what you really want is for me to marry an Irishman."

"An Irishman? Of course not. Let me point out your brother is a marquess. He and his wife are part of the established and perfectly respectable English aristocratic community there. It is not as if I am turning you loose in Dublin to make your own way."

"Perhaps Dublin is better than you think," Melissa snapped, and turned to continue to march up the stairs. "I very much doubt my father would have exiled me to Ireland," she tossed over her shoulder as she reached the top and headed for her bedchamber.

Ireland! Now what was she going to do?

London

THE LETTER LAY ON THE table in the front hall, next to the silver basket where his mother's friends left their calling cards.

Ethan Hawthorne poked at it with his finger. "Is this the letter you mentioned?"

His mother, who had just come out to the front hall—not quite grand enough to be called an entrance hall—looked at him suspiciously. "Of course. How many letters from Ireland do you normally receive?"

The obvious and accurate answer would have been "none," but Ethan jerked his eyebrows up and down instead. "Then I will read it," he said, glancing over at his mother in part to see if she recognized she was being teased.

She did not.

"Well, I should hope so," she huffed, and turned to return to the morning room.

Ethan unfolded and flattened the letter out on the table. It was, as he expected, from his uncle, the Earl of Kendall.

My dear nephew:

I was riding with my steward over the fields today and it came to me sharply that I will not be the master here forever. This land that belongs to us—me now and you in the future—is good land and will repay richly whatever effort is expended on it.

It occurred to me that it would be well if you could come here to learn some of what I was taught by my father, and he by his. You do not know this land and this country, and it would be unfortunate if the progress we have made should be compromised by the

8

necessity of your learning what needs to be done without guidance from those more experienced.

If you come in the next month or so, you would have the opportunity of taking part in the harvest.

The Countess and I welcome you if you choose to come.

Yours faithfully
Charles, Earl of Kendall

Good Lord, the man expected him to come to Ireland. Immediately, it appeared, as he suggested he be there for the harvest. Although Ethan spent most of his time in London, his father had left him a modest estate in Kent, and he knew enough of the agricultural calendar to appreciate that the harvest would be beginning in September. It was now late August.

He considered what he knew about travel between London and Ireland, which admittedly was not much. He did know there was the Irish Sea in between, which would have to be crossed. He scrubbed his memory for the location of his uncle's estate in Ireland, and after a moment of pondering, came up with County Meath. That sounded about right. As he understood, that was on the eastern side of Ireland, which would be a benefit. At least he would not have to travel across the country. If he went, that is.

It did not look as if there was a great deal of choice in the matter.

"What did dear Charles want?" His mother's curiosity had clearly overwhelmed her pique at her son's casual attitude. She was now standing in the door of the morning room, as if she were mid-errand and not hovering.

"He wants me to come to Ireland for the harvest." Ethan was discomposed enough to abandon his usual enthusiasm for ruffling his mother's sense of propriety.

"How nice of him," she said, her tone happy.

"Mother, this is Ireland we are talking about. Not Brighton." Everyone knew of the Prince Regent's revels at his remarkable Royal Pavilion there.

His mother refused to rise to the bait. "I would think it makes great sense for you to go while Charles is still alive. You will have enormous responsibilities later and the more you learn now the easier you will find it then."

Ethan glared at his mother. "You sound as if it is settled that I will go to Ireland when Uncle Charles dies and I inherit the title and estate."

"Your father always told me that should we inherit, we would go to Ireland, and that was back in the days when it seemed quite likely Charles and Elizabeth could have a son. But they only had the two daughters—twins, they were, and it's fortunate both of them lived." A trace of an old worry crossed her face. "Both of them married now, with children. So you will not be trapped in the society of aging relatives only. Although I believe Aunt Tryphena does still live with them," and her voice trailed off as she turned to return to the morning room.

Ethan looked at her retreating back in amazement. His mother thought he might choose to live in Ireland? Miles away from London and the brilliant life he enjoyed there?

"Live in Ireland?"

She stopped where she was, perhaps startled by the outrage in his voice. "Well, that is where your land and responsibilities will be."

"Mother, Ireland is a very long away from here—a long way from everything important. The distance is only one problem. Worse, the place is full of Irishmen, people of no culture or refinement, but apparently restless and rebellious. Do you seriously contemplate the notion I would choose to live in danger of violent rebellion so far from civilization?"

Her hands, holding the needlework she had been working on, dropped to her side. "Ethan, from everything your father ever told me, Kendall House is a substantial residence on an extensive estate. Your uncle Charles is a man of integrity and considerable refinement. Generations of the family have lived there for many, many years, almost back to the Normans. It is not as if you have been invited to Africa."

"But they are Irish."

"They are not, any more than you are. They are English, English in their speech and English in their manners. I begin to believe that you must go there, Ethan, to find out what is true and what is not about the history of your family. Your father missed Ireland to his dying day. It's a great pity you never had the proper opportunity to speak about Ireland with him."

This was not the first occasion his mother had lamented that Ethan had only been eleven years old when his father drowned in a boating accident. He sighed heavily.

"There was another one of their rebellions in 1803, for God's sake. Do you want to have to worry about me every moment I'm there?"

"I'd never taken you for a coward." His mother, having loosed the heavy artillery, turned with a sweeping motion to return to the morning room, leaving him the choice of following her to continue to argue, or to remain in the hallway, seething.

He remained in the hallway, but he had the unpleasant presentiment he would not be spending the autumn moving pleasurably from one friend's house to another's. Since London after early summer was largely abandoned by the better and the best of society who retreated to their country estates, he had planned, as usual, to accept their hospitality. Instead, it seemed, he would be tramping around Irish fields, attempting to remedy his almost complete ignorance of what grew in them.

He had, however, not entirely committed himself to that course yet.

For the next two or three days there was no discussion of the subject unless he counted his mother's gentle enquiries as to whether he had booked his passage yet. Since he had not, Ethan chose to avoid her whenever possible. If avoidance was impossible, his invariable reply was "All in good time, Mother," followed by a complete change of topic. At times he found himself in the extraordinary position of actually inquiring how she had spent the previous day. He would even ask about the truly remarkable bonnet or the new scarf lying on the table. Whatever had caught his eye.

"Do you care, Ethan?" his mother would murmur.

His younger sister, Emmeline, showing more tact than he would have given her credit for (she was, after all, only fifteen years old), asked no questions about these bizarre exchanges, at least until the third day.

Then, she and Ethan finding themselves alone in the library, her control broke.

"What on earth is going on?" she asked, casting a quick look at the library door to make sure it was still closed.

"Whatever do you mean?" Ethan kept his voice deliberately bland.

"Ethan, I am not an idiot," she said with some spirit. "I have done my best not to pry, but I am very curious. What are you and our mother talking about?"

As he was ten years older than she was, he attempted at first to take refuge in his seniority. "I cannot think how that concerns you."

The year before, Emmeline would have dealt with her frustration by bursting into tears, but she was clearly gaining some maturity. "I believe that when more than two people are present at some common gathering—at dinner, for example—politeness requires the conversation be general. I thought I had been further taught it is rude to discuss secrets when others are present. Am I mistaken?"

Ethan could not entirely prevent his mouth from twitching. When had Emmeline learned the art of the gracious set-down? He bowed his head slightly in recognition of her new skill. As he contemplated what to say, it suddenly occurred to him since she was obviously growing up faster than he had given her for doing, it might be interesting to see what her opinion of the expedition to Ireland might be.

"Our uncle in Ireland has invited me to come there to learn something about the estate I am presumably going to inherit."

"Presumably?" Emmeline turned to him with what appeared to be genuine confusion. "Who else could inherit? You are the son of Uncle Charles's brother, and as far as I know, there is no one else with a claim."

Ethan shrugged. "If I should predecease Uncle Charles, the title and estate would pass to someone else. There must be second cousins somewhere about."

"Are you feeling faint?" she inquired. "Or perhaps you propose to end it all in the village pond."

"I'm sure I could find a body of water closer than Kent," Ethan said, "but no, it was not my intention. Although it might be narrowly preferable to going to Ireland with what would appear to be the intention of taking up residence there one day."

"What's wrong with Ireland?"

Maybe education for young ladies left out salient facts. Ethan fixed her with a steely gaze. "Apart from the fact it's on the wrong side of the Irish Sea and it rains there more often than not, it is populated by a host of uneducated, slow-thinking Irish people. These people, from all I hear, drink incessantly and are bound to priests and superstition. They seem to spend most of their time planning rebellion and treachery against the sensible British who have been able to raise the place to a level of prosperity the native Catholic population can neither match nor understand."

"Oh." Emmeline looked thoughtful. "But Uncle Charles and his family must not find Ireland such a despicable place. Our ancestors have lived there for generations."

"You asked me what was wrong with Ireland. I have no idea why our family has thrived there for so long."

"Then perhaps it would be a good idea to spend some time there yourself and find out."

Ethan held his head—a trifle theatrical, he knew, but desperate times call for desperate measures. "What is wrong with the females in this house?"

Emmeline's mouth curved wickedly. "Perhaps it is not the females who are mistaken, but the male."

He eyed his sister, and unwillingly noticed that not only did she now argue more sensibly, but she was turning into an exceedingly attractive young girl. Her hair, as dark as his own, was thick and glossy, and her eyes flashed with life, whether she was laughing or arguing with someone. A nice nose, too, and without thinking his hand moved to his own face. He had always taken secret pleasure in the classic shape of his nose. The rest of his face had little extraordinary to offer except perhaps long eyelashes, which his mother was prone to remark on to his embarrassment.

Would Emmeline be one of the successes when her turn came to make her debut at the Season? He would be quite proud to escort her, which would also give him the opportunity to make certain the more unreliable of his acquaintances did not get within a mile of her.

Unless of course he was in Ireland. He groaned.

"What is wrong with you?" she asked, her look suddenly changing to one of concern.

"Nothing of great importance," he answered promptly. His life would not be improved by focusing his mother's attention on his health or lack of it. Even Ireland would be preferable.

Emmeline raised an eyebrow. "Well, for whatever it is worth, I think you should go to Ireland and see what it is really like. It probably has little resemblance to the dreadful place you are imagining. Then too I have heard terrible stories about how mercenary and cruel some of the middlemen employed by English landowners are. When it becomes your responsibility, I would rather have you deal with our Irish tenants. I understand that many owners of Irish property leave them to the mercy of the middleman, who has no interest in the welfare of people who have probably lived on our family's land for generations. Middlemen generally would rather line their pockets with the rents, do nothing to improve the property, and send as small a proportion as he dares of what he collects to you."

"Heaven above!" Ethan could not prevent a broad grin from stretching his face. "I had no idea we had such a powerful voice for the Irish right here in our very own house."

"You can laugh all you want." Emmeline's offended dignity was impressive. "But I believe I have listened more to people who know what they are talking about than you seem to have done. I do think you should go to Ireland."

Ethan could not prevent himself from reaching over and mussing her shining dark hair, even as she squeaked in protest and tried to twist away.

"Now I am absolutely convinced you should go to Ireland or Timbucktoo or somewhere a long long way away from here!" Her voice was becoming quite unladylike.

"You would miss me," Ethan said, letting her loose.

"Give me a chance to find out," she muttered, using both hands to restore her hair to an approximation of its former order.

He stared gloomily at the floor. What had started out as a bare possibility of his being away from England for a considerable period of time was becoming more and more likely.

3

ETHAN WAS NOT ENTIRELY SURPRISED to find his feet walking him onto the mail boat sailing from Holyhead in Wales to Dublin.

His final decision to agree to his uncle's suggestion was not made gladly. In fact, he managed almost two weeks without discussing it at all. Two weeks during which every time he passed his mother she eyed him significantly. His sister was not much better. Every time he passed her, she asked him why he was being so stupidly stubborn. Lord knows what they would have said if he had ever been at home long enough for a conversation. Ethan made it his business not to find out.

Most of his meals he ate with friends, the same friends with whom he spent most of his evenings, evenings requiring a high alcoholic content for full enjoyment. It was much easier that way. By the time he came back to his home (on those evenings when he had not fallen asleep on somebody else's convenient chaise longue or other horizontal surface) the lights were out and not only his mother and sister but the servants were abed. In the mornings he roused himself to face another day, washed, shaved, and dressed and took care to eat his morning toast and egg and cup of black coffee when neither mother nor sister were about. Should he encounter either of them in the hall his mother looked at him significantly, and Emmeline asked him why he was being such an idiot. Ethan would escape again.

It was at some point during the second week he returned earlier and more sober than had been his recent pattern. Fortunately both Mrs. Hawthorne and Emmeline had already retired, but there was still a fire in the sitting room as the day, summer or not, had been chilly.

Ethan sank into a chair and happened to glance over at the small table next to the chair. There was the wretched letter from his uncle—had his mother thoughtfully placed it there? He had had blurry moments when he wondered vaguely where it had gone.

Now he picked it up and looked at it again.

It was not written in an unpleasant tone, nor did it order him to do anything. In fact, when he read it over two or three times, he had to admit what he had always known: it was a friendly, pleasant letter from one man to his successor, offering to provide preparation for a job for which he may never have asked but was inevitably to be his lot in life.

Perhaps it was time to stop running away.

There were a few necessary questions to work out. How soon was harvest? Was it humanly possible to get there in time? There was most certainly no time to write his uncle and ask for answers to either of those. Not to write and receive an answer, at least.

So that night, hoping his head was clear enough to allow him to write intelligibly, he wrote a brief answer to the earl explaining he would shortly be on his way, and left the letter on the table in the front hall, confident that his mother would make sure it went out with the morning post.

Feeling nobly the had done his duty, and more than slightly uneasy about what he was getting himself into, Ethan went upstairs and fell into his bed.

Traveling from London to Holyhead was about what Ethan had anticipated. The first day was the worst, with the coach being most crowded and his own head causing misery because of a more than generous farewell party hosted by several friends. The brandy and wine had been better than they ordinarily drank, which meant they slipped down the throat more easily, but also contributed to difficulties in deciding when enough was enough. Ethan managed to pull himself together sufficiently for a farewell breakfast with his mother and Emmeline, although he ate little. He was surprised and more touched than he expected to be by Emmeline's heartfelt farewell, delivered with tears and a close embrace. His mother used the time at the breakfast table to deliver an examination into what Ethan remembered of the family connections she had been trying to make clear to him since he'd read his uncle's letter. The exercise would have gone more easily and harmoniously if he had been prepared for it. He was not, and the pain in his head—which he chose not to mention under the circumstances—was undoubtedly responsible for the blankness of his mind. At the moment of departure his mother was more exasperated than mournful.

On the second and third days, the numbers of fellow travelers fluctuated, and sometimes Ethan had plenty of space and other times it seemed the coach was crowded with women and children, for whom more space was required due to their propensity to move around. Few of the children seemed to notice when they trod on the other travelers' feet or fell against them when jostled by the coach's swaying.

On the fourth day the coach worked its way to Holyhead, and as the packet boat was not due until the next day, there was another night in a travelers' inn, which was to say it had basic facilities and few comforts. The packet arrived late in the morning, and by the time all the incoming passengers and their possessions were removed onto dry land, it was obvious they were not going to be able to leave until four or five o'clock, which at least allowed Ethan to have his dinner at the inn. He had been advised by some of his fellow passengers the food there was unexciting, but still better than what would be available on the packet, so he ate at the same table as three others taking the same boat. It was hard to imagine that the food on the packet boat would be worse.

All things considered, it was a relief when the time came to get on board.

The cabins had already been reserved when Ethan bought his ticket, so he found himself in the central lounge or gathering room with the other general passengers. He located an unoccupied bench, and did his best with the carpet bag he had brought with him. His heavier luggage was wherever the crew handling the baggage had taken it. Fortunately the voyage was a smooth one, but Ethan could have done without the disturbed sounds from the horses on the deck below when the packet set off under sail and the unfortunate creatures had to adjust to the constant movement of the boat under their feet. Either he grew accustomed to the noises or the horses ceased to complain, but when he was awakened from his restless sleep, his head cushioned by the carpet bag, it was dawn and the port of Howth, just outside Dublin, was in sight.

There lay Ireland ahead of him, and whatever was about to happen next. Ethan shook his head, tried to straighten his hair and his clothing, and considered how he was to get to Drogheda, wherever that was, where his uncle was to meet him.

All around him the other passengers were gradually gathering themselves together, collecting their hand baggage—in some cases remarkably extensive—and moving to the windows to see what was to be seen.

Ethan glanced out and saw, to his amusement, that the coach of one of the men he had eaten with at the hotel in Holyhead was right outside that particular window, and the man was bustling around it. He abruptly seemed to focus on Ethan on the other side of the glass and motioned to him. Ethan's surprise must have shown on his face, because the man gestured even more imperiously, beckoning him.

Ethan hesitated for a moment, and then decided it was probably easier to go on out to see what the man had in mind than to try to communicate in dumb-show, and so grabbed his carpet bag and went down the short corridor and up the stairs—really more like a ladder—to the deck.

The packet seemed to be in the midst of sidling up to the dock as he glanced around to see where his one-time tablemate might be. Momentarily torn between fascination with the docking procedure and the obligation to find out what the man had wanted him for, he decided to locate the coach first and then see if the packet was still being eased against the dock.

He had just turned in that direction when the man, from all appearances gentry, came toward him.

"How was your night?" he asked, with a slight grin.

"Not as bad as I was prepared for it to be," Ethan replied. "And yours?"

"Worse than I had hoped. The coach rocked with the wind as well as with the motion of the sea!" He shrugged and laughed, and then extended his hand. "Thomas Halleck, of Chelsea."

"Ethan Hawthorne of Gorse House, Kent," Ethan replied, giving his country address rather than the less distinguished neighborhood where he lived in London, although Chelsea was rather on the fringes of Town.

"It occurred to me when I saw you at the window that you might be unfamiliar with Dublin," Mr. Halleck said. "Do you have someone meeting you?"

Ethan shook his head. "I was hoping there would be some hacks at the dock who could take me to the place where I could catch a coach for Drogheda. My uncle is expecting me there."

"Have you a great deal of other luggage?" Mr. Halleck indicated the carpet bag with a motion of his head.

"Just a small trunk."

"Well, I could certainly take you to the coaching inn," Mr. Halleck said. "We could stop for a breakfast on the way. It would be more palatable than the last time we dined together." He raised one eyebrow and they both chuckled.

"That would be very kind of you." Ethan did a sort of half-bow. It *was* kind of him. Was this sort of generosity typical of life in Ireland? He considered and gave his own head a quick shake. Ireland had nothing to do with it. Mr. Halleck of Chelsea was as English as he was himself. Perhaps he just wanted some company for breakfast.

Which was apparently true. Ethan was able to be of some assistance during the complicated procedure of lifting the coach off the deck and setting it on its wheels at the dockside. The horses were retrieved. They stamped their feet uncertainly when the coachman first led them onto solid ground, but fairly soon seemed to grasp that the insecure footing on the boat had come to an end. Their normal expectations were correct once more: the ground stayed put.

By that time the other passengers had dispersed and the dockside was quiet as Ethan and Mr. Halleck, having rounded up his driver and footman, climbed into the coach and were carried off towards the city. The city itself seemed to be a curious mix of wide streets and gracious Georgian houses—like some of the finest townhouses in London—but at the same time there was a somewhat shabby air to the place.

"You should have seen it twenty years ago," Mr. Halleck said, as they pulled up in front of another inn and climbed out of the coach. "This is a reliable place for a meal," he explained briefly, and then went back to talking about Dublin. "Most of the prosperous English residents who were here in government service of one kind or another have left after the Act of Union when the Irish parliament was dissolved and Irish representation was moved to London. So did many of the noblemen who decided they would be more influential if they lived in there as well. It didn't happen all at once, of course, but Dublin now is not what it was before."

Ethan tried to remember when the Act of Union had taken place—back when he was a boy, almost certainly. Mr. Halleck must be a fair bit older than he was, but he had not been so aware of it before. Following him into the inn, Ethan glanced about, seeing for himself what Mr. Halleck had reported. The furnishings had once been elegant, but the place had a neglected feel to it. The curtains were of fine fabric (his mother made enough fuss about such things that Ethan had learned more than he intended to about the quality of such things as drapes and upholstery) but just faded enough to be noticeable.

When they reached the residents' dining room, however, it was obvious the food was still plentiful and delicious. Ethan ate more than he intended, reminding himself he had hardly been tempted to gluttony by the meals on the road, and he would be back on the road later today, heading north to Drogheda.

"Do you know Drogheda?" he asked Mr. Halleck.

Mr. Halleck shrugged. "I've not been there. It has history—so many places here in Ireland do—but I doubt there's much to attract a visitor now."

Ethan sighed. "A pity. I will be living near there for a time. That will be the closest town."

"Well, there are few towns of any size outside of Dublin—well, apart from Belfast, of course."

Ethan nodded. It had, apparently, been fruitless to hope there might be anything more interesting than learning about agriculture in the vicinity. The conversation wandered on in other directions; it seemed that Mr. Halleck had business in Dublin often enough so that he was familiar with the city, but never stayed long enough to develop friendships that were more than casual. It was the obvious explanation of how he knew it was possible to bring his carriage over on the packet with him, and why he welcomed having company over breakfast.

After they had dawdled over coffee—deliciously strong and hot—they had the carriage brought round again and went off to the inn from which mail coaches north to Drogheda and Belfast were dispatched.

"If there is not a coach leaving this afternoon, we can return to the inn where we had breakfast for tonight and then come at the proper hour tomorrow," Mr. Halleck said easily. Ethan nodded at him with gratitude. He had been wondering what to do with himself if in fact he would have to spend the night.

This was his first experience of travel outside of England and Scotland. Ireland was technically part of Britain. Formalizing that was what the Act of Union in 1801 (the date came easily to mind now; perhaps he had paid more attention in school than he had thought) had been about. Still, it seemed distinctly foreign to him, and he felt more out of place than he had ever done in the course of his ramblings between country estates on the other side of the Irish Sea, even traveling in Scotland. It was not a comfortable feeling.

It was therefore with inner rejoicing that he discovered a coach was due to depart for the north within the hour. He and Mr. Halleck bid each other a warmer farewell than Ethan would have predicted from their joint experience of the sorry inn in Holyhead, and made arrangements to keep in touch. If by any chance Ethan would be coming south to Dublin again he would contact Mr. Halleck to find out whether he planned to be in Dublin then as well.

It was much more comfortable to wave Mr. Halleck off with the firm knowledge the coach for Drogheda had his trunk already loaded. Behind him in the courtyard two husky men who spoke such a thick Irish brogue Ethan could hardly understand them were loading the last items to be carried on the coach. It was a considerable relief to him when the man who sold tickets for the coach spoke English clearly enough for Ethan to comprehend, Irish flavor and all. He could be confident he had the right ticket in his possession.

Of course, he still did not understand exactly how he was to make his way from Drogheda to his uncle's estate, but so far he had followed the instructions in his uncle's brief note that had come just before his departure, and all had turned out as planned.

This was just the next step.

Irish roads were worse than English roads.

Of course Ethan could have predicted that, but having had what he expected confirmed did not make the jouncing of the coach any less trying to the human body. There was one brief pause on the way to change horses, and to give the passengers (there were five of them) the opportunity to purchase something to eat and drink so long as they did so quickly.

The other passengers seemed cheerful enough, chattering much of the time among themselves—again Ethan found them too difficult to understand to follow the conversation easily. Besides, the fatigue of his journey from London to Holyhead followed by the restless night on the packet boat was more and more difficult to overcome. In the end, he allowed himself to doze, Irish voices buzzing in his ears, and the bumping of the coach over the rough roads rocking him to sleep. Surely they would rouse him when they reached Drogheda.

In fact they did.

"Mr. Hawthorne, sir?" A voice shouted through the open door into the coach.

Ethan shook himself into something closer to wakefulness.

"Yes?" he asked thickly.

"Ye for the Earl of Kendall?" The questioner looked Irish to him, if better dressed than many he'd seen.

The Earl of Kendall? Ethan forced himself to sit up straight and pay attention.

"Yes, I am his nephew," he said, making the words as clear and distinct as possible. Suppose these Irishmen found it as difficult to understand him as he found them?

"Right. I be 'is groom. I 'ave a horse for you. Leave yer trunk here, and we'll pick it up w' the cart tomorrow."

Ah. So here he was on what was bound to be the final stage. He was glad he'd caught some sleep on the coach; better to nap there than doze on horseback. There was the bustle of getting his trunk removed from the coach—they were again at an inn, but this one had no courtyard. The coach simply stopped where it was and anyone else trying to use the road had to either make a way around it or wait until the coach moved on.

When the horse was brought to him, already saddled, it was clearly a fine one. Well, it would be. Irish horses had a famous reputation, after all, and it was reassuring his uncle chose to keep such a splendid horse for ordinary errands, which collecting him from Drogheda had to be.

Under the supervision of his uncle's groom, Ethan sauntering along behind, the trunk was safely stored at the inn, and with the groom riding out slightly ahead, the two of them set off down the road to Kendall House.

It was farther than Ethan might have expected, but the ride was a pleasant way to travel after being shut into the coach for so long. The countryside was magnificent as they left the town behind them. Ethan was grateful he had the luck to make the trip on a beautiful day, when the sky was bright blue with puffy white clouds sailing by now and then, as if they had been selected for scenic value. There were wildflowers growing here and there, but what mainly impressed him was the incredible variety of green colors. It seemed as if each tree and bush and shrub had picked out its own shade, and the grasses of the fields had chosen from a different slate of greens. The air was fresh. He could almost smell the tang of the sea, although they were riding inland, away from the coast.

He was abruptly quite relieved he was making this journey now, when his uncle was alive and in complete charge, rather than coming after his uncle was gone, the estate had fallen into possible shambles, and he responsible for picking up the pieces. He was, in fact, grateful to his mother for pressuring him to take up his uncle's invitation. Not that he had any immediate intention of telling her that. Not all of her advice was quite so much to the point, and to give her credit for getting this one right would almost certainly open floodgates to a great deal more.

The information he had been given about Drogheda being the nearest town seemed to be quite accurate as well. The road continued before them as it did behind, with not so much as a village to be passed through. The countryside looked to be cultivated, however. Somebody presumably owned all this land and was putting it to good use. There had been several herds of well-kept cattle that they passed, as well as corn of various varieties. From time to time he saw a lane leading off, either to the left or the right. Lanes leading to other houses, he supposed.

He had a host of questions he would have liked to ask the groom, but they kept moving forward at a steady pace, and Ethan was not entirely confident he would understand what the man said if he caught up and rode alongside. This Irish brogue problem he was going to have to master, and soon. There was no use being dependent on family members, who presumably spoke intelligibly, to explain what everyone else was saying.

His mind went on rambling. The road seemed much smoother when he was on horseback than he had imagined it when riding in the coach. Even so, it would be good to arrive somewhere and stay there, for a while at least. Travel—at least serious travel from one part of the world to another—appeared to be the sort of thing to appreciate most when not actually doing it.

He was enormously relieved when the groom ahead slowed and turned down one of the lanes, horse and rider hesitating before going forward to make sure that Ethan was still following. At last. Surely a lane must lead somewhere reasonably soon.

The question, apparently, was what was "reasonably soon." The two men continued on for considerably farther than Ethan would have expected. Just as he was about to ask, probably more sharply than he should, how far away this Kendall House was, the groom turned and called to him over his shoulder.

"We be comin' by the back way, sir," he said. "This road be t' the stables."

Ethan nodded. He expected he probably grunted as well, but decided not to attempt further conversation.

Then it was there. The stables were to his right, a well-kept handsome building, and to the left in the near distance was the substantial stone bulk of Kendall House. It was an impressive mansion. His mother probably would not be surprised by it, but Ethan had to admit he was. His uncle, an earl (he reminded himself), was clearly a man of considerable wealth. He followed the groom past the open door to the stables, and rode on, slowing, to the portico protecting the entrance to the mansion.

There, at long last, he could stop. As the groom ahead of him had done, he dismounted, his legs for the first few steps feeling unreliable. Had it been that long since he'd had a long run of riding? As he walked toward the steps leading up to the massive front door, the door itself opened, and a neatly dressed butler stood there to welcome him.

"Mr. Hawthorne, sir," he said as Ethan came up the steps toward him. Behind him in the hall Ethan could see two other figures approaching, the first presumably the earl, and with him his wife.

"Ethan," the earl said with more warmth than Ethan had expected, "it is good to have you here at last."

"Welcome." The countess was smiling and her voice welcoming. She was slender and surprisingly elegantly dressed, at least compared to Ethan's expectations. His vision of life in Ireland was undergoing rapid reconstruction.

"Yes, indeed," the earl said, coming out to take Ethan's hand and shake it heartily. "Welcome to my house"—his smile was more like a grin—"and yours to be."

IT FELT VERY GOOD TO sit down on a chair that wasn't moving.

It seemed the last time Ethan had done so was vastly long ago, but when he devoted his mind to the problem he realized it was only that very morning, when he had breakfasted with Mr. Halleck. It felt it had been much, much longer.

His aunt and uncle brought him into the music room to sit and have a cup of tea and unwind a little. He first tried to address them by their titles, but Aunt Elizabeth stopped him immediately.

"We are family and family know each other by their names." Her voice, although light and cultivated, had been quite firm. "It is Uncle Charles and Aunt Elizabeth, please."

He had not anticipated so warm a reception.

"We were not sure when you would arrive, so we thought it better not to attempt a family dinner today." His uncle's dress was the same as any English gentleman at home, right down to his carpet slippers, plainly visible as he had one knee crossed over the other. "But tomorrow our daughter Anne and her husband Hugh, the Marquess of Ashbourne, will be here to join us with their two small children."

"Not at the table," Aunt Elizabeth put in hastily.

"And they too have a guest from England." His uncle continued serenely with no notice taken of the interruption. "Hugh's younger sister Melissa has just recently arrived here to spend some time with her brother and sister-in-law. Since their daughter is still very, very young—"

"Only one month old," Aunt Elizabeth explained.

"—I'm sure Melissa's help will be appreciated by Anne."

Ethan wondered how many husbands would accept a wife breaking into his conversation so placidly. It seemed as if his aunt and uncle had mutual understanding between them.

"I will look forward to meeting them," he said. "I understand your other daughter is married as well?"

Aunt Elizabeth sighed. "Yes, and very happily, too, but she is living in Dublin with her husband and daughter. We really ought not to complain, since they have a cottage near here, and Caroline and her little girl come up to visit regularly. But they are not here now."

Ah. So Caroline was the daughter married to the Irishman. Interesting.

A tea tray had been brought in, and Ethan was more grateful than he expected to be for a fresh, hot cup. It was the strong Irish tea he had been served since his arrival, but it tasted good to him then, as did the shortbread biscuits served with it.

"Would you like the chance to rest for an hour or so? We planned on a later dinner tonight, so you would have a chance to nap for a bit, if that would suit you." His aunt was obviously keeping an eye on him, because no sooner had he lowered his empty cup than she made the offer.

Ethan could imagine nothing more desirable. Somehow it seemed a very long time since he had slept in a bed, although he must have done— two, three nights ago, would it be? Certainly not the night just before, because he had been on the mail packet crossing the Irish Sea, and in retrospect the day felt as if it had gone on for a very long time already, although it was still full light.

"Thank you, Aunt Elizabeth. I would appreciate that." He hoped his voice conveyed some of his gratitude, but feared what he mainly sounded was tired.

That may have been true, because his aunt rose to her feet at once, and guided him up an impressive staircase and down a corridor to a large and pleasant bedchamber overlooking the grounds behind the house.

"I will send one of the footmen to waken you when it is time for dinner," she promised. "We had thought of arranging a valet for you, but did not know if you would be bringing one. Fergus can fill in for the time being." She smiled, and let herself out, quietly closing the door behind her.

A valet. Ethan looked all around the room, admiring the furnishings and the view from the window, but most of all appreciating the wide and comfortable-looking bed. As he walked over to it and took off his boots and his coat it occurred to him the day would come when all this would belong to him. As he lay down on the bed his eyes wandered over the ceiling, appreciating the decorative moldings. All this would be his.

But he was too tired to appreciate it. Within a minute or two he was fast asleep.

Melissa was enormously grateful that it was time to turn Charlie over to his nanny. Of course Joanna, the new baby, was still very young, and it was not unreasonable that Anne could not keep up with what seemed to Melissa to be Charlie's remarkable energy. Of course when Anne asked her so nicely she really could not refuse to take Charlie out to play on the vast lawn. Anne said she did not want to turn Charlie over entirely to the nanny's care, and she had tried as long as she could to continue to spend some time each afternoon playing with him, but since Joanna's birth she simply had not been able to do so. It was a great relief to her Melissa was there and could take her place for a bit.

So Melissa did, but it was not with any great sorrow that she turned her nephew, who was still bouncing enthusiastically, over to his nanny to feed him supper and put him to bed.

The question was what she was to do with herself.

Ballymuir was a lovely name, and the house was all right. It was certainly big enough, but both her brother Hugh and Anne had said that it had not been looked after well until Hugh had taken over the estate. They had been working on it as time and leisure allowed. Indeed, the primary rooms were freshly decorated and the walls newly painted and wallpapered. Nor could she complain about her bedchamber, prepared as nicely for her as she could possibly ask, with new bed hangings and wallpaper with posies and roses interlaced with ribbons.

The rest of the house was still shabby.

Of course, she only had reason to know that because she had wandered through the house from attic—which was, of course, where the servants' rooms were and completely uninteresting—to basement, which she discovered was a maze of intersecting rooms for the kitchen and all the accessory rooms for food storage and the pantry and scullery and meat locker and the wine cellar which was locked tightly. Neither attic nor basement had yet been refurbished and repainted, nor did either offer anything in the way of interest, even when Melissa's requirements were minimal.

There was really nothing much to do. Hugh was away almost all the time, working with his steward on the estate. He did offer to take Melissa to show her the new tenant houses he had had built. "The old ones were simply appalling," he told her. "Dogs live better in Gloucestershire than people in Ireland."

She had not taken him up on the offer. Tenant houses, no matter how improved, were nothing in which she had any particular interes. Still, she almost regretted having refused when she saw him lift his eyebrows and turn away. He had not suggested anything else for her entertainment.

She had assumed she and Anne would go out together, shopping in a nearby town or visiting other ladies, but the recent birth of Joanna, who was only four weeks old, made outings unlikely even as an idea, and the longer Melissa stayed there the more she realized that it was unlikely in any practical way as well. There was nowhere to else to go, for one thing. Her brother had met her in Drogheda, which was a wide spot in the road in her opinion. She had not expected Hugh to be spending as much time on farming as he was. Of course, harvesting was beginning, but how long was it to go on? At home she and Hugh had gone for long walks together, and one thing there seemed to be plenty of here were lanes to explore. But alone? The countryside in Gloucestershire had always seemed more closely populated. Domesticated. The nearest house she knew of here was Kendall House, and they took a carriage to reach it. On her own, how could she make sure she did not get lost down these anonymous Irish lanes?

She had assumed Anne had friends to visit, but she didn't speak much about them if she had, and the only house to which Melissa had been taken was Anne's family home, Kendall House. It was very grand and kept in perfect order. She had to admit Anne's mother (or Aunt Elizabeth as Melissa was invited to call her) was a gracious hostess with an unexpected sense of fun. Still, going to Kendall House was an event. It was not the sort of place where Melissa could arrive uninvited any day she chose. At least no one had suggested it, and Melissa was hesitant to ask.

She could go riding, of course. Hugh had some nice horses. But where was she to ride them? There did not seem to be any such thing as signposts, at least not on the roads leading to Kendall House. Much as she would love to escape from Ballymuir to almost anywhere else, finding herself hopelessly lost in the Irish countryside was an unpleasant possibility.

When Anne was up in her sitting room feeding Joanna, Melissa asked her about what she had done when she was a girl living near here.

Anne's face lit up. "That was a marvelous time," she said, looking over the baby's head and out through the window. "I rode, of course—you'd be surprised at what interesting places there are all around here."

Yes, Melissa would be. "Where?" she asked.

Anne's gaze returned to her face. "Well, it's hard to explain," she said. "When I am riding again—Hugh wants me to wait for another month—we'll have to go out together and I can show you some of them."

"A month?" Melissa's voice was faint.

"Yes, not long at all. And there are some good walks around the property right here. Have you walked across the lawn to the line of bushes and trees to the west? There are some paths there you can follow. When Caroline was here with her daughter for a while she was terrified half the time Henrietta would wander off down one of them, but they are far too overgrown for a baby to manage. But if you wear a heavy dress you don't care greatly about, I think you might find it interesting to see where they lead. It was one of my favorite pastimes."

In the morning, alone in her bedchamber, Melissa considered the idea. Walking outdoors—at least when it was not raining, which unfortunately it was this grey morning—was something she did like to do. She had hoped Anne might suggest something less solitary. She hated to admit it, but her mother was indeed revenged for her daughter's lack of enthusiasm for London. There she had felt smothered by the continual press of people, and she never had figured out how to meet the expectations the beau monde seemed to maintain for young ladies of her age and class. The moments she spent alone felt like a breath of fresh air.

Here she was totally isolated.

What was there to do besides aid Anne with child care? Cheltenham had certainly not been her idea of exciting but at least it was close enough to reach easily and there were places to stop for a cup of tea and people to visit there. From what she had been told, the only towns of any size here in Ireland were Belfast and Dublin, both of them were well out of reach. Here she was, and apparently here she would have to stay.

She sighed, and started down the staircase, smiling politely at the butler—what was his name?—who always appeared whenever anyone stepped into the grandeur of the entrance hall.

This time he actually spoke, instead of wafting out of view.

"I believe Lady Anne is in the parlor," he volunteered.

Melissa blinked at him and remembered to say, "Thank you," before starting off in that direction. Goodness. Was her aimless wandering so obvious even the servants were noticing it?

Anne was indeed in the parlor, sitting with some needlework in her lap. When Melissa came into the room, she looked up and smiled in greeting.

"I wish I were one of those people who finds great satisfaction in working with a needle, but I'm afraid I'm not," she confided.

Melissa shrugged. "Neither am I. My mother does quite beautiful work, and she seems to enjoy doing it, but it always seemed so pointless to me."

"What do you enjoy doing?" Anne asked.

Melissa glanced at her swiftly. Was she trying to figure out what might interest her house guest? She must know this visit had not been Melissa's idea. That was not the sort of information her mother would be inclined to keep confidential. But Anne's face remained tranquil until she picked up the linen in her lap and frowned at it.

"It's so unfair," she grumbled. "My sister does lovely things as well. I think she got the talent for both of us when gifts were being handed out."

Melissa hesitated and then plunged forward. "What do you think your gifts are?"

Anne's smile was nearly a grin. "I'll tell you mine if you tell me what yours are."

Melissa took a quick breath, and let it out. "All right. Tell."

Anne let the linen drop into her lap again. "Well, I love to read. So that is one. I can play the piano, not expertly, but I enjoy doing it. I love adventure, but being a respectable wife and mother makes that a difficult gift to cultivate. I tried adventure once and found I had bitten off much more than I could possibly chew, so I suppose what I really enjoy is reading or hearing about other people's adventures. I do love having children around and I didn't know that until I had my own. It is great fun watching them discover the world." She looked over at Melissa again, still smiling. "Is that enough? Tell me yours."

Melissa took another breath, deeper this time. "I don't know if I am good at it, but I enjoy talking to people. It was my greatest weakness at school, I was told, but I made some very interesting friends there. I shall miss being away from them." She paused and thought. "I do like shopping, too. I like the challenge of finding exactly what I want at a price I can pay. We live close to Cheltenham, and there are enough shops there so that you can find the same sort of thing at more than one shop, and I find it challenging to work out which shop offers the best value for my money." She hesitated again. "And I like dancing, and have been told I'm good at that. So there are three things."

Anne shook her head, laughing a little. "Well, we have little enough to offer in the way of shopping and dancing here. That is unfortunate!"

Melissa shrugged. "I think my mother thought I was doing too much of both, which is possibly why she sent me here. I can't imagine it was just because I cut my hair!"

Anne tilted her head to one side, inspecting Melissa's hair closely. "Well, I'm not exactly in the first wave of fashion of course, but I think your short hair suits you. It's true I don't know of anyone else here in Ireland who has cut her hair, but I don't see how that matters. Your hair is so full and bouncy and you are so petite I think a great mop of hair would be overpowering."

Melissa leaned forward, eagerly. "That was exactly it! I had masses of hair and it was curly and wild and would not behave itself unless I put in enough hair pins to start a shop by myself. They would fall out and my hair would try to burst out of the ones still there—I seemed to spend half my life stabbing in pins. Or finding others to replace the ones I lost."

Anne flashed a smile of understanding. "I have to admit my hair is always slithering down, so I am no example, but I can see what you mean about yours." They were sitting close enough to each other that Anne reached out to touch Melissa's hair cautiously. "Oh, my, it's soft enough but good gracious, how curly it is, and how thick!"

Melissa nodded. "Exactly. I cannot tell you how glad I am that the idea crossed my mind to hack it off. Well, I did the front and sides, and more or less ordered my maid to do the back."

Anne tilted her head back to examine the sides and back more closely. "I think you did a good job. And so did she."

"Well, I told her what to do." Melissa grinned. "Maybe cutting hair is another of my talents. But what a completely useless one! Can you imagine my mother's face if I set up a stall on a corner in Cheltenham and offered to cut other people's hair?"

They laughed together at the mental picture. Melissa wished she had a piece of paper to sketch out what it would look like, but pieces of paper were not what you were likely to find lying around in a parlor. Perhaps sketching could be one of her talents, but what she did best was caricature, which was not appropriate for ladies, as her mother and school mistresses had made plain. But perhaps here in the wilds of Ireland?

She suddenly realized that Anne was speaking and she had not been paying attention.

"—some sociability for you. My mother sent over a message this morning that our cousin Ethan was arriving today. He will be too tired today to do anything but fall into bed—remember how exhausted you were when you arrived? He has come all the way from London. But tomorrow we are going over to have dinner at Kendall House so you will have a chance to meet him. It is not often we have guests at both Ballymuir and Kendall House!"

In spite of herself, Melissa felt a quiver of interest. Somebody from London? She had always longed to go there herself when nothing was expected of her. Not during the Season. The idea of being exhibited again as a prospective bride seemed to her the far side of tiresome. Yes, she had to admit now it might be nice to meet other people, and yes, there would be dancing, but she could not imagine being put on display a second time—and the cost of it! Particularly when she had no ambition to marry. To marry meant she would become the possession of some man, like his boots or his cravat.

But London! The city itself—that would be magnificent. If she enjoyed Cheltenham, how much more fascinating would London be.

She closed her mouth firmly. Anne certainly was more companionable than Melissa had imagined, but enlightening her on what her mother thought was her unreasonable antipathy to marriage and all the folderol of the Season might be enough to horrify her.

Better to concentrate on the coming family party the next day. That was what had to be high excitement in the quiet world of Ballymuir.

CLEARLY, THE KENDALL ESTATE WAS run with precision and genuine effort. Ethan may have had the first day to rest and gather his resources, but the following morning he was expected to arise early enough to accompany the earl on his day's work with his steward. His uncle had made that quite clear over dinner, and when Ethan came in for breakfast the next morning it was obvious the earl was waiting for his arrival.

Fortunately Ethan was not voraciously hungry, but during the day he regretted he had not eaten more. Eating in the middle of the day did not appear to be part of the earl's daily nourishment. His breakfast, it appeared, lasted until dinner. Ethan wondered bleakly how much the earl had eaten. It was not that he was accustomed to luncheon with ladies, but he was used to having some coffee and perhaps a pasty or a roll with ham around about eleven o'clock. The hour of eleven came and went on the Kendall estate with no perceptible pause in the business of showing Ethan the land he would be responsible for, what was grown on it, and what kind of care it needed.

It was the longest day of his life.

As he followed his uncle and his steward, Mr. Bowyer, on the meticulous survey of the land and grounds, he probed at his own attitude. He was not bored—well, not exactly. It was more that he found it all supremely uninteresting. The requirements of different kinds of corn were the sort of information he feared would not stick in his head. He thought he could probably grasp the divergence between sheep and cattle—for one thing, the different sorts of fields they inhabited—but his initial opinion on moving about with them was that they were both

stupid and seemed unfortunately liable to get into trouble as a direct result. Fortunately, the major part of the estate was given over to grains—corn they were called as a general term—and one did not expect corn to think.

The distances they rode did not trouble him. He enjoyed riding on a good horse, and his initial impression that the earl's horses were exceptionally good was confirmed. It was the time spent dismounting and walking around to examine some area or particular crop he found tedious. At first he genuinely tried to concentrate and remember what he was told, but as the day wore on it appeared he had absorbed his maximum capacity of new information, and after that he simply stalked around after his uncle and Mr. Bowyer and tried to appear at least superficially interested.

The day started out cloudy but dry, a circumstance his companions remarked on frequently enough so it seemed clear this same exercise would have been carried out even if rain had been pouring down. By the grace of God, however (or so Ethan attributed it), the weather seemed to clear until in the early afternoon the sky clouded over again.

"I think we may be in for a fair downpour, sir," Mr. Bowyer remarked.

Lord Kendall inspected the sky, his head thrown back and his eyes concentrated. "I fear you are right. It would be a pity to drown Ethan on his first day here, would it not?"

A shadow of something like a smile passed over Mr. Bowyer's face. "We may not have done all we wanted to, m'lord, but we got a bit done. Tomorrow's another day."

Ethan's heart sunk as he tried to imagine how much had been planned for the day. It seemed to him the distances ridden and areas chosen for close inspection had been enough to fill up a couple of days of work. But there was, apparently, a perceived necessity to acquaint him with the whole estate all at once.

He glanced up at the sky himself, hoping his thankfulness for the dark clouds rolling towards them was not obvious in his expression.

"Better head for home," his uncle pronounced. That he was reluctant was plain.

Mr. Bowyer touched his forehead, half bowing to both of them, turned his horse, and headed away at a reasonable speed. They had passed the steward's cottage just before, pointing it out to Ethan, and it occurred to Ethan now the steward would be home and dry in a few minutes, whereas he and his uncle had a fair distance to cover.

He should have added to his thankfulness for clouds a request to get under cover before the approaching downpour began.

They very nearly made it, but there was not any gentle rain to begin with. One moment the sky was dark and threatening, and the next it was as if someone had torn open an immense bag, dumping quantities of rain down over them.

To his surprise, his uncle seemed exhilarated by the torrential rain. His face streaked by the deluge, he grinned in apparent delight.

"We can hope for good crops with all this rain on the richness of the earth we're blessed with," he shouted over to Ethan.

He smiled warily back, wondering if the man was impervious to the cold rain dribbling down the collar of their coast, inevitably soaking shirts as well as what had been warm bodies underneath. Fortunately he could see the stables of Kendall House ahead of them, and urged his horse forward. The horse, apparently less hardy than the earl, gladly picked up speed and it was not long until he and Ethan reached the open door to the stables. Ethan dismounted and horse and man rushed into the warm, dry space within. Fortunately his uncle was not far behind him. Ethan would have felt a pretty fool if Uncle Charles had continued his leisurely approach. Ethan would have had to wait in the stables, wondering if he should have stayed with him, deluge or no deluge.

They got wetter still, of course, walking to the house.

Aunt Elizabeth was watching for their return, and made anxious squeaks as they came up the front steps and into the house, dripping all the way.

"Good heavens, you might have drowned!" She went on marveling at their degree of wetness as she peeled soaked coats off both of them, and ordered them to sit on the chairs Duncan, the butler, produced so they could take off their boots before they tramped mud through the entire house.

"It's a good solid rain," the earl said with satisfaction as he walked in his stocking feet to peer out one of the long sidelights by the massive front door.

"It made you solidly wet enough." Clutching their coats at arm's length, his Aunt Elizabeth waved Ethan and her husband up the stairs. "It will be most unfortunate if you wind up with lung fever," she threatened, as she followed behind, as if in fear the earl would suddenly reverse progress and go back to admire the rain a little longer.

When they reached the top of the stairs and came to the point where they went different directions to their rooms, Aunt Elizabeth paused to hand Ethan his wet coat with instructions to leave it for Fergus to cope with and told him he was to take the hot bath she had ordered for both him and Uncle Charles, and then dress properly for dinner as she was expecting that Anne and Hugh with the children and Hugh's sister would come for dinner, rain or no rain.

"If we were to wait for fine weather, we might not see each other for weeks at a time," was her parting shot.

As Hugh turned gratefully into his room, he could hear his aunt's voice, still organizing her husband all the way down the corridor to their suite. He relaxed into anticipation of a hot bath—wonderful!—and a chance to actually get something to eat. His stomach told him breakfast had been a very long time ago.

Even if the evening at Kendall House could hardly be called a dinner party, Melissa had to admit she felt a frisson of excitement as she pulled out two of her nicer frocks to choose between. Just because she was unenthusiastic about the prospect of a second Season in London did not mean she wished to give up sociability entirely. As it was, the only people she had seen other than Anne and Hugh were their very young children.

Then, too, there was the promise of some drama. If this was the cousin who would inherit Lord Kendall's estate, how did that sit with the two daughters? Of course, only Anne was here, and both of them were married—Anne very happily so, from all she could observe—but wouldn't it be a little hard to see everything they'd been most familiar with pass to somebody presumably they'd never laid eyes on?

Not that she expected open conflict. But everything seemed so placid here. She couldn't help wondering if there might be some excitement lurking in this place where everybody seemed so content with their lives just as they were.

Oh yes, she reminded herself. She was supposed to be getting dressed. She looked at the two white muslin frocks in her hands, and sighed. Yes, it was the height of fashion—or at least it had been during the Season. However, from what she had seen before leaving London, it was more or less what everybody would be wearing next season as well. And plain white was so boring!

It was so reminiscent of those ballrooms of the beau monde—night after night, all the young ladies in white they tried to distinguish by adding jewels and embellishments which to Melissa made them even more drearily similar.

She turned back to the wardrobe, sighing, and fished out one of the dresses remaining there. It was blue—a pale blue, of course—and she could drape a shawl over her shoulders with some blue woven into it but also a medley of pastel colors and paisley shapes. Maybe not a gown that would stop all in awe where they stood, but at least different from what she had worn in London, evening after predictable evening.

"Melissa!" It was Anne's voice in the corridor.

Melissa opened her door to peer out.

"Oh, dear. I'd hoped you would be dressed by now. Do you think you could get yourself ready as soon as possible, and then come give me a hand with Charlie? The baby's fussing, and I don't like to have her get really upset when we are just about to go out, and that's what will happen if no one is holding her."

"Of course," Melissa said, closing the door again and starting unbuttoning. Anne had said they would get a maid to help her, but no one had appeared yet, and under the circumstances she was reluctant to ask Anne for the loan of hers. More, she could not understand why the baby had to be brought along with them in any case. Wasn't that what nannies were for? There were times when she really felt that Ireland—at least this bit of Ireland—was on the very edge of civilization. She didn't remember seeing anywhere near as much of her sister Penelope during her entire babyhood as she had seen of Charlie in the days she had been there.

Melissa sighed again, and stepping out of the day dress she had been wearing and into the blue dress for dinner, began the process of buttoning all over again. Fortunately the buttons on the blue dress were fewer and larger, intended as part of the decoration. There was also a nice lace ruffle around the neckline, keeping it well inside the bounds her mother considered respectable. And a blue sash just below her bosom. *That* she could not tie in the back without aid, so holding it in one hand, she left her room and headed in the direction of the nursery, where she could hear Anne's voice as well as the piping young sound of Charlie.

"Oh, good," Anne said as soon as she came into view. "I really do appreciate your help. Do you need to have your sash tied?"

"I do," Melissa said, wondering briefly if this would be a good moment to mention her lack of a maid and then, taking in Anne's haste in tying the sash into a quick bow (but was it centered? or tied neatly?), came to the conclusion it was not.

"I have a ball," Charlie told her.

"So I see," Melissa replied.

"Thank you so much," Anne said, and rushed out the door.

"I want Mama." Charlie marched over to the door after her. Fortunately, Anne had closed it, and Charlie had not yet the height, or the mastery, of door handles. He turned back to face Melissa. "I want Mama now," he said, as if she might have misunderstood his first request.

"Where's your nanny?" Melissa asked, thinking it was just her luck to have the planned time of departure be the time when Anne had excused the nanny so she could have time with her son. Or, in this case, have Melissa have more time with him.

"Dunno," Charlie said with no particular interest.

"Do you want to roll me your ball?"

He still had it clutched in his hand. "No," he said. "Frow it." And throw it he did, right at Melissa's middle. He had more strength than Melissa thought it reasonable for a two-year-old to be capable of.

"Ooof." The noise was involuntary, but it amused Charlie, who giggled and ran over to retrieve the ball for, presumably, a second go at her.

"No," Melissa said firmly. "You may roll it to me on the floor and I will roll it back. Good little boys do not throw balls in the house." If that was not the rule here, it certainly should be. "You may throw your ball outside."

Charlie gazed at her, clearly measuring to what degree she meant that. Melissa stared back, trying to look determined. She was also simultaneously resolving that should she ever be unfortunate enough to find herself increasing, she would devote most of the period between discovering her condition and producing an infant to picking out a really superior nanny, who would bring the child to her at carefully controlled short periods until the child was maybe 10 years old, at which point the periods could be lengthened.

The impasse between Charlie and Melissa was resolved by the door flying open again, and Anne appearing, with baby Joanna over her shoulder, wrapped in a blanket.

"Hugh has the carriage ready downstairs," Anne said. "Are you both all ready to go?"

Melissa, startled, took a quick look at Charlie. She had not realized that getting him ready for departure was part of her assignment. The quick look convinced her that he was certainly ready enough to go to his grandparents' house, particularly as his grandmother at least seemed completely convinced that the sun rose and set in his shining face.

"Does he need a jacket?" she asked Anne.

"Umm," Anne murmured, clearly debating. Melissa went over to the wardrobe up against the wall, opened it, and took out the nearest one.

"We can take this one just in case," she said.

"Oh, no, not that one." Anne crossed the room quickly to join her. "It's the wrong color. Let's take the red one instead."

As Charlie seemed to be wearing one of the apparently identical loose smock-like garments that seemed to be what children of either gender at his age wore day in and day out, Melissa could not see what difference it made if the jacket were red, green, or purple, but she obediently replaced the green one and took out the red. As she approached Charlie she could see that in fact there was a very subtle reddish pattern in the fabric of his smock, so she supposed it made sense.

"There," she said, getting one arm into the jacket quite easily, but having to be firmer than she liked to be (particularly in the presence of his mother) to get him to relax the other arm sufficiently to stuff it into the sleeve.

Anne, fortunately, was not inclined to be critical. She shifted Joanna's position slightly on her shoulder, and took a deep breath.

"Hugh is too obliging to be truly impatient down there, but it would probably be more thoughtful if we go down the stairs now so he can have the satisfaction of fitting us all into the carriage," she said.

Melissa said nothing. This was not the first time Anne had mentioned what she saw as Hugh's really remarkable personal qualities, few of which Melissa remembered being impressed by when they had both been living in Gloucestershire. It was nice to think that love had such a splendid effect on the character. Of course, she considered as she followed Charlie who was following his mother down the staircase, it could be the effect of love was on Anne, who had become lovingly uncritical rather than indicating any improvement in Hugh himself.

Something to think about, when she wondered whether anybody would ever be sufficiently overwhelmed by her own virtues not to notice that the elements of her personality that her mother had been trying to modify for years remained pretty much as they had always been.

A depressing thought, that. She lifted her chin defiantly, and continued after the others out the door and down the steps to where the carriage was awaiting.

6

IT WAS NOT FAR TO Kendall House. It had seemed a very long distance to Melissa the first time she had traveled from Ballymuir, but that had not been long after her arrival there, and the experience of being bounced and jolted again in a carriage was not one she welcomed.

This time it seemed shorter. Possibly it was because she was beginning to recognize the bends in the road and particularly memorable trees as they passed them. Anne and Hugh were engaged in bubbling conversation almost all the way, mostly teasing each other. From time to time Charlie's voice piped up, and Melissa observed her brother, never before to her knowledge particularly interested in children, was usually the first to answer whatever he asked quite sensibly, as if he expected the child really was trying to learn something when he asked a question. Even a question that sounded fairly pointless to Melissa.

She thought about the young men she had encountered during the Season and felt her own eyebrows lift slightly. Undoubtedly some of them had been fine young men, but as a group they had impressed her as being most interested in the masculine worlds of the card rooms and long intensely boring stories about hunting and shooting parties. Of course there were men who did dance in the ballroom with the elegantly dressed ladies whirling around the dance floor. Neither the dancers nor the young blades gathered in their laughing groups seemed to see the other girls, just as carefully dressed, sitting along the edges trying to appear fascinated by the conversations of their mothers or chaperones who gathered in small groups, their eyes flicking rapidly from one set of dancers to another.

She had not always been one of the wallflowers. She had danced quite frequently. But she remembered sitting on the sidelines more vividly. At least that was one thing she did not need to worry about happening here in Ireland, given the dearth of sociability she had experienced so far.

Then, amazingly enough, they were there. Melissa, sitting quietly with her back to the horses, suddenly realized they had passed through the great gate and were coming to the curve that led to Kendall House itself. Charlie had started out sitting next to her, but bobbed back and forth from that seat to the one opposite where his parents sat, his mother cradling baby Joanna in her arms. No one seemed to pay any attention to the reality, so startling to Melissa, that they were actually there. Already.

The carriage gradually came to a halt, and there was the usual re-organization of everyone for alighting, as if it had been a considerable journey rather than just a short run. Joanna's blanket had to be straightened, Charlie's jacket pulled back into position over the smock. Melissa's hands moved automatically to smooth out her dress, although it could not have become very wrinkled, especially since Charlie had done all of his climbing over his parents, and she had been left uncrushed.

The door was opened and steps set in place by a footman. Hugh nodded at her to be the first one to step out. Once outside, she allowed herself one furtive poke at her hair, hoping it looked presentable, as she waited for everyone else to join her.

Hugh confined Charlie with his arms, keeping him out of the way while Anne gathered herself and the baby up and was gently handed down to the ground. Then finally Hugh and Charlie came out, and all of them could turn ready to climb up the stone steps to the magnificent front door, opening now to receive them.

Melissa let the rest of them move ahead of her, and followed along afterward. This was, after all, just a family dinner—although there was the interesting prospect of the heir. From London, was he?

Of course Ethan had heard the rattle of the carriage approaching. As it happened, he had been sitting with his uncle in his uncle's comfortable library cum study. Both of them had shed the wet clothes from the day, and after his bath—he assumed Aunt Elizabeth had made sure his uncle had had a warm bath as well—he felt considerably more cheerful about the evening. His uncle poured each of them some brandy to continue the warming process. Ethan sipped slowly and cautiously, being familiar from regrettable times past that drinking enthusiastically on a completely empty stomach was the path to an evening of great cheer and a morning of doleful repentance.

His uncle's head was up, listening. "They're here now." He rose to his feet.

Ethan stood, debating whether to tip the last swallow in the glass down his throat or leave it behind. Prudence, and the sight of his uncle halfway out the door, induced him to set down the glass and follow.

As he walked down the wide passage to the front door, his uncle well ahead in his eagerness to see his daughter and grandchildren, Ethan found himself wondering what Hugh's sister would be like. If he had understood what his aunt had said about her correctly, their family in England had packed her off to Ireland out of exasperation, since she had had a single Season in London and was apparently unwilling to consider another. He was not sure what conclusions he could draw about her on the basis of that. He had been in London himself during the Season this year and necessarily, since he stood to inherit an earldom, was considered eligible by too many eager mamas surveying a field somewhat decimated by the Peninsular Wars still in progress.

Would he recognize her? In some ways he would rather not, as if he did, she might recognize him as well, and there had been episodes he would just as soon keep from the common knowledge of his relatives here in Ireland. Nothing greatly out of line, but there had been more drinking and gambling than he suspected these upright Anglo-Irish would approve of. So far he had not stumbled into serious problems with either, a course he intended to continue. But still—well, it would be interesting to see who this sister of the marquess was.

She was coming through the door just as Ethan reached the great hall. Ahead of her had been Charlie, scrambling up the stairs himself as he was proudly proclaiming to his grandmother, tugging on her skirt to gain her undivided attention. Then came Anne carrying the new baby and behind her Hugh. Then the girl, and Ethan's heart sunk.

Oh yes. He could not remember her name, but the color of her hair was memorable. Only as he recalled, there had been a great deal more of it. It had been piled on her head, obviously requiring heroic efforts to get it there, and over the course of the evenings when she danced with energy, the restraining power of the pins or whatever she used to hold the whole structure in place would loosen, and the volume of hair would gradually expand. "Bush-head," some wit had named her, and after drinking for a couple of hours, the name seemed far more clever than it sounded when cold sober. Did she ever know of the sobriquet? He had an uncomfortably clear memory of a lot of hearty laughter pointing out the phenomenon. He most profoundly hoped he had not been identified as a member of that laughing crowd. Had he ever used that unfortunate name himself? Unfortunately he could not remember, although the sinking feeling in his interior suggested he had.

She was certainly not Bush-head now, although not a beauty either. Her chin was too decided and her nose, instead of being aquiline was snubbed. With the mass of hair gone—what had happened to it?—he was far more aware of her blue eyes than he had ever been before. Bright blue they were, with long thick eyelashes.

"Melissa," his uncle was saying, "I'd like to present Ethan Hawthorne to you. He is my heir, and has come to Ireland to learn a bit about the estate before he is wholly responsible for it."

There was a pause while they took the measure of each other.

Oh dear heaven. She most decidedly did remember, and from the expression on her face, the name of Bush-head must have been used within her hearing.

She curtsied, neatly and with ice in her eyes. "Mr. Hawthorne," she said. "A pleasure to meet you." Clearly she had no intention of admitting to the gathered relatives they had ever encountered each other before

Fair enough.

He bowed. "The pleasure is mine."

His aunt said, "And here is our daughter, Lady Anne, and her husband, Lord Ashbourne."

Ethan bowed. "Who is this charming young man?" he asked, moving over to acknowledge Charlie, who stared warily at him. He bowed to them all, and Anne, carrying the baby, made a courtesy dip and pushed down gently on Charlie's head so that he bowed as well.

The circle of onlookers all beamed as if the introductions were the start of beautiful friendships, and they all made their way down to the music room, chattering with the intimacy of family as they walked.

Ethan and Melissa followed behind, silently.

The music room looked quite splendid. A table with a sparkling white cloth was set out in the middle with chilling champagne bottles and delicate glasses.

"We never welcomed Joanna properly and now we have two guests to welcome as well." Lord Kendall was visibly pleased with himself, especially as everyone else seemed astonished by the elegant display.

Anne looked the most taken aback. "And here I've just asked Sophie to take the children," she said.

"Well, not for a few minutes," Lord Kendall said. "We have some lemonade for Charlie, and surely Joanna should be present at her very own celebration of birth."

"Of course," Anne said, just as Sophie—one of the maids here at Kendall House? Ethan had not noticed her before—came into the room with the ease of long familiarity and reached for Charlie.

Lady Kendall turned to her. "We are having a celebration," she told her. "Come back in about five minutes or so, and the children will be ready to go upstairs then."

Anne settled down into a chair and settled Joanna propped on her lap. "This is all for you, sweet pea," she said.

The gentlemen waited for the ladies to seat themselves. The gentlemen were then sitting down when Melissa stood up, murmuring some apology, went over to the piano, fussed about with something, and then returned to the group, this time choosing a seat as far away from Ethan as the seating arrangement allowed.

Ethan nodded at her, just to let her know that he had in fact noticed.

She stared back at him expressionlessly.

This had the makings of an interesting situation. Ethan made a trifling adjustment of the tails of his jacket, and paid exaggerated attention to the discussion the marquess and his uncle were having about how crops were coming this year. Not as well as they had hoped, he gathered, but better than they had feared. There was a lot of chat about the weather. The ladies, at least his aunt and Anne, joined in enthusiastically. Melissa did not contribute, nor did he. He would have liked to participate, but the course of recent weather was not exactly what he felt most qualified to discuss.

As arranged, the maid Sophie returned and collected the two children after Joanna had been taken around for everyone to admire and kiss goodnight. Ethan, assuming this was the family pattern, dutifully lowered his lips to the baby's soft cheek, but observed a minute or two later that Melissa simply touched her finger to the baby's cheek, shooting him a scornful glance as she drew her hand away.

Battle lines had apparently been drawn. It was unnecessary, Ethan thought, since judging by today, he was going to be spending most of his time out in the fields where Melissa was unlikely to go. He could not decide whether it was unfortunate or not that given the circumstances, he was unlikely to ever find out what, specifically, his offenses in London had been to earn such enmity. For the sake of curiosity it would be interesting to know, but it was probably better he did not. It seemed highly unlikely the two of them would spend any extended time in each other's company, which quite honestly suited him quite well. He had not been overwhelmed by Miss Melissa Preston's charms in London, and nothing he was seeing here persuaded him to think differently now.

Dinner, therefore, was the opportunity for family-centered conversation. The two households brought each other up to date on what had gone on since they had last met, which must have been less than a week ago, from what Ethan gathered. There was some more interesting information about Anne's sister Caroline—a twin sister, apparently— who was in Dublin with her Irish husband. He was apparently a businessman of some substance, and Caroline was getting a chance to enjoy the entertainments and music available there. They had also been engaged in rehabilitating and refitting a cottage, not far from Kendall House, for Caroline and her daughter to use when they came for extended visits with the earl and his wife.

Anne explained to Ethan that Mr. Gallagher was Caroline's second husband. She had been married to the Earl of Linnell, heir to his father, the Duke of Apthorp, but her husband had been unfortunately killed in a riding accident very shortly after their marriage, and after the birth of their daughter, Caroline and her baby had come home to Ireland.

It all fit in with some gossip Ethan had overheard but paid little attention to in London. Curious that he should find himself in the very family that had been under discussion.

The dinner was delicious, country fresh and all well-prepared. Ethan ate, at last, with great pleasure. Anne confided to him that not only was their cook, Maeve, gifted in the kitchen, but also an Irishwoman of strong principles and in a real sense, the one who knew most comprehensively what was going on in the house, upstairs and downstairs. Anne said that she still came to Maeve when she was having difficulties dealing with her own servants.

"And she used to make me little pies with jelly and tell me wonderful stories when I was small. I think I will have to bring Joanna over here in a few years and make sure not to pay attention when she strays down to the kitchen," she finished.

Her mother looked at her with raised eyebrows. "I think you may need to exercise some caution rather than just leaving the child to learn whatever Maeve has to tell her. Remember the difficulties you got yourself into." Her voice diminished into a murmur at the end, which

Ethan thought was a pity. It sounded as if there might be an interesting story there, but when his aunt finished it with a warning nod of her head it seemed unlikely he would ever hear it.

It was shortly after that the countess rose. Would he really be able to call her Aunt Elizabeth as she had asked? The other ladies rose with her, and Ethan remained with the gentlemen for port and a cigar. He accepted both. As cigars no longer made him feel ill it was his practice to accept one, but he did not look forward to smoking them. With the port they were accompanied by a great deal of agricultural discussion.

Ethan tried to keep his mind on what the men were saying. It was obvious that both Uncle Charles and the marquess were genuinely fascinated with the business of running their estates. So far he had found what he had seen of it to be a matter of routine and drudgery, but when he caught the lift in their voices and their obvious pleasure, he wondered if somehow he was seeing the whole process incompletely.

After all, what he was here to learn was what he would be doing—or responsible for making sure was done—for the rest of his life. Even if he chose to go back to London and leave a middleman to run the estate, whether it prospered or not would define how comfortably he would live himself, and what he would pass on to his own heir, whoever and however that would happen. He might wind up beggared. Gossip said other men had.

It all seemed, for better or worse, he should be paying more attention to what there was to learn from his uncle and the marquess. He looked back over his day, marveling in a way that he was still awake and alert. Even giving a passing thought to bed was probably a great mistake, because there was clearly going to be some time before he would be able to climb into his own. Worse, if there was anything he had learned from today, it was that the day started early and Uncle Charles and his steward were both iron men who were capable of working the entire day straight through.

Was it cowardice to hope for rain? At least he had learned to eat a hearty breakfast.

Unbelievably enough, it was only his second full day in Ireland. He sipped slowly at his port and listened to the two other men talk.

OH, SPLENDID.

Melissa sat listening to Lady Kendall—no, she had instructed Melissa to call her Aunt Elizabeth, since they were really part of the same family now. All right. She was listening to Aunt Elizabeth and Anne talking, and Aunt Tryphena was rocking in a rocking chair, her stubby legs short enough so that they did not touch the ground. Melissa had not been prepared for Aunt Tryphena. She was apparently a distant relative, not an aunt at all, but from what Melissa gathered, she had been living at Kendall House for many years. In any case, she seemed to have all the typical eccentricities of most elderly women, plus a few all her own. The first time Melissa had come to Kendall House, she had been treated to a muddled reminiscence of sorts in which somebody—Aunt Tryphena herself?—had been burned out of house and home by some dreadful pack of Irish rebels still lurking dangerously close.

Anne had swept in before the story had been completed, murmuring, "Yes, yes, Aunt, but we need Melissa here for a moment," which they did not, and as a result she had never heard the point of the story, assuming there had been one.

So Aunt Tryphena was there, but not contributing to the conversation, since it mainly circled around the exploits of Charlie and an extensive discussion of whom Joanna might resemble. Melissa had nothing to add to that, since as far as she was concerned, all new babies looked very much alike, small with squashed faces and not much hair. All things considered, she would prefer not to be listed among the people Joanna might look like.

Goodness knows, Melissa hoped for the baby's sake that she would not grow up to have hair like her own.

And was it not the most unfortunate luck in the world that the only other person around who was not sunk up to the knees in Irish soil should turn out to have been a member of the most objectionable group of young men she had encountered during her Season in London. Oh, she remembered them well.

Not him so much, although she believed she had danced with him once or twice. He was an excellent dancer, if she remembered properly, but then most of them were. But they danced as they behaved, as if it was the most amusing thing in the world to drop in and out of the strange courting ritual of the Season. They were all well dressed, moneyed, and none of them, as far as she knew, were yet old enough to have come yet under serious pressure to marry and multiply, as was the explicit duty of title-bearers and the presumed fate of the simply well-born. Ethan Hawthorne fell somewhere between the two. He was due to inherit a title, but as he was a nephew, not a son, he was not now a viscount or carrying some other subsidiary title possessed by the present earl.

So he and his friends laughed and played cards and more than sometimes had drunk too much by the end of the evening. When it suited them, they came out to join the dancing for a set or two. But then they retired back to the card tables, usually laughing a little louder and undoubtedly sharing their less-than-flattering opinions of whatever girls had been unfortunate enough to be their dancing partners. They certainly had been given to dubbing the poor girls with nicknames. Melissa still burned when she thought about the one she had overheard being applied to herself. Bush-head. As if the only notable thing about her was the unreasonable quantity of hair she possessed!

She was more than ever grateful she had chopped it all off. Hell would freeze over before she let it grow out again. (It did not count as coarseness if she did not speak the word out loud.)

"I was thinking it might be interesting to go over tomorrow to see how Caroline's cottage is coming along," Anne said, obviously speaking directly to Melissa.

She blinked, hauling her attention back from the bad old days during the Season to this summer evening in Ireland.

"Cottage?" she said, trying to remember when anybody had discussed a cottage.

"Oh, yes. Had I not mentioned that before? Caroline's husband Martin bought a cottage here for her to use with Henrietta when they came up here to visit us, but it was in poor condition and needed quite a lot of repairs before they will be able to use it. My father and Hugh have been keeping an eye on it, but it has been some time since I have seen it myself, and I thought we might go over and see what the state is."

Aunt Elizabeth's face lit up. "Or you could come here. I could have Maeve make some of those delicious maids of honor cakes that she's made a few times before." She nodded at Anne, her eyes twinkling. "And perhaps you might like to take some home for Hugh."

For no reason that Melissa could see, Anne was blushing rosy red and shaking her head at her mother. Nobody, however, seemed inclined to explain.

Just then the door opened and Uncle Charles, Hugh, and the detestable Ethan all came in together, smelling distinctly of cigar smoke.

The ladies turned to greet them with smiles and Aunt Elizabeth moved to the tea table to serve them some tea. Well, all the ladies with the exception of Aunt Tryphena, who went on rocking in her chair, looking thoughtfully into the distance. That had to be one of the advantages of being old, Melissa decided. No one expected you to behave just like everybody else. A pity old age had so many other disadvantages.

The conversation, when Melissa turned her attention to it, seemed to be mainly concerned with plans for the next day. Much was based on the weather. Apparently Uncle Charles and Ethan had one set of plans if the weather was fine, and another if it rained again. Or at least Uncle Charles had plans. Melissa had the fleeting sense Ethan looked less than excited about the possibility, which was satisfying.

"We thought we might go over and see how they are coming along on Caroline's cottage," Anne said.

"Is the cottage just for Caroline to use occasionally?" Melissa was curious enough to join in the conversation.

"That's what Martin purchased it for. I must admit that Lord— Uncle—my husband and I were surprised when he proposed it in the first place, but it's very thoughtful of him." Aunt Elizabeth's blush when she couldn't decide what name was most appropriate had begun to fade by the time she finished speaking. "It has no land with it, so it was not very desirable for anyone else around here."

"What does he do in Dublin?" Ethan asked. Melissa glanced over at him. The note of genuine interest in his voice was something she had not heard before.

"He deals in investments, for himself and others. From what I hear, he has a very sure touch with them and an impeccable reputation in

Dublin." It was Hugh's turn to speak up. "He quite often travels to London and back again. Even to New York in America," he added, and Melissa noticed Anne's quick look at her husband. Did she wonder if her husband ever wished he had wider scope than an estate in Ireland? Melissa would. How much more interesting it would be to travel and see new places and meet people who lived in entirely different ways. Of course she did not think New York itself was on the edge of the frontier, but it would certainly offer different challenges. Had she only been a man herself...

"A bunch of Irish in New York," Aunt Tryphena suddenly volunteered.

Everybody's head swiveled in her direction.

"They should send all the Irish there," she continued, unperturbed. "Then we could have a sensible country here."

That was apparently not the general opinion, because Aunt Elizabeth, Uncle Charles, and Anne all burst into speech to direct the conversation in some other direction, which would have been much more successful if each of them had not come up with a different subject to pursue.

As it was, the awkward moment was swallowed up in general laughter, followed by Uncle Charles inquiring of Melissa if she sung at all.

It was the last thing she had expected. "A little," she said cautiously.

"Wonderful! Anne and Caroline used to make some music for us after dinner," he said enthusiastically. "Anne, can you show her the music you used?"

Anne rose, making her way to a cabinet, and looked at Melissa with some concern. "You don't need to feel you have to," she murmured, as Melissa walked over to her. "My father loves music, and I think he really has regretted that he no longer has anyone regularly available to provide it."

"Well, if he is not expecting great things, I think I can keep up." Melissa kept her voice low, as Anne had done. "I am certainly no great singer, but usually I can carry a tune."

"That's as much as Caroline was capable of—is capable of, I should say. I am no threat to the great pianists of the world, either. We'll probably muddle along as well as Caroline and I used to."

Melissa was somewhat surprised at the number of music sheets available, but it did not take the two of them long to find a piece Melissa had sung before at some house party, which fortunately Anne knew how to play.

"I think we have found something," Anne told her father.

"My dears, that is most satisfactory." He settled back in his chair with visible pleasure. "Just begin any time you are ready."

It was certainly not anything Melissa had visualized herself doing in the strange land of Ireland—least of all in the presence of one of the young men who had been such a torment to her in the very recent past of her Season in London. Even so, when Anne began to play, it was easy enough to sing along with her. Like Uncle Charles, she did genuinely enjoy music and it was indeed an agreeable way to draw the evening to a close.

When they finished that piece, they were applauded, and Uncle Charles asked wistfully if there were any other pieces there that they both knew.

"Papa, Melissa and I will look through the music another day," Anne said, rising from the piano. "It is getting late, and I have two sleepy children here who need to be taken home and tucked into their beds."

Melissa was surprised to realize she was tired herself. The long summer evenings of Ireland confirmed what the clocks indicated: it was not late yet. But she supposed she was living among country folk now, and days started and ended earlier than she was accustomed to.

The group in the music room dissolved into movement. Aunt Elizabeth and Anne went up to get the children. Melissa offered to come to help, but was assured that they could take a child each downstairs. Perhaps if she could hold Charlie on her lap in the carriage…

Hugh and Uncle Charles shared some last bits of mutual advice and information, Ethan behind them apparently either trying to listen or trying to look as if he were listening. Then there were the muffled sounds of Anne and Aunt Elizabeth coming downstairs, each carrying a sleeping child.

When they heard the sounds in the music room, Aunt Tryphena slid forward in her rocking chair until her feet touched the ground and then came out into the entrance hall, Melissa coming after her, to go up on her tiptoes to deposit a dry kiss on each child's forehead. She looked like such a funny old woman, and Melissa found herself wondering if she had ever had children of her own. Probably not. But although being a dependent relative might not be the most desirable condition of life, at least she was still part of a family.

Melissa had never thought of that as an advantage before.

It was not fine the next day, but it did not rain enough for Uncle Charles and Mr. Bowyer to cancel their plans to visit the far fields. Ethan, of course, went with them and genuinely tried (he told himself) to be interested in what they were inspecting. Unfortunately, even now as close to harvest as it was, the fields all looked to him like expanses of dirt with plants of various sizes growing in them. Although the other two seemed to be quite comfortable inspecting the plants and making estimates of when each field would be ready for harvest so the most efficient distribution of tenants and farmworkers could be arranged, Ethan was unable to distinguish the difference between one field and another, let alone what constituted readiness for harvest.

Presumably this would be the sort of expertise he would develop with time, but the thought of the number of hours it would require for him to gain any familiarity of his own was a daunting prospect. So for the present he rode along, a silent presence behind the other two, chatting busily back and forth between themselves.

Was this really where he intended to spend his lifetime? The more stories he heard of middlemen—conversational patter between his uncle and Bowyer—the less he liked the idea of hiring such a person to function unsupervised, making (as so many seemed to do) the lives of the tenants a misery, and potentially skimming off much of the wealth of the estate. The tenants seemed inoffensive enough to him, although he suspected that they were implacably Irish and Catholic and would not care greatly if the English in the big house disappeared off the face of the earth. But in their stolid way, they seemed to appreciate the reasonable treatment they received from the earl, and the possibility of anything changing did not seem to be an immediate concern.

With determination he turned his attention back to whatever the other two men were talking about.

"Trying to fit in harvest at exactly the right time and having the best weather for it are two of the puzzles of running the estate," his uncle was confiding over his shoulder.

Ethan nodded knowledgeably, he hoped.

"Mr. Bowyer, here, is one of the best at making sure it all fits together well," he went on to say.

Ethan looked at Mr. Bowyer, hoping again that his expression indicated appreciation for the steward's skill.

Mr. Bowyer's mouth quirked. "It is no great problem if it all seems a bit vague to you now," he said.

Oh, dear heaven. Had his incomprehension and ignorance been that clear?

"It takes years to be entirely comfortable in making these decisions, which is one of the reasons I think it is so sensible that you have come over to learn about it before you have to start making the decisions yourself. After a couple of years the choices will seem obvious to you, and then you can do whatever you wish without fearing that you are leaving the estate to flounder. Of course we all hope the earl will be with us for many years to come."

Ethan nodded vigorously. But good Lord, although he was perfectly sure Mr. Bowyer considered two years almost nothing, his heart sunk when he imagined two years off here in the deep country of Ireland, with dinner with the relatives likely being the most exciting revelry. Two *years*? He had been thinking more along the line of maybe as long as six months—less would be better.

He vaguely remembered—must have been years ago—his mother had given him a stern lecture on the responsibilities of a title. Might have been shortly after his father died, when he abruptly found himself the heir. Whenever it had been, she had waxed long and eloquently how under English law one person who took on the burden of responsibility for the title and estate that had been handed down through the generations and would continue to be handed down, and the benefits of wealth and power attached to the title and estate came with the price of carrying that responsibility until it was his turn to pass it on to his own heir.

She had declared that it was God's own plan for the organization of land and property down through the ages.

Feeling the price of that responsibility heavy on his own shoulders, Ethan sighed as unobtrusively as possible, and turned his head to contemplate the grain growing in front of and around him. Now how was he to remember it should look when it was ready for harvest?

IT MUST OBVIOUSLY BE DIFFERENT if they grew in your own body.

Melissa lay on a rug stretched over the lawn, watching Anne giggle at Charlie's lack of skill at throwing a ball. The first two or three times had been amusing, but he had been tossing the ball now for much longer than Melissa had any interest in watching. She had to admit it was funny when the ball flew backwards out of his grip, and he was left turning around in a bewildered circle to see what had happened to it. But that only happened once.

Baby Joanna meanwhile slept in the woven basket Anne had placed her in to bring her outside. Melissa was close enough to her so if the baby squeaked she would hear, but Anne still came over every few minutes to make sure all was well.

If this was what she would gain if a second round of the Season ended in matrimony, Melissa was not at all sure the reward was worth the trouble. Yes, it must be wonderful to be loved as single-mindedly as Hugh obviously loved Anne. The two of them together exuded happiness. Melissa's father had died when she was too young to have memory of him with her mother, but her mother had never had Anne's warmth in her voice when she had talked to Melissa about her father over the years since.

But even if you were deeply in love with some man, would that make up for spending years of your life tending babies? Of course Anne had a nanny, but Melissa was convinced no nanny ever had an easier life. Now in London, the clear and obvious purpose of a nanny was to free a young mother for sociability and taking advantage of the riches of London. But here in country Ireland? Take right now for an example. Here they were, out on the lawn, with the babies. Joanna was no trouble; she was asleep. Charlie was all right, if Anne was really interested in what he was doing.

But even if Anne had arranged to have the nanny supervising the children, what would she be doing instead? Needlework? Reading a book? Sitting and watching puffy white clouds slide across the blue sky?

It seemed to Melissa a little of that would go a long way.

What should she do herself? Go through all the fuss and bother of preparing for—and *enduring*—another Season? Persuade some young man who lived in or near London he was wild about her and wanted to spend the rest of his life responsible for her? Someone well enough off (she didn't care greatly about a title) so that he could keep her supplied with servants, most importantly nannies, and enough wealth so she could use her free time as she chose? At least there were a variety of entertainments in London, and interesting people who did not spend their entire lives thinking about crops.

"Had you ever thought about doing anything other than getting married and having children?" The question popped out of Melissa's mouth before she had decided to ask it.

Anne turned to look at her, with an odd smile on her lips. "I don't think I had given much thought to what I wanted to do with my life," she said. "I knew what I did not want to do. I did not want to leave Ireland and meet an assortment of strange Englishmen, even if they were handsome and danced well, and thus be committed to living there instead of here." Her smile widened. "I was just fortunate your brother came when he did to take up the title and the estate, and that he cared about Ireland as well. Caroline was different. She had been set on going to London and marrying an Englishman for ages. Years, even. But of course it all ended badly for her."

"Her husband died?" Melissa was curious what the whole story had been. There had been glancing references, but nothing more.

Anne sighed, and looked out over the lawn to the distant trees. "Yes. They had only been married five or six months when he died in a riding accident."

"But she has a child, doesn't she?" Or was that something that should not be talked about?

Anne's smile returned. "Yes. A daughter that was the focus of her life until she met Martin. Martin is wonderful, Melissa. Huge. If you ever meet him you will be so surprised. He's not fat—he's just tall and built—" she laughed "—by the same builder who did Stonehenge."

Melissa, immediately picturing one of the great stone monoliths she had seen in drawings with a hat on its head, laughed, too.

"And Irish," Anne went on, with her tone softening. "The very best sort of Irish. Down to earth and plain-spoken and very, very kind. Sometime while you are here we should go down to Dublin and stay with Caroline to give you a chance to get to know them and the city. Everyone says it is not as grand as it was, but I am looking forward to seeing it, and Caroline seems very happy there. Certainly happier than she was in England, but of course the circumstances are different."

"Umm," Melissa murmured, sitting up on the blanket and realizing Anne felt free to talk because Charlie had climbed into her lap and was well on his way to sleep. It must be lovely to be a child and able to drift into a nap whenever you were tired or bored. A pity she could not remember when she had been that small. Did anybody remember? She had never thought to ask.

"I sometimes wonder what I want to do with my life," she heard herself saying. She almost clapped her hand to her mouth. Had she lost all control of what came out of her mouth? What had possessed her to say something so revealing of her most private self without considering whether she should do so or not?

Mercifully Anne did not look horrified. "Well, of course the problem is that we are women, and our choices are so few." She was running one hand down Charlie's back as she spoke. "I have been very lucky. But whether to get married or not—well, that depends so much on the person you think about marrying. In a way, it is the greatest risk of all, because when you marry, the law says you belong to your husband. If your husband chooses to be stingy or cruel, you must live with stinginess or cruelty. So you hope to be more fortunate.

"But if you do not marry—" Anne let the words lie there for a bit before she continued. "If you do not marry, unless you have wealth of your own, and only few women do, you will be dependent on others. Usually relatives, and they may be kind to you or may not."

"Like Aunt Tryphena?"

"Actually Aunt Tryphena was married. I don't think she ever had children. If she did, they must have died quite young, because I've never heard of them. She was one of those caught up in the bitterness between the English and the Irish. The Rebellion of 1798, if you've ever heard of it. The Irish call it The Revolt. Her house was torched by Irish rebels and her husband died in the fire."

"Oh," Melissa said in sudden enlightenment. "That was what she was talking about."

Anne nodded. "According to my father, she doesn't remember what really happened, which is a mercy. What she thinks she remembers is what she read in the newspapers then and heard from other people, which is why it changes every time she tells it. It seems comical until you think about how dreadful it must have been. She's related—I've never known exactly how—to my father, and I gather we lived nearest, so she came here. She came when Caroline and I were still little girls, and has been at Kendall House ever since."

Melissa shivered. "A house torched by rebel Irishmen—that sounds horrible. Do things like that still happen?"

"N—no." She hesitated. "But that's not to say nothing like that will ever happen again. You have no idea how badly the Irish are treated here. It's their country, and they—too many of them—live like dogs, scrambling for food, using whatever they can find as shelter. No wonder they look at us who are English and wonder why we have all the privilege and all the big houses. We have the money and worst of all, the control of their lives. Which, officially, we would wish to increase by having them turn Protestant and give up the church they believe in."

Did Anne's voice tremble a little? Melissa looked at her, guardedly. "Caroline's husband is Irish, is he not?"

Anne gave her a quick glance, and nodded, equally quickly.

"Does he feel that way?"

She could almost feel Anne relaxing. She even smiled. "You know, I have never asked him. He is such a warm and generous man I would find it hard to believe that he holds resentment in his heart anywhere. But that's all right. I'll resent it for him." She shrugged. "It's not fair. But then we did not ask to be here. The English government sent us—well, encouraged us strongly to come—hundreds of years ago and we've been here for generations. So it would be reasonable we should have some rights as well. But they deny us those rights as forcefully as we deny them virtually any rights at all, and the anger and bitterness keep growing. I don't know what the answer is. I don't think anybody does, except the entrenched interests on either side and what they want really is the disappearance of the other community. I thought once you could choose which side you want to be on, but I don't believe that now. You are who you are."

Melissa leaned back, propped up by her arms. She really wasn't very good at predicting what people are like. She would never have guessed that Anne, the docile and agreeable wife who took such devoted care of her children, was a cauldron of molten opinion when she started to talk about the Irish. She wondered if Hugh knew that about her, and then answered herself silently. Of course he must. The two of them were too close for her to keep her strong opinions to herself. After all, Melissa had hardly badgered Anne to weasel out the truth about her thoughts. They had just been talking on a summer's day, and it had all come tumbling out.

Of course, fascinating as it was, it still did not answer Melissa's problem. What was she to do, assuming she had any choice in the matter? Was she to surrender and have another stab at a Season in the hope of finding herself a suitable (and hopefully satisfactory) husband? What reasonable alternative was there? It made her want to howl at the moon. Yes, she knew she was more privileged than many. Yes, if she chose not to marry it might be possible for her to become a governess or some wealthy lady's companion, but the thought of either was stifling. She had given her own governesses—there had been two of them— enough misery to make it only fair to feel some herself, but it was not a life she was eager to undertake.

In fact, was there a life she was eager to undertake? Living at home in Gloucestershire was nothing she wanted to do forever. She could feel a smile creeping over her face as she considered that her mother would not be eager for that either.

"What's so funny?" Anne asked. Clearly she had been watching her more closely than Melissa had realized.

Her arms were getting stiff. She rolled over onto her front and chuckled a little. "I was thinking how relieved my mother probably is not to have me at home for a while. She wishes I were a more amenable girl and would do what she thinks I ought to do with pleasure. The difficulty is I'm not certain what I want to do. But the idea of going back for another Season in London is not something I would choose. It's so expensive, and such a waste of money. I do like wearing pretty gowns, but not when the whole point of wearing them is to be acceptable in the eyes of everyone around me. I hate the desperate feeling I must be chosen by someone or I will be a failure. And there's no escape. That's the whole point of the Season—to be snatched up as a wife by some eligible man who has to marry just as you do." She pulled herself back up to a sitting position. "But the most boring fate is being reduced to talking about poor me, poor me, poor me. I apologize, Anne!"

Anne was laughing at her. "Poor old Melissa! We will have to see what we can figure out to amuse you while you are here."

It was on the tip of Melissa's tongue to ask if Anne had any idea how long Hugh and her mother expected her to stay here, but mercifully this time she did have some control and folded her lips together casually rather than let the words spill out. At least a prisoner has some idea of how long his term is, she thought, sighing. Was she in Ireland until her hair grew out? Well, that might be forever. She saw no reason at all to let it grow. She was happier and freer with the great mass of hair reduced to a manageable pile of curls she could run a brush through and call it done. If she had to be especially presentable, she could tie a ribbon around her head.

"Oh no!" Anne's sharp cry of exasperation broke into Melissa's reverie, and she suddenly realized rain had begun to spatter. "Bless this Irish weather," Anne exclaimed, grabbing at the basket with Joanna in it, trying to capture Charlie—who still half-asleep was trying to get to his ball—and kicking at the rug they'd all been sitting on.

"I'll get that," Melissa said, reaching down to grab the rug and pick up Charlie's ball in the same sweep. She handed the ball to Charlie. He took it, mollified enough to stop squirming quite so vigorously. "Do you want me to take Joanna?"

It was raining a little harder. Where had that black cloud come from? It had been a nice day.

Anne looked harassed. "Yes, if you take Joanna I think I can manage Charlie and the rug." She scrambled to her feet, handed the basket to Melissa, taking back the rug and adjusting her hold on her son. "Don't try to run—none of us are going to melt in a little rain."

Belying her own words, she took off close to a run, with Melissa coming after her. She tossed the light blanket that had been at the end of the basket over the baby so that she would not get wetter than necessary.

The rain was coming down briskly by the time they came running up the steps to the house. The butler mercifully had already thrown the door open, and quickly took the rug from Anne, who put down Charlie and his ball as soon as they were safely indoors, and turned to Melissa to relieve her of the basket with Joanna.

"This wretched country," she said. "Can't let us have a peaceful afternoon in the garden without having a shower to go with it. Well, that's the end of our excursion to see Caroline's cottage. I was going to suggest we ride there, taking the horses so I could show you some places to explore when you get restless, but obviously not today."

Charlie let the ball roll away under a table in the entrance hall and began to howl. Joanna, gathering all was not as it should be, commenced a half-hearted wail.

Anne looked ruefully at Melissa. "This seems more of an argument against marriage and consequent child-raising than the comfortable cozy example I'd hoped to set. One minute you are contentedly at rest and the next minute uproar is all about you."

Mercifully, from Melissa's point of view, the nanny heard the noise and came running down the stairs, and within minutes everything was restored to order, the children being taken upstairs to the nursery, and only Anne and herself left standing there, shaking off the rain they had picked up during the course of the run.

"Would you like to go upstairs and dry yourself off?" Anne asked. "I'll do the same, and we can at least have a cup of tea in the morning room like proper ladies."

So she would not see the cottage today, Melissa thought, as they climbed the stairs together and went off in different directions to their rooms. She had been curious to see this place that Caroline's Irish husband had apparently purchased on the spur of the moment, so that his beloved wife—only at that point she must not yet have married him—could visit her family and still have the comfort of her own place for herself and her daughter. Wouldn't it be lovely if it was something like what she had imagined: a gift of love from a man to the woman he wanted to marry.

Maybe, if marriage could be something like that, it would not be so much to be dreaded. Perhaps it would be endurable to belong to a man who wanted that much to have you happy and surrounded by your own possessions, your own place, even when the two of you were not together.

But where were you to find a man like that? From her experience of the young men she had encountered during her experience of the Season in London, they must be thin on the ground. She had no confidence that the men of good family and some fortune she had danced and dined with cared two pins for what she might be like as a human being.

No. They were like that unpleasant Ethan Hawthorne. He and his friends had apparently seen the whole process of meeting and marrying—which, after all, was the point of the Season itself—as a tremendous joke, and used their limited wit to point out to each other anything unfortunate that might strike them as less than perfection.

Bush-head, indeed.

ETHAN'S INTEREST IN AND MASTERY of the details of estate management did not appear to increase day after day. In fact, the grim truth was that seldom had he been so bored. His uncle was unfailingly kind and encouraging. Mr. Bowyer, Ethan suspected, recognized he was an idiot, but continued to be informative if he was asked a question, and did not intentionally show him up as a fool. Occasionally that was what happened, but Bowyer was always apologetic, apparently genuinely so, and made extra efforts to clarify whatever the confusion had been about.

No. He could not blame the lamentable state of affairs on anyone but himself. Information he had no interest in would not find a place in his brain to stick. He feared he could be told the same thing 47 times in a row and be just as uninformed at the end as at the beginning. He began to worry about the poor tenants once they were turned over to his management. Of course he assumed that Bowyer would continue to serve as steward, which would be of some help, but as everyone else confidently supposed, he would be the one in charge who had the answers.

But what if he did not? It made his head ache.

Finally there was what Uncle Charles chose to describe as a rest day. Of course, there had been Sundays all along, but those days were devoted to church in the morning, and then dinner that day rotated back and forth between Kendall House and Ballymuir, with the entire family in attendance. On those occasions, Ethan and Melissa had as little to do with each other as possible without drawing anyone else's attention.

But this was on a Wednesday. Apparently Aunt Elizabeth wanted to go to Drogheda to purchase something there, although from Ethan's quick look at the place he could not imagine what a lady as elegant and tasteful as his aunt would find to buy.

What was important, however, was that he had the day to himself.

He took one of his uncle's better horses and decided to enjoy himself with a completely purposeless, self-indulgent ride. He would not look at crops, he would not check where the cattle were grazing, he would not check to see if the tenants were in need of something, he would not do anything except what he wanted to do.

It was a fine day, and he found riding in the sunshine—not high summer sun, fortunately, and just a lick of autumn in the air—the most pleasurable thing he had done in weeks. The air was fresh, except when he rode past the cattle, and the vivid green of Ireland was all around him. Ireland, in fact, was rather an inviting place when you could just ride through, rather than studying it.

Unless you suddenly found yourself face to face with Melissa Preston.

What on earth was she doing out on some nameless country lane, riding a rather nice horse all on her own?

"Oh." She pulled up sharply. "It's you."

Ethan took care to make a polite on-horseback-bow, not quite from the waist. "Indeed. A good day to you."

She lifted her eyebrows. "Good day to you. What are you doing, wandering around without supervision? I thought you were having heavy tuition in the fields."

Ethan managed to smile. "I understood that young ladies did not wander about unchaperoned on country roads."

For once, the girl gave him a wholly unstudied grin. "I escaped."

He responded with the same, not really meaning to. "So did I."

"What are you supposed to be doing?" Her voice actually sounded interested.

"For once, nothing. The earl has taken Aunt Elizabeth to Drogheda for some shopping."

She wrinkled her nose. "What's there to shop for?"

"I couldn't tell you. Mercifully, I was not invited along." By now they were idling along, side by side. "What should you be profitably engaged in?"

Melissa sighed. "Looking after children, I suppose. I told Anne I'd like to have a morning ride, and she was busy organizing the nanny, and just murmured, 'Fine,' so I didn't wait around for her to change her mind. I just left."

It was Ethan's turn to lift an eyebrow, which he did. Just one. "And how are you enjoying your stay in Ireland, Miss Preston?"

She did not answer. Instead she countered, "And how are you enjoying yours, young Hawthorne?"

He grinned. "I believe in fact I am older than you are."

"Oh probably so," she snapped back. "The last leaf on the tree and all that." There was a not entirely hostile pause, and then she asked, "How old are you?"

"Twenty five."

"And I am but twenty. You're right. But even at twenty my mother seems convinced that I am destined to be a last leaf. My cutting my hair pushed her from pessimism to despair, and here I am."

"How is Ireland supposed to improve your prospects?"

Melissa sighed heavily. "I'm not sure. I think the goal is to make me realize how terrible it is to be single and forced to live in some other woman's house my whole life long."

"Is it terrible?" He was genuinely curious.

"Well, it's not exactly what I'd like most to do. I would hope that if they were my own children it would be easier to take care of them. But going through another dreadful Season with unpleasant people like you and your friends is not a delightsome alternative."

That silenced him. He had truly not considered that any of the girls he had encountered during the continual social whirl might not be there by choice. Why he had not he could not really justify. Perhaps it was because his mother did not care whether he went to the balls and dinners and garden parties on the lawns of estates set on the Thames or not. He knew enough to realize that in a few years' time—maybe less—the pressure would be on him to find himself a wife to procreate and carry on the title and the family name. But it was not now. But of course it was taken for granted females should be in their first youth. He had never thought that being very young and encouraged to perform, not entirely unlike a trained seal, might be a miserable business. But he had watched it, and laughed when something embarrassingly amusing had happened.

For the first time, he felt he might have behaved differently.

"I might well not be there next Eastertime," he said. It was not an apology, but if she would think she had not to deal with him, would it make the prospect more attractive?

"My mother, of course, says that I will not be either. It's the hair. According to her, I cannot possibly set off for another Season with my hair cut short, and it's so much easier to keep it this way that I have no intention of ever growing it again. So unless we resolve that sticking point, I suppose I will remain in Gloucestershire." She looked squarely at him. "Unless I am not released from my Irish bondage."

"Oh."

"Yes. I have been given no fixed term."

"What do you think you'll do?"

A tentative smile appeared on her lips, and disappeared. "Think I'll do or would like to do?"

Ethan shrugged. "Either."

"Given my d'ruthers?" She laughed, but not with amusement. "Run away."

Ethan found himself genuinely horrified. "Run away? By yourself?"

Now Melissa looked positively challenging. "Want to come?"

"God, no." He repented the blasphemy the moment he said it, seeing Melissa recoil just a bit, almost as if he had slapped her. "Sorry," he muttered. "I beg your pardon. But that would be madness."

Her chin was high and her cheeks were pink. "I apologize. I misjudged you." They were approaching a crossroads, and she tightened her reins to make the turning. "Good day," she said, and galloped off into the distance.

Ethan looked after her, partly regretful and partly—mostly?—relieved.

What a really peculiar girl.

Stupid, stupid. And even more stupid. What had possessed her to open her mouth and admit all those ridiculous things? Melissa shook her head briskly, as if by doing so she could shake out her whole recollection of the absurd conversation. She'd slowed down, once she was sure she was far enough away so that Ethan would not be able to follow her, even if he was inclined to do so. What an exasperating man he was.

Of course she wasn't going to run away. Why did he have to take that so seriously? How on earth would she be able to manage anything like that? She was a female. A respectable female—well, all right, a lady—would never be seen wandering around the countryside on her own, except on the shortest of rides, like the one she was taking today. Going to Dublin or anywhere else in this godforsaken country on her own? Of course not. Much less back across the Irish Sea. Ethan, like all men, had no idea how smothering the rules applying to women were.

No, her options were strictly limited. In fact, she had none. She would remain here in Ireland with her brother—not that she saw much of him; he was out with his steward most of the time—and she would help Anne take care of two small children. Well, to be fair, she helped Anne with one. Joanna was so young that the only care involved was feeding and changing her, and Anne, from what Melissa could see, did that. She did manage some time to spend concentrating on Charlie, and when she was in the middle of her Charlie time and Joanna needed attention, she asked Melissa to make herself available to distract and entertain him. The nanny picked up times in between, for example during meals or in the evening, or when she and Anne had some other activity, like taking a short ride together.

That would be her life in Ireland, unless she could think of something else interesting and socially acceptable for her to do. At Ballymuir? The mind boggled.

Perhaps if she were reported to be docile enough, her mother would permit her to come back to England. In that case she would be sent off to London just after Easter-time. Did she dare to hope it might be in the spring of the very next year? Possibly, if her mother could be persuaded she would not be totally ostracized because of her short hair. Maybe this next time she would be obliging enough to try to make friends with some of the other girls. Not all of them had been betrothed, and subsequently married, during that last Season. She could share with them their concentration on pretty dresses and absurd little hats and keeping track of which of them had more callers bringing flowers the day after an important ball. Maybe, if she were *really* fortunate, some young man whose family maintained a large house in London would become infatuated with her, and she could become a wealthy young wife who lived in Town and still went to concerts and picture galleries and danced at Almack's or not, as she chose, because she had a husband and did not need to charm another man. At home she would have a nanny to take care of whatever children she bore for her husband's family, and a footman to carry her purchases on Bond Street. That was the best she could hope for.

It all sounded unutterably bleak. Almost as bad as riding alone down a country lane in Ireland with tears rolling down her cheeks.

Why did she have to be female?

Before she turned into the drive leading to the portico at Ballymuir she pulled off her glove to fish into her pocket and pull out a handkerchief. If she was silly enough to cry about nothing, she did not have to admit it to Anne or whoever else might be around. She scrubbed her face briefly, tucked the damp handkerchief away, and lifted her chin.

She was more than ordinarily glad she had done so when she heard the sound of hooves behind her, and turned around to see her brother riding up to join her.

He pulled up side by side with her, beaming. "And where have you been?" he asked.

Melissa found a smile. "Anne didn't need me for a bit and I thought it had been a while since I'd gone riding in the early morning. So I did, and now I'm coming back for breakfast."

"That's satisfactory." He started to move forward, and Anne touched her heels to her horse so that she stayed even with him. "I was having breakfast thoughts as well."

"I thought you might have eaten before you went out."

"Well, today Sheehan had some things of his own he wanted to check out, so I took a look at how the rebuilding is continuing, and thought I'd come back here. I've hardly seen you since you arrived. I'm glad we happened upon each other."

This time Melissa's smile was unforced. So Hugh had noticed they'd seen so little of each other. It was not that she'd expected they would spend all the time hand in hand, but it would be good to have a chance to have breakfast with him and maybe a chance to talk over what he thought her long-term plans were. To the extent there were any.

They took their horses to the stable, and on the way back to the house as they chatted about nothing, Melissa tried to plan how to ask him what their mother had said to him. What did he expect about her future? Her concentration made her responses to what he was saying absent-minded, and suddenly remembering how he had withdrawn when she had been less than enthusiastic about being shown what he'd been doing on the estate, she pulled up a brilliant smile and started to pay attention.

It might have been just barely in time—Hugh looked at her warily when she smiled—but they were companionably chatting when they went into the dining room where breakfast was laid. Fortunately no one else was there.

They both selected what they wanted to eat from the sideboard. Melissa noticed that Hugh must be a great deal hungrier than she was. But then, she thought, he spent most of his days away from the house, so did not have the occasional biscuits or fresh fruit that at this season was still available in bowls around the house.

Hugh had happily begun on his loaded plate when Melissa sat down.

"Did Mama say anything about how long she meant for me to stay here?" she asked very casually.

He glanced over at her, chewing. Eventually he said, "Why? Are you bored here?"

Melissa was prepared for that. "Not at all," she said. "I was just wondering if I should be preparing to go to London immediately on returning home, or if Mama thought it better for the following year." She glanced at him, making a point of smiling. "It's more difficult if you have no idea of what you are expected to be prepared for."

"She didn't say." Hugh concentrated on his plate for a minute or two while Melissa tried to remember what she was planning to ask next. "She seemed mostly exercised that you had cut your hair," he suddenly added. "She said you were deliberately making yourself unmarriageable. That struck me as odd."

"It struck me as odd as well." Melissa muttered, not caring if she sounded grumpy. All this fuss because she had cut her hair? Her mother should try going about with an unruly unmanageably curly weight of hair on her head. And if the hair was supposed to make men fall in love with her, it had not exactly made her irresistible in London when she had been there, after all. She had returned home as unmarried as she had left it.

"What do you want to do?"

She looked over at her brother with surprise. "What do you mean? When do I want to go to London?"

"Not wholly. What do you want to do with your life?"

She shrugged. "I do not have a great number of choices, do I? I suppose I shall get married at some time."

"That is what most people expect." He went back to eating his breakfast. After a bit, he asked, "Would you want to live in England or in Ireland?"

"Ireland?" Melissa was plainly dumbfounded. "Why?"

"Well, you've not seen much of it. Neither have I, but I was interested in what Martin, Caroline's husband, had to say about Dublin. Now that Caroline and Martin are there, I hope to go down to see the place. But there's no reason why you should not go before I do."

Melissa looked at him, still perplexed. "Why would I want to go to Dublin?"

"Well, I'm sure Caroline and Martin would be able to find some interesting young men among their friends."

Of course. Realization began to sink in. "What do I want with interesting young men?"

"As you did not find anyone in London, perhaps it might be an idea to see if you are more taken with life here in Ireland. Dublin seems a more likely place than round about here."

"You mean to marry."

Hugh looked up from his eggs and bacon. "Well, of course. What else are you going to do?"

For a moment Melissa did not have the heart to say anything. Well, of course. How had she ever come to the idea that Hugh might have something else to suggest? What else was there?

She finished the last swallow of tea in her cup. "I should go up and see if Anne needs any help," she murmured.

Hugh put down his fork and knife for a moment. "I should have said before how much I appreciate how much help you are being to Anne. I think she is finding taking care of two children more of a challenge than she expected."

"There is the nanny," Melissa pointed out, dully.

"I know, but Anne so valued the time she had with Charlie on his own that she wants to give Joanna the same attention, and with two I gather it's difficult. But she has always been full of energy. I am sure she will find a way to manage."

Melissa rose from the table. "I'll go find her."

Hugh gave her an especially warming smile. "I'm glad we had this chance to talk. We should see more of each other while you are here."

She nodded, and did her best to smile back. Yes, of course. What she really had not wanted to hear was confirmation of what she already knew was true. Sooner or later she would have to resign herself to marrying someone.

Or think seriously about becoming a governess, God help her.

HARVEST WAS PROCEEDING WELL. AS far as Ethan could tell, it was better than Uncle Charles had feared. Mr. Bowyer was more difficult to read, or perhaps a good season meant less to him it did to the owner of the estate. From what Ethan gathered, there had been a sequence of difficult years, each one offering a hope of the more abundant harvests of the past, and each one disappointing in its turn. Seeing the carts full of grain, lumbering off to be weighed and ground, it was hard for him not to see the wealth that was there, rather than the wealth there may have been at an earlier time.

It was hard work. Hard work for the tenants and extra men hired on to help with the job, even hard work for an earl, his steward, and his heir, riding from one field to another to supervise what was going on, making sure all the grain was going where it should be, rather than being unlawfully poured into small bags which would disappear as quickly as they were filled. As his uncle had explained, it was his custom to make sure all his workers had some share of his success, but years of tales of absentee landlords and dishonest middlemen had convinced almost all the tenants and workmen you could only count on what you could hold in your own two hands. Plenty later was no substitute for a little bit now.

Ethan was tired of being so weary. Tired of rubbing dust and dirt into his face when he swiped away the sweat. Tired of the monotony. Ride to one field; ride about within it, checking on what was going on, laughing a bit with the workers but keeping your eyes open, riding about again as you left, taking a sweep in the opposite direction so the simple-minded ones who might have thought you would go the obvious way would be unable to hide their bags before he spied them and dismounted to jerk them out of their hands.

"Don't punish them," Uncle Charles had told him. "Just make sure the contents of the bag go on the carts with the rest, tell them they'll get their share when all the crops are in, and be sure to take the bag with you. We don't have time at this season of the year to deal with resentful bunches of men gathered to complain. Easier to stop it where we see it, and move on."

Other nearby landlords might consider the earl's methods as mollycoddling where discipline would do better, but Ethan could see the sense of it. There was no dangerous murmuring among his men, simply a sheepish recognition that when they were caught it was a grab fair and square, and nothing more to be done about it. Of course real success would mean there would be no pilfering, but this was Ireland, and it seemed to Ethan his uncle had achieved about all that was possible under the circumstances.

Round and around, up and down, the sweat ever on his face and dripping down the back of his neck—not what Ethan had visualized when he had received the summons to come to Ireland. Still he had to recognize what his uncle preached was true: it was better to be out in the fields in the middle of what was going on rather than to stand behind the glass windows of the big house and speculate about the mood and temper of what the workmen. As much as Ethan found himself temperamentally unsuited to this life, he had to agree Uncle Charles had worked out a successful way of managing it.

Still, the days were long, and Ethan was not exactly sorrowed when Uncle Charles called him and Mr. Bowyer together, saying he was going back to the house to do some of the necessary paperwork. He rode off, and then as if taken by an afterthought, turned back to where Ethan and Mr. Bowyer still remained.

"Ethan, perhaps it would be good for you to see how the records are kept. Bowyer, I would suggest you close down the two fields where we started, and send those men home. That way you will only have the other two, which you can keep an eye on yourself. Maybe another hour? Use your own judgment. When you are weary, you can be sure the men will be as well." He jerked his head at Ethan as he turned his horse. "Ethan, come with me."

So they rode back to the house together.

Once there, Uncle Charles told him he saw no reason to do paperwork dirty and sweaty. He was going to take a wash before they settled in the library and suggested Ethan do the same.

Ethan thought the best part of the day was standing beneath the pump and letting the water—wonderfully cold—run over his hot, dirty body. Infinitely better than a warm hip bath, which might be better from a temperature standpoint (once he had begun to cool off) but presented all the problems of trying to submerge his head and underarms, which needed the washing most. Obviously having learned this was his preference, Aunt Elizabeth made sure there were large towels out by the pump so that he could discard his sweaty clothes there and pass through the house wrapped up in towels, not concerned about encountering housemaids along the way. She herself kept busy elsewhere.

So it was he was able to come down to the library, clean, freshly dressed, and feeling like a human being rather than a half-baked reincarnation of the Green Man.

His uncle was already there, freshened and clean himself, and better yet, there was a tea tray. His uncle had his cup of tea in his hand, and there were a few biscuits as well. Ethan had learned to eat a substantial breakfast, but he did have to hold himself back from falling on the tea and biscuits like a starving man. Altogether he felt as if he had by a splendid chance returned to civilization when he had expected two or three more hours in the sun and dirt.

Of course, he reminded himself, he should be grateful for the sun. Harvesting in the rain would be agony, and how much of the harvest would you lose from men and horses squelching about in the mud?

"Bring that chair over, and come sit with me," Uncle Charles told him. "We both need to see the papers."

Ethan did as he was instructed, and sat down. He was more intrigued than anything else. He had always enjoyed his schoolwork, even the Latin. But maths had been his special favorite, and it rapidly became obvious keeping the records involved a great number of figures, and working out their relationships with each other.

The earl was obviously the kind of person who wanted to keep track of how this year was doing in comparison to last year, and the year before that, and for the next hour or so Ethan was in heaven. Instead of struggling with the obstinacy of plants, animals, and men, he was manipulating figures according to rules he already knew. Time flew past.

When Duncan, the butler, put his head in the door to announce dinner, Ethan was, for the first time, aware of disappointment. There was still a fair amount to be done, and nothing would please him more than continuing with it. However, Uncle Charles was the master here, and Ethan only the heir.

"Well, you have given me a wonderful start," his uncle said, as they rose to go to the dining room to meet Aunt Elizabeth and the peculiar Aunt Tryphena. "I shall enjoy doing the rest, and you can keep an eye on Bowyer—and he keep an eye on you—tomorrow while you finish up those fields."

Ethan glanced back at the papers still strewn all over his uncle's desk in the library and felt his heart sink. So he was to spend his time out in the dirt with the grain, while his uncle did the record-keeping. It was enough to make a man weep. This was the first work he had done since he came to Kendall House he thoroughly enjoyed, and now he had shown he could do it, he was exiled again to work he disliked—even hated.

He was very silent over dinner.

It must have been two or three weeks later Ethan came to the stark realization that he simply could not stand any more of it

There had been no further opportunities to bury himself in the bliss of facts and figures and to draw conclusions from what he found there. Instead it was more days out on the estate, moving from field to field and from problem to problem—none of which interested him. He stood there watching his uncle and Bowyer argue out the best way to handle whatever it was—surly tenants, corners of a given field that failed to prosper, heavy rain on the day when harvest of one particular crop had been planned—and felt absolutely no compulsion at all to jump in and offer his suggestions. Do it one way or the other: it made no difference to him. Just tell him what he was to do, and he would trudge off and do it.

But he didn't *care*. That was the part that finally made it unendurable. This was going to be his land, his responsibility, his choice of whether he was going to continue to develop the wealth-producing potential for the family in years to come, or let the estate gradually deteriorate. How was it that enthusiasm for the job somehow skipped his generation? Let him do the planning. Let him make the decisions about what was to be done. But do not, for God's sake, make him supervise the work out in the fields. His uncle was clearly the sort of man who liked to have his own hands in the soil, to be involved at the most basic level. Not that he was about to plow whole fields by himself. But he wanted to see the plowing being done.

Ethan could not care less. Were he in his uncle's position, he would leave all the day-to-day work to Bowyer, or some equally capable successor, and he would retreat to his study, to work out the plans and possibilities. Once he had them firmly fixed in his mind, he would sit in his own comfortable study—or library, if he left the arrangement as it was—and summon Bowyer to give him the instructions. When Bowyer left, he would know exactly what he was expected to do. Then Ethan could read a good book, or take an afternoon nap, or drink himself into a stupor. It would not matter, as long as he pulled himself together to take Bowyer's report and added that information to his master plan so whatever he did tomorrow, or a year from now, would have developed from practical experience with the same field the year before.

But the problem was that was not the way his uncle worked. Uncle Charles believed as firmly as he believed the sun would rise the next day the proper way to run an estate was to run it: to be out there day after day. Not necessarily 365 days a year, but from what he'd seen, not a great deal less.

So what was Ethan to do? Remain here and be driven slowly out of his mind? Return to England and be across the sea and totally unable to see from time to time how matters were progressing? Or would it not be better to be somewhere else here in Ireland, capable of returning whenever needed or just because he wanted to take a look?

It was then he thought of Melissa.

God knew she was not like any other girl he had ever chosen to spend time with. She was wasp-tongued and clearly found getting along with him neither necessary or desirable. But she had sounded nearly as desperate and reckless as he felt. Was it not she who had talked of running away?

Why should they not run away together? The obvious destination made him smile. Dublin. They would go to Dublin.

Why Dublin? Well, why not? There was really nowhere else on this benighted island to go. Dublin was not London, most certainly, but it was a city of sorts, and must have potential. Once there, he could deposit Melissa on this Caroline he had heard so much about. That would take care of her, although he doubted Dublin would settle her restless spirit. Quite obviously London had not. But once she was settled with Caroline, he could investigate what was possible for him to do in the city.

Business. There must be a great deal of business in any city of any size. True, he was a gentleman—an aristocrat-to-be—and according to the rules of gentlemanly behavior he should never soil his hands with the sordid practicalities of business. But to him business was infinitely preferable to soiling his hands with the dirt of his estate.

Would learning something he might be able to apply on the management of his estate make sense? It certainly struck him as a useful way to spend the years before the responsibilities of Kendall Hall and the estate were yoked around his neck. Uncle Charles seemed to be very fit, and please God, long should he continue to be so. But if Ethan contrived to find some way of life he genuinely enjoyed in Dublin, perhaps he might find some way to spend part of the year in the south, the rest of the time north, living on the estate.

Who could say? But the idea had possibilities.

There would be no way to explain him going to Dublin by himself when he logically should be on the estate learning his business. Melissa would give him a way out. If she were as unhappy as she claimed to be, Aunt Elizabeth would certainly have noticed it. Aunt Elizabeth was rather the noticing kind. So if he let his aunt know he thought a spell with Caroline might do Melissa some good (which it might well do), then the two of them taking off together would not seem remarkable after all. She would have a male relative with her so she would not be a defenseless young woman on her own. In fact, if push came to shove along the way, he could always claim to be her brother. They were not wildly dissimilar in looks.

He gave a passing thought to her remarkable bush of reddish gold hair and dismissed it. His own was an unremarkable brown, but quite often there might be one with ginger hair in a family and the others have more ordinary colors. In any case now she had cropped it, her hair was not the first thing you saw when you looked at her.

He had been so deep in his own thoughts that when he glanced up he had a nightmare moment or two of wondering where he was and then panicking that somebody had done something completely irresponsible and he had been standing right there not seeing it.

Fortunately not. He had been sitting mounted in the shade of a tree, and his horse had had the good sense to shift as the sun moved, so he was still shaded. The work on the field he had in theory been supervising was continuing without any outrageous deviation. It was another hot day—his uncle would be giving thanks for that, and indeed it was easier to harvest on such a day, but Ethan would have been grateful for a thin cloud cover to take the edge off the heat.

Odd. In his casual life back in London he paid little attention to what the weather was doing. Here the variations in the Irish climate were of continual absorbing interest, and made all the difference in whether his day would be just ordinarily boring or a physical misery to be endured and forgotten about as rapidly as possible.

Looking about, he saw another shady spot under a tall tree that would be nearly as good an observation point, and he touched his heels to the horse and was just moving over to it as his uncle came cantering into the field.

"Had enough?" he called over.

Ethan smiled and did not remark that he had had enough ten minutes after they reached the fields this morning. "I was thinking it might be getting time to go in.'

"Indeed. We can leave them to finish up. I have some correspondence at home I need to attend to, from Martin, Caroline's husband."

Ethan glanced at his uncle, his interest immediately caught. He'd like to know more about this Irishman who had married into the Anglo-Irish aristocracy. He seemed to be very comfortably off—he was, after all, apparently doing extensive renovation on a cottage for Caroline that would be used only occasionally. What did he do in Dublin to make him so prosperous?

That was critical enough to ask about.

"What did you say your son-in-law does in Dublin?

Uncle Charles shrugged. "Investments. He must do quite well with them, because Caroline's original father-in-law, the Duke of Apthorp, has Martin handling his investments as well. That was how Caroline met him in the first place: he had come to dinner at Apthorp Manor. Caroline was in mourning at the time, but the Duchess felt they knew him well enough so it would be appropriate for Caroline to be present that evening. They saw each other again a year or more later when Caroline was bringing her baby, Henrietta, back to England."

Ethan was perfectly sure there was more to the story than that, but that was not the part that interested him. Investments. It would be interesting to see exactly what that involved, and if it was anything that he might be able to learn. If he might wish to learn.

Yes. Dublin was a good idea. He just needed to get hold of Melissa and explain the possibility to her. His only problem was they had not parted on good terms.

He did not plan to be hindered by a minor problem.

MELISSA ROCKED IN THE ROCKING chair and tried to be as interested in Charlie's mastery of the spinning top the tenth time he wanted her to watch him as she had been the first. Anne was feeding Joanna across the room, and making appropriate encouraging noises whenever Charlie turned to her.

Melissa was so bored she thought she might die of it. Worse, by the time Charlie outgrew this stage Joanna would be nagging her to dress her French doll or goodness knew what else. Maybe she would be called upon to admire how Joanna could dance a few steps. Or build a house of wooden bricks. Assuming Melissa was still in Ireland and still attached to Anne and Hugh's household.

Or perhaps she might be in England, preparing for her fifth Season. Did people have a fifth Season? At what point were they declared unmarriageable and sent home?

She stood up abruptly and walked to the window, the chair rocking wildly behind her.

"Look at the chair, Mama!" Charlie cried out, charmed it was still making jerky motions, all on its own.

"My goodness, yes," Anne said, lifting Joanna from her breast to her shoulder. The baby was getting older. Her head no longer wobbled as if it were dangerously loose, but was held more or less erect, and her wide blue eyes stared across the room at Melissa. Her hair was thicker, too. Melissa had a moment of terrified pity: would the poor child be unfortunate enough to inherit Melissa's great mass of curly hair? She was Melissa's aunt, after all.

She sighed and turned back to the window.

For heaven's sake. There was Ethan, of all people, riding up the drive.

"Did you invite Ethan over here?" she asked.

"No," Anne said absently, her attention now on changing Joanna. "Why?"

"He just rode up."

"How odd," Anne murmured. "Maybe Hugh wanted to see him for some reason."

Dismissing the problem, Melissa watched the flight of two birds across the pale blue sky, almost free of clouds. They had had wonderfully fair weather the last week, which Hugh had enthused about each night at dinner. Apparently it greatly simplified the harvest.

It would have been lovely weather for garden parties and taking long walks, Melissa thought. She had in fact been doing some walking, across Ballymuir's extensive lawns and down the country lanes, past sprawling hedges and rolling green meadows. Reluctantly she had to admit that Ireland could be a very lovely place. No, there was not much in the way of entertainment, but the place itself was beautiful. When she said so, Anne had been plainly happy Melissa could see the beauty, too. It was that about Ireland she had always loved, she said. She could not imagine living anywhere else.

There was a discreet butler-like knock at the door.

Anne took a quick look to make sure she was dressed properly, and called, "Yes?"

It was Mr. Jenkins, the butler. "Madam, Mr. Hawthorne is here. He says Miss Preston asked him to come by."

Melissa goggled at him. *What?* "He did?" she asked faintly.

"Yes, m'lady."

Anne looked at her.

Melissa shook her head, bewildered. "I don't know what he's talking about."

"Well, why don't you go down and see what it's all about," Anne suggested. "I'll just stay here with the children."

Mr. Jenkins nodded and withdrew

Melissa walked toward the door, puzzling it out. She had asked Ethan to come here? When? She had absolutely no recollection of ever doing such a thing.

She opened the door, looking back over her shoulder at Anne. "I can't imagine what he's referring to," she said as a last protest before she closed the door.

When she came down the stairs, Ethan was in the front hall.

Melissa looked at him questioningly.

"Is there somewhere where we might talk?" Ethan asked, as if he appeared there regularly.

She looked around, uncertain, until Mr. Jenkins took control.

"May I suggest the drawing room, Miss Melissa?"

"Oh yes. That would be fine. Thank you." She followed the butler, Ethan coming behind her. Mr. Jenkins opened the door and then went about the room, opening the heavy drapes. The room looked far more approachable with sunshine flooding across the floor.

"Thank you, Mr. Jenkins," Melissa said, sinking down on a convenient sofa.

Ethan sat down on a nearby chair. Mr. Jenkins bowed and withdrew, leaving the door slightly open.

As if we were a courting couple, Melissa thought, exasperated.

She turned to survey Ethan straight in the face. "Well?"

"I needed to talk to you." His voice was low.

Melissa continued to stare at him, waiting.

"I had an idea."

She still waited.

"You talked about running away."

Her eyes widened a bit with alarm. "Yes?" she asked cautiously.

"It made me think you might wish to be elsewhere, too."

The last word caught her interest. Could it be that Ethan was as restless and dissatisfied as she was? "What do you mean?"

He glanced at the door, and, his voice still low, said, "I would rather slit my throat than spend another day out in those miserable fields."

"Oh." It was not so much a word as an indrawn breath. "I had no idea."

"Good. I hope no one else does either."

For a moment they sat, simply looking at each other.

"What do you have in mind?" Melissa's question was cautious, her voice as low as Ethan's had been.

"Two steps." He looked suddenly serious, as if he had planned something out carefully. "I thought I would start by finding an opportunity to tell Aunt Elizabeth I thought you were restless here so far out in the country."

"Ye-es," she said, drawing the word out.

"I hope she might suggest a visit with Caroline in Dublin."

Melissa watched him. "And if she does not?"

"Then I will suggest it. Uncle Charles was talking about them yesterday."

Her head went on nodding absently. Then she met his eyes again. "But how does that help you?"

He grinned. "You will need someone to travel with you. You cannot go all the way to Dublin by yourself. I am the only one free to go."

"Unless Aunt Elizabeth suggests she go instead."

Ethan's face was comically dismayed. "I had not thought of that. Do you think she would?"

She shrugged. "I don't know. Joanna is still very young. Aunt Elizabeth might want to wait to visit Dublin until Anne is able to go with her."

His mouth jerked up at one corner. "Is there any way to guarantee that? I am not going to stay here. I can't stand it."

Melissa raised her right eyebrow. "I have told you why I am unhappy here. Why are you? You're going to be the heir. Your whole life is organized ahead of you and you have all the freedom of a man. Where is there a problem?"

He spoke through his teeth. "I have never been involved hands-on with running an estate. I am a city man. The only time when I have not hated every minute of the day was when Uncle Charles and I went over the estate records and figured out where we were in relation to last year and the year before and what plans we should be making. That, to me, was satisfying work. What I need to do when the estate is mine is have Bowyer or someone like him take over the practical management while I do all the planning and record-keeping."

"What? You would have a middleman?"

"No, I would have a steward I am familiar with. I would be in Dublin, working there on something more congenial to me, and come up here frequently enough to see how affairs are progressing and to check on how our projections have worked out. It is only a day's journey, after all. I would not be in England, paying little or no attention. I would be doing what I can be good at, and hiring someone else—hopefully Bowyer—to do the rest. He is responsible and knows the tenants and local people well."

"So why would you be going to Dublin now?"

"Because I hope to learn from Caroline's Irish husband or whoever else I can find the skills I need for what I want to do. I am not saying I am capable now. I am saying I will never be capable of caring for this land with the passionate attachment my uncle has, and presumably all his ancestors had as well. One way or another they've kept this place wonderfully prosperous. I am cut from different cloth. I just need to work out how to make my cloth fit the circumstances."

Melissa sat silent for a bit. It was curious how odd people were, often so different from what she saw first. When she remembered the crowd of supercilious young blades Ethan had hung about with during the Season, from all she had known not a serious thought had passed through their minds. It seemed impossible this reflective young man could have been one of them.

But the practicality of what he proposed! Was there really any way it might come about? In a way she was still tempted to just pack up her bag and run away tonight rather than go through a process that might take days, working through everyone's objections. She was sure there would be many of them. But this Ethan who was coming to the end of the harvest in Ireland was not the carefree lightweight she had thought him before. If they followed his plan they would not be burning bridges behind them.

Her mother would not come screeching over to Ireland to bundle her back—back to where? Melissa could not guess what her mother's next move would be. It hurt her heart, somehow, to know she was giving her mother so much grief, although if the silly woman would just look at her and for once try to see who she was…

"So how would we start?" she asked.

Ethan's mouth quirked again. "I thought you had gone to sleep." He did not sound pleased.

Melissa glared at him. It would of course be much more pleasant if they actually liked each other, but as there was no one else around in a position to assist either one of them, she supposed they would have to put up with the situation as it was.

"As I had not, perhaps you could explain your plan to me in greater detail," she said acidly.

He nodded, as if acknowledging an adversary. "I hope to talk to Aunt Elizabeth this evening."

"Before or after slitting your throat? It is surely inevitable you will have to spend a day or two more in the fields."

His head snapped up, and from the flash in his eyes he was on the edge of jeering at her in return, but he swallowed and managed something close to a smile. "If all goes well, I will come back tomorrow to arrange our plans in more detail."

"And if it does not?" Melissa could have bitten her own tongue, but the challenge was already out there. Why was she so determined to be such a harridan?

Ethan smiled sweetly. "Then you may go to hell and make your own plans."

He rose, bowed politely, and went out.

Melissa shut her eyes and pressed her fists into her cheeks. Why, why, why did she have to be so disagreeable? Did she want to get away from this indescribably boring place or not?

She resolved to work out an appropriate apology for when she saw him tomorrow. If she saw him tomorrow.

Well, he had not been wrong, thinking her peculiar. Ethan rode through the gate back onto the road. If she were not his ticket to freedom, he would abandon any further attempt to deal with her. Prickly? A porcupine ready for battle would be cuddlier. But this was the best method he could think of for obtaining his own opportunity to learn if what he was thinking of would be practically manageable or not.

This Irish Martin—what was his last name? Ah, Gallagher. That was it. Gallagher would be an invaluable source of information. But it would undoubtedly be more impressive to Martin if Ethan showed the initiative to search out some facts independently rather than just showing up asking questions as if he were incapable of doing anything else. Presumably Melissa would be invited to stay with Caroline—she was, after all, the sister-in-law of Caroline's sister.

Of course, he was Caroline's cousin—which relationship was closer? He supposed it would depend on the personal relationships. If there were only room at Gallagher's house for one of them, it would of course be Melissa. She was, after all, a female in need of sheltered housing. How large could their house be? If necessary he could stop at a coaching inn while making inquiries around Dublin for a room to rent and for a place to work to learn elementary principles of accounting and so forth. Then, if he were asked for dinner with the Gallaghers (and Melissa, of course), which would surely be likely, there would be plenty of opportunity for the two men to talk on their own and hopefully for Gallagher to give him some further direction.

Once they were in Dublin they would probably spend little time with each other, and it could not take more than a day or so to get there. He had left Dublin in the morning and been in Drogheda later the same day. Even dragging along an argumentative female could not add more than one day to the journey.

This remained the only plan he'd been able to devise which supplied him with a plausible reason to head down to Dublin himself. His reason had to be believable. Otherwise, Uncle Charles might doubt his commitment to the estate. He had grown fond enough of his uncle not to want him troubled through his old age believing his heir was likely to lead the estate into rack and ruin. Not at all. Ethan was as committed to the well-being of the estate as Uncle Charles was. He just intended to run it on an entirely different pattern. His goal was not to make the tenants' lives harder to bear or allow some greedy middleman to siphon off substantial chunks of the profits made by their labor. If eventually his own son—now there was a awesome possibility!—had the same love of the land that Uncle Charles had, that son could come back to Kendall House and thrust his hands in the soil day after endless day.

But, dear Lord, Ethan did not want that for himself.

He rode directly to the stables, and turned his horse over to the first groom he saw rather than hang about chatting as he usually took pains to do. Then he went straight to the house.

It was only as he was running up the steps to the front door that it occurred to him his aunt and uncle might not yet have returned from the shopping excursion to Drogheda. He stopped dead, almost tripping over his own feet.

Duncan had the door open, waiting for him in any case.

"Good day, Duncan," Ethan said cheerfully.

The butler nodded his head politely in response.

"Has Lady Kendall returned?"

Duncan nodded again. "She is in the music room, sir."

Well. So far, so good. Rather than inquire about the whereabouts of his uncle, Ethan would take the opportunity to speak to his aunt.

Aunt Elizabeth was indeed in the music room quite alone. She was working on some form of needlework—Ethan had never been interested enough to learn what the various sorts were—and looked up with a warm smile when she saw him.

"How was Drogheda?" he asked.

"I was able to get the few things I needed," she said, looking pleased. "There is no point in thinking you will be able to shop seriously there. I'm afraid I was spoiled forever when I was in London for Caroline's come-out and first wedding. But all I needed now was fabric for new pillowcases and sheets, and plain linen or even cotton on occasion is available in Drogheda.

"How did you entertain yourself while we were gone?"

"I went riding for a bit. It's interesting to see what the land around here looks like. Gives me time to think as well."

Her hands went still, and Ethan realized he had her full attention. "And what were you thinking about?"

He decided to go straight to it. "I came across Melissa the other day."

Had her attention tightened a bit?

"I got the impression that she is"—he took a moment to look as if he were searching for a word—"perhaps not entirely happy."

His aunt's brows came together, and she sighed. "I was afraid of that. I had hoped that Gloucestershire was rural enough so that it would not be greatly different here. But of course there are no young people around except Anne and Hugh, and both of them are busy and quite domesticated, I suppose."

"She was in London for the Season this spring," Ethan put in.

"Well, after that anything would seem dull, I suppose." His aunt sighed again. "I don't know quite what to suggest. Perhaps she might enjoy spending some time in Dublin with Caroline?"

Ethan's heart nearly skipped a beat, but he managed to keep a straight face. "Do you think she might?"

"It would be a change. I would think Caroline might have some friends closer to Melissa's age."

Ethan tried to look as if he were thinking it over. "Could she travel down there by herself?" He hesitated, and corrected himself swiftly. "No, of course not. But I would like to see more of Dublin myself. If Uncle Edward could spare me, I could take her down there so she would not be travelling alone."

Aunt Elizabeth brightened. "What a splendid idea! Aren't you all coming near the end of the harvest? I'm sure under the circumstances he would be willing to have you leave. I have been fretting about Melissa myself."

He drew his hand over his face as if he were deep in thought. This was working out to be all too easy. He felt almost guilty—well, he supposed he should feel properly guilty, because he had been playing fast and loose with the truth. But would it not be to their greater good if he could find a way to fit the requirements for management of the estate into something he could imagine himself doing?

He looked his aunt directly in the face. "Would it be better for you to speak to Uncle Edward, or should I?"

His aunt considered, her brow wrinkling. "Let me talk to him. If there is a difficulty, the three of us could get together to work out a solution."

It was the best of all possible arrangements. Ethan nodded, being scrupulous to keep his face solemn and let none of his relief and excitement show.

"I will leave it to you, then," he said.

There the matter rested.

12

ETHAN DID COME TO BALLYMUIR the next day.

Melissa and Anne were together—for once without the children—when Mr. Jenkins came to tell Melissa he had arrived.

Anne, who was out on the newly-built terrace arranging some plants, looked at Melissa with some surprise.

Melissa, who had been assisting with the planting, caught sight of her dirty hands. "Oh dear."

"What on earth does he want now?" Anne caught herself, and grinned sheepishly. "That sounded more unfriendly than I meant. Don't mind me."

"I have no idea," Melissa said untruthfully. "I'll go wash my hands and find out."

She scrambled up the stairs and washed her hands quickly. Fortunately she glanced at herself in the looking glass and discovered she must have touched her nose at some point, so she washed her face while she was at it.

Then she came down the stairs, hoping she looked serene and not as eager to hear the news as she was.

Ethan had been installed in the drawing room.

He waited until Mr. Jenkins withdrew before he spoke. "I think we've done it."

Melissa did not even try to control the great smile that spread across her face. "That's wonderful! When do we go?" She sat down, Ethan taking a seat across from her.

He shrugged. "That's still up in the air a bit. Aunt Elizabeth suggested you going to Caroline herself, and when I proposed going as your escort,

85

she seemed to feel that was acceptable. She was going to mention it to Uncle Charles, and this morning when I saw him at breakfast, he said 'Dublin, eh? What next?' to me and shook his head. But pleasantly."

Melissa's smile diminished a bit. "Oh. When do you think you will know for sure?"

"I think we can plan on it as approved. How soon would you be able to go?"

"Today? Tomorrow?"

"That eager?"

Melissa could only interpret Ethan's look as patronizing. But he was her key to freedom. She took care not to bristle.

"Do you wish to remain here longer? Perhaps until the end of the harvest?" She tried to keep her tone pleasant.

He looked at her sharply. "No, of course not. Perhaps by the end of this week?"

She nodded, ever the docile young lady. Well, he would see. Once she was in Dublin, she had no intention of being set down in Caroline's household like a potted plant. How she was going to arrange for greater freedom she had no idea, but Caroline had a young daughter, and probably was as much engaged in her care as Anne was with her two. Melissa had had quite enough of small children for the time being. Exactly how she was going to manage in Dublin she did not yet know, but she felt sure inspiration would strike.

"Just let me know. I did not bring that much with me, so I don't have a great deal to pack." She started to rise, then hesitated. "What should I tell Anne?"

"Now?"

Melissa did not roll her eyes. When did he think she meant? "I believe she is a little curious about why you have come over twice in two days."

He laughed out loud. "Perhaps she thinks we are courting. That would complicate things."

"I'll be sure to set that straight," Melissa snapped back. Courting? Where did men get the gall to assume such things? By virtue of simply being male, they thought any female would be flattered by their attention?

"Yes, that would be as well." Ethan obviously put his mind to the problem. "If they get the idea we are interested in each other, then I am no good as an escort."

"Exactly. Fortunately, that misunderstanding can be taken care of by the bald truth." She leveled a stare at him. "You think I am an ugly shrew and I think you are an unsuccessful run-of-the-mill would-be rake. That should be sufficient."

Ethan blinked. "I believe your opinion of me has rather more adjectives than my opinion of you."

"Rearrange them as you will."

He looked thoughtful. "I don't think 'ugly' quite meets the case. You're better looking since you cut your hair."

"Off." She could not seem to control the melancholy in her voice. "My mother insists I cut my hair off."

He shrugged. "Either way. But obstinate and peculiar—those would be more accurate."

The very slight softening Melissa had felt when he refused "ugly" hardened instantly. "As you choose." She wished she could kick him sharply in the shins as she had done with Hugh when he was an irritating schoolboy and she was still too young to be taken firmly in hand. She would have to be continuously in Ethan's company for at least one full day and possibly parts of two. Did she want to be in Dublin that desperately?

Yes. Unfortunately she did.

"So what is your master plan now?" She tried to mellow the edge in her voice somewhat, but she could still hear it, and from the jerk of one of his eyebrows, so could he.

"I'm not sure it earns the title 'master' plan, but I had thought I would talk to Uncle Charles to make sure of his agreement and find out how often the post coach goes down to Dublin. Then we could be driven to Drogheda in the carriage to wherever it is the post coach stops, and go to Dublin from there."

"And how am I to be informed of the arrangements?"

"I could always come back to tell you, but as you point out, that might be misunderstood. Perhaps Aunt Elizabeth could come over to make sure you agree, since as far as she knows, you have not been involved in the idea yet."

Melissa nodded slowly. Yes. There was no doubt that Ethan was extremely competent when it came to planning, whether she liked to admit it or not. "That should work out well," she said. After all, one should give credit where credit was due.

Ethan stood up and gave her a brief bow. "It should not be long now. Maybe the end of the week?"

It was Tuesday. Melissa dipped a routine curtsey. "I will wait."

He went out the door—Mr. Jenkins had left it properly open, again—

and Melissa took a deep sigh. Well. She assumed the die had now been cast. She had given her permission for him to proceed, and reversing any of the plans would involve more questions than she had any desire to answer.

Somewhere, very very deep down, she could feel herself rejoicing. Once she heard the front door close, she came out of the drawing room and went back out to the terrace where Anne was still laboring with the plants.

Her head came up as soon as she heard Melissa approaching.

"What did he want?"

"I'm not quite sure. He was going on about Dublin. Apparently he passed through the city on his way to Drogheda, and found it quite impressive."

"So I have heard," Anne said wistfully. "Now that Caroline is there, I am very much looking forward to seeing her and getting to explore a little. But Joanna is still so young that I think it only makes sense to wait until spring for a trip. We won't have her outside much after autumn is over, and it seems foolish to go all the way to Dublin and have to stay inside there as well. From what she says, they have a rather grand house, but I want to see more than just her house."

"Mmm." Hopefully a noncommittal noise was better than a proper answer. "Do you want me to go back to planting the rest of these?"

"Yes, please." Anne pushed the hat she was wearing in the sun farther back on her head and then, squinting, moved it forward a little. "We're lucky to have such a fine day."

Melissa agreed, and the conversation moved on.

Ethan, on the way back to the part of the estate to which he had been dispatched (fortunately in the same direction as Ballymuir), had the satisfaction of knowing his plans were underway. Melissa was prepared to go, Aunt Elizabeth had spoken to Uncle Charles, and he did

not seem to be displeased by the idea, and now all that was required was to set the whole enterprise in motion. That, he supposed, would require him to consult with his uncle about the post coach schedule (if he knew it), the location where the coaches stopped in Drogheda, and the best method of being delivered there. All of which would be better done at the end of a day of work rather than interrupting him now. The prospect was cheering enough so that Ethan did not even mind the prospect of being a responsible part of the harvest supervising team for another day. Or two. But he was more than impatient to leave.

Unfortunately that night his aunt and uncle had been invited out for dinner. What Ethan wanted to discuss could not be crowded into five minutes while Uncle Charles's valet perfected his neck cloth.

Ethan ate his dinner in solitary splendor in the dining room. He would have been just as satisfied eating at the kitchen table, as he had been known to do at home, but here the option did not appear to be open. He debated bringing a book with him to the table, as he was alone, but decided against it. Mr. Duncan, the venerable butler, might be offended.

A solitary dinner lasted a very long time. He did not linger for port, on his own, nor for a cigar, which was not the part of the after-dinner ritual he enjoyed most.

Instead, he went to the music room.

Love of music seemed to run through the family. He had even, at one point, been given some piano lessons. It was not the usual thing for a gentleman, but his sister Emmeline had broken her arm falling from a horse, and his mother, who had engaged the piano teacher mostly out of pity because his wife was sickly and he had three children to support, was reluctant to dismiss him. Obviously it was impossible for Emmeline to continue, so Ethan, under protest, was drafted as a student.

Now, he took a look at the music available in the room, piled neatly in a folder. He found a piece he thought he might be able to manage, and took it to the piano.

He was still playing when the door opened, and his uncle came in, in the more elegant evening clothes he had worn for the dinner away from home.

"I didn't know you played." He glanced around the room, clearly noticing the music scores now loose around the piano. Ethan had abandoned a few as too difficult. Most of them he had tried, discovering immense pleasure in the effort.

Ethan turned around on the stool, grinning. "I didn't know I did, either. I did have some lessons many years ago, and when I saw the music I thought I might have a try at it again."

"It sounded pleasant as I approached." His uncle picked up one of the scores, looking at it with a faint smile. "This is one I think Anne used to play. She and Caroline would give us music in the evenings. Caroline sings—not a strong voice, but a very pleasant one. I remember that time with affection. It is a pity that the years pass so swiftly."

It was the kind of thing Ethan had heard older people say quite often before. He smiled agreeably, not having anything to add. It seemed to him the years had sometimes more than enough duration as it was.

"My wife was talking to me about the possibility of Melissa going down to Dublin for a while."

The remark brought Ethan to immediate attention. "Yes, she and I had talked about that as a possibility," he said. "Aunt Elizabeth seemed to think she was somewhat restless here, with no younger people around."

His uncle nodded. "Yes. Anne is not that much older than she is, but I suppose she sees Anne with an established life, a husband and two children, as in an entirely different situation, which of course she is. But the problem is how Melissa would get to Dublin on her own."

"Aunt Elizabeth and I thought it might be possible for me to escort her down there. I would love to have the opportunity to look around Dublin myself for a bit, but since I came to take part in and learn about the harvest, this might not be the best time to go." Ethan almost held his breath, fearing that his uncle would agree with him and the whole scheme be necessarily abandoned.

"Well, you have been here for most of it." His uncle stretched his neck and rolled his shoulders. "It's been a long day," he murmured, abruptly resuming his normal erect posture, only then apparently aware of what he was doing. "If Melissa is as restless as my wife suggests, a break might be an idea for both of you. There's little enough for you to do here once the harvest is in."

Ethan met his eyes in surprise. Did Uncle Charles realize how temperamentally unsuited he was to agricultural work? Thinking swiftly, he forced himself to relax and shrugged. "I would enjoy the change, I must admit."

"Then let us plan on it. How soon would you want to leave?"

Ethan shrugged again, this time to give the impression he was thinking it over. "As soon as the end of this week?"

"A post coach leaves Drogheda on Thursday. Would that be too soon?"

Had the man been reading his mind? Ethan swallowed. "Would we need to let Caroline know that Melissa is coming?"

His uncle smiled. "I would not be surprised if my wife has already communicated with her about it. Knowing my wife as I do, and knowing we have had a few letters from Caroline, I rather suspect it is your Aunt Elizabeth's opinion that Caroline could do with some company as well, and this is her complicated plot to pull the untidy edges together."

Well. Perhaps plotting ran in the blood—although of course Aunt Elizabeth was not the blood relative. It would be rather comical to think she had been working out her own plan for dealing with Melissa's restlessness at the same time as he had been trying to find some way of coping with his own.

"Do you think Aunt Elizabeth would be willing to propose the plan to Melissa?" he asked. Better put all the pieces in play. "I have the feeling she is not over-fond of me. We knew each other, slightly, during the Season, and she has indicated she felt some of my companions were not as respectful as they might have been."

"What happened?" His uncle looked at him closely.

Ethan sighed. He had not planned to tell the story at all, but perhaps it would be better to share part of it. It would certainly make it clear they were not trying to work out some way to run off with each other.

"It was her hair," he admitted.

"Her hair? Because it is short?"

"No, it was not short then. She has rather a lot of it, and it was very curly, and hard to control. It tended to overwhelm her face. My friends thought the effect was unfashionable and even unattractive." He had been feeling progressively more ashamed he had not discouraged some of the unkind remarks at the time, especially now he realized she had been hurt, but there was no way to rectify that now. It was probably better to let it sink into the past.

He sighed and continued. "Since they were my friends, Melissa associated them firmly with me and has made her displeasure with me plain. I discovered that when we happened to encounter each other a day or so ago when we were both out having an early morning ride. I went over to Ballymuir later to explain I had not participated in whatever it was she found offensive, but she was not open to discussion about it."

His uncle frowned. "That is unfortunate. Do you suppose she will refuse to have you as her escort to Dublin? Because it would be difficult for me to leave…"

"Oh, no." Ethan spoke as quickly as he could manage. "It is just a day of travel, after all. It is not as if we are going to be traveling companions for any considerable stretch of time."

"Pity about that." His uncle spoke regretfully. "I cannot say I have seen many women with short hair, but I must say I find it is quite suitable for Melissa. Her hair is a lovely color and I like the curls. But I am an old man, comparatively speaking, and what do I know?" His face settled into a reluctant smile. "And being an old man, I must continue on my way to bed. Next evening we must be sure to ask you for some music here, if you would be so kind."

He rose from his chair and started toward the door, pausing to turn back slightly.

"Let this be a lesson to you, my boy. Never remark on a young lady's appearance in anything but clearly complimentary terms. They are as unpredictable as vipers."

Whereupon he left the room, chuckling.

MELISSA COULD HARDLY BELIEVE IT had happened. There she was, sitting in the post coach, somewhat squeezed, it was true, between a large lady who had come from Belfast and a smaller but much encumbered older woman who was taking a considerable number of parcels to her daughter in Dublin. Ethan, not entirely hiding his enjoyment of her situation, had much more room on the bench across, but she could see it would not be appropriate for a man to sit where she was when a female was available to do so.

One more example of the advantages the male gender enjoyed in this world.

Crowded or not, she was actually on the way to Dublin, with not a small child in sight, and the prospect of seeing something of the world. How everything had fallen into place so neatly she could not quite understand, although she was determined to quiz Ethan once they were somewhere more private.

It had all been organized with amazing swiftness. Aunt Elizabeth had come to ask her opinion of a visit to Caroline in Dublin. When Melissa had said calmly she would be delighted to go (being quite proud she had not shrieked with joy), Aunt Elizabeth had suggested she start packing because the most convenient time to go would be the next day.

Melissa's eyes widened with surprise, but she agreed promptly, and made her way to the bedchamber she had been using to start sorting out clothes for taking with her. There was fortunately no problem of having to take a maid, as she had not had anyone in particular at Anne's house. Anne's maid had come to help when needed or one of the upstairs maids had offered to lend a hand. Fortunately she did not need much in the way of assistance. Her hair she could manage herself, which was another benefit of it being short. All she needed to do was to run a brush through her curls and then perhaps, if she felt like it, to coax one or two curly strands to lie around her face into a position she thought might be more attractive.

Dressing was more of a problem, so she chose to take with her only the dresses she could get in and out of on her own if need be. She hoped there would find someone available at Caroline's house to lace up her stays at the back, but if worst came to worst, she was fortunately small-breasted and slender enough so that she could make do with just her shift.

In any case, one way or another, here she was in the coach with Ethan, and enough other people around them so that they did not need to talk all the way. She had wondered what on earth she would find to talk to him about if they were alone in the coach.

At Balbriggan mercifully the large lady from Belfast left the coach, and no one else joined them. Melissa was able to take her seat by the window and use the side of the coach to lean against and drift into a kind of half-sleep. She remained vaguely aware of what was going on, but floated in a lazy daze where she was not required to pay attention to anything. The road seemed to be somewhat smoother as they came farther south, although Melissa was not sure if that was something she was actually observing, or simply that she was growing accustomed to the coach's bumps and jolts.

It was perhaps two hours or so later when Ethan reached across to jiggle her elbow.

"Hmph?" She struggled back toward wakefulness.

"We are coming into Dublin."

She blinked and forced herself to sit up and look out. The old woman next to her, who must have been sleeping as well, shook herself awake and began to collect her parcels, which had spread both on the floor and the seat. Melissa handed her the one or two that had been jolted over nearer to her, and then turned her attention to the window.

Dublin seemed to be a queer mix of shabby small buildings on dirt roads, and then as the coach kept moving southward the buildings grew taller and more prosperous-looking. At last the coach rattled over a bridge crossing the River Liffey, and slowing down a rather unimportant-looking road, came to a halt at an inn.

This was clearly the terminus, because everyone was gathering their possessions, and the door was thrown open for them to disembark. Ethan motioned to Melissa for her to remain until he had the chance to jump out, and then reached out his hand to help her descend.

"Where are we?" Melissa looked around.

"I saw Trinity College, so we cannot be far from St. Stephen's Green." Ethan picked up his case and Melissa's bag. "There's a hack over there. We can take that one."

She looked at him. They had not discussed how much money either of them had. She knew she would be staying at Caroline's house, but she had taken the money she had brought from Gloucestershire. It was not a great amount, but there had been nothing near Ballymuir to spend money on so she still had all of it. Had Ethan brought money with him?

"How much will it cost?" she asked.

"I have money," Ethan said grandly.

Standing in the midst of a group of strangers did not seem a good place to discuss how much he had, so she followed docilely as he led the way to a hack cab, waiting on the street just past the inn. He helped her in and went to speak to the driver.

Ethan had said it would not be far, but Melissa was surprised first by the amount of traffic on the roads and secondly by the route the driver chose, which seemed to involve a great deal of turning.

"It's probably because of the traffic," Ethan suggested. "There. I can see the Green now."

Melissa peered out at it. It seemed a pleasant place, and if the house of the Gallaghers faced on it, it would probably be a pleasant house.

Just then the cab came to a stop. The house they faced was more than pleasant. It was large and elegant, like the houses around it. Melissa kept staring at the magnificent fanlight above the front door, and the important-looking brass knocker on the door itself.

As it happened, no one needed to knock it. Ethan helped Melissa out, and was paying the driver when the door flew opened and a small enthusiastic woman came running out.

"You must be Melissa!" She threw her arms around a rather startled Melissa and went on talking. "I'm Caroline Gallagher, and I am so pleased to have you here." She hugged Melissa and went on to take Ethan's hand, beaming as if he were a long-lost friend. "You must be my cousin Ethan. Welcome to Dublin. Don't worry about the cases— O'Malley will organize them."

Darting back to Melissa, Caroline took her arm and led her into the house. A middle-aged butler, elegantly dressed, bowed to her as he passed, going out to pick up the cases that Ethan had set down on the pavement before he followed the women through the front door.

It was all far more spacious than Melissa had imagined. She had been told Caroline's husband was prosperous; it was now plain he was wealthy. They were in an entrance hall, with wonderful plaster moldings up the walls and decorating the ceiling. Just in front of them was another entrance, with a fanlight that was a twin to the one over the front door, but under this one the door was open and apparently kept so. Beyond the door was a grand staircase, curving up.

Melissa hesitated, taking just a minute to admire the elegance around her, when suddenly she heard a brisk single bark, and a small dog came scampering down the staircase, followed by what had to be one of the biggest men she had ever seen.

"Welcome to you," he said, his voice tinged with an Irish accent.

Melissa stared at him wide-eyed. First of all he was tall, although with the elevation of the entrance hall ceiling his height was not as remarkable as it certainly would be in an ordinary house. But more than that, he was large all over. Not fat—not at all fat. Large. Compared to him, Ethan looked almost scrawny.

Caroline went straight to the giant, put her arm around his waist, or as far as it would reach, and beamed up at him. "They're here, Martin," she said. "Isn't it wonderful!"

The expression on his face when he looked down at his wife caught Melissa by surprise. It was as if he was savoring his connection with something so fine and remarkable he could not quite believe it was true.

If any man ever looks at me like that, Melissa thought, he will have my heart forever and I won't care if the law says I am his possession as much as a pair of shoes. Should any man ever look at me like that.

"Who have we here, Caro?" he asked.

"They're family, although I've not met them before. This girl with the wonderful hair is Melissa Preston—she's Hugh's sister. And the fine young gentleman is Ethan Hawthorne, the future Earl of Kendall. Anne and I shall have to teach him where all the best hiding places are in Kendall House so that when he's earl—a long time from now, I hope— he will be able to find where his children have hidden."

Melissa and Ethan shared a look. Caroline was not at all what either of them had expected, although neither of them probably could have specified exactly what they thought she would be like. She was small, fair-haired, and very pretty. Anne had explained Caroline's tragedy to Melissa, and she was sure Ethan knew of the story as well. But the woman they were meeting did not seem tragic in any way.

Ethan was squatting down on the floor with the dog. The dog appeared delighted to have somebody friendly available, and was dancing about, wriggling with pleasure and trying to lick whatever bits of Ethan were available.

"Ah. Ethan—is that right?—seems to have discovered George," Martin said.

Ethan looked up with one of his friendliest grins, looking not at all like the scornful young blade Melissa remembered from London.

"He's a great dog." He looked genuinely fascinated with the dog. "George, eh? And how does he come by such a distinguished name?"

Caroline knelt down by them. "He was named by the stable boy at Apthorp Manor, really more like a castle, where I lived with my first husband. I was devastated when my husband died, and his father let me have George. He was a particularly friendly puppy, and the stable boy said that he thought he was the king."

George, obviously excited by the attention, continued wriggling and butting his head against any receptive legs.

"George!"

Melissa and Ethan looked up at the child's voice, and saw a very young little girl—a little younger than Charlie? Melissa wasn't much good at guessing children's ages—coming down the stairway.

"George dancing," the child said.

The giant picked her up and she giggled happily at being swept through the air and settled into what was obviously a familiar position on his shoulders.

Melissa looked nervously at the ceiling height. Fortunately they were all on the stairway side of the interior fanlight, and the ceilings were the same level as on the next floor.

"You must meet some new relatives," Martin said.

Caroline reached up to pat the child's back, whether to make sure she was balanced safely or just to let her know she was there Melissa couldn't decide. "This is Henrietta, our daughter," she said.

"And the nice man playing with George is Mr. Hawthorne." Martin spoke with authority.

"But since he is a relative, you should call him Ethan," Ethan said. He was now rubbing George's stomach, sending him into ecstasy.

"Caro?" the agreeable giant asked.

"I suppose so," Caroline said, half unwillingly. "I suppose I should be insisting on proper politeness, but as you will be here for a while, it would seem very odd to be calling you Mr. Hawthorne when shouting up to say that dinner is ready."

"Oh, I was not going to be staying here," Ethan said quickly.

"You're not?" Melissa and Caroline both spoke at exactly the same moment, as if it had been rehearsed.

"No. I had thought I would be staying at the inn where the coach stopped," he said, straightening up, leaving a baffled George to scramble to his feet.

"Why ever would you be doing that?" Caroline sounded confused.

"Well—I mean, I'm not a close relative, I mean directly—" Ethan sounded as confused as she did.

Henrietta reached down from her perch to pull Ethan's hair.

"Hey!" One of Ethan's hands went up to his head, to bat whatever it was away, and then when he realized he had hold of Henrietta's hand, he shook it instead. "Thanks so much, young lady, but I'm hoping to keep this hair as long as possible. My father was bald, which worries me."

Henrietta giggled—Ethan was now playing with her hand, sweeping it back and forth—while Melissa stared at him with awe and amazement. She had never heard him sounding so much like an ordinary friendly person before. Was it the presence of a child and a dog that had uncorked this unexpected display?

Caroline was meantime apologizing to Ethan and trying to get Henrietta down from Martin's shoulders while she explained to her that pulling somebody's hair is not what nice little girls do, all at the same time.

Martin obligingly bent down so his wife could retrieve Henrietta more easily.

"Well, I hope you're part of the family now," he said. "I do not allow my daughter to attack strangers in such an intimate way."

"It's not as if we don't have room enough," Caroline added, once she had Henrietta captured and set down on her own feet again. "I don't know if the builders of this house had a huge family or dozens of guests, but there are enough rooms for all of us, including the inhabitants of both Kendall House and Ballymuir, if everyone chose to arrive at once. With some to spare."

Ethan looked around.

"It's futile to argue with her," Martin observed fondly.

Ethan shrugged. "If you're sure it will not present difficulties. I don't want to be taking up space that should be used otherwise."

"Well, then." Caroline spoke with obvious relief. "Let me take care of this baggage here—she does have a nanny!—and then I'll sort out the dinner problem. Or maybe I should show you your rooms first." She looked at Martin as if she were undecided.

"She has a fine mind, but prefers to use mine," Martin said, still regarding her as if she had been especially constructed to please him.

Caroline beamed at him. "Then I'll show Melissa and Ethan to their rooms first. If dinner is a little delayed, you will not be disturbed, will you?"

"Not at all. I shall restore Henrietta to her nanny, shall I?"

"That would be very kind of you. Melissa and Ethan, just follow me up the stairs. Don't worry about your cases now. I'll make sure they're taken upstairs." Caroline, still almost twinkling with good cheer and hospitality, headed for the stairway, looking over her shoulder to make sure Melissa and Ethan were coming after her.

Was it the difference between the country and the city? Or was it that Caroline and Martin had not been married for as much as a year yet? Somehow it seemed to Melissa this house shone and sparkled with good humor and delight, with both Caroline and Martin much happier than any other people she had known.

Oh, her brother and Anne seemed very happy together, but it was in a more settled, domesticated way. Uncle Charles and Aunt Elizabeth (although they were not truly her uncle and aunt, but some complicated sort of in-law) were more staid and used to each other, which was what would be expected.

But these two? Caroline had not a breath of tragedy hanging about her, although undoubtedly her first marriage and her husband's early death must have been very difficult. Martin did not behave as if having his wife be the daughter of an earl and himself plain Mr. Gallagher caused him so much as a passing thought of feeling lesser than she in social standing. He was comfortably confident, and they were clearly and plainly devoted.

If she could have a marriage like that—well, that would require rethinking everything. A pity she was not at all certain she would be capable of that kind of relaxed relationship. She knew she was a prickly person. How did you stop being prickly and be as gracious and joyful as Caroline seemed to be?

The stairway swept up in a double-height space, with a drawing room on the right as they reached the top of the staircase. The rest of the open area was a great balcony overlooking the stairway, and by the side of it, a row of railings. Melissa noticed someone had run a length of firm-looking linen fabric in and out through the balusters—presumably, she gathered, by direction of Caroline so that a small child given to exploration would be unable to wedge herself into a position where she might fall.

Caroline clearly knew how a small child would think.

Melissa was surprised at the depth of the house. When she remarked on it, Caroline laughed and said she had been equally surprised. There was another staircase that led up to the floor above, and that was where the bedrooms for Melissa and Ethan were. Melissa's windows looked out into St. Stephen's Green, the park across the street, and she assumed Ethan's did as well, as he was in the second bedroom down from Melissa's.

Caroline ordered Melissa to take a short rest. Traveling was hard work, she said. Then she left them alone. Melissa could hear the sound of her feet retreating. She thought of going down to see how Ethan was doing, but the bed suddenly seemed to be singing a siren song to her and she sat down for just a moment, mulling over the new aspects of Ethan she'd seen.

It seemed easier to think lying down, so she did.

Her dreams were confused muddles of the very large Martin, small Henrietta, Caroline wafting in and out of rooms and staircases, and Ethan.

Mostly of Ethan.

MELISSA WOKE UP MUDDLE-HEADED and inexplicably cross.

The first thing she noticed was that it was morning. Then she realized that although she didn't remember taking her shoes off, they were lined up neatly by the side of her bed, and there was a blanket tossed over her, although she was still wearing what she had been wearing the day before.

None of it made any sense.

She ran a hand through her hair—at least that seemed to be as she would have expected—and pulled herself up so she was sitting with her legs hanging over the side of the bed.

Someone must have been close outside the door, listening, because although Melissa was unaware of having made any noise, there was a gentle knock on the door.

"Yes?" Melissa had absolutely no idea who it might be. Caroline? Ethan?

The door opened partially and a maidservant's head came around the edge to peer in.

"Miss Preston? Would you take a bit of tea now?" Clearly Irish. Well, what did Melissa expect? Chinese?

Tea sounded wonderful. It occurred to her to wonder what had happened to dinner. She hoped that Caroline had not planned anything special for their first evening in Dublin. Melissa seemed to have missed the evening entirely. Had she really slept the clock around?

"Yes, please," Melissa said, trying to sit up straight and look less like somebody who had slept in her clothes all night.

The maid apparently was a mind-reader as well. "Miz Gallagher thought 'twas best to just let you sleep," she confided.

"I slept," Melissa agreed.

"'Twould you like to take a bath now or have some tea to start?"

Melissa considered. The thought of changing out of her travel-worn clothes was certainly tempting, but so was a cup of tea.

"Maybe I'll have the tea to start," she said, unconsciously echoing the girl's words. "Do you know, is my case somewhere handy?"

The maid nodded. "'Tis right here in the room." She motioned to it, partially hidden by a comfortable-looking chair. "'Twas my thought to put your clothes away while you had the bath. Miz Gallagher made it plain you was not to be disturbed so I couldna do it before."

Melissa suddenly realized her own head was bobbing up and down in agreement. She stopped sharply. "And what is your name, please?"

The maid looked surprised and colored slightly. "I'm Moira, please," she said.

Melissa took a firm grip on herself. "Well, Moira, let's start with tea, and then I'll take that bath, and you can put my clothes away, and maybe we can get the day started in a more organized way."

Moira smiled—she had a lovely broad smile, even if a couple of teeth were missing—and nodded. "I'll do that, ma'am."

The tea was excellent and so was the bath and Melissa was overjoyed yet once more because washing her hair was not the major production it had been back in the bad old days when she seemed to have more hair than head. Washing and drying it had taken forever. Now her hair was slightly damp when, dressed and organized, she set off to see what was going on elsewhere in the house. Even so, it looked acceptable from what she could see in the looking glass thoughtfully provided in her bedchamber.

That was good enough.

She started down the staircase cautiously, looking for whomever might be around, but Caroline still startled her when she popped out of a room, leaving the door wide open. It looked like an inviting room behind her, light and blessed with a high ceiling.

"Oh, Melissa, are you starving to death?" Caroline demanded.

Melissa composed herself enough to answer relatively calmly that she was still most definitely in the land of the living.

"I felt terrible letting you go without any dinner, but you were sleeping so peacefully that I could not persuade myself to awaken you. I left some bread and an apple outside your door so that if you did wake up in the night and you were hungry there would be something there."

Melissa automatically looked behind herself as if she could see up the staircase and around the corner to the door of her bedchamber.

Caroline laughed. "Oh, I had it picked up this morning. I had visions of you getting up out of bed and stumbling over it."

Melissa shook her head. "Oh, no. Moira was there to help as soon as I woke up."

Her hostess looked pensive. "I must ask her if she ate the apple. The bread would have gone stale, but it would be a shame to have taken the apple all the way to the kitchen, when she could have just eaten it herself." She took Melissa by the elbow. "Let me take you down and see what we can find for you to eat now."

"What time is it?"

Caroline frowned. "I would think it must be close to ten o'clock. Martin and Ethan had breakfast together and then I think Martin took Ethan with him to the office. But we can check the time properly from the clock downstairs."

"Ethan went to the office?"

"I think so. At least I haven't seen him here."

Melissa found herself feeling unexpectedly bereft. She and Ethan had made no plans together, but somehow she hoped they would do some initial exploring of Dublin together. Had they talked about that, or had she thought it up all by herself?

"Breakfast?" Caroline asked brightly.

Unfortunately at just that moment Melissa's stomach growled. Fortunately Caroline seemed to be not easily horrified, and in fact they broke into giggles together.

"If you don't mind," Caroline said, pulling herself together with cheerful determination, "I think they've probably cleared up in the dining room on the entrance floor. Would you mind going down to the kitchen?"

Melissa tried to remember where she might have seen a dining room as they came in. All she could remember were the two fanlights, identical, one over the front door facing the street, and the other between the front door and the staircase. There must have been rooms there, but she couldn't remember seeing any.

"Not at all," she said, wondering where the kitchen might be and how it was reached. The main staircase was certainly too elegant to be the way of getting food from the kitchen to the table.

"Come with me." Caroline turned a corner, not in the great corridor that led from the staircase to the back of the house, but a much less conspicuous passageway, where she opened a door. There was yet another staircase—it would be interesting to know exactly how big this house was, Melissa thought—but this one wound down past yet another door.

"That goes into the dining room," Melissa to her. "There's another more elegant entrance in the entrance hall just before the staircase."

They continued down. After another turning of the stair, there was a door straight ahead which Caroline pushed open.

They were in the kitchen. It must have been toward the back of the building, because there were high windows that looked out into the sunshine of the back garden. The kitchen was large, but fundamentally the same as all other kitchens Melissa had known: a big table occupying the center, a sink along the side, shelves with pots and pans, and a great kitchen stove, taking up all the space within the fireplace that clearly had been the place for serious cooking for many years before.

The interesting part was that Ethan was sitting at the table, with a newspaper, a large cup of tea, and two pieces of toast.

"Oh!" Caroline turned to Melissa, shrugging, and then back to Ethan. "I thought you went to the office with Martin."

"He invited me," Ethan said. "But Melissa and I had vaguely planned to take a look around Dublin together and I thought I'd wait until she woke up to see if she were still in the land of the living. Good morning, sleepyhead."

Melissa knew he was teasing but wished he hadn't. It reminded her that she seemed to be some sort of joke to him. Still, he had waited to see if she was planning to go out exploring with him, and that was extremely kind. Why did he have to be such an enigma?

Caroline was summoning a maid to set up some breakfast for Melissa.

"We usually eat breakfast sometime between eight and nine o'clock, because Martin wants to get off to the office, so I'm afraid they clear everything away once we're done," she said apologetically, as if her normal household routine was something unusual that she should reorganize for the convenience of temporary guests.

"Well, the toast and tea would be fine for me," Melissa said.

"Nonsense. You had no dinner. You should be hungrier than that," and Caroline bustled off to arrange things properly—at least in her eyes. Very shortly there was the delicious smell of bacon and eggs, and Melissa realized her nose knew she was hungry, even if her stomach was not entirely convinced.

Ethan was happy to share, admitting after an impressive mouthful of bacon and egg that he had already had one breakfast with Martin. "I am pleased to discover breakfast is the sort of meal you can enjoy twice," he said, beaming at both Melissa and Caroline.

It did not take the two of them long to lay waste to the food supplied on the table. The cook must have made it her business to stay out of their way, because the only servants they saw had none of the dignity of the cook in such a grand house. But a fresh teapot was supplied when they had passed the stage of eating enthusiastically, and since Caroline had long since disappeared upstairs to see what was happening with Henrietta, Melissa and Ethan were effectively alone.

"Do you want to take a wander through Dublin?" Ethan asked, when he was drinking what he claimed would be his last cup of tea. "Martin says it is much more compact than London, with some rather grand buildings."

"I would." Melissa set down her own cup. "Thank you very much for waiting for me. I had not realized I was so tired."

"Actually, part of my reason for waiting was purely selfish." Ethan set down his cup as well and rubbed his hands together as if preparatory for some major action. "I wanted the chance to talk to you. Using you rather as a wall to bounce my ideas against, if you don't mind."

She looked at him dubiously. "Me?"

Ethan made an odd quirk with his mouth. "Well, not to be uncomplimentary, but you are the only one around who has known me more than a month or so."

"Known you?" She heard her own voice squeak. "You mean we went to some of the same social gatherings and knew each other's names. Generally speaking. Although as I recall, you and your friends had some other names for me."

He started to shrug, and then tossed his hands out imploringly. "Look, Melissa, I have apologized for that, have I not? If I have not, then I most heartily apologize now. It was unkind and certainly unhelpful—although if that's what spurred you into cutting your hair, you look greatly improved now."

"I don't know what to make of you," she grumbled.

This time Ethan did shrug. "Then try it out as a friend. Look, I need to talk to someone about what I am thinking."

She opened her mouth to tell him just to start then, for heaven's sake, and then closed it. Perhaps she should cut him a little bit more slack.

"So I came over here to work with Uncle Charles, and learn some of what I'll need to know eventually, even if he is at present so hale and hearty it looks as if he has a chance of outliving me." His mouth tilted again.

She said nothing.

"You know I hate the day-to-day business of keeping an estate. But one day Uncle Charles showed me what he calls the accounts, how he keeps track of everything and projects what he will need for next year, what did well and what did not. Melissa, I suddenly saw what it was I wanted to do. Let Mr. Bowyer run the fields. Keep me in touch with what is going on, of course. If there are problems or unusual successes, I want to see them. But the year-long drudgery out in the fields—I would despise that. Let me keep the facts and figures. Let me compare years; let me compare types of seed, find out what is available, what has been, or could be, improved. That I am eager to do. More than eager."

He half-smiled, apparently just taking in the intensity of her interest. "So what I need to do is learn how to do the paperwork. The planning. Martin asked me if I would like to see his office. I would like nothing more. Only I want to do more than see the office. I want to be there, to work there. He works with investments, but much of it must be forecasting, working from records to see what has happened in the past. I believe I could learn from that. Maybe eventually I could spend part of my time here and part there—well, to be realistic, probably most of my time there. But have time to spend here to get away from the pressure, away from those damned—excuse me. Away from those fields."

He dropped his glance down to the table, and moved his cup and saucer to one side and then back again. "Or am I being a fool? I had to ask someone."

Melissa started to speak, and realized her mouth was too dry. She swallowed, and then said very quietly, "I do not think you are a fool." Her eyes flicked back up to his face. "I do not think I know who you are. This man talking to me here is not the man I saw in the ballrooms and soirees in London."

His face still looked anxious, but he attempted a smile. "You did more than see me. I am quite sure we danced together more than once."

"Are you?" She smiled. "Did they tease you about it?"

His eyebrows jerked. "Not that I remember, but it would not matter. Most of them are fools anyway."

"Did you recognize that at the time? Remember, they will eventually be the great men of England and the world."

He shrugged. "Well, I was a fool as well, so probably not. If they are tomorrow's rulers, God save the king." His look fastened on her again. "Do you think my plan has even a breath of rationality to it?"

The words "how should I know something like that?" almost rose to her lips, but she hesitated instead. "I like that you are thinking so seriously about it," she said. "But I am a girl, the most trivial of creations. Girls are not allowed to have opinions about anything so important."

He stared back at her without expression. "But if you were allowed."

"Then I would try it. I would not tell anyone else I am trying it, which might make it difficult, because you would need to stay here in Dublin longer than I think anyone expects you to stay. But I am sure you are clever enough to think of an excuse."

"Would you stay?"

Melissa frowned. "What does that have to do with anything?"

"If you go back—unless by chance Caroline chooses to go back as well—I would have to go back to escort you."

She laughed without amusement. "Oh, fine. So it is up to me."

Ethan shook his head impatiently. "No, of course not. I'm sorry. I did not mean to dump the burden onto your shoulders. I was just trying to think practically."

She considered. This was requiring a whole new way to think about Ethan. He was apparently not the supercilious young blade he'd been in London. She should stop talking to him as if he were. "Well, if Caroline is willing to keep me around…"

He suddenly rose to his feet. "There is no reason for us to spend the day here in the kitchen. The cook is probably waiting impatiently for us to go somewhere else. Shall we take a look at Dublin?"

Melissa stood up as well. "By all means," she said. She cast a quick glance around the kitchen as she walked toward the door. She should remember this place. She had met a whole new Ethan here.

THE WIND WAS SHARPLY COLD when they stepped out onto the street.

It looked to Ethan as if Melissa was trying to huddle deeper into her pelisse and scarf. "How can it be this cold? It's just barely October," she complained.

He pulled his own coat closer around his neck as well. "If we walk rapidly, it will be warmer. Perhaps the house is heated more than we thought."

As they walked, a sharp gust blew across St. Stephen's Green.

"No," Melissa said. "It's the weather."

They turned onto Grafton Street, out of the wind, and walked along, silently but companionably. Melissa seemed to be looking around with fascinated interest at the houses, an odd jumble of fresh-looking buildings up against older, more worn structures. Ethan found himself looking as well, wondering where Martin's office would be.

"Where are we going?" Melissa asked.

"Probably not as far as I'd planned." He grinned at her. "But we must see the River Liffey that separates Dublin into north and south. And I'd like to take a look at the Customs House. It's a fine elegant building, even if there's not much use for it since the Act of Union. At least that's what I've been told. Martin said the best way to see it is from across the river, so if we just turn right when we get there, we can walk down and it will be right there."

Melissa shivered.

"Then afterwards we can stop in at the inn—I think it's just down one of the streets here—and get a hot cup of tea or coffee."

She nodded, glancing gratefully in his direction.

"If we walk faster, you'll be warmer."

She halted. Then she wrapped part of her scarf around her head like some of the Irishwomen they saw scurrying along the streets. "Faster?" she challenged, and picked up her pace.

He laughed and stretched out his legs a little to keep up with her.

The river was dark and far narrower than the Thames when they reached it, but the road—or Essex Quay, as it said on a sign—was broad enough so there was no chance of bumping into anybody coming the other way, even wrapped up as they all were and concentrating on getting to wherever they were going as rapidly as possible.

Still he had to admit to himself it felt good to be walking so vigorously after the long day cooped up in the mail coach. The exercise was in fact warming him up. He hoped the same was true of Melissa, because now that he thought about it, men seemed to dress much more warmly than women. The overdress thing she was wearing—what would Emmeline have called it? a pelisse or something?—looked too thin to be much protection against the wind.

Even so, it was interesting to be out and having a look around. But the city would certainly present a more attractive face if everybody else was not hurrying, as they were, to get inside out of the cold wind.

Melissa obligingly slowed a little when Ethan waved off to the side to show her Trinity College, established by Queen Elizabeth more than 200 years before. He assumed students would be nearby, but they all were presently proving their intelligence by remaining indoors.

"How can it be this cold in October?" she grumbled.

"We're farther north here than in London," he pointed out

"Not that much. I suppose it must be colder yet in Scotland."

He looked at her. She did look cold. Her lips were not exactly blue, but her face looked pinched. He tried to muffle his own sigh. He would like to see the building—there were 14 carved keystones representing the rivers of Ireland—but this did not seem the day for it.

"Never mind the Custom House then. I think it has become more important to get you indoors," Ethan said, taking her arm to guide her down a small street to their right, and then in through a door to what was clearly a travelers' inn.

Had he ever taken her arm like that before? He couldn't remember doing so, and he was surprised by how slim and delicate her arm seemed to be. Almost as if he had a bird in his keeping. She shook off the shawl over her head, and he found himself impressed by how bright and shiny her headful of golden red curls was. How had he missed before how attractive her hair was? Well, of course it had been somewhat out of control back then in London, with its length and abundance only minimally held in place, but he should have noticed the magnificent color. Odd.

But here he was standing, looking at her, and she probably was wondering if he'd gone dumb.

"Would you like coffee or tea?"

She did not reply. Instead she rearranged the shawl around her shoulders, and slipped gracefully into a chair at the empty table where they were standing. It was much better inside. When the door closed behind them of course they were out of the wind and in a warm, close atmosphere with perhaps too much smoke, but still a great improvement over the outside with the wind roaring down the river.

She clearly thought so. He could almost see her opening up like a flower, even in the stuffy atmosphere of the inn. But she had not yet answered him.

"Is it that major a decision?" It was still surprisingly satisfactory to tease her.

She blinked up at him.

"Excuse me?"

"I asked if you wanted coffee or tea. You were messing with your shawl, but you didn't say anything."

"Oh." She didn't seem to recognize he was teasing her. Emmeline would have flared back at him. "Thank you. Tea, please."

He moved over toward the counter. The room was fairly full already, and from time to time the door opened—he hoped their table was out of the line of the draft—to let in other refugees from the cold. If October was like this, he did not like to think what it would be like in December. Or January. Or, as far as that went, crossing the Irish Sea. Did this mean that he would be here in Ireland until spring at least?

Could be. Fortunately his turn to be served came up, and he headed back to the table with the hot mugs warming his hands.

"I'm sure there are some shops around," he said, handing her a mug of tea, "but I don't know where they are."

"There's nothing I need right now." She sipped at the tea, and then set the mug down. Her forehead wrinkled again. "Who paid for my passage on the mail coach?"

His mug stopped midway to his mouth. The workings of a woman's mind had always been more than he could keep up with. Both Emmeline and his mother continually bewildered him with curious comments like that. What on earth made her think of such a thing sitting here in Dublin, drinking tea?

Then, through the windows out onto the street, he saw a coach pulling up, and smiled. She must have seen it as well. There was still some logic in the world.

"You need not worry about it," he said. "Uncle Charles gave me enough to pay for both of us."

Melissa nodded. She turned a bit more to look out the window.

"Poor people," she remarked, as the travelers, almost in a bunch, came hurrying into the warmth, holding the door open for each other. A distinct cold draft through the entire room accompanied them. "But I wish they would hurry up and close the door," she added.

Ethan half lifted himself out of his chair, thinking he would go close it for the sake of everyone else inside as well as Melissa, but fortunately the last in the queue came shambling through and the door closed. He settled back, only to have the door flung open again by a white-bearded old man, certainly the last of the coach passengers, and noticed with some amusement the latecomer was being glared at by others besides himself and Melissa.

The door shut and stayed that way.

"How long are you thinking of staying in Dublin?" she asked.

He glanced at her quickly. In spite of the discussion in the kitchen of the house on the Green, she did not sound resentful. It was more like ordinary curiosity.

"I am not sure." He drank more of his tea, to give himself some thinking time. "I'm hoping to go into the office with Martin tomorrow and see if my idea of working there for a time is practical at all. Once I know that, I'll be better placed to make longer term plans. But if matters go as I hope, it certainly will be a month or so."

Melissa nodded. "I have the feeling Caroline would be disappointed if we returned to Ballymuir—well, back north, much sooner than that. I would like to go around with Caroline a little to explore more of Dublin."

"I thought you were not interested in the shops."

This time she realized he was teasing. "Well, I'm sure there are more things to look at indoors than shops," she said, obviously working to keep her mouth from curving. "Besides, if I am to shop a female companion is much more desirable."

"I sense I am rejected."

"Not at all. Any time I choose to walk by the side of a river with a cold wind howling, I will certainly call on you."

They grinned companionably at each other. It was the first time they had done so, Ethan realized. He would not have expected it.

After a brisk walk just this side of running, they scuttled through the front door of the Gallagher's house almost side by side. Fortunately the butler had seen them coming. How, Ethan could not imagine unless he stood facing the glass panels surrounding the front door continually, because there certainly could not have been much time elapsed between them turning to the couple of steps leading to the door and the door swinging open.

"Brisk out there," the butler remarked in a friendly fashion as he shut the door behind them.

"More than brisk," Ethan agreed. He unwrapped the scarf around his neck and took off his hat and outer coat to hand to him.

"I'll just run these upstairs." Ethan watched Melissa run lightly to the staircase up to the piano nobile level, look briefly through the drawing room door, and then disappear into the depths of the house.

He turned back to the butler. "Is Mr. Gallagher in?"

"Yes, sir. He asked for you when he came in." The butler, seemingly on his way to hang up Ethan's outside clothes, paused.

Ethan hesitated, trying to remember if he had been told the butler's name. If so, he had forgotten it.

"I'm sorry," he said, "I do not remember your name."

"O'Malley, sir," the butler replied, and continued on his way.

It was on the tip of Ethan's tongue to say, "Well, that should be easy enough to learn," but he restrained himself. "Thank you, Mr. O'Malley," he said to the butler's retreating back.

So Martin was in the house, but he had forgotten to ask where. He had only the most general idea of how the interior of the house was laid out. There was the ground floor, which had the dining room. He had seen the table through an open door, but had expected that was where it would be, as it was in many London houses. Behind that? He did not know.

Then came the piano nobile floor up the staircase. That was where the drawing room was, and possibly the library, or a study: either of those seemed likely. It was unlikely Martin had ascended to the floor above, where the largest bedchambers would be, nor higher still, which was where his bedchamber and Melissa's were. Henrietta's nursery would be at the top, and behind that were only the attics for the sleeping arrangements of the servants.

All things considered, he should investigate behind the dining room first, and then try up the grand staircase.

He found what he was looking for first try. A door was partly ajar, which helped, and he could see a large, very masculine looking room through the crack.

"Martin?" he asked, hoping his voice didn't sound as tentative as he felt.

"Ethan, is it?" The comfortable ever-so-slightly Irish voice greeted him, and in a moment the door was swept open.

Ethan admitted that was who he was, and he was welcomed into the room, supplied with a warming glass of brandy—"The cold out there is enough to freeze a man's ears off his head," Martin said—and seated in a comfortable leather chair.

"Did you carry out your design to see a bit of Dublin, then?"

The brandy burned deliciously down his throat. Ethan allowed himself to savor it for a moment before he answered. "A bit. We got as far as the Liffey and were heading for the Customs House when I realized Melissa was getting far too cold."

Martin's eyebrows lifted. "Not much of a walk, that, when the weather is more pleasing, but a fair distance with the wind howling."

"Exactly." Ethan buried his nose in his glass again, savoring the warmth.

"Pity the old city did not see fit to welcome you more kindly. Never mind. There will be better days." Martin settled more comfortably back in his chair. "If you choose to come with me to the office tomorrow, it'll not be quite so far, but I hope it will be warmer even so."

"I would like that."

Martin looked at him squarely. "Why?"

Ethan was startled enough so that he nearly coughed over his brandy. Well, he supposed it was a fair question. True, he had not known any men who went to an office regularly, but he supposed it was not ordinarily seen as a place to visit.

He paused for a long moment to think over his answer.

"I find myself in something of a dilemma."

Martin, still watching him closely, nodded.

"I have been working with my Uncle Charles on the harvesting. In fact, that is why I came to Ireland at this time of year. My uncle suggested that it would be a good idea for me to become more acquainted with the estate and what went into running it as someday I would be the one responsible, and it would be easier to learn if I had those with more experience to teach me rather than trying to figure it out on my own."

Martin nodded again. "Wise counsel."

"So I came." He sipped at his brandy again, working out his words in his mind. "I have been out in the fields with my uncle and Mr. Bowyer, his steward, and I have learned a great deal."

Martin did not speak.

"What I have mainly learned is that I am not a born farmer. Nor an enthusiastic one."

The Irishman's face quirked into a smile. "I see."

It was becoming easier to talk. He was able to explain his short experience with his uncle's recordkeeping and his wish to concentrate on that part of the estate business reasonably sensibly. Martin listened intently.

"I see. So you see my office as—as what?"

"A place for me to watch and learn. Now, I realize you have no time to set aside to teach me. Also I cannot claim to know exactly what it is that you do. But I would think forecasting and analyzing would be part of it."

"Much of it."

"If I could be allowed to watch what goes on and teach myself by what I see—"

"Much of what we do is confidential."

"I do not believe I am loose-tongued."

"Nor do I. But the details of what you learn must be kept confidential." Martin, who had been leaning forward somewhat, settled back into his chair. "So you wish to come into the office and observe and learn."

"Yes, sir. With the understanding that if I stray into any material you wish to keep entirely private you will warn me off, and I will ask no questions."

Martin nodded. "T'would be fair enough. Shall we start tomorrow?"

Ethan took a deep breath. So he was almost launched. Was he sure that this was what he wanted to do? This would mean tying himself to Ireland, in all probability, for the rest of his life.

"Yes, sir," he said.

16

WHEN MELISSA CAME DOWN TO breakfast the next morning she found Caroline sitting at the dining room table, contemplating the world outside the window over a cup of tea.

"Good morning!" She turned around to face Melissa with a broad smile. "I am glad to see you. Martin and Ethan were disinclined to talk to anybody but each other and left far too early, to my way of thinking, to get to the office so presumably they could go on talking there. At least we need not worry they do not get along."

Melissa slid into a chair. "I hope it's not as cold as it was yesterday. Is the office far?"

Caroline shook her head. "Not far at all. Dublin is still a fairly compact city, although it must not have felt that way yesterday when you were out in that dreadful cold. I'd thought to take Henrietta for a short walk in the Green, but although she was willing enough to go out, I knew she would take her own sweet time moving from one interesting spot to the next and I would freeze to death while she investigated one thing after another. I don't remember who told me a child is going to explore things no matter what you do, so you might as well allow time for it, but it is true. Yesterday I couldn't imagine spending that much time outside without having to chip off frozen fingers and toes. Hers *and* mine."

Melissa laughed with her. "Is it always this cold in Dublin in October?"

Caroline shook her head again, emphatically. "It is not. We seldom even have snow in January and February. So I hope our usual October weather will come back from wherever it's hiding and we'll get back to things as they should be."

"So what would you normally be doing today?"

Caroline sipped from her cup, looking thoughtful. "An ordinary Monday," she mused. "Well, I suppose I would take Henrietta out for a bit, unless it's as cold as yesterday, but I have to step outside and see. It really depends on whether it's an inside day or fit for being outside. If it's an inside day, there's a tablecloth I'm working on, so I would spend some time on that. If it is nice out, I most likely would take a walk in St. Stephen's Green, and bring Henrietta along to run and get some exercise. We sometimes meet other children there. Henrietta is still mostly in the watching stage—she's just past a year old, although she has been walking for months now, so she seems older. But she certainly likes being with other children. She and Charlie had a fine time together. My mother insists they were talking together, but that seems unlikely to me."

Melissa nodded. So a day not unlike the days she had spent with Anne at Ballymuir. She had hoped in a city…

"Are there any art galleries about?" she asked. "Any places with pictures?"

Caroline looked at her, surprised. "I would think there must be, but I haven't been to any. I'll talk to Martin—he'll know where they are. Would you like to go see one?"

"Very much. I like to draw myself, but I'm not really good at it. I can do odd or funny drawings—you know, like caricatures. But that's not proper drawing."

"I know there are shops where they sell pictures, and display quite a few. I'll have to ask Martin about places like public art galleries or museums, I guess…" Her voice drifted away as she sat with puzzlement furrowing her forehead.

"Thank you." Only then did Melissa glance up and notice the footman who had apparently been waiting for her to express some preference for what she wanted to have for breakfast. "Oh. My mind wasn't on food," she said, and quickly asked him to bring her some coffee and toast.

"With marmalade," Caroline put in. "We do have some lovely marmalade."

Caroline was quite right. It was.

It was not until an hour or so later that Melissa extracted herself from the dining room and Caroline's company. The nanny had brought Henrietta down, and after some chatter Melissa thought Caroline probably wanted to concentrate on her daughter single-mindedly. She slipped away after murmuring some feeble excuse she did not think Caroline really heard anyway.

She went to the front hall, peering out of a side window to see if she could deduce from the clothing of passers-by whether it was so cold today as well. Naturally, the first few who walked past their door were all men, who seemed to dress very much the same whatever the temperature.

"May I help, ma'am?"

It was the butler. What was his name? Something very Irish, she remembered that.

"I was just trying to determine whether it is as cold as it was yesterday," she admitted.

The butler, who obviously believed in the direct approach, swung the door open and walked as far as the steps. "Not as cold as it was, I don't believe, but I would not go so far as to say it is pleasant out," he told her when he came back in.

Since she'd had the benefit of the gust of cold air as the door was opened, Melissa was inclined to agree with him.

"Thank you so much, Mr.—Mr.—" she floundered, scrubbing her memory for the name.

"O'Malley, ma'am."

"Mr. O'Malley." She beamed at him with appreciation and relief. How had she forgotten such an Irish name as that?

With courteous nods they both backed away a bit, Mr. O'Malley to go wherever he had been before he materialized in the front hall, and Melissa to start up the grand stairway, pausing to admire the wonderful plaster decorations on the walls as she passed them.

When she reached the top of the flight, she looked back down at the graceful elegance of the stairway and the space it occupied, and had a moment to contemplate the oddity of Martin, plain Mr. Gallagher, who owned this magnificence, particularly compared to the relatively plain manor her brother owned—the one that she, her mother, and her sister occupied—in Gloucestershire. And her brother was a marquess! Of course he had Ballymuir as well which was certainly a pleasant enough establishment, but it was nothing like this house in Dublin.

Obviously Martin did very well at whatever it was he did. For a moment, still looking down over the stairway, Melissa wondered exactly what it was that he did. Whatever it was had plainly earned him a fortune. But what on earth did Ethan think he would learn from him?

Ethan presumably would still be spending most of his life on his estate. So what use would it be to him to discover what Martin did each day at his office? It was such a pity everyone seemed to assume that only men were interested in those sorts of questions. She had no idea whether she herself would have a "head for business." Wasn't that what it was called? But she would certainly never have an opportunity to find out.

Maybe her mother was right and there was something wrong with her. Anne and Caroline both seemed adept and perfectly comfortable living within the limits confining the way a lady should lead her life. Neither of them was dull or uninteresting, either. Caroline's horizons were possibly a bit wider than Anne's, but then Caroline had been exposed to more. She had gone to England, she had married—twice!— and she had undoubtedly associated with people both when she had been in London for her season and later when she was living with her first husband's family.

What had that been like?

Almost ashamed of her curiosity, Melissa whirled about to continue her way up to her room where she hoped she would find the little packet of colored pencils and paper that she was almost sure she had brought along with her.

She almost walked straight into Caroline.

"Oh!" she said, backing up with alacrity.

Caroline, holding Henrietta in her arms, laughed. "My goodness, from the expression on your face you must have been settling the major issues of our civilization."

"Well, you know, somebody has to think about them," Melissa said, keeping her face straight with some effort. "The men do not seem to be handling the whole matter brilliantly, or the English and the Irish, for one example, would be working warmly in harmony."

"For all I know, they may do," Caroline said vaguely, clearly not particularly interested in the problem.

"That's not what I hear from Anne." As Caroline seemed to be going in the same general direction as Melissa had intended, they walked together.

"Oh, *Anne*." Melissa could hear the genuine warmth in Caroline's voice. "Anne has the heart of an Irish rebel. Fortunately she also has the common sense of an Englishwoman, and was fortunate to meet your brother, but to hear her talk, once she gets started, there is almost certainly great trouble to come."

"Does Martin share that point of view?"

"Martin?" The special gentleness in her voice that Melissa could hear every time she spoke about her husband was there. "I don't think he wastes much time on that. He just gets on with what he does well, and lets the rest of it flow around him. Dublin is a Protestant city in a Catholic country, and fortunately, he is successful enough not to experience the grievances Anne is so upset about. Besides, he lacks the temperament of a rebel, poor dear. Martin likes people and prefers getting along to disagreement. Even when once he was very angry with me he was, at the same time, working out the way for us to find our peace."

They had reached the nursery, and Henrietta's nanny came out to take the little girl in her arms.

"I don't know if she is restless or simply tired," Caroline said. "Perhaps if you could rock her in a chair with a book it would settle her into a nap. She and I have been hopping around in the dining room having a splendid time, but I think she needs some quiet now."

Henrietta contentedly laid her head on the nanny's shoulder, and the two of them retreated into the nursery.

"There's no doubt that Martin is an extraordinary man," Melissa said, picking up the thread of their conversation.

Caroline smiled with the contentment of a cat in cream.

"Was your first husband like him?"

As she heard the words coming out of her mouth, Melissa was horrified. Yes, she had certainly wondered, but she had never imagined she would actually ask such a question.

Caroline looked at her shrewdly, but still smiled. "Come with me to my sitting room. I'll tell you the story."

The sitting room was to one side and slightly behind the bedchamber that appeared to be shared by her with Martin. There was a door connecting the two, which Caroline pulled shut, as there seemed to be a maid cleaning out the fireplace in the bedchamber.

"These houses have walls so thick that even in the bitter weather they stay reasonably warm. But we will still want a fire later on this afternoon, when it is as cold as it has been. I tell you, I dread to think of what January and February will bring if it's this cold in October." There were two chairs close to each other, one a great large rocking chair. Caroline tilted her head, looking at Melissa. "Would you prefer to rock, or have a chair that stays in one place?"

"I'll rock, thank you." She settled herself in the chair. "I've never seen one so large."

Caroline laughed softly. "It comes from Martin making an uneasy trial of an ordinary rocking chair. He liked it, but he was too large. So I had that one made for him. It's sturdy enough so that I believe two Martins could sit in it."

They settled themselves, and Melissa rocked back and forth, back and forth, in the silence.

"You asked about my first husband," Caroline said at last.

"I am sorry," Melissa put in quickly. "It was none of my business. I do apologize."

"No." Caroline looked at her hands. "It's an interesting story, one easier to tell than live. Besides, it's too cold to go out today, so it's a good day to talk." She gave Melissa a quick, almost mischievous smile.

"I have been very lucky. First there was Henry. That was only—well, less than three years ago, and I feel I must be ten, twenty years older now. We were so young, and so much in love, and we thought we would have forever. We met at the ball my aunt gave for my debut, and there was something between us at once. It lasted for the whole Season, and we knew it would be real forever. He was to be a duke, and I was the daughter of an earl—although an earl in Ireland, which is slightly less grand—so it was suitable. We married at St. George's in Hanover Square, which as you know is the appropriate place to marry, and went to live at Apthorp Manor in Suffolk, which Henry would inherit some day."

"Manor?" Melissa's puzzlement was clear in her voice.

"Well, that was its name, but the original manor must have been built centuries ago and they have been adding to it ever since. It has wings here and there, and several substantial additions, not all in the same style. It's very odd, but Henry loved it."

"Did you?"

"I think I would have, except that only five months after we came there, Henry was killed."

Melissa murmured something.

Caroline shrugged, but pain was clear in her eyes. "Yes. It was terrible. He jumped over a wall, forgetting there was a ditch on the other side or thinking he would clear it. I don't know. He was reckless in a lot of ways. I thought it was cavalier and charming, and still thought that when the recklessness took his life. I sometimes wonder what our marriage would have been like, if he had lived long enough for us to have the kind of marriage that counts."

"But Henrietta..." Melissa started to protest.

"Well, yes. But it took a while for me to know that I was increasing, and then there were all the months when we all—me and Henry's father and mother—waited for Henry's son to be born. But it was not a son. That was hard."

Melissa said nothing.

"Now that I think about it, I guess it was hard for a long time. Really from the time Henry died—was killed—well, whatever. Perhaps that's why I feel I am so much older than I was when Henry was alive.

"From that time on I was never sure what was going to happen, what my life would be like. The Duke, Henry's father, could not have been kinder, but I could no longer be the mother of the heir. I was just one more woman living in the house, with a female baby. The Duchess was more of a problem for me. I think she saw me as an extra dependent, and she had her own ideas about how I could make myself useful.

"What finally made me realize that I needed to take Henrietta and come home was when she decided it was my duty to accompany her daughter Dorothea when she made her debut during the Season this spring. She was going herself, of course, but she thought—I don't know. Maybe she genuinely thought Dorothea would be more comfortable with me there. By then we were very good friends, Dorothea and me. But I couldn't see how I could manage spending much time with Henrietta in London, and of course there was my dog George to consider. For the Duchess it was all just a matter of leaving them at the Manor. There would be people to take care of them there."

Melissa looked at her face. Caroline looked composed, but knowing how important taking care of her own children was to Anne, she could imagine Caroline's distress if she was expected to leave her daughter to nursemaids and not see her for months on end.

Caroline, seeing Melissa's intent regard, smiled. "So that was when I decided to come home to Ireland. I talked to the Duke about it, and he could not have been more helpful. So much so that he came with me all the way to Holyhead in his traveling carriage, so Henrietta and her nanny and my dog George and I could all make the journey in reasonable comfort.

"And then when we got to Holyhead, there was Martin." All of a sudden the half-hidden unhappiness was replaced by a mellow glow.

"Is that where you met him?"

Caroline shook her head. "No, I had actually met him, once, at a dinner at Apthrop Manor. A couple of guests had begged off at the last moment, and so the Duchess pressed me and Dorothea to take their places. It was not that long after Henry had died, so I was in deep mourning and increasing as well, but she said the other guests were all close friends of the family so it would not be inappropriate for me to be there. Then she added there would be two or three gentlemen from London, and one of them was Martin. I had never met anybody so large!"

"He is big," Melissa agreed. "So then you met him again at Holyhead. Did he take the mail boat as well?"

"He did." It was obviously a good memory for Caroline, because her eyes were shining. "It was a horrid voyage, I suppose. The English girl who was Henrietta's nanny was wretchedly sick on the boat. It got very rough overnight, and how I would have managed without Martin's help I still can't imagine. He was just there, kindness personified, and reached out to do things for me before I even realized they needed doing. I suppose I fell in love with him there and then, but it took a while once we were in Ireland for me to recognize it."

She smiled and shook her head a little, as if to put the memories to one side. "Which is more than enough about me. And what have you been doing with your life up until now?"

Melissa sat motionless for a minute, trying to think what on earth she had been doing. It seemed uneventful, compared to the dramatic unfolding of Caroline's life.

"Not much, really, I suppose. When our father died, Hugh inherited the family estate, which was reasonably prosperous, but nothing of course like Uncle Charles's, and as our father was gone, that meant Hugh would inherit the title of marquess, as well as Ballymuir and the estate. We had not known our uncle or aunt, at all, and there was no invitation such as Uncle Charles extended to Ethan, so it was only after the uncle's death that Hugh came to Ireland. From what he has said, or more exactly not said, I gather the estate was rather a mess, and Hugh has been trying to return it to something closer to its possibilities. Meanwhile, I was sent off to my debut Season in London this year. Hugh was very generous with making it possible for me to have the right clothes and all, but I was not a tremendous success. I thought we should not spend that much again for me to go to London next year as well, but if I did not do that, our mother had no idea what to do with me. I think that's mainly why she packed me off to Ireland, although I think what sealed her determination was that I cut my hair."

"But you have lovely hair!" Caroline protested.

Melissa rolled her eyes. "My mother says that her hair should be a woman's crowning glory and no man would be interested in me as it was now gone. Therefore I might as well be sent away all the way to Ireland until I grew a new headful. Which is not going to happen because I trim it now as it grows. It was horrible when it was long. It was so heavy and unruly and it would not stay properly bound up, and I was forever dropping hairpins and stabbing replacements in. Short hair is even fashionable nowadays for some ladies in London, but it would make no difference to me if it were not." She ran her fingers through her hair defiantly. "I am never going to let it grow again."

"Would you go back to London for the Season if your mother permitted you to go with your hair short?"

That took a minute to think about if Melissa was to answer honestly. "I would rather not," she said, speaking very slowly. "The Season is not designed for someone like me. I am too prickly and I really do not care enough about beautiful dresses or having just the right bonnet or making the right sort of chatter with mindless young men who have no intention of marrying for years, but are pressed into coming to the parties by their mothers or aunts or mothers of their best friends who are trying to persuade their own sons to attend. Everyone is on display."

"I suppose all that is true." Caroline looked thoughtful. "Isn't it interesting how different people can be? I looked forward to the Season in London for years, and I loved every minute of it."

"Didn't you meet your first husband right at the beginning?"

Caroline nodded, smiling. "And that made all the difference, I suppose. So here we are. And what are we to do with you, Melissa?"

IF NOT EVEN CLOSE TO warm, the weather was certainly better than it had been the day before. Ethan was able to walk home mulling over the day he had spent in Martin's office.

Whether it was a typical office or not he could not say, never having set foot in an office before. Gentlemen did not. But did that mean Martin was not a gentleman? Presumably. Ethan didn't know what to think about that.

Martin's office was in a rather elegant building, encompassing the whole of the ground floor. There was a large room filled with clerk's desks, and then a few separate offices around the edges, the largest and most elegant belonging to Martin, of course. Even after a day there, Martin only vaguely understood what all of them were doing, but the atmosphere there was what he noticed first, and what he was thinking about as he walked home through the late afternoon chill.

What had caught his attention first of all was the genuine interest the people working there seemed to show in what they were doing. What he noticed next was the general good humor in the place. Not standing around chattering—there was none of that. But requests were made pleasantly, rather than as rough orders. Courtesy seemed to be the general rule.

Martin had taken him into his own office at the beginning to show him what was being accomplished in a general sense, and although Ethan could not grasp all of it after an hour's discussion he could see what was required was sharp attention and the ability to spot patterns quickly, as well as a good memory for a whole variety of information being presented almost simultaneously. As far as he could see, the men working with Martin were concentrating fiercely on what they were doing, but still seemed capable of dealing with each other (and Martin, of course) with habitual politeness.

It occurred to Ethan as he walked that Martin's methods of dealing with the men who worked for him might be the most important thing Ethan could learn from him.

The details of the business, yes. Ethan hoped that he would pick that up over time. Clearly it was too complex for him to grasp in one day, and he suspected Martin had only explained a very small part of his business. Still, there was clearly a difference between the management of investments, which was mainly what Martin's business was, and the management of an estate.

What he needed to learn immediately, he thought on this very first day, was the combination of civility and efficiency. Surely that was not something that came naturally to every man who crossed Martin's threshold. But it was the overriding impression Ethan had on coming away. He wanted to work like that himself.

Having come to that conclusion, Ethan looked around with more interest.

It was not far from Martin's office to the house on the Green—a walk of probably ten, fifteen minutes. The streets he walked were filled with businesses, large and small. There was some shopping available, but he suspected there had to be other areas of the city that offered a greater variety of shops and commodities for sale.

He wondered where Caroline went shopping. She was nicely dressed; clearly she had a good sense of style. Thinking about it, he could not remember properly whether Anne had impressed him quite the same way. His attention was not naturally given to the details of how the ladies around him dressed. But he noticed Caroline's way of combining colors and the fabrics she chose. She must be very good at it.

Melissa? It was hard to work out what he thought of Melissa. She attracted him more now than she had when he first encountered her here in Ireland, and far and away more than had been the case in London, which now seemed not only miles but years away, although it was not yet November now, and they had both been there throughout the length of the Season this very year. He doubted he had noticed her presence at once. He did remember he had danced with her, but he had no distinct recollection of any particular occasion. It had been made obvious to him she was more distressed than he would have thought by the senseless joking that had gone on about her unmanageable hair, but she and her hair had been only of passing interest to his friends and himself. It was just one of the peculiarities of appearance they had taken pleasure in pointing out to each other.

Stupid, really. The thought they might be overheard was not anything he remembered considering. They were talking for their own amusement, not thinking of anyone else. It occurred to him now it was not only those who were the butts of their humor who might have heard their conversations, but other more polite members of the *ton* attending the same functions who likely formed a less than favorable impression of their conduct.

Well, that did not matter as much now. Here he was across the Irish Sea, on his way to becoming an earl and doing his best to work out a responsible way to manage the estate he would be responsible for. What his former cronies were up to he had no idea.

He did feel badly about Melissa's distress. Not that her hair was unattractive now. It might have been rather glorious then, if he allowed himself to imagine her with all that hair flowing freely over her shoulders and down her back. But proper young ladies kept their hair under tight management, and what had been slightly comic about Melissa's hair in those days was that it tended to bulge out one place or another, doing its best to escape whatever young ladies did to keep their locks tidily tucked under their bonnets or decorated decorously with plumes or leaves and flowers or whatever else they added.

Of course now Melissa's hair was more or less the same day and evening, with what looked like soft curls all over her head. He surprised himself by liking it, by wishing sometime by some unimaginable circumstance he might be able to run his finger through those curls. They were certainly a wonderful color.

Pausing to cross a street, he gave his head a shake. What he should be doing was paying more attention to what he could learn from the admirable and successful Martin Gallagher. Brooding over the beauty of any woman's hair at this time of his life made no sense whatever.

Particularly not Melissa Preston's hair.

Ethan was not prepared for a hand to grasp his arm.

He turned quickly and warily to encounter a man who looked vaguely familiar.

"Uh," he said, wondering how on a Dublin street corner he could come across someone he was sure he had met before. Surely everyone he knew was in England.

The not-quite-stranger touched his hat. "Thomas Halleck. Of Chelsea," he added, his lips quirking in an amused smile.

Of course! The Mr. Halleck with whom he had spent most of his first day in Dublin.

"What a pleasure to see you again, Halleck," Ethan said. "I must apologize. I was wool gathering."

"That does not surprise me. From your absorbed expression, I feared you were about to step straight into traffic. How do you happen to be in Dublin? If I recall correctly, you were headed to the general neighborhood of Drogheda when last I saw you."

Ethan shrugged. "I have indeed been there until a few days ago, when I accompanied the sister of my cousin's husband down here to visit another cousin." He smiled himself. "That sounds unnecessarily complicated, but there is quite a lot of family living close around up there. I believe both of us were eager to escape the blandness of country life for a time. Dublin is a city, after all."

Halleck looked at him keenly. "And how is your introduction to prospective estate ownership in Ireland going?"

Ethan made a seesaw movement with his hand. "Interesting. But complicated."

"That sounds as if it might be a story worth telling." Halleck glanced around. "If you have a minute, there is a public house I know well close at hand. Can I persuade you to stop for a glass of ale and some conversation?"

Ethan started to shrug, and then it occurred to him it was still early, and Martin would not be returning to the house on the Green for dinner for some time.

"That would be very pleasant," he said. "Thank you."

They turned together and walked a short distance down the road Ethan had been about to cross, turning into the first public house they came to. It did indeed appear to be a rather better than ordinary establishment. They passed the open door into the public bar where there were a crowd of men, some of whom were making music with pipes and a fiddle. Passing by, they took their seats in the well-furnished saloon bar on the other side. There were fewer men there, and from their dress and manner, reasonably prosperous as well.

It was a quick business of ordering their ale, and it was pleasant to feel the warmth from the fire. It was not as cold as it had been the day before, but it was still chillier than Ethan would have expected, and he said so.

"It's been as bad in England," Halleck told him. "No one knows quite what to make of it. Everyone agrees that if it is like this before November, it will be well nigh unendurable in January. Public opinion seems to believe ordinary commerce will come to an end because the rivers will freeze over and everyone will be home huddled by their fires." He hitched himself closer to the table as the ale was served to them, and regarded Ethan curiously. "So how is the relationship between you and the land you will inherit complicated?"

Ethan hesitated for a moment, and then decided as long as he gave no details about the Hawthorne family or their properties it was his story to tell, and since Halleck, from what he had told him before, was familiar with matters of business in both London and Dublin, he was interested in what his opinion would be of Ethan's plan to concentrate more on the business side of the estate in the future. Would such an arrangement be practical in his opinion?

He practiced one of the skills he had seen Martin use in his office—and, for that matter, when dealing with friends and servants at home. He made his account as brief and concise as he could, while concentrating on presenting the situation clearly.

Halleck listened with obvious interest. "I would think it would require capable and conscientious people to carry out your instructions both in Dublin and on your estate, since you would not be in either place enough of the time to supervise them closely. But other than that, Hawthorne, I see no reason why the arrangement would not work successfully."

One of the bar attendants opened the door of the saloon bar, and for a minute or two, until the door banged shut again, the music and garrulous voices from the public bar floated into the saloon. The music was infectious and for a moment Ethan wished he could hear more of it, until the door closed and he turned his mind back to what they were discussing.

Halleck looked at him curiously for a moment, and then spoke abruptly, as if he had debated asking the question. "With whom are you working now? I cannot help being impressed by what you say about the management skills of the individual you mentioned."

Ethan laughed. "It is none other than the husband of the cousin I am staying with. He is indeed an interesting man in many ways. He is Martin Gallagher, and among his other qualities I should mention he is one of the largest men I have ever met."

Halleck burst out laughing as well. "He is indeed that, but also one of the cleverest. You are a fortunate man, Hawthorne. Gallagher comes closer to genius in handling money than any other man I know, whether it's his own fortune or the fortunes of others persuasive enough to convince him to manage them. I cannot be surprised he manages his employees equally well. You could not have a more qualified tutor."

Ethan raised an eyebrow. "Well, that is certainly a glowing recommendation. As host, he cannot be faulted, and today he was kind enough to let me prowl around his office to see what I could learn from watching what was going on. I hope to spend several other such days there. There seems no shortage of opportunities for educating myself."

"To what end?" Halleck looked at him curiously. "Have you an interest in financial business yourself?"

"Not directly. But I am planning a different method of handling the estate when I inherit it than the hands-on method my uncle prefers."

Halleck gave a low laugh. "I think I can perceive your difficulty. Would it be possible for you to stay here in Dublin for a time? Now the harvest is completed there cannot be that much to draw you back to the estate immediately, and I would think you would find continuing to work with Gallagher more to your taste."

"Is it that obvious?" Ethan chuckled as well, and finished his glass. "I should be getting back to the house, however. Even one as absorbed in his work as Gallagher eventually goes home for dinner."

Halleck nodded and began the business of collecting his hat and gloves. "We should get together for dinner. I am here for the winter it seems. I have not had company before, so I cannot highly recommend my cook yet, but she seems quite competent at producing reasonable food. You mentioned that your cousin had come down with you. Do you suppose she would care to come for dinner as well? I hesitate to invite Gallagher and his wife under the circumstances, but if we find my cook rises to the occasion we could see about that in the future."

Ethan brightened. "Actually, inviting Melissa would be an act of compassion. She is not my cousin, actually. She is the sister of the Marquess of Ashbourne, who married my cousin. They live in County Meath. Her mother sent her to her brother, to spend some time with his family, but Melissa was more involved in aiding her sister-in-law with the two small children than she would have chosen. Now that I think of it, she has probably spent most of today doing much the same thing, although my cousin Caroline has only one little girl, whereas her sister Anne has two under the age of three. I had hoped to take Melissa for more of a walk about Dublin today. We tried yesterday, but took refuge in an inn much sooner than we would have chosen had we not been chilled through."

"Well, by all means, do bring Melissa along. I have no handy female relatives at home—would that make it awkward for her?"

"I doubt it." Ethan wondered if he should say something about Melissa's independence of mind, and then decided it was probably more politic to wait and see how much of that independence she chose to exhibit. He would feel a great fool if he went on at length about what he perceived to be her temperamental difficulties in fitting in with the social expectations of young women of her age and class and then discovered she was behaving in as maidenly a fashion as he had observed her during the various social events they had both attended in London that spring. Besides, what business was that of Halleck's?

Perhaps he could suggest to Melissa she keep her more unusual observations to herself during the evening.

No. He surprised himself by arguing internally she was entitled to present whatever social face she chose. Halleck might find as much amusement and pleasure in Melissa's company as he did himself.

He was even more surprised to realize in fact Melissa did interest him, and he would be quite proud to bring her to Halleck's Dublin residence.

How odd, even laughable he would have thought that last spring!

MELISSA SAT QUIETLY AT THE dinner table, only half-listening to the conversation Martin and Ethan and Caroline were carrying on. She hoped the astonishment she felt had not shown on her face when Ethan had told her she was invited for dinner with him at his friend Mr. Halleck's house that Friday. He had not seemed to be joking, not at all.

Now she was trying to conceal not only that she had been amazed but that she was pleased and excited to be going out for a dinner not surrounded by family. After all, she and Ethan were not related at all, although after all this time spent between Ballymuir and Kendall House everyone had made it plain they all were considered family somehow.

But Ethan had told a friend of her existence! He must have, or how else would she be included in the invitation? That was the astounding part. Sitting there at the table trying to make it look as if she was eating more of the very nice lamb than she actually was, her mind was far more on what she was to wear than on the food in front of her. She did not want to shame him, or remind him of what he had obviously found odd-looking when they had met during the Season. Or had it been only her hair?

She could go shopping on the morrow, if Caroline would tell her where to go. She still had the money she had brought with her, almost all of it. Her mother had given her a comfortable amount, but either Hugh or Uncle Charles had covered any expenses she had so far. The only time she might have had to spend money in Dublin was when she and Ethan escaped the cold in the inn, and Ethan paid for that. So if she wanted a new bonnet or a scarf or perhaps a new pair of shoes, she had enough to do so without worrying. Unfortunately, she had brought little of what she had down to Dublin, since they had left in such a hurry. She would be content with anything that would make that little somewhat more elegant.

"Don't you think so, Melissa?" Caroline sounded quite heated, as if there had been some difference of opinion.

Melissa had not the faintest idea of what they had been talking about. She blinked at Caroline blankly.

"Now Caro, dear heart, that is not fair," Martin said. "Melissa has been far from us. I am sure she has been settling matters in her own mind much more important than the question of whether females should be admitted to Trinity College."

Melissa smiled gratefully at him, and wondered if she could confess she had been worrying about what she would wear Friday. As it happened, she had quite strong opinions about the learning capabilities of women, and she was rather sorry she had missed the discussion.

"Actually," she said, deciding on telling the truth, "I was wondering if Caroline could tell me where to find a new bonnet to wear Friday."

Everyone laughed, but Ethan was laughing like the others, not unkindly but with genuine amusement.

"Trust Melissa to be honest about it," Caroline said with enough fondness so that Melissa could feel her face flush.

"I am not very good at inventing explanations on the spur of the moment."

"Just as well. The truth is quite endearing," Martin said. "Caro, can you take our guest out to show her where you buy the quantity of bonnets that are falling out of your wardrobe?"

"Of course I can. Or she could take her choice of the number you clearly feel is excessive right here in the house." Caroline drew her face into something approximating a frown, and then laughed. "But truly it is more fun to buy one in a shop, so we shall add to the supply."

"Wonderful. That solves the problem," Melissa said with satisfaction. "Now what were you talking about when I so rudely let myself become absorbed with the question of what to put on my head?"

"It is enough to tell you I was right, and these two gentlemen entirely wrong." By this time the pudding had been served and consumed (Melissa discovered to her surprise she had apparently eaten it), and Caroline rose gracefully from her seat. "We will therefore leave them with their errors of judgment and have some coffee in the drawing room. After they have finished with their brandy and smelly cigars, they are welcome to rejoin us."

As she followed Caroline up the elegant staircase, Melissa thought watching the relationship between Caroline and Martin was almost enough to persuade her there was something to be said for the institution of marriage. She had really had so little exposure to it, since her father had died when she was very young, and most of the family and close friends she had known in Gloucestershire seemed to have placid, unremarkable marriages. One or two of them could probably be described as actively unpleasant, even from as little as she was permitted to observe. She was sure that Hugh and Anne were very contented with each other, but she thought Hugh worried that since she was much younger and his sister, she might feel excluded if he unbent with Anne in her presence. Or perhaps he thought their marriage was their private affair.

Either way, Martin and Caroline were entirely different. Their fondness for each other was almost palpably present whenever they were together, almost as openly demonstrated as their love for Henrietta. Caroline had said that she was fortunate in his attachment to the child, and Melissa could see what she meant. No one would guess Henrietta was not Martin's own daughter from his manner with her.

If marriage could be as close as that, perhaps it was worth considering.

But then she and Caroline turned into the drawing room, and Melissa's attention was entirely absorbed with the fascinating details about the most likely shops available and where they would start out, and which establishments Caroline would recommend most highly…

Friday evening seemed to bear down upon them like a runaway carriage. Before they went shopping, Caroline and Melissa decided together which of Caroline's excess gowns Melissa might be most comfortable wearing. Ignoring her hesitant objections, Caroline dragged her into her own dressing room.

"Martin is far too generous with me, and I have more gowns than any woman not in the midst of the Season in London has any need for. You and I are not so different in size: let us take a look and see if among the dresses I have not worn or worn only once there is one that would give you the pleasure of something new. You have been so good about helping with Henrietta that I would love to do something for you."

In the end, they found a pea-green crepe frock Caroline had never worn.

"This was one originally made for Anne, but when she married and was staying in Ireland, several of her dresses were made over for me. Anne has green eyes, but green is really not my color, which is why I never actually wore this one. It had a lovely white satin slip with lace sleeves—yes, there it is. The lace, you see, matches that deep flounce of lace around the hem of the frock." She stepped back, looking between Melissa and the dress. "Yes, the green will be lovely on you, with your wonderful curly hair. I don't think we need a full bonnet, more of a white satin bandeau, with your curls tumbling over it. I think I've seen something like that. We must go see if it's still there."

It was, and there was further satisfaction in finding pea-green slippers, just about the same shade as the dress, even if Caroline and Melissa only located them on Friday morning. It was delightful to feel she was dressed in appropriate finery when Ethan knocked politely on her door to ask if she was nearly ready and tell her he was going downsairs.

She swept up her white French kid gloves. Fortunately Caroline had a fur cape and matching muff for her to wear, since the weather was no warmer than it had been. When she came downstairs, Ethan and Martin were both standing by the top of the staircase.

"You look lovely," Martin said. "If this young man here attempts to abduct you, you are to come and pound on my door. I will be a safe refuge, since I already have a beautiful wife of my own."

Ethan smiled and nodded his agreement, but Melissa could see admiration in his eyes she had not seen before.

Martin's carriage was in front of the house, awaiting them. "It is far too cold to walk even a short distance." The firmness of Martin's jaw when he told them it was there made it plain he was not open to argument. "Besides, this gives the horses some exercise."

So Ethan handed her into the carriage, and she settled into the seat, enjoying the luxurious interior and the faint fragrance of soap or whatever it was that hung about Ethan. As the carriage pulled away, he leaned forward a little to look at her properly.

"They should see you in London as you are now." His voice was warmly appreciative.

Melissa smiled back at him. "Would you agree to tell my mother that? She is convinced short hair has ruined any chances for admiration."

Ethan reached out with one gloved hand to touch her curls by the side of her face, careful not to disturb the silk bandeau. "I will be a gentleman and keep my hands in my gloves, but I am sure your hair is as soft as silk, and the color is wonderful. I have to admit the color was magnificent even before you cut it, but now people notice it rather than how much hair you have." He paused, looking slightly sheepish. "That was meant to be a compliment. I hope it sounded like one."

Melissa could feel herself blushing. "I will take it as that," she said. It was nice of him to say it, even if it was phrased somewhat oddly.

"I met Halleck—Mr. Halleck—on the ferry coming here." Ethan cleared his throat, clearly meaning to extract himself from the marsh he'd found himself in. "Well, no, actually I met him at the inn there at Holyhead the night before we left. But in the morning we became somewhat more acquainted, and then had breakfast together in Dublin. He was kind enough to take me to the coaching inn so I could get to Drogheda." More comfortable now, he smiled at Melissa. "Yesterday on my way back from Martin's office we encountered each other. He has rented a house as he will be spending the winter in Dublin, and invited us warmly to come for dinner, although he made no claims for the quality of his cook."

"Well, dinner is more for sociability, is it not?"

Ethan started to nod and then shrugged his shoulders. "Let us hope so. I know very little about what his business is, or why he needs to be in Dublin when he lives in Chelsea, but that is not what is important."

"Not at all," Melissa agreed.

"He is acquainted with Martin. He thinks very highly of him."

Just at that moment the carriage came to a lurching stop. Ethan peered out the window, and said, "I believe we are here," just as the footman came to open the door for them. Ethan stepped out first, and held out his hand for Melissa as she stepped down.

The house was well cared for, although not nearly as large as Martin's house on the Green. Martin's house had the front door placed in the middle of the house. Mr. Halleck's house was smaller. He had a similar front door and elegant fanlight, but to the left of his door was the door of his neighbor.

Ethan extended his elbow to Melissa, and she laid her hand on his arm as they walked up the three steps leading to the door. Clearly they were expected, because the door opened even before they lifted the handsome brass knocker, and Mr. Halleck himself beamed at them.

"Hawthorne," he said with obvious pleasure. "Do come in. So far I have only a minimal number of servants, and the housekeeper is arranging the table, so here I am answering the door myself."

Melissa dropped her hand from Ethan's elbow as she stepped through the door first, and he followed, shaking Mr. Halleck's hand as he came in.

Mr. Halleck bowed politely to her, and she dropped a curtsey, wondering if businessmen were more comfortable shaking hands than bowing to each other. If that was so, she was glad Ethan knew what was expected.

"And this is—your cousin?" Mr. Halleck asked.

Ethan and Melissa looked at each other. "Not exactly," Melissa said. "My brother is married to Ethan's cousin."

"Ah," Mr. Halleck said.

"Melissa, I would like to introduce Mr. Thomas Halleck of Chelsea, now temporarily of Dublin. Halleck, this is Miss Melissa Preston, my cousin by marriage—I suppose we could phrase it that way?" he asked, turning to her.

Melissa nodded, looking curiously at Mr. Halleck. He was older and had the look of a gentleman, although from what Ethan had told her of him, he was more likely a cit. His face was friendly, not precisely handsome. His jaw was decided and his ears did not lie neatly against his head—Melissa wondered if he had been teased when he was at school. He wore trousers, but his neckcloth was neatly tied and his jacket well-tailored, just as she would expect of an Englishman. But then of course, she reminded herself, he *was* English. He simply happened to be in Ireland, as she was herself.

"Please come in and sit down," he said, leading the way to the stairway. "Miss Preston, it is indeed a pleasure to meet you. And how are you enjoying your time in Dublin?"

Since he was preceding them up the stairs, essential since neither of them knew where they were going, Melissa waited until they were all the way up the stairs to respond. There, just as in the Gallagher house, they turned right into the drawing room. In fact, from what she could gather from taking a swift look around as they came to the top of the staircase, his house was very similar to that of the Gallaghers, only on a smaller scale.

"I have not seen a great deal of it," Melissa said, as she was shown to a seat and given a glass of white wine, "but I am looking forward to getting to know it a little better." She looked over at Ethan. "We did go out together, but it was so cold that when we were walking along the quays by the river, we had to take refuge in an inn. But I am very grateful to Ethan for trying to show me some of Dublin."

"I have not been a regular resident of Dublin before, but I must admit I have never known an autumn so cold." Mr. Halleck, having handed a glass of wine to Ethan, took one for himself and sat down in am armchair. Over his shoulder, through the window behind him, Melissa could see the corresponding window in the house across the street, and behind the gauzy curtains, as she sipped her wine, she watched the dim shapes of one or two people moving around inside. It was odd. Even in London she had never been able to peer directly into someone else's life as she could here.

By the time Melissa was giving the conversation between Ethan and Mr. Halleck full attention, the subject had moved on to new construction being done around town.

"I had thought the impulse for new buildings would have diminished almost entirely, but there still seem to be some beautiful buildings going up," Mr. Halleck said, coming over to refill Melissa's glass. "There is the splendid new building recently finished on the west side of St. Stephen's Green, the Royal College of Surgeons, and work is going on the new General Post Office on Sackville Street. So in spite of the Act of Union, there is considerable optimism among the people of Dublin."

Ethan answered something about how his cousin lived on the north side of St. Stephen's Green, as Melissa sipped at her wine. It tasted very good indeed, better, she thought, than the last glass, although she was not accustomed to drinking very much wine at all. But this wine was really delicious.

Mr. Halleck had poured a third glass for her before the call came to go down to the dining room. It was unfinished, but he told her to bring it with her—he had a glass to finish himself—and so they all came down the stairs with a glass in hand. The dining room was very pleasant, and Melissa was glad to find the first course came promptly, because with two glasses of wine on an empty stomach she felt a little blurry.

Nor did the situation greatly change over the course of dinner. Ethan and Mr. Halleck carried almost all of the conversation, while Melissa listened, or did not. The dinner was delicious, and the wine more so— they had moved on to red wine now, which was very nice, although Melissa had not much cared for it before. She found herself floating off into a quiet contemplation of the muffled noises of carriages moving past on the street outside and the tempting smells of the roast meat course on its way upstairs from the kitchen below. Mr. Halleck and Ethan were apparently having a fairly earnest discussion, judging from their expressions, but she rather lost track of what they were talking about.

Instead she concentrated on the heavy maroon draperies at the window, covering most of the thinner silk gauze-like fabric shielding the room from the street. It was a wonderful feeling to be so close to life outside the house, but protected from the cold evening air by the warmth of the room itself. From time to time Ethan glanced over at her and smiled, as if to reassure her, but then would return to his conversation with Mr. Halleck. Melissa smiled back, and would take a small bite, but for all the delicious smells, she found that she was not very hungry. Two or three bites would satisfy her, and then it was a business of moving food around her plate as subtly as possible to make it look as if more had been eaten.

In the end the meal was finished, but they sat for a time longer, the conversation carrying on as before.

"No point in sending Miss Preston off on her own," Mr. Halleck said comfortably, so he and Ethan drank some port, and then brandy, with her at the table, but did not smoke cigars. Melissa chose not to try the port, but to continue with the wine she had been drinking, half listening, half floating in a pleasant fog.

When they rose from the table, Melissa a little unsteadily, Ethan took her elbow, and leaning against him, she felt safe. He and Mr. Halleck were laughing about something. She heard Mr. Halleck say, "I do apologize, I should have been more observant," and Ethan laughed and said something else—Melissa didn't quite catch it. Somehow they were at the door and dressed in their outdoor clothing. Mr. Halleck must have given instructions to someone, because there was a carriage there.

Between them, Mr. Halleck and Ethan helped Melissa make her way into the carriage. After cheerful farewells, they moved through the quiet streets of Dublin, she leaning against Ethan's shoulder, looking out the window on her side. Somehow it had come to be late at night, and the streets were dark, except for the light of the moon, which was fat and yellow and hung low in the sky.

19

IT TOOK LONGER THAN SEEMED reasonable to get back to the house on the Green. When Mr. Halleck's carriage stopped at the door to let them out, the coachman waited on the street while they made their way to the door. Melissa found it curiously difficult to walk across the footpath and up the steps without Ethan's support, and reached out to lean her hand against the doorframe, just as it opened. When the butler appeared, the coachman nodded at them before pulling away and clattering down the street.

Once they were inside, Mr. O'Malley took their coats. "Mr. and Mrs. Gallagher have retired already, but they said if you wished for some hot milk before bed, I was to arrange it for you."

Melissa giggled. She didn't mean to, and she put her hand over her mouth. When she dropped it, she spoke carefully. "Thank you very much, but I don't think we need you to go to any trouble."

Ethan cast a quick look at her and then turned to the butler. "If you could arrange to take some hot milk to Miss Preston's bedchamber, it might help her sleep."

Melissa started to object, but Ethan nodded to the butler, who responded with a single tip of his head and disappeared in the direction of the stairs down to the kitchen.

"Come with me," Ethan said to Melissa. "Let me take your arm going up the stairs."

"My legs have gone all wobbly."

"I can't say I'm walking really straight myself," Ethan said, and laughed. Melissa had never heard him laugh quite that way. It was more like a giggle. It made her giggle back at him, and the two of them went up the stairs arm in arm, chuckling and giggling back and forth. Neither of them was walking entirely steadily, but fortunately Ethan seemed more sure-footed than Melissa felt, and she leaned on him.

When they went up past the floor where the main bedroom suite was, they looked at each other and then, grinning at her, Ethan placed his hand over her mouth. For a moment Melissa tried to pull away indignantly, and then she giggled a little, putting her own hand over his to muffle the sound. Then, breaking loose and trying to step silently, she made her unsteady way to the stairs rising to the floors where their bedchambers and the nursery were, clutching for the stair rail. Where had Ethan gone? She was too blurry to wonder.

When she reached the top of the stairs, she went straight to her own room and fell gratefully on the bed.

Ethan appeared in the door a moment or two later.

"Are you all right?" He kept his voice low.

Melissa, who had fallen on her face, rolled over. "I'm fine," she said, but the words came out oddly. She giggled again, and Ethan looked down at her.

"I have your hot milk," he said. "The maid was bringing it upstairs."

"I hate hot milk," Melissa said, and giggled again.

"Maybe it will help settle your stomach."

Melissa put both hands on her stomach and turned to him. "Is something wrong with my stomach?"

Ethan was still standing there, looking down at her. "There's nothing wrong with your stomach." His voice was suddenly almost...almost tender. "Nothing wrong with any part of you."

Melissa blinked at him. "I must have had too much wine. That sounds as if you like me. I didn't think you did."

He sat down next to her on the bed. "I like you. I like you a great deal."

She drew her eyebrows together. "Not in London. You laughed at me then."

He leaned over her, and his hand curved around the side of her face. "If I did, it was foolish of me."

Melissa turned her face even closer to his hand. "It's all right. I didn't like you either." She looked up at him and smiled. "I like you very much now."

"Silly girl. You don't know what you are saying."

"No," Melissa agreed, somehow regretful. "I had too much wine. Everything is fuzzy now."

"Too much wine will do that to you." He nodded wisely. "I must be fuzzy as well. Your face is so soft."

She reached up and caught the side of his face with her hand. "Your face isn't fuzzy. It is rough. Prickly." She reached up with the other hand as well. "Both sides are. Are beards prickly as well? I have always wondered."

Ethan laughed. "I have not felt many beards, I must admit, nor tried to grow one. It is not the fashion just now. But your face is soft and inviting."

"Inviting what?" It was suddenly perfectly clear to Melissa what she wanted most. She wanted him to put his face against hers, to wrap her in his arms and hold her very close, so close that there was no space between them.

Just as suddenly, Ethan's hand left her face, and his arms went around her and she found herself lifted up and enclosed within the circle of his arms, his warmth all around her, and his lips moving slowly, deliciously across her face until they met hers.

"Ohhh," she sighed into his mouth and for a moment the fuzzy feeling gave way to a sense of spinning in the room, kept from floating away only by the warmth of his arms and the wonderful trust she so surprisingly found in his strength and sureness. It felt right to be cradled in his arms, to feel his hand moving down from her face to her shoulder and then to the neckline of her dress, to slide beneath it until her breast felt the unfamiliar sensation of a hand moving over it, cupping it.

She thought she would melt with the pleasure of it.

"Melly-girl, you should stop me," he whispered in her ear.

She looked up into his eyes glowing down at her. "But I don't want you to stop."

"This is dangerous—we ought not to..." His voice, so low and intimate, was the only sound she could hear in the quiet house. They were high enough up in the building so that street noises—if there were any—were muffled by distance, and it was only the two of them there, in the flickering light of the candle they had brought upstairs with them.

In the shadows and the silence it felt as if the only matter of importance was to experiment with how close they could come to each other. When Ethan's fingers found the buttons down the front of her dress and clumsily began to open them, she pushed them away to unbutton herself because she would be much faster at it. Once her dress lay open around her, with only her stays and her shift between her and nakedness, she reached for his coat, and tried to push it off his shoulders, but it fit so tightly that he laughed with her, softly, and pulled it off himself. Then his shirt came off over his head, and Melissa was able to run her hands over his back and chest. Delightfully, the hair there was soft enough to rub her cheek again. Skin of one pressing against skin of another: why had no one ever told her this wonderful sensation existed?

The rest of their clothes were removed in a haze of urgency and anticipation. Exactly what their bodies were racing toward Melissa was not sure, but through the haze and the kisses there was the steady sureness that this was what was meant to be.

"I should stop—I could stop—" His voice was husky in her ears.

"No, no, no," she whispered back. Stop? When her heart was beating as hard as it was, and she could feel the warmth spreading through her whole body, to places that had never known this warmth before? It was like the warmth of the wine but trebly more inviting.

And when she was there on the bed, wide and welcoming, she wondered why no one had ever told her how wonderfully two people could fit together, and even the stab of searing pain was not enough to jerk her out of the daze of warmth and confusion and little licks of pleasure that followed, delights she had never known existed.

"Oh, Melly-girl," Ethan breathed into her ear, and suddenly the sensation exploded, and she slid back down a delicious slope into calm. The frenzy was over, and what was left was the warmth of being together, still wrapped around each other. In the quiet, she felt all over again the delicious fuzziness of the wine and the bliss, and it seemed the most natural thing in the world to close her eyes and sleep in his arms.

When Ethan awoke, he was in his own bedchamber, his clothes a tumbled mess on the floor, and at first he felt nothing but a vague sense that something unfortunate had happened for which he needed to make amends—but what?

Recollection came creeping back as he struggled to sit up in his bed, his head troubled by the sense that a headache was there somewhere in close proximity, not ready to settle yet exactly, but definitely lurking in the wings.

Then he remembered. Dear God, what had he done?

The headache landed, clearly with the intention of taking up residence.

What had he been thinking? Obviously, he had not used his brain at all; other parts of his body had taken priority. The first obvious example of his lack of good sense was that he had had considerably too much to drink, for which he could blame no one but himself. True, Halleck had been very free-handed with the wine and the brandy later, but Ethan had not been roped or tied and forced to drink it. Worse, Melissa (oh, lord in heaven, *Melissa*) was purely and simply drunk, and he had known that. Gentlemen do not take advantage of young ladies—young *virgins*—under those circumstances.

Most unfortunately of all, how it had happened was now of only historic interest. The fact was that it had, and the only question he should be dealing with was what were they going to do now?

No, there was a bigger one. How was Melissa? He had never imagined she could be as she was last night. The prickly, disagreeable girl he had known and regrettably laughed at in London had been transformed into a soft, yielding woman who leapt into passion with as much eagerness as he had felt himself. He had come to like her during their journey and this time in Dublin much better than he had expected, but he had never imagined that so much fire lay beneath her conventional surface. But what would she be like when he saw her next? She would have every right to treat him with open contempt. Unquestionably, he had taken advantage of her.

A complete change in the relationship between them would be difficult to explain to the Gallaghers. Yet telling them the truth was plainly impossible. Dear heaven, they had trusted him! They had observed the two or them were like brother and sister, and since his uncle and aunt had allowed them to travel together, they had not insisted on chaperoning them and had arranged rooms for them perilously close together. Because they trusted him.

Dear heaven. Ethan's head sunk down into his hands. What was he to do now?

Should he have gone straightaway to her bedchamber this morning to find out how she was? It was clearly too late to do so now; he could hear footsteps—presumably of servants?—in the rooms around him. In fact, there was a knock on his door, which turned out to be the manservant Martin had assigned to serve as a valet as Ethan had not yet replaced his man in England. His uncle had made similar arrangements at Kendall House, and since he had not required much in the way of services, it had worked out well.

So whatever the day would turn out to be, it was underway. He had not known it was possible to go through the familiar routines of washing and dressing in the morning, exchanging necessary words with a servant, with such a sick heart.

The sound of his shoes seemed impossibly loud as he made his way down the staircases. Would Martin be waiting for his appearance to accompany him to his offices? He hoped not. This day what he needed most was to find some private time with Melissa to determine how she was and what she was thinking. That would be almost impossible if he vanished with Martin before she came down in the morning, and returned with him in the evening. The only hope for a few words with her would be if he came to her bedchamber again, and he promised himself he would never step into that room again.

Martin was not in his study, and the drawing room was equally empty, so Ethan continued down the grand staircase to the ground floor. In the dining room he could hear women's voices, so he took a deep breath, and opened the door.

Caroline and Henrietta were there, as was Melissa. Henrietta gave him a big smile and shouted out, "Unca Ethan!"

Caroline laughed out loud. Melissa, across the table from him, glanced up at him as a quick half-smile flitted across her face.

So. She was not going to give him the cut direct, which would be difficult to carry out in the present circumstances anyway. But it seemed she was prepared to offer limited cordiality. That would make it— whatever "it" was—easier.

Ethan murmured an all-purpose "Good morning" and sat down in the closest available chair.

"Tea, Ethan?" Caroline asked.

"Yes, please," he said, and reached out for the filled cup. He seemed to have exhausted his conversational capabilities.

"Toast!" Henrietta told him with all her earlier enthusiasm. "Toast 'n jam!"

"Plain toast will be fine, thank you," he said. A glance showed him Melissa had made the same choice. Strangely, his stomach seemed to have weathered the excess of the night before rather better than he would have expected, but he feared she might not be so fortunate. She was drinking her tea without milk, he noticed.

"Here, poppet," Caroline said, seizing a cloth to wipe some of the jam transferred from the toast to Henrietta's face. "She does love jam, but not much of it actually gets into her mouth, as far as I can tell."

Henrietta endured the cleaning operation in the same way as every other child Ethan had observed, admittedly few. She pulled her chin in and leaned back as far as her child's chair would allow trying to escape the cloth in her mother's hand. The moment she was set free she pushed more jammy toast into her mouth, restoring the smears that had just been wiped away.

He found himself smiling with genuine amusement, enough so that he dared to look at Melissa directly. "And how are you this morning?"

Melissa lifted her eyes momentarily to meet his, and then dropped them. "Fine, thank you." Her voice was low.

"I don't think Melissa has properly wakened yet this morning," Caroline said, giving her a fond look. "She's been quiet as a mouse. So I will ask you instead. How was dinner last night?"

Ethan continued to look at Melissa, but she did not look up again. "It was very pleasant, thank you. When I spoke to Halleck about the invitation he seemed uncertain about his cook, but I thought the food was excellent."

"And the wine," Melissa offered. "It was excellent as well, and he was very generous. I'm afraid I had a bit too much."

That he had not expected. He watched her with some confusion.

"Oh dear." Caroline was warmly sympathetic. "How do you feel this morning?"

"I think I will drink less next time."

"Sensible girl." Caroline beamed at her. "Is there anything in particular I could get for you?"

"No, thank you. I am fine. Just not very hungry yet," Melissa explained, pushing her plate away.

"Probably just as well." Caroline turned her attention to Ethan. "Are you feeling somewhat the same?"

He found himself in somewhat of a quandary. It would be untrue and unfair for him to say he had been cold sober the night before, but it was against a gentleman's code to admit to ladies he had been drinking too much, whatever the facts of the matter.

"The toast and the tea suit me well, thank you," he finally said, rather too late.

Henrietta had abandoned her toast and was just about to spread the jam still on her hands through her hair when Caroline, distracted from Ethan, grabbed her.

"I believe it is time to return this child to her nanny for something close to a full bath," she said, lifting her out of her chair carefully and holding her a little less closely than she usually did. "If you'll excuse us?"

Ethan said, "Of course," heartily, and Melissa made some indistinguishable noise, and Caroline bore her daughter out of the room.

Silence lay heavy across the table.

Well, better to start as he had intended first thing this morning. "How are you?"

Melissa lifted her head and looked directly at him. "Fine. And you?"

That was not what he had anticipated. He hesitated, and then spoke quickly. "We need to talk."

She was still watching him. "Why?"

Now he was completely nonplussed. Could she have forgotten the entire episode entirely? In some ways, that would make many things easier, but what if there were consequences? In fact, there were bound to be consequences. She had been a virgin. Now she was not. How was he to explain that to her if she did not know?

Dear God, where was he to go from here?

Her eyes were still fixed on him—her wonderful blue eyes under those thick lashes. Had he ever told her how beautiful her eyes were? And the mass of golden curls, brightened by reddish gleams? How had he never seen the promise of that when they were in London together, at the balls, circling through the dances, her beauty illuminated by the light of hundreds of candles?

"Melissa," he began tentatively, "last night—"

Her gaze did not waver. "Oh. Last night. Much of it is very vague to me, but I do remember—some things." For the first time her glance dropped, but almost immediately lifted to meet his again.

He hoped his breath of relief was imperceptible. "And that is why we must talk."

Now her eyes did move. She studied the arrangement of the cutlery on the table and shifted the position of a spoon slightly. "Why? Nothing has changed."

"Melissa!" He feared he was speaking too loudly and deliberately lowered his voice. "It is quite possible everything has changed."

She shook her head. "It just happened. You were drunk, and so was I. I've never been drunk before. It's a strange sensation, is it not?"

Ethan felt strongly tempted to pull his hair out. Or hers. "Everything between us has changed now, Melissa. That cannot be overlooked. It is possible that we must marry."

She looked—there was only one word for it. She looked indignant.

"Why must I marry you?"

How had he ever found himself in this incomprehensible situation with this maddening woman? "Melissa, we may have made a child." He almost spat the words out.

"Or might not have." Her chin was up, and her eyes were flashing. "I suggest we save the melodrama for actual events. As things are now, nothing has changed. Nothing."

Melodrama? What was wrong with the woman? Here they were, balanced precariously on the edge of disaster, and she was claiming they stood firmly on level ground?

"Let me make it very clear. I am prepared to marry you, Melissa Preston, if it happens we have made a child between us."

She stood, brushing a few crumbs from her skirt as if perfect grooming was the most important element of her life.

"Let me make it equally clear. I am not prepared to marry you."

With which she turned from the table and walked out of the room without a glance behind her or in his direction.

20

SOMEHOW THE ATMOSPHERE AT THE Gallagher house rocked back to normal.

At least Melissa was certain it was as close to normal as possible. She made a point of speaking to Ethan whenever they were with Caroline or Martin, but made sure the two of them were not alone together. He was spending most of his time with Martin, and from his quietly increasing confidence, their association was going well.

Melissa herself felt her moods had turned from reasonable to inexplicable. She would wake in the middle of the night with the memory of Ethan wrapped around her, whispering in her ear, and by the time she managed to get back to sleep she knew she was as unreasonably cross as she had ever been. Or she would be suddenly, pointlessly happy. None of it made any sense.

She tried to keep these wild fluctuations from anyone else. For once, spending time with Henrietta and Caroline was her chosen way of spending time, because dealing with a baby not yet two was easy compared to dealing with adults, and when Caroline was with Henrietta, her entire attention was focused on her daughter. Melissa was free to let her thoughts rumble around in her head, whether she understood them or not.

Then there was George. Melissa had paid hardly any attention to the dog from the time they had arrived, but he had always been around, usually in the general vicinity of Caroline, although he was apparently also attuned to Martin. When it was roughly the time he might be coming home, George haunted the entrance hall, waiting. If he came home unexpectedly, George would hurl himself from wherever he happened to be down the staircase to greet him, his hind end wriggling with joy.

Now George became Melissa's blessedly nonverbal friend.

When it was not too cold, she would volunteer to take George for a walk, and they came to know St. Stephen's Green well, walking down one of the tree-lined walks to the splendid statute of George II on his horse. On the fine days that were increasingly infrequent there would be other people walking there as well, and Melissa, not used to dog handling, was relieved George was a mannerly dog and endured canine sniffing from fellow leashed dogs, sniffed himself, and then trotted off when she tugged at his lead.

It gave her time to think. Or, more accurately, to try to organize her thoughts into some kind of order. She made up a list of principles for herself.

First. She must never, *never* drink too much again. It was horrifying to see what a few seemingly harmless glasses of wine could do.

Second. She had seen glimpses of what closeness there could be in marriage between Caroline and Martin. Martin so loved Caroline that she was free to be whatever she most truly was. If Melissa could not have that kind of love herself, she would not marry. Not anyone. Certainly not Ethan, who had laughed at her in London and had never said, let alone shown, that he loved her now. He had been nearly as intoxicated as she had been. What had happened had not been love. It had been loss of control.

Third. It was preposterous to think she must have conceived. Given how pleasurable it had been, people must indulge in those activities all the time. If child-bearing were the inevitable result, one would not be able to walk in St. Stephen's Green for the crowds of people taking up space there.

Fourth. It was good to have had the experience once. Once.

Every time she walked she went over her four principles. Tried to keep them firmly in mind. Tried to believe them.

Back at the house on the Green, Melissa was increasingly concerned about Caroline. When they had first arrived, Caroline had been vividly alive with energy and enthusiasm. She was still great fun to spend time with, still reported the fascinating stories Martin had told her about the astonishing world of business and people outside her experience, but when she was not talking, or when Melissa unexpectedly entered a room where she happened to be, she too often looked worn and weary. When she saw Melissa, her face would brighten and she would pull herself erect.

"How was the walk today?" she asked.

This time they were in the ground floor entrance hall. Melissa had released George from the lead, and he was wriggling with joy to find Caroline coming out of the dining room. She bent over to give him a warm welcome.

"It was cold again. Not many people out today." Melissa continued with her process of unwinding the muffler she was wearing over her outdoor woolen cape, then the cape itself, and the pelisse and silk scarf wrapped around her throat, and eventually down to her warm long-sleeved morning dress, and outside gloves. She peeled off the gloves and reached into her reticule for her lighter inside gloves, pulling them onto her hands. "There," she said. "Down to the basics. But I needed every bit of the rest of it."

The butler standing there received each of the items as she discarded them, and walked off to put them away.

"It was that cold?" Caroline asked with some concern. "If it's that cold here, it must be terrible up at home for all of them there." She sighed. "Well, there's no need to stand here in the hall. There's a nice fire in the drawing room." Turning, she started up the stairs, but instead of her steps being as light as usual, she was almost plodding. George raced ahead of her.

"I know." Melissa frowned as she followed, watching Caroline anxiously. Maybe there was something about the cold that drained a person's energy. She was a guest, after all, not Caroline's caretaker. Unless Caroline said something about it herself, she should not worry about matters that were none of her business. She had plenty, after all, that were.

"I don't know how long Ethan intends to stay here," she said as she climbed the stairs. "But I worry that winter is going to set in any time now—it is the end of November—and I don't know how difficult travel will be once it does." She followed Caroline into the drawing room, and found it was blissfully warm.

Caroline, although her eyes still looked weary, found a broad smile as she settled herself in a comfortable chair, waving Melissa to one close to her. "I'm sure it will be terrible. Wouldn't it be marvelous if you were marooned here for the whole winter? I would love that. Just think, someone to talk to and do needlework with and just have as a very special friend all winter long!"

Melissa smiled back, hoping her lack of enthusiasm did not show. Yes, a winter with Caroline would have its advantages, but she was not at all sure those advantages would compensate for being trapped in the same house as Ethan for the whole winter long. Of course if he continued to head off to the office with Martin every day and not return until both of them came home, he would not be around that much, but even so…

"I don't know what Ethan is planning," she said, which was true enough. "We certainly never thought of spending that long here. I know he is enjoying working with Martin—that is obvious enough—but I don't know if he should be working with Uncle Charles on the estate."

Caroline shrugged. "I am certainly no expert on running an estate, but from what I remember, Papa was home a great deal of the time when it grew cold. There were not a great number of bitter winters I can recall, but even during the milder ones there was not so much to do. I'm sure he would be writing to ask Ethan when he planned to return if he was concerned about it. My letters from my mother give no hint that they thought he would be back before now. In fact, what she has said is she is relieved the two of you are not trying to come back when it is this cold."

"Unfortunately, at this time of year it's not likely to get warmer." Melissa got up and went to the windows overlooking the Green. From what she could see, even fewer people were out than had been there when she was walking. What was Ethan planning? She had no idea. When would he have learned what he needed to learn? She was too wary to open any serious conversation with him. He had a way of earnestly studying her when she was paying attention to something else. She would suddenly feel uneasy, and look around to meet his eyes and he would be watching her. Just watching.

She dreaded the post coach ride back with him—hours of being together—but certainly there would be other travelers, which would put paid to any personal conversation. But what if there were not? She shuddered.

Perhaps time just needed to pass. Once he was convinced there was no substance to his worst nightmares, he would let her go, and not follow her around with his eyes whenever they were in the same place together. Perhaps it did not matter whether they were here, or in the coach, or back up at Kendall House and Ballymuir. Except that there they would be living separately. Still, thinking of the journey, it might be best to let the time pass here with the Gallaghers, with Ethan gone most days with

Martin, and Melissa able to hide herself, more or less, behind Caroline's skirts.

Turning from the window, Melissa returned to her chair. How long would it take to discover if she were increasing? Two or three months? She knew nothing about the process of bearing a child. There was something about missing one's courses, but she had only overheard that in snatches of a conversation, and was not sure she had it straight. Hers would be due any time now, she thought. How many did you have to miss before it mattered? The only person available to ask would be Caroline, and she was the one person Melissa could not say a word to.

"Perhaps tomorrow I may go out for some more silk thread," she said. At least the prospect of going somewhere other than the Green would be distracting.

Caroline, who had been gazing fixedly into the fire, glanced over at her. "What colors are you missing?"

Melissa hesitated. She could hardly say she didn't know, but exactly what she did need was unfortunately vague in her mind. She was doing a fine piece of linen to place across a chest of drawers, or a table, and for the life of her, she could hardly remember the pattern.

"Green," she said. She was sure the pattern had leaves.

Caroline's weary face brightened. "Green? The color of Ireland. I think I have several shades—certainly one of them would be right. I'll go fetch it."

Melissa started to protest, but Caroline was already on her feet and almost out the door, George behind her.

Melissa, after starting to rise to stop her, sank back into her chair and stared into the peat fire, noticing all over again its distinctive smell. Fragrance, Martin would say. He had learned to read by a peat fire, and it was the essential scent of home, he'd told Melissa. Some people now were coming to rely on coal, but if for no other reason than nostalgia, he wanted peat burned in his house.

She liked the smell herself now. How odd. Here she was in an Irishman's house—and apparently would be for some time—and sometimes it felt as if her own Englishness was slipping away.

However, if she had remained in England, she would never be facing the complications she faced now. What had her mother been thinking, dispatching her off to Ballymuir?

The door opened, and Caroline came in, a wonderful variety of green silk threads hanging over her hand. Melissa looked up at her and smiled.

Time to cover all the anxieties up again and pretend nothing in the world could be wrong.

Ethan trudged along in the cold, deliberately taking a longer way to the house on the Green. Martin had told him he had sent for the carriage, but Ethan had pleaded errands he needed to run—he had none—and chose to walk off in the wrong direction, should Martin be glancing out the window. He desperately needed time to think.

What was he to do with such a stubborn woman?

Here she was teetering on the edge of ruin, which she did not seem to recognize, and she would pay no attention to him nor to his attempts to discuss the situation. It was as if that unfortunate evening had never happened. Instead of the warm, welcoming girl he had held in his arms, he was now faced with a remote, cold beauty—yes, unfortunately he still saw the beauty he had not recognized before—who treated him as a vaguely familiar, but unwelcome, acquaintance. She was polite; why did he wish for the days when she had snapped at him?

When he saw her at dinner—well, that was about the only time he did see her. When she and Caroline rose to leave him with Martin for cigars and brandy, it was increasingly often the last time he saw her. When he and Martin went to the drawing room to rejoin the ladies, it was usually Caroline alone there. Caroline and Martin could be wonderfully amusing company, and from Caroline he learned a great deal about Ireland and details of his own family background his mother had never told him. Probably had never known.

But the distance between him and Melissa continued to grow.

He turned a corner, and found himself on an unfamiliar street. For just a moment he paused to look around. He was not far from the River Liffey. If he walked a bit farther he would be on College Green, with Trinity College on one side and the Bank of Ireland across the street. Dublin was such an odd mixture. Buildings of such beauty surrounded by small houses and shops, elegant and not, and then the grand houses both north and south of the Liffey. He really should spend more time wandering around the city, but the cold was already creeping into his bones.

He should not have thought about that. Once he realized how cold he was, he felt the cold even more sharply, and the only direction in which to go was straight into the closest pub.

He stepped inside the muggy warmth with gratitude. The pub was nearly full, which made sense because it was the end of the working day for many and he could not be the only one to feel the chill outside. He stepped to the bar, ordered a warming whiskey, and looked about casually.

"Hawthorne!"

He turned to see who was calling his name, and there was Halleck, who lifted his glass to him and moved in his direction.

He had a welcoming smile, and Ethan found a smile to answer him. After all, it was certainly not his fault the evening at his house had had such a calamitous finish. He had not forced either of them to drink, and of the two of them Ethan was more guilty for not realizing how inexperienced Melissa was with the effects of wine. He should have drunk less himself so he could have stepped in much earlier to protect her.

"So how is the educational effort in Gallagher's office proceeding?"

"Very well, thank you. Sometimes I fear I am becoming addicted to the challenge of investing."

They both laughed. Then, glancing at Ethan with just a touch of wariness, Halleck asked, "And how is the lovely Miss Preston?"

Ethan rebuilt his smile. "Very well, thank you." It occurred to him that he was repeating himself, and he decided it was necessary to elaborate at least slightly. "She is enjoying her time in Dublin as well, although unfortunately it has been too cold for her to be able to do as much exploring of the city as I think she would like."

Halleck sighed. "It does not bode well for the winter. I was considering bringing my wife over since it looks as if I will be here even longer than I had thought, but I would not want her crossing the Irish Sea at this time of year. This winter looks to be a severe one. It is as bad in London, by the way, so it is not as if she is going to be much warmer there, unfortunately. But the crossing—the Irish Sea can be nasty even under normal conditions."

He paused. Looking almost sheepish, he admitted, "But I confess I miss her. When I came over this time I did not anticipate that my stay here would be so long."

Ethan had not known he was married. Of course he must be lonely now. He briefly considered asking Caroline if it would be possible to invite him for dinner, but swiftly dismissed the idea. It might be good for Halleck, but he had no idea what effect his presence would have on Melissa, and at this point he was not of a mind to experiment.

"It seems likely that we will be having a hard winter, wherever we are," he said.

Halleck nodded. Then he turned his head to look directly at Ethan.

"I'm sure it is out of line for me to say this, but doing without my wife has made me appreciate the virtues of marriage more than before. I miss the companionship most. I find I am not eager to return home at the end of the day when she is not there. I look forward to her letters as if we were still courting, and fortunately she is proving to be a faithful correspondent. When I think about the winter, I confess I think about the perils of the Irish Sea, and fear the regularity of her letters will suffer with the difficulties the post boats will certainly encounter."

Ethan smiled sympathetically. At least he tried to. Although he could certainly sympathize with Halleck's situation, it seemed an odd topic for two men who knew each other so casually to be discussing.

"Miss Preston is not related to you?" Halleck abruptly asked.

Ethan hoped he did not look as startled as he felt. "No."

"She struck me as a very suitable young woman." Halleck stared into his drink. "Pretty and bright and sweet-tempered. You could go farther and not find many like her."

Ethan was sure by now his expression could only be described as wary. "Indeed," he said noncommittally.

Halleck glanced at him and laughed. "You young men are all alike," he said. "Fearing that matrimony would infringe upon your freedom. It is only when you are married, if you choose well, that you discover the greatest freedom of all is to be yourself, and to have that self valued by another person."

Ethan was surprised—no, more than surprised. Astonished. Astonished to feel a wash of real longing. He could imagine that. He could even imagine that with Melissa. Perhaps, if there were the necessity to marry, it would be a good thing. Maybe even as much as wonderful.

But how in the world was he to persuade her of that?

MELISSA WAS BECOMING SERIOUSLY CONCERNED that Caroline was ill.

When she came down to breakfast, Caroline was not there, day after day. Sometimes Henrietta came down looking for her, and although she would stay and chatter for a few minutes—only about half of which Melissa understood—she would soon wander off to find her mother, her nanny lurking in the hall waiting for her.

When Caroline eventually emerged from her bedchamber, she was pale and clearly tired, even at the beginning of her day. Increasingly she left walking George to Melissa or one of the footmen, so much so that Melissa found George following her hopefully when he believed his time for a walk was coming close.

Martin seemed to be watching over Caroline closely, but did not seem to be worried about her. He was adoring, as usual, good company with everyone else, and as always, warm and self-assured. Melissa watched him wistfully. Would there ever be anyone who would look at her with the kind of intimate warmth Martin so continually showed with Caroline? It was as if she were the sun he circled, content, sure of himself. But he was focused completely on whatever would make her happy.

It was all very bewildering.

At dinner the mystery was revealed.

All four of them were there, which had been happening less often recently. Caroline had begun having her dinner brought upstairs to her, and Ethan was occasionally absent, but Melissa did not know where he was. Apparently Martin did. He would murmur something to Caroline, if she was there, or apologize charmingly to Melissa if they were the only ones there. He took a consistent interest in what Melissa was up to during the days, and made a point of directing her to places he thought she would be interested in, whether places to shop or particularly remarkable buildings. He would dismiss any of her tentative questions about Caroline with easy confidence.

"She is not feeling well today," he said if asked. "But she will be fine."

That evening, everyone was there, and Caroline seemed to have more appetite than she had had recently. She even remarked on how delicious the soup was.

The bread with it was wonderfully fresh as well. Seeing Caroline better than she had be increased Melissa's appetite as well. Perhaps she had been fussing unnecessarily. Everyone had times when they were off color.

Ethan had some comical stories about what had been happening at work, apparently when Martin was away from the office, and he laughed as hard as Caroline and Melissa did. Caroline was particularly amused. She seemed almost glowing, her eyes most often fixed on Martin.

Then, with a radiant smile, she turned to Melissa. "You have been so patient with me, Melissa, that I must tell you first. I am increasing. Again!" Her delight was obvious.

Melissa's eyes instantly locked on Ethan's. She shook her head as imperceptibly as she could manage, with a great rush of relief. Caroline was not sickening for something dreadful. She would be having another child!

"How wonderful!" she said with all the enthusiasm the relief gave her. "Won't Henrietta be lucky to have a sister or brother!"

Martin laughed. "I'm not entirely sure she will see it that way. More likely she will see it as a challenge to her supremacy. But we certainly have enough love for two of them, and I believe Henrietta will be rational enough to understand that she is the older, and thus more likely to set the rules once our new one is past infancy.

"For me, though, it is brilliant news. I am so proud of my dear wife."

Caroline colored charmingly. Melissa felt she could hardly breathe for the thick happiness in the room.

Ethan congratulated both of them. For the first time, Melissa could look at him without a sinking sensation in her abdomen. Caroline was increasing; she was not. She had not been sick in the morning, as Caroline was confessing she had been, and she had not been unusually tired.

She gifted Ethan with a whole-hearted wide smile. He looked at her, obviously bewildered, smiled back and returned his attention to his dinner.

The celebration continued after dinner. Instead of the ladies leaving the dining room to the gentlemen, Martin insisted that they stay and brought out chilled champagne (apple juice for Caroline) to drink with the lemon ice he had somehow acquired for their sweet. Melissa drank one glass, and not all of that. As she set down the glass with some champagne still sparkling at the bottom, she looked across the table at Ethan, as if challenging him to say anything. He smiled again and glanced away.

The evening ended earlier than it might have done. They did move up to the drawing room for after-dinner coffee, and talked for a short while, but very soon Martin took Caroline's hands and pulled her to her feet. Melissa had the feeling he would pick her up in his arms if they had not been present. He told them that mother and baby both required lots of rest, and led her off to their part of the house.

Ethan and Melissa glanced at each other, and with a single impulse, lifted their cups to their lips at exactly the same moment. Melissa tried to swallow a giggle, and Ethan snorted, clearly attempting to muffle a laugh.

"This is ridiculous, you know," he said after a minute or two of silence.

Melissa lifted her chin. "What is ridiculous?"

"You and me. Pretending we hardly know each other."

She looked down at her lap and smoothed her skirt. "Well, we do not really know each other very well."

He cocked his head and surveyed her. "Compared to what?" His voice was a challenge.

Melissa heaved a sigh. Why could he not just let it pass? She had been stupid, she fully realized that. When she had been in London, she was never offered more than a single glass, and since she had not particularly cared for most of the wines she had tasted, she had often not finished that one. She could not remember how many she had drunk at Mr. Halleck's house, and was glad of it. The crucial fact was that she had clearly drunk too much, and Ethan had taken advantage of it.

She glanced over at him and repented. No. It was not fair to blame him. He had drunk too much as well, she was sure. He had apologized the next day—she remembered that quite clearly—but she had been so embarrassed that she had not known what to say and therefore had said little. He had been worried that she might have conceived.

Conceived. What a strange word. How odd she should know it, when she knew so little about the whole process of reproduction! At least, if they were planted here in Dublin for the winter, she would have the opportunity of watching Caroline and learning so that if it ever came about that she *should* conceive, she would have some idea of what was likely to happen.

It was so stupid that girls were told so little. Nothing, really, until they married. She had learned tidbits here and there from friends of her mother talking, but those instances had been few and far between since her mother had taken care that neither she nor Penelope were anywhere around when she and her friends were talking.

Her lips tightened with annoyance, and she looked up to realize Ethan was still studying her.

"Well?" he asked.

Well what? She had lost track of whatever he had said last. She shrugged.

"May we at least have peace between us?" His voice sounded genuine. Genuinely earnest.

"Of course." She made sure her tone was easy. "We have been friends of a sort all along."

He shook his head and looked away, almost as if he were exasperated. Melissa looked at him as blank-faced as she could manage. He had asked for peace, and she had responded with an offer to return to the friendship they had had before. What more did he expect?

It was only when he rose, bowed politely, and excused himself that Melissa, sitting in the now empty drawing room, considered whether they had ever been friends at all.

The days dragged on and added themselves into weeks. Caroline said that the morning sickness was better than it had been, and she was now almost always down at the breakfast table, laughing and giggling with Henrietta, who seemed relieved her mother was behaving more normally. Henrietta and George were developing a closer relationship as well. He was always gentle with her, and she thought he was the funniest companion of all.

Generally, the atmosphere around the house was returning to more what it had been before Caroline had been poorly. On days that gave the hope of being warmer Melissa and Caroline went out together, sometimes to walk with Henrietta and George, sometimes to peer into the shops to see if there was anything interesting. There usually was.

Melissa still took George on independent walks, because when Henrietta was with them progress was slow and they returned home far sooner than George was prepared to come in and settle down in the house.

Unfortunately, the warmer days became fewer and fewer as November slid into December. Correspondence between Kendall House and Dublin increased in tempo as the question of Christmas was debated. Aunt Elizabeth had hoped initially that the Dublin wing of the family— now including Melissa and Ethan, at least for the present—would come north for the holiday, but as the cold set in more and more firmly both north and south, eventually Uncle Charles wrote a firm letter saying that there would be many Christmas days in the future, and he did not like the idea of Henrietta and Caroline (especially now that she was increasing) getting stopped by snow somewhere between Dublin and Kendall House. True, there was seldom heavy snow in Ireland, but this winter to date had seemed to indicate that snow was not only possible but likely, and all of them up north would celebrate it more happily knowing that the Dubliners, temporary or not, were warm and safe at home.

Which put paid to any idea Melissa might have had about leaving Dublin.

Nor could there be any question of returning to England at this time of year, although Melissa wondered gloomily if either her mother or Penelope had given a thought to that. She had fairly regular cheerful letters from her mother, none of which (thankfully) had anything to say about the importance of matrimony. Nor did they make any reference to the likelihood of Melissa returning to England any time in the foreseeable future.

She did not know quite what to make of that. Was her exile in Ireland intended to be permanent?

Having just received yet another letter from home, Melissa was pondering the problem over her breakfast tea when Caroline suddenly spoke up.

"I think it is about time to order our Christmas goose."

Melissa looked at her in some surprise. They were not that deep into December yet, and she had given barely any consideration to the holiday

"When do you ordinarily do that?" she asked.

"Well, that is just the problem. Last year we had Christmas with the family at Kendall House, and my mother was in charge of the dinner. So this is my first time at it, and I'm not sure when to do what."

"There's the Yule log," Melissa prompted, to be helpful.

"I'll let Martin take care of that." Caroline looked thoughtful. "It's the food that concerns me. Let's see. Fish to start, and then the goose, and do we need roast beef as well?"

"There will be only the four of us."

"Perhaps not. Ethan asked if he might invite his friend Mr. Halleck. His wife is in England, and he is alone over here. He doesn't like to ask her to cross the Irish Sea at this time of year."

Mr. Halleck? Melissa hoped Caroline did not notice her automatic recoil. Which made no sense, really. True, she had been a silly idiot, but that was all safely in the past, and she would have a single cup of Christmas cheer, and hope no one commented on it. Just because he had offered—and she had accepted—more wine than was reasonable was no reason to wish the poor man to be alone on Christmas day. She just hoped he would make no reference to their prior encounter.

Caroline stretched luxuriously, and pushed her breakfast dishes away. "I should go find Henrietta. She must have slept late this morning." She sighed pleasurably. "I know it is indelicate to say so, but now that I am not so sick every morning, I have to say there are advantages to my interesting condition. It is lovely not to have the mess of my courses every month! I did tell you where the rags are kept, did I not?"

Melissa suddenly felt an icy chill that started at the top of her head and moved swiftly all the way down her body. Her courses. This was now December. They should have begun already. Had she had them in November? Surely she could not be remembering accurately. Could she remember even looking for those rags since she'd been here in Dublin?

She sat staring straight ahead. She was not overwhelmed by fatigue. She had not been sick to her stomach. Wasn't that enough to be sure?

"Melissa?" Caroline asked.

She found a smile. It had been one month for sure. Two months possibly. "Do you want to take a walk this morning?" She hoped Caroline did not hear the crack in her voice.

IT WAS OBVIOUS TO ETHAN when he came home that evening something was wrong with Melissa. What it might be he could not guess, and any tactful attempt to find out—at least he meant it to be tactful—was turned away.

"I am fine," was the most cordial reply she would give him.

He was unsurprised that his mind rapidly moved to disastrous alternatives, but as there were several of those, his worry was free to wander in many directions. Had she written her mother about that fateful evening? She had no father, but would her brother Hugh be preparing to descend upon him, threatening God knew what unless he married her? Well, he had asked her already.

He had asked, had he not? Or had he simply told her that was what they must do? His memory of that evening was certainly foggy in places, but he was quite certain he had suggested they marry the next day. Had she not consulted with anyone, but finally grasped the difficulty she would face marrying someone else when inevitably he would discover she was no longer virginal? He had never mentioned precisely that to her, as far as he remembered, but she would have to be either unbelievably unworldly not to have thought of it all by herself. Was that what was eating away at her usual good temper?

Or, of course, the most catastrophic possibility. Was she with child? If she were, would this be the way she would react?

He was most horribly convinced that she probably would. But she had told him—true, only with the slightest possible shake of her head—that she was not.

Thus he returned to the start of his circular thinking all over again.

On this night, as luck would have it, Martin was in a mellow mood. He had stopped at a jewelry shop on the way home, and bought a pair of diamond earrings for his wife (as he explained it, "One for you and one for the baby"). So she was flushed and glowing with joy, and it was almost as if the two of them were in a golden circle of mutual admiration. Ethan sat at the dining room table with them, fiddling with his glass to keep his eyes from remaining fixed on them. He wished he could sit and stare: such felicity was not something that a person saw every day.

Melissa was staring at the window, past the curtains, presumably, to the street. Was she also reluctant to pay too much attention? He wished he knew. They had had moments of genuine companionship, but moments did not last, and when he looked at her now, all he felt was empty longing. Longing to run his fingers through her red gold tumbled hair. Longing to know what she was thinking when her eyes seemed to be following people passing the windows or the occasional carriages moving slowly down the street between themselves and the Green. Longing just to talk to her when neither of them was guarded and wary, so that he could speak truly and so would she.

Was all that so impossible?

"How the diamonds glitter in the candlelight." Melissa broke the otherwise contented silence, and Caroline beamed at her.

"I am so happy tonight," she said. "I cannot quite believe that I am fortunate enough to have all this happiness now. It makes me look back to that whole hard year and more after Henry died, and it seems incredible that I have so many wonderful things piled in the space that was empty for so long."

"Did you have any inkling that your life would change so?" In Melissa's question, Ethan could hear the wistfulness.

Caroline considered for a full minute or more, and then slowly shook her head. "No. It had never occurred to me before such sorrow existed, and when I was caught up in it, I did not think there was a way out. I just kept putting one foot in front of the other and tried to endure." Momentarily Ethan could see on her face the hopelessness she must have felt, and then the shadow lifted. "Funny. George was the first bit of happiness. I am so grateful that the Duke agreed I could have him with me in the house, although the Duchess had always disliked dogs."

"Funny old George," Martin murmured fondly.

"He is that," Caroline agreed. She leaned toward her husband. "Have you noticed how Henrietta is coming to play with him? I am so grateful! I no longer need him as much as I did, and I would hate it if he felt abandoned. But she thinks he is the funniest creature around, and he would follow her anywhere. Which reminds me."

She turned toward Melissa and her face became businesslike. "Do remind me to speak to O'Malley tomorrow. I saw Henrietta working on getting the front door open this afternoon. O'Malley was somewhere else in the house, and in his absence she very nearly succeeded. We will have to remember to fasten that upper latch she cannot reach. If she opened the door—and I'm sure she will continue trying—George would undoubtedly follow her right across the street to the Green, no matter what traffic might happen to be in the way."

"Perhaps George would bark to let us know she might be in danger," Martin suggested.

Caroline laughed at him, her face alight with love. "You have greater trust in George than I have, my dear. I would hope something like that might happen, but I have more faith in sturdy latches than in George's reliability as a watchdog."

Ethan chuckled as well, but his eyes returned to study Melissa, who was now watching her finger run down the linen tablecloth with the same intensity as she had been devoting to the activity on the street outside.

She was unhappy. He could see that. But he had no idea why she was so, or what he could do to relieve her of whatever the problem was. All he had was a sick feeling somewhere in his interior that she needed something from someone, and he wished more than he could remember wishing for anything before that he could be the person to supply whatever she needed to dispel her unhappiness.

If it were a pair of diamond earrings, he would rush to the store where Martin had bought the beautiful ones he had given Caroline and buy a pair for Melissa first thing in the morning.

But he did not think it was diamond earrings that were needed.

The next morning neither Melissa nor Caroline were up and about when Martin and Ethan set out for the office.

It was cold enough so that Martin hesitated for a minute or two on the doorstep debating whether it was worth the time to get out the carriage. The two men stood there looking at each other until they started to laugh at the idea that two grown men were thinking over the practicalities of getting out the horses and the carriage to avoid what amounted to probably a ten- or fifteen-minute walk, even considering the cold. Of course the carriage, kept in the unheated mews, would not be significantly warmer until the journey was almost finished.

At which point they shrugged at each other, pulled their mufflers up high enough so that the soft wool nearly met their hats, and shuffled off together, promising each other a race to the coffee that with any luck would be hot and waiting for them once they reached the office.

No snow had fallen yet, but there was ice where miscellaneous drips had collected and frozen. Ethan discovered he was marching along keeping his eyes on the ground in front of him lest he only discover a patch of ice as he slid over it and, because this was that sort of day, crash to the cold, unwelcoming pavement. When he lifted his eyes for a moment and saw Martin's building ahead, he allowed himself to notice that brisk walking was doing what it always did, and he was no longer as miserably cold as he had been.

Still, they both went directly to the cubbyhole where the housekeeper for the offices tended a small stove used exclusively for coffee or tea. Standing there in their coats, gradually unwrapping mufflers and discarding hats and gloves, life seemed much more promising than it had done up until then.

Ethan made his way to the high desk that had gradually become his work area, and leafed through the mail from the first delivery that morning. His mind was still restless and seemed disinclined to settle on any of the matters that he now could handle himself, nor could he seem to persuade himself to think of a coherent summation he could present to Martin requesting help with difficulties he still encountered from time to time. His mind was too undisciplined to remain rigidly on task. Perhaps he was simply too much a gentleman still to be able to work regularly and unhesitatingly as the men around him did. As Martin appeared to do with such calm and easiness of manner.

Of course the only direction his wayward attention strayed was toward the puzzle of Melissa and what he was obliged to do—what he *could* do—about her. Compared to that, the ornate and polished phrasing of the correspondence now littering his desk concerning the buying and selling of instruments of finance seemed trivial indeed.

He was still only going through the correspondence in a desultory fashion when Martin's voice was right behind him.

"Do you have the letter from the Duke of Apthorp?"

To his mortification, Ethan actually started, not having seen him approach. He straightened up to a more businesslike posture, and pawed at the disorganized pile of correspondence in front of him. Had he seen a letter from the Duke? He honestly could not remember. The only possible course of action was to go through the pile again now, this time paying attention to what he was looking at. He began at once.

A hint of disapproval passed over Martin's face. Ethan had seen it before—even seen the full-blown version—but this was the first time it had been directed at him. He cringed, invisibly he hoped.

But the gods were merciful. At exactly that moment the letter Martin wanted was the one he turned over.

"Here it is." He started out sounding confident (or so he wanted to believe), but then remembering what a generous benefactor Martin had been, he added, "I do apologize. My mind has been wandering this morning. It makes me doubt my suitability for detail work."

Martin, surprisingly, smiled. "Every man in this office, most definitely including me, finds from time to time that our bodies have arrived here somewhat ahead of our intelligence. Perhaps on a cold morning like this our better selves stopped off at the pub to warm up and let the rest of us get along to the office." He clapped Ethan's shoulder. "Here, take a look at this and see if you can figure out exactly what His Grace is wanting. I must confess it is beyond me."

Ethan took the letter back gratefully. "Thank you. I'll do my best."

"Perhaps at lunch we can go out to the pub and see if we can persuade our minds to join us for the afternoon." Martin made the invitation as he was turning away to return to his own office, and Ethan looked at his retreating back with appreciation.

There was so much to learn working with the man, and not all of it was about the details of investment and sensible use of money. If he set up the plan he was contemplating, Ethan would have employees as well, and after spending his days here for a time, he knew the most important knowledge he could pick up was to observe and learn from Martin's skill in dealing with those who worked for him.

Determined on renewed dedication, he firmly placed Melissa in the to-be-dealt-with-later compartment of his mind, and picked up the Duke's letter. He began to read it closely, and managed to find peace for a while in total concentration, applying himself to a matter completely removed from personal considerations.

When the two men arrived home that evening, Melissa was elusive as she had been of late. Caroline was there to greet them, and explained that Melissa was feeling poorly, and she had insisted on sending her to bed and would send her dinner up to her. Caroline herself was feeling splendid, she assured Martin, whose eyes looked worried at the mere notion of Caroline catching any possible ailment.

"I think Melissa is mostly just tired," she explained. "And bored, probably. It is such a shame that it remains so much colder than it would normally be at this time of year. It is even worse than I remember it when I was growing up at home, and that is well north of here. I'm sure she was hoping to be able to wander around the city with me, poking into shops and going to some of the entertainments that are not available in the country. I truly doubt that there is much wrong with her besides fatigue—she says she has been sleeping badly recently—and weariness with being housebound."

The creases around Martin's eyes eased out, and he was cheerful as they went in to dinner. Ethan's concern only increased, and he spent most of the time at the table trying to plot out a way to have a private conversation with Melissa. If she was established in her bedchamber, he would have to go there. Such a visit would require making sure Martin and Caroline had retired for the night, but recently they had been doing so quite early. Martin was determined Caroline must be tended and coddled and watched over lest she overtire herself trying any activity that could possibly be considered unwise.

This had its advantages. Once the Gallaghers were settled for the night, Ethan could take the chance that if he walked in his stocking feet, they would not hear him from below as he crept as quietly as possible from his room to hers.

It was of course flagrantly against all rules he had ever been taught, and he did not like to think about the consequences should they be discovered. Still, Ethan was blessed with only so much patience, and what he had was exhausted. He was determined to find out what was wrong with the girl. There was always the possibility that when she discovered him in her room, she would scream with fright or outrage—possibly both—but he had to take the chance.

It seemed to him his charming hosts stayed up later that night than usual. Continuing to chat lazily around the fire, he consoled himself with the thought it was more likely his impatience than any change in their schedule. But eventually they excused themselves and went up the stairs to bed.

Ethan sat on in the drawing room, trying to determine from faint sounds from above the stages they were reaching in the process of retiring. The house, he discovered, was really very well and solidly built. No matter how intently he listened, he could not hear much. A whisper of sound here and there—perhaps a step or two toward the bed? But no reassuring squeak resulting from them actually climbing into the bed penetrated to the floor below. Ethan had to sit and wait until he was sure there had been no sound at all for a considerable time before he felt safe in making his own way upstairs as quietly as possible. Surely if it was impossible to hear the second floor from the first floor, it would be equally impossible to hear the third floor from the second.

It was supposition, not proof, to be sure, but it was the best he had.

Once up in his own room Ethan took off his boots and set them as silently on the floor as he could manage. He was determined not to alert anyone to the possibility of movement up there. In his stocking feet, he walked as lightly as possible out of his own door (he had left it open so that neither sounds of opening nor closing would betray him), and went to Melissa's door, past the two empty rooms between them.

He eased her door open.

There was no light in the room, save the dim light cast by the moon, just past the full. Melissa had apparently blown out her candle and settled down into her covers. She was not yet asleep, judging by the speed with which she sat up, facing him.

"What are you doing here?" Her voice was not friendly.

"Shhhh," Ethan cautioned her in a whisper. "Do you want to wake up the household?"

"That depends. What do you want?"

Ethan found himself repressing a furtive grin. That sounded like the Melissa he knew, plainly enough. "I wanted to talk to you. You have not been available much lately."

"Did it cross your mind it was not accidental?"

He pressed his lips together to keep the grin from breaking through. Ah, Melissa!

"I need to know how you are."

"Fine."

"I don't believe it." There. He had said it. He had just admitted to her, and more importantly to himself, that something was wrong.

She opened her mouth to speak—he had been in the dark room long enough so that he could see that now—and then closed it again. She turned away to look in the direction of the window, as she had done so often when they were dining, but of course now there were heavy draperies to hold in the warmth, except for the narrow space between them through which the dying moon shone.

"Are you with child?" He made his voice as gentle as he could.

She took a quick breath as if she were about to answer, and then exhaled slowly. Sadly? He could not see her clearly enough to know.

"Yes."

It was as if a glad exultant cry and the leaden weight of disaster finally faced warred within him.

"We must marry, then." The words were automatic.

"No. Not yet. Please." Her voice was not defiant, but forlorn. "Please let me wait."

"Wait? For what?" He remembered that they might be overheard and forced back the impulse to shout at her.

"All conceptions do not end in a birth," she whispered. "This would not be a marriage either of us chose for ourselves. Please, let us wait just a little longer. To see. So many women lose, so early on. Please let us wait."

"How long?" It was more and more difficult to keep his voice down.

She shrugged. "I don't know. Until I am sure? Perhaps until I have to dress more carefully? There is no sign yet."

"Then how do you know?" She had to be the most maddening woman he had ever met.

She shrugged again. "I have missed my courses three times now. Sometimes—not often—I am queasy in the morning. So far I have not been really sick. I heard somewhere morning sickness means the baby will be healthy, so maybe something is wrong, but I don't know. Please, Ethan. Please let us wait. Just a bit longer."

He wanted to shake her until her teeth rattled. He wanted to clutch her into his arms. He wanted—oh, most of all he wanted to *know*. Were they truly linked together now, for the rest of their lives?

No. If it were true, if they had made a new life between them, it would not be a disaster. The worst thing was not knowing, and now he knew. But not much else had changed.

He stepped over to the bed, and leaned over to kiss her forehead. But she shrank away from him, and so he picked up her hand, lying on the bedclothes, and kissed that instead.

"Thank you for telling me," he said. "If you wish it, we will wait. But don't hide from me. Please don't continue to hide."

Even in the dim light, he could see gratitude in her eyes.

23

THE DAYS DRAGGED ON, BUT for Melissa nights lasted forever. She resisted admitting to herself a baby's welfare might depend on her own health. Even so, in the middle of the night as she tossed and turned the uneasy thought of how sleeplessness might affect the life she had within her—willingly or not—made her cross and sleep even more impossible. If there were a baby there (she still clung to the "if"), it would have to look after its own survival. No sooner had that thought shaped itself in her mind than overwhelming guilt would strike again.

Most women rejoiced in the discovery that they carried new life. Good women did. If she had any doubt of it, all she had to do was look at Caroline, who glowed with happiness and content. It made Melissa that much more aware of her own failure at womanliness. If only the whole problem would just go away, disappear like frost on the windows when a fire had warmed the room.

Their mutual rejoicing had deepened the relationship between Caroline and Martin. Melissa had envied them before; that envy was now doubled. When Martin returned to the house in the evening, he no longer went first to his study. Instead, still carrying whatever materials he might have brought home with him, he went to find Caroline as soon as he came in.

Ethan, following him, would make a business of taking off his outside clothing, looking around to see if he could locate where Melissa was. Or at least that was what he seemed to be doing when she positioned herself at the top of the grand staircase. His eyes would search for hers. Melissa wondered what message he was looking for. That all was over and he was a free man? Or was he still awaiting her permission to admit what was

170

happening was indeed happening, and it was time to speak about it freely?

She didn't want to. She couldn't bear to. She now had no more morning sickness, so any day now there might be a pain, a rush of blood—she didn't know exactly what to expect—and this agonizing time of uncertainty would be over.

Or time could just go on, agonizing or not, and after a while—not quite a year, she knew that much, but nobody had ever told her anything exactly—she might be in really deep trouble. Ethan would still be there; she could trust him for that. But did she want him to be? Well, she had no choice.

Her mother would take her back. She could be reasonably confident of that. But she would be shamed, and the thought of that ate into Melissa's conscience. It wasn't her mother who was a fool and drank too much, and it wasn't her mother who gave way to Ethan's appeal, but it would be her mother who would be shamed and maybe even not welcome in the homes of women who had been friends. No. She could not let that happen.

If she was truly carrying a baby now (and it was becoming harder and harder to persuade herself that she was not), she would have to marry Ethan. Have to be grateful that he offered. Have to live whatever life he thought would be suitable for her, what he thought would be endurable for him. What Caroline and Martin had between them would never be hers, but whatever she had would last a lifetime, his or hers.

If only it did not all feel so *hopeless*.

"Are you coming down or shall I come up?" Ethan called up to her.

"I think it is warmer up here." She looked over her shoulder into the drawing room. "There's a nice fire going."

"I believe I could stand that." By then he had been relieved of his overcoat and hat and outdoor gloves and the muffler that kept the tips of his ears from freezing off his head, and looked more like his normal self than like some roughly man-shaped pillar wrapped in wool and leather against the icy wind.

Melissa knew exactly how cold it was outside. Now that Caroline was officially delicate, Melissa had taken over the job of escorting George the dog on at least one of his daily outside excursions. In the evening one of the footmen put him out in the garden at the back, and kept an eye on him until he came running back to the door to be let into the warmth. In the mornings, though, cold as it was George wanted to have a brisk run, so Melissa would take him over to the Green. At that hour there were few other people walking down the paths of the Green, although there were bundled-up shapes presumably going to work who scuttled along the outside edges, all heading north towards the shops and buildings of Dublin itself. Some of them, poor souls, would have to cross the River Liffey itself, with the wind rushing down across the bridges over the cold, dark water.

Melissa made a point of keeping them in mind as she and George marched down one path to the noble figure of George II on his horse, and then marched down another and around to the footpath that took them back to the northern edge, to the house on the Green with the butler just inside to open the door the moment they approached and welcome them back into the warmth of inside.

"Warm is good," Ethan said with contentment as he held his hands out to the fire.

One way and another the furniture that had been originally decorously placed around the walls of the room had moved closer and closer to the fire, so that there was now a cozy choice of places to sit to which warmth would spread.

Ethan politely waited until Melissa chose an armchair to sit in, and then perched on the edge of a settee where he could extend his feet a bit closer to the lumps of peat on the grate with flames dancing over them.

"I don't know if peat produces more warmth than coal, but the smell is distinctive." He seemed to be watching the fire with close attention, until he suddenly swung around to face her. "And how are you today?"

"I am fine, thank you." She had promised not to hide, but she had not agreed to confide in him.

"I worry," he said abruptly. "If it is unwise for Caroline to go out into the cold, you should not go out either."

She pressed her lips together. "I am fine," she repeated.

"Please, Melissa—" he started to say, but just then Caroline and Martin, she wrapped in a pretty quilted overdress, came into the room.

Melissa looked up to greet them with a smile as genuine as she could manage. She saw Ethan was doing the same.

"Dinner is very nearly ready," Caroline said.

"Would you like a splash of warming whiskey before dinner?" Martin asked Ethan. Ethan allowed that he would, and Martin produced two glasses and poured a neat amount into each of them. While he was busy with the glasses, Ethan caught Melissa's eye and shrugged ruefully.

Martin glanced at her. "Would you like a glass of wine?"

She shook her head and murmured, "No, thank you," noticing that he made no similar offer to Caroline. It didn't matter. Melissa had already resolved never to drink another glass of wine for the rest of her life.

After dinner, Ethan found he was only half-listening to the casual conversation rippling around the circle before the fire. Caroline was talking about what she and Melissa had been doing at home that day. From the guarded expression on Melissa's face, her account made it sound much more interesting than it actually had been. Or perhaps for Caroline, it had been a satisfactory use of time.

He thought back to this morning, walking briskly on his way to work. As was more usual now when the mornings were so chill, he and Martin spent little time in conversation. The goal was to get into the warmth of the office as rapidly as possible. Even so, he found himself looking into the faces of the people who were hurrying past them, wondering where they came from and where they were going. It would be interesting, would it not, if by some form of magic he could read what their thoughts as they scurried down the streets. Were any of them, as he was, wobbling on the edge of something that might determine the pattern of the rest of their lives?

When would Melissa be certain she was carrying his child?

He had never thought about such a possibility before. He was still somewhat dazed by the reality of it. He had never been given to pulling a blanket over his head and pretending, and he did not know how to cope with Melissa, who apparently was.

No, marriage and family had always been somewhere in the far distance as part of what his life would include, more so since he stood to inherit a title and then would be obliged to produce an heir to take his place when he was gone.

He had not thought this would happen when he was still only halfway through his twenties. But it had, and he found it more and more difficult to mask his impatience from Melissa. If this was where they were, he wanted to have it settled so that he could get on with the rest of his life. But there it was: she was too frightened to face it.

And he, apparently, was unwilling to force her to do so.

How long could they go on like this?

True, she was still slim. He doubted she was eating as much as she should. What did they say? A woman who was increasing should eat for two? From what he could see at the dinner table, she was barely eating enough for one. If that did not improve, he was going to force himself to speak to her about it, even if he had to pay another late night call to her room to talk to her alone.

But sooner or later her figure was bound to change. He wished he knew how soon. At present Martin and Caroline were entirely absorbed with Caroline's condition, which, he realized, was a mercy. But neither of them was stupid, and in the enforced intimacy of sharing the same house, they would be bound to notice at some point. Surely, *surely*, before they did Melissa would give up this idiotic pretense that nothing was happening.

Or would he have to force her to it? Where did the distinction lie between being manly and being gentlemanly?

"Don't you think so, Ethan?" Martin asked. Ethan's head jerked up, and he vaguely realized that Martin had just said, "More so today."

What was more so today?

He smiled, weakly he was afraid. "I do apologize. I'm afraid I was wool-gathering. What did you say?"

Martin laughed. "I'm sorry. It's not important. I suspected you were miles away from us. Anywhere interesting?"

"Afraid not." Again, as so often, Ethan was grateful for Martin's easy manner. He had to be the most difficult man to annoy Ethan had ever encountered. "Mainly brooding over the weather, I'm afraid, and wondering how much my absence is inconveniencing Uncle Charles."

"At this time of year—especially with it being as cold as it has been— he has almost certainly been staying home in the warmth," Caroline assured him. "I daresay he has had Mr. Bowyer out checking on the condition of the tenants and making sure they are managing in this bitter cold."

"I assume my brother will be doing the same with his." Melissa spoke quietly. "He was so proud of what he has done making their houses more sound. I wish now I had gone with him to see what he had been working on, but at the time I thought I could do that at any time. I certainly did not expect to be here in Dublin for the winter!"

Caroline reached over and grasped her hand. "I, for one, am glad you are. I really would find it difficult to be stuck here in the house all by myself, and with the best will in the world, Martin would not be able to stay home from work to keep me company."

"Wait until the child is due to be born and you'll be surprised at what I am able to do," Martin half-growled.

"When will that be?" Melissa asked.

Ethan glanced at her in surprise. Even he knew it takes nine months for a baby to be born. How was it that Melissa did not?

"It's nine months, as I learned with Henrietta," said Caroline.

Did that mean she had not known either? Were girls so innocent even when they married?

"So that means"—she counted on her fingers, although Ethan suspected she had long since worked out the calendar—"June. A lovely month, I think. She and Henrietta will be just two years apart." She turned to Martin, her face glowing. "And what a two years it has been, has it not?"

"June," Melissa murmured. Ethan was still watching her, trying to read her expression. Was she showing more than interest? Pleasure perhaps? He hoped so. If she was carrying a child—his child—he wanted that child to be born into some kind of happiness, some kind of love. Of course he would be there. But how hard would it be should the child's mother be counting her regrets?

Surely Melissa would not be. But until she had made up her mind to accept the inevitable, he would have to prepare to love this child for both of them. He leaned back in his chair, watching her. Her eyes flicked in his direction, and then away when she saw he was looking at her. He smiled a little, and continued watching. After a minute or so, she moved restlessly in her chair, glancing back at him, her mouth twitching sheepishly when she realized his attention was still fixed on her.

But there they were, with Caroline and Martin mercifully still absorbed in whatever they were talking about. Reminiscing about when they'd first met, as far as Ethan could gather from the scraps that came to his attention from time to time. On the mail boat from Holyhead to Dublin, if he remembered correctly.

Not that he cared about it, right at the moment. Working out some peace with Melissa was a sufficient challenge, thank you very much, and one of the most challenging elements was that it had to be done almost entirely in public. He had resolved never to invade her bedchamber again, but it appeared to be the only place where he could talk to her freely. Would she scream and throw the door open if he came to her tonight? He knew this time had to be agonizing for her, and wished somehow he could take part of the burden from her shoulders. He was not going to leave her alone to manage what neither of them had intended to happen. Had she dreamed of love and romance? Was that what girls hoped for? He could not promise her that—for one thing, he was completely uncertain of what she felt for him—but constancy had to be worth something, did it not?

He smiled more openly at her, and before she dropped her eyes and turned away, he saw she had allowed him a faint curve of her lips.

Yes. He would have to invade her bedchamber again tonight.

24

MELISSA OPENED THE DOOR OF the wardrobe in her room and thumbed through her clothes folded in neat piles. How many of them would continue to fit? There were not a great number there as she had not brought all of her clothes from Gloucestershire to Ireland in the first place, and only brought her favorite and most useful from Ballymuir to Dublin, since originally she planned to stay there for a few weeks at most. That had been in late September, and it was December now. She had been wearing the same dresses over and over again, which was unavoidable, but not possible forever. She was uncomfortably aware she had always been proud of a rather neat waist, but it was beginning to disappear. Oh, it was happening very, very gradually, and thank goodness high waists were in fashion, so no one would have noticed yet.

Even so, reality was beginning to close in on her.

Whether she wanted to face it or not, she knew in her heart of hearts she was increasing. For better or worse, she had not felt sick much of the time, as Caroline had. But there had been no trace of her courses for three months now. Nobody had remarked on it, of course. Moira, who was basically an upstairs maid, had been pressed into service to help Melissa dress. But she did not know her with the intimacy Melissa had had with her maid in Gloucestershire. Moira organized a bath for her when she wanted one, and helped her wash her hair. Arranging her hair was something Melissa could pretty much take care of herself. She brushed it herself at night, and would only ask Moira's help if she wanted to add a ribbon for a change. Every two or three weeks, it would need trimming. Melissa would cut the parts she could see, and Moira would trim around the back. That had happened at least three times so far—more evidence time was passing.

Melissa could not in all honesty believe nothing was happening. For one thing, she felt different inside. She could not define what the difference was, precisely, but it was there. Worse, although she had not admitted it to anyone, she was inexplicably weary much of the time, which was something Caroline frequently mentioned with exasperation. The unwelcome but obvious conclusion was that both of them were increasing.

True, women did miscarry. It might still be a possibility. But it seemed less and less likely, and although it had seemed a door to freedom when she had first begun to suspect she had conceived, time had changed her. If there was new life growing in her, she felt the responsibility to take care of it.

She had moments of resenting that sense of responsibility, but there it was. She had more to consider than herself, now.

At first she did not identify the tentative knock at her door. It was very quiet. She stilled, wondering if she had heard something, but not sure if there had been a sound. Then it was repeated, marginally louder, and she frowned. Everyone had gone to bed, had they not? Moira had helped her into her nightgown and warm robe, but then she had been dismissed to do whatever she would have been doing at that hour had Melissa not been there.

"Yes?" She could hear her own voice, wary and tentative.

"It's me." The door was pushed open very quietly, and Ethan stepped into the room.

Melissa moved backward. "What are you doing here?"

Ethan placed his finger on his lips. "Hush," he whispered. "We need to talk."

She slipped down to her feet to stand stiffly facing him. "What about?"

It seemed to her Ethan's shoulders sagged for just a moment. "Melissa." He spoke so softly it seemed that all she heard was the gentle hiss of the s's in her name. "Please. There is no point in pretending. We are together in this. We need to talk about what we must do."

"Do? It's already done." She felt a flicker of shame at the bitterness of her tone.

Ethan just looked at her. She dropped her eyes and inspected the slippers on her feet as if they were new and interesting. How did he come to be so patient? Back in those long-ago London days when they had been acquaintances, she would never have guessed his capacity for patience and self control.

She surrendered now. "What must we do?" she asked, still studying her slippers.

Ethan spoke quietly but firmly. "We must marry."

She felt her shoulders lift and drop with a sigh. "Yes."

They both fell silent. Melissa lifted her eyes and they looked at each other.

"It will be good if we make it so," he said. He reached out to take her hand, and she allowed him to hold it but couldn't quite make herself curve her fingers around his. Of course he was right. Under the circumstances they had no other possible choice. She should feel wonderfully fortunate. After all, he could have refused to take any responsibility. He could have simply disappeared—well, no. He did not really have that option. He was the heir to an earldom. An earl-to-be couldn't just disappear, leaving behind the man who currently held the title and all his family. It wouldn't do, poor thing.

The logical consequence was that one day she would be a countess. A countess! Not like the average countess, of course, if there were such a creature. The countess she would be would be restless sometimes, would sometimes be sharp when she did not entirely mean to be, unless she could train herself out of that. She would certainly have short hair. No matter how fashion changed, Melissa would never let hers grow again. She had had quite long enough of battling the burgeoning bush on her head.

Aunt Elizabeth seemed to do a serene and elegant job of being a countess. Perhaps while Ethan was learning from Uncle Charles how to be the master of an estate, she could be learning how to be the mistress from Aunt Elizabeth.

But whatever each of them learned, they would never have a romantic attachment that was almost tangible, like that between Caroline and Martin. She had imagined what love might be like before, but until she had come to Dublin she had never seen love living and breathing in front of her, warming everyone around them with its glow.

They would marry, not because neither wanted a life without the other, but because it was necessary. Surely they could make a reasonable, practical marriage between them. She had wanted a marriage that glittered with fire and passion, smoldering with the lifelong warmth two people could have who dreamed of their lives entwined together.

Their marriage would be sensible. Polite.

"My mother will be astonished," she said. "Relieved, of course, but mainly unable to believe it at first."

"Believe what?" His face, like his voice, was puzzled.

"That I am to be married. I was sent here for many reasons, I expect, but the event that settled the matter was that I cut my hair. I am sure one of my mother's main purposes for me being away from England was the opportunity to grow my hair back in decent obscurity. What I looked like in Ireland didn't bother her. All she wanted was for me to be marriageable again when I came back to England. I don't know why she thought I was going to let it grow out here."

Ethan's mouth quirked. "She miscalculated. I prefer your hair short." He reached out to tousle it and his smile widened. "Will the title help?"

His hand on her head was no longer tousling her hair, but wrapping itself around her head. She had forgotten how good his hands felt on her body. Without meaning to she turned her head into his hands, taking comfort from the warmth. For a minute she just rested against him, letting herself take in that she was no longer alone. She never had been, really. She had just been too stubborn to take the hand reaching out to her.

Still resting against his strength, she sighed again. "My mother will love the title," she said. "What she wanted most was to get me married. In her mind it would be proof positive she had failed if I remained a spinster all my life. The title will be like the cherry on the top of the cake." She glanced at his face. "Now she can focus her energy on Penelope."

"Poor Penelope."

Her conscience stirred. "She's not that bad about other things. She just has a fixation on making sure our futures are secure, and to her mind that translates to having a husband. Maybe she's right. Otherwise why would so many people marry? For a lot of them it doesn't seem to lead to lifetime happiness."

"I don't really remember what my parents' marriage was like," Ethan said thoughtfully. "But he was off sailing with friends and she was at home with us when my father drowned. So I assume they spent at least some time separately."

Melissa sat down on the bed. "Odd, isn't it, that both of us lost our fathers when we were children."

He sat, too, but at a distance, leaning back against the post that supported the canopy over the bed. "I wonder if you will like my mother. True, I do not suppose you'll have much chance to get to know her, unless she happens to come here. She has my sister Emmeline to launch into society, so I expect she will remain in England, for the next few years at least."

For a moment Melissa allowed herself to contemplate the horrifying possibility of his mother coming to help her learn to run Kendall House when Uncle Charles—odd to think that he would be her uncle by marriage now—was gone and she was taking over the responsibilities that Aunt Elizabeth handled so gracefully.

Well, that would not be for many years, she hoped.

"When shall we tell Martin and Caroline?" Ethan's tone was matter of fact, and she abruptly was aware that he was now speaking at normal volume.

"Shhh," she said, putting her finger to her lips.

His eyebrows jerked upward and he nodded agreement. "I forget they are below us," he said, his voice much lower.

She considered. "That's difficult. Do you suppose they will believe it is their fault because we were allowed to go unchaperoned?"

Now it was Ethan who sighed. "No, of course the fault was ours. Mine. But if we had been the married couple, and they were unwed and staying with us, I am sure that would be what I would accuse myself of."

"I suppose everybody at Ballymuir and Kendall House thought of us more as brother and sister." She rubbed her hands over her face. "Oh, dear. I suppose I thought at first telling people would make it all simpler. But it looks as if—"

"—it only complicates everything," he said, completing her thought.

They sat for a minute or two, not speaking. Melissa expected he was trying to figure the way to untie this unforeseen knot, just as she was.

"I am not showing yet," she murmured.

"Showing?" He looked perplexed and then his face rapidly cleared as he comprehended what she meant. He looked at her intently.

She straightened up indignantly. How dare he look at her like that? As quickly as her temper flared, she forced herself to calm. How did she expect him to know what her shape might be at this stage? Her day gowns were fashionably loose. She was in her nightclothes now, her robe bunched around her.

He persisted. "When do you think you will?"

Self-conscious, she glared at him. "How do I know? I've never been—" She suddenly realized her own voice had increased in volume, and clapped her hand over her mouth. "I'm sorry. I really don't know," she whispered. She started to add that her breasts did seem to be larger and she thought her belly was rounding, just a little, and then realized she couldn't possibly mention such anatomical parts to anyone, least of all a man. She blushed at the mere thought of telling him anything so intimate.

Again they sat in silence. Trying to take calming deep breaths inconspicuously to cool down the hot reddening of her face, Melissa suspected he was as unable as she to find a way to discuss the matter.

With a move so sudden it startled her, he jerked to his feet and stalked over to the window. Grabbing the curtains in one hand, he pulled them back to stare out at the Green, so far below them in the dark.

"I can't think of how to tell Martin," he confessed.

She nodded. "I know. I feel the same about Caroline. I keep thinking how horrified they will be. They have been so good to us I can't bear them feeling themselves responsible."

"I know."

Another silence. Where could they go from here, Melissa wondered. She had imagined the necessity of them marrying would be the awkward part. She had not foreseen the shame of admitting the state of affairs to the Gallaghers. Her hand moved automatically to her midsection, as if to comfort the baby. "It's not your fault," she wanted to say. When had her hope for miscarriage transmuted itself into protectiveness? She could not remember the turning point.

A deep sigh from Ethan. He turned away from the window.

"Would it be possible for us to marry secretly, and then when we tell them, we would be married already?" he asked.

She had never considered that. "What about calling the banns? How could we do that without them knowing? Or where would you get a special license?"

He shook his head. "The laws are different here. What they are exactly I don't know, but I believe the banns are not required here." He paused, searching her face. "I suppose I could find out."

"How?"

He grinned a little sheepishly, but it was good to see a change from the grimness. "I don't know that, either. But it should not be impossible to find out." He ran his hand through his hair absently. "I suppose I could just step into a church and ask."

"I suppose so." Melissa stared at him with wonder that he could come up with such an obvious solution to what she had been imagining was an intractable problem. "That's very clever of you, to think of that," she added admiringly.

He looked embarrassed. "Do you have any inspiration on what we should say to Martin and Caroline?"

She shook her head. "None. I think I will have to rely on you to be the clever one in our partnership." She looked straight at him with sudden anxiety. "That is what it will be, won't it? I'm afraid it will be very difficult if what you expect is a dutiful wife. You should know I think the law is horribly unfair that insists when we marry I become your possession, like a pair of shoes or your overcoat."

"It's not as bad as that," he protested.

"But it is. For example, unless we have it specified otherwise in a cleverly crafted marriage agreement, all my money is available for you to make use of. As it happens, I don't have enough to be worth fussing over. Which is lucky, as I don't see how under the circumstances we're going to be able to have a proper marriage agreement unless you have a tame lawyer here in Dublin." She thought for a moment and then added, "In fact, it would be a problem even if everything was normal and we had time to work details out. Neither of us has a father to negotiate on our behalf. I guess Uncle Charles could be your representative, but I don't have an idea whom my mother would appoint. And whoever it was would certainly be in England, which would be unhandy to say the least."

"Just as well we don't have time for it," Ethan said. "But I do not intend to consider you my possession, as if you were a particularly beautiful silver tea set."

She briefly debated with herself whether she should allow herself to feel pleasure in being compared to a valuable tea set—one that was "particularly beautiful"—and let the subject drop, or try to do a more comprehensive job of explaining her objections to the conditions of marriage for women in Great Britain.

He forestalled further discussion of the subject by coming from the window to her side as she sat on the bed. "I have no idea what time it must be by now, but it certainly is late, and you should have plenty of sleep, I am certain." He ran his hand through her hair again, smiling as the curly locks slipped through his fingers. "I do want you to know how relieved I am, and really, honestly pleased we will marry. I may have to creep into your bedchamber again to let you know how we will be able to arrange it, but my mind is at peace now we are in agreement. And I will try not to be too officious in making private suggestions I hope you will consider concerning the welfare of our child. Please, Melly, take care of yourself so that the babe will grow strong and healthy."

"I will." She looked up at him with surprise and some wonder. He had not used that nickname since the night—well, That Night when all this had been so foolishly set in motion.

"Let me kiss you to seal the promise," he whispered, and his lips came down to meet hers. It was a lovely kiss, warm and endearing, with just a hint of the passion she remembered too clearly. "Good night, dear one," he said quietly, and turned to leave the room.

Melissa sat on the bed watching the door as it closed nearly silently behind him. She had no way at all to describe even to herself what she was feeling.

THE NEXT DAY IT WAS very difficult to act as if nothing had changed. Ethan slept more heavily than he had done for weeks, and as a direct result overslept. When he awoke, full morning light was coming into his room. The curtains had been drawn back, and there was a well-established fire. Consequently the room was warm and cozy and the temptation to roll back under the bedclothes and sink back into sleep was almost irresistible.

He must have made some noise, or possibly the manservant serving as a temporary valet had been coming into the room from time to time to see if he was awake yet, because very shortly after he roused, the door opened part way, and his manservant peered through the space available, pushing it farther open when he saw Ethan propped up on his elbows and blinking sleepily.

"Good morning, sir," he said. "Are you ready for your coffee now?"

Ready? Still half-asleep, Ethan grunted, which the manservant apparently took as an affirmative response because he nodded and disappeared, closing the door carefully behind him.

Ethan fell back upon the pillows.

The details of the day before were somewhat muddled in his mind, but as he lay on his pillows contemplating the underside of the canopy over the bed he gradually recalled the day bit by bit, and, with increasing clarity, the night. As the memory unfolded, he realized the night before had been the most relevant event of the day. He had gone to bed more peacefully than he had been able to do for days, even weeks.

Melissa had agreed to marry him. The child they had so injudiciously created would have a recognized place in life, and so, by extension, would its mother. Or perhaps it was the other way around. Melissa would not be that horror of conventional society, an unmarried mother, and so their child would be born into security. Any way he looked at it, it was a much better prospect than had seemed likely for long weeks before.

Not that the future was necessarily smooth. There were a few formidable hurdles yet to jump. For one thing, if he remembered properly—and his mind was clearing enough so he was sure he did—he and Melissa had agreed mutually that telling Martin and Caroline about the disaster resulting from the two of them going out to Halleck's house that evening unchaperoned, and, worse, returning the same way would be so awkward at best that neither of them could see a reasonable way to do it.

Neither could bear to think about what would happen if they said nothing now but it eventually became apparent Melissa was increasing. Presumably he would talk to Martin, and Melissa would talk to Caroline, but neither of them looked forward to those conversations. Surely it would be less painful if they could also tell them they had already married.

Whether that was entirely true Ethan did not want to investigate too closely, but it had given him something practical and useful to do besides watching Melissa with hawk-like concentration, worrying about what could happen to her and the child.

She was to be his wife, and the child to come would be his legitimate son or daughter.

His immediate task was to find out how one went about getting married in Ireland. If he had to go to a church to ask, the parish church for the Gallaghers, St. Ann's on Dawson Street, was the closest.

Would the rector have some sort of office at the church? Going by English churches he remembered, it seemed reasonable. If the rector was not there, somebody else would know his name and where he could be found. At least it would be a place to start.

That was what he would do today.

When the manservant returned with a tray supplied with a cup of black very strong coffee, exactly as he liked it, Ethan thought the day showed definite progress. He sat up in bed, supported by the pillows, and contemplated what he would tell Martin to explain his absence from the office today.

As it happened, he didn't need to tell him anything. When he had dressed, ready for the day, he came down to find only Melissa and Henrietta at the breakfast table. Henrietta had obviously already eaten.

186

Her high chair was there, but she was standing next to Melissa talking to her earnestly.

Melissa looked up to see him and for a flashing moment he saw greater warmth in her eyes than he had seen for several weeks. She gave him a faint smile and turned back to Henrietta, still chattering obliviously.

Ethan served himself from the buffet, had fresh hot coffee poured, and waited until Henrietta distracted herself with a spoon she could reach on the table, standing on tiptoe.

"Has Martin already left?"

Melissa shrugged one shoulder. "I believe so. When I came down, Caroline had just reached the stairs with Henrietta, but she did not look as if she felt well, so I took Henrietta downstairs instead. She murmured something about Martin as she went back to bed, but I didn't hear exactly what it was."

"Where's Henrietta's nanny?"

"Nanny!" Henrietta shrieked exuberantly.

"Upstairs, I think. Caroline usually likes to have breakfast with Henrietta. You're always gone by that time." Melissa's voice was matter-of-fact, but her eyes were warm.

He took a quick, hopefully unobserved look around. No one but the child seemed to be within earshot. "I thought I would start with a quick stop at St. Ann's."

She kept her eyes on her plate, but nodded. "I hope all goes well," she said obliquely, since the nanny was coming in to recapture Henrietta.

"I am sorry, Miss Melissa," she murmured. "I thought she was with her mam."

"It was fine," Melissa said. "I could have gone upstairs to get you, but we were having a good time together."

The nanny nodded in response, scooped up Henrietta, and left the room with her, Henrietta's head bobbing over her shoulder, the little girl watching the two of them as she was carried away.

"A pity Caroline's not feeling well." Ethan looked at Melissa. She did not seem to be delicate, which was a mercy. At least she didn't have to invent some explanation for repeated episodes of feeling poorly.

She only nodded, but he could see she knew exactly what he was thinking. When his mother had shown her ability to read his mind, he felt hunted. How odd was it that now the same competence was reassuring?

Before his thoughts could confuse him completely, he stood up.

"Time for me to get going," he said. He looked at Melissa meaningfully. "Take care, Melly." Her head jerked slightly at the nickname. He smiled at her. "Get some rest."

"Sleep my life away?" But her voice was teasing.

"Whatever you need." He bowed, very slightly, and went out the door.

St. Ann's Church had been built almost a hundred years before, but compared to the much greater antiquity of many of Dublin's buildings, it seemed a relative newcomer. From the outside it was a plain but elegant Georgian design, but when he went inside Ethan discovered its richness of brilliant stained glass windows made the interior splendid in the multi-colored light. There was no one in sight when he first entered, but he was quite content to settle his nerves walking into the sanctuary and admiring the details of the windows.

He was standing, leaning back to see the top of one, when he heard footsteps, and saw a smallish man in clerical dress had come in behind him.

"May I help you?" he asked.

Ethan had made a point of paying attention to the sign in the entrance foyer which listed the names of the rectors since the church was founded, and he asked, "Is the Reverend Bewley around?" that being the name of the current holder of the office.

"I am Bewley. Is there something you are in need of?"

Ethan bowed. "I find I need some information."

The little man looked up at him solemnly. He was indeed small. Ethan doubted he would come up to his own shoulders if they stood back to back. His features were built to scale, as were his feet and hands—Ethan found himself wondering vaguely if he had to buy shoes designed by the cobbler for children—but his eyes were warm and sympathetic.

"I assume the matter is of some importance?" His voice was clearly English, but Ethan would guess the Irish intonation came from long years of residence in Ireland.

"Of great importance for me." Ethan spoke earnestly and for a moment feared that his voice had wobbled just a bit, but Reverend Bewley's attention did not waver.

"Then I suggest you come with me to my office," he said. His feet nearly soundless on the stone floor, he led the way to a small office around to the side of the sanctuary. "Will you have a seat?"

It was a plain, simple room, decorated mainly by a crucifix on the wall over a desk that appeared undistinguished except for the beauty of the wood. He motioned to Ethan to take the chair to the side, and sat down at the desk itself. Like the desk and the room itself, the chairs were plain in design but lovingly created from wood perfectly smooth to the touch and faithfully polished over many years of dutiful care.

Ethan sat, and took a deep breath. "My name is Ethan Hawthorne."

"How may I help you?" the rector prompted.

"My question is about marriage." Ethan wished he had taken more time to plan exactly what he wanted to say, but now faced with this small but self-assured man, all he could think of was the bare, unvarnished truth.

"In England, in order to marry, banns must be called in the parish church for three weeks prior to the ceremony," he began.

The rector nodded. "I am aware of that."

Ethan wished he had started some less obvious way not leaving him feeling such a fool. "Of course," he said. "But I have been told that this is not required in Ireland."

The rector nodded again. "It is true that the Hardwicke Marriage Act of 1753 does not have force in Ireland."

"I see." Ethan felt a wash of relief. "What is required to marry in Ireland?"

The little rector's eyes twinkled. "A willing bride."

Ethan's nerves were so on edge that he laughed outright. The rector laughed with him.

"Fair enough," Ethan said. "That I have."

Rev. Bewley still smiled. "I assumed it was for yourself you were asking."

Ethan wished more than ever he had taken the time to work out a sensible if untrue explanation for the necessity of a speedy marriage, but he was coming to hope that the rector would not be fiercely judgmental. In any case his mind was as blank as if it had been wiped clean. He had no recourse except the truth.

"Let me start by saying it is entirely my fault."

The rector nodded but did not speak.

"There is an unmarried girl who is carrying my child." There. He could hardly state it more baldly than that.

Rev. Bewley nodded again.

"We met initially last year during the London Season. Neither of us was much impressed with the other, and I am shamed to say some friends of mine—and me, unfortunately—made inappropriate remarks about her hair. She has truly remarkable hair. It is a shining red gold and there was such a lot of it we called her Bush-head."

"Unkind," the rector remarked.

"Indeed," Ethan admitted. "My only defense is a weak one. I did not—I assume we did not think she was aware of it. But she was."

The rector continued to listen.

"We did not see each other again until the late summer. I am to inherit a title and property from my uncle, who has only two daughters, and he proposed I should come to Ireland to learn about the estate that will someday be mine. By coincidence, this girl was dispatched to Ireland to stay with her brother, who happened to be married to one of the two daughters, my cousins."

"Dispatched?" the rector asked.

"Yes. I believe her mother was primarily upset because she had not chosen to marry anyone during the Season, but the final straw appears to be that she cut her hair."

"Ah," the rector said. "This was an improvement?"

"She is beautiful." Ethan spoke quietly. "As it happens the two estates are close together, and since her brother's wife is my uncle's daughter, we saw more of each other. At first neither of us was any more drawn to the other than we had been in London during the season, although I did believe she was much better looking now.'

Once he had started it was easier to continue. He had not realized how he had longed to talk about what had happened with someone besides Melly herself. He had longed to tell someone how endearing she had become. So he began there and went on to explain how the family had come to think of them more as brother and sister than a young man and a girl, particularly because at the time they still did not like each other very much.

He related how they had been allowed to travel to Dublin together, and around the city (until it was too cold) based on the same belief. That they had been invited out for dinner and each of them had drunk more than was wise, she of wine, and he of whiskey and brandy afterwards.

How when they reached his cousin's house late that night the house was still, everyone else retired, and seeing attraction in each other they had never been aware of before, one thing had inevitably led to another.

The rector nodded, in the way of a man wise in the world's imperfections.

Somewhat later, his cousin told them with delight that she was increasing. As time went on, he was more and more troubled by the girl's paleness and fatigue, so similar to what his cousin was experiencing. Once when he found a way to speak to her privately he pressed her for information, and she finally admitted she was with child. He told her they must marry. She refused, telling him that many pregnancies ended early, and they should wait. Only very recently had she agreed marriage would be wise.

"So," Ethan finished, "now I have to learn how to go about it."

"Have you told your cousin and her husband about these circumstances?"

He shook his head. "We were both afraid they would blame themselves for not chaperoning her adequately, when the fault was entirely ours. Eventually, of course, they will have to know, but we—I thought it would be better if when we tell them, we could also tell them we were now married."

Silence lay between them. Eventually the rector spoke. "So it is not only a marriage you are inquiring about, but a secret marriage, at least for the present."

"I'm afraid so."

They sat looking at each other.

"I cannot keep it secret forever," the rector said.

"Nor can we hide the reality that she is increasing." Ethan shrugged. "Sooner or later she will deliver the child."

The rector smiled. "Obviously. But even if she should lose the child, you are resolved to marry her?"

That one was easy. "Yes." Ethan said it as firmly as it was possible to speak without raising his voice inappropriately. "She is very dear to me now, and not just as the mother of my child."

"What about her?"

"She seems resigned to it. This morning she was even friendly." As he spoke the words he wondered if they told too much about the impasse they had reached.

"Is she looking forward to the birth of the child?"

Was that relevant? Or maybe the good rector needed to hear something positive about their relationship and the unplanned birth so relentlessly approaching.

"I believe she is. I am sure that I am, now. I had not thought much about children, but being around my cousins' children—both here and up north, where my uncle lives—has given me the chance to see how they enrich their parents' lives."

The rector nodded, and his head went on bobbing as he seemed to be considering something. "I must report all marriages," he said at last, "but I believe I can mislay the records of a single marriage for a while. A matter of months. Will that do?"

Ethan felt as if a weight of at least a ton had rolled off his shoulders. "Yes, Reverend Bewley. It will. Thank you."

"But you must tell them soon. All of them."

Ethan met the rector's eyes. "I know. We will. I hope a marriage will make it easier for them, to show we have taken steps to fulfill our responsibilities to each other. And the babe will be legitimate."

Another silence fell between them. Then the rector spoke.

"When will it be convenient for you to come? You will not have witnesses? If you have not, it would be better if it could be in the day time on a week day."

"Name the day." Odd to think all he had seen initially was the size of the little rector's body. Now he was far more impressed by the immensity of his heart.

26

IT WAS NOT LONG AFTER Ethan had left that the door to the dining room opened again and Caroline came in. She was pale, but she had been pale for some time now. Her shoulders were covered with a warm shawl, but when Melissa looked at her carefully—just for a moment, because she did not mean to stare—it was obvious to see her shape had begun to change already. She was more buxom than she had been, but then Melissa was more buxom as well. Would it not be peculiar if their babies were born at or close to the same time?

"I found two or three more shawls in a cupboard the other day," Caroline said absently. "I was thinking that some of them might suit you."

"Thank you." Melissa had thought of going out to the shops to find some warmer clothes for herself—shawls at a minimum, but a warmer frock or two and a new spencer would be nice as well. But when it came to the point of putting on her heavy outside clothing and venturing out into the cold to go from shop to shop, it was generally easy to decide tomorrow would do just as well, or possibly the day after that. To have a new warm shawl without having to go out to get it would be splendid.

"Where's Henrietta?"

Melissa glanced up. Caroline had obviously been on the point of sitting down when it occurred to her that her daughter was not there in the dining room as well.

"Her nanny came and fetched her. She had quite a reasonable breakfast and was determined to get down from the high chair, so I lifted her out. We played together a bit and talked until Ethan came in."

"Ethan? Did he not go with Martin, then?"

193

"Not today. I gathered they had some special arrangement, but I confess I wasn't paying much attention." Which was certainly not accurate in detail, but if it explained his absence it would do.

Of course her mind returned immediately to the thrumming worry of how he was doing on his errand to discover how their marriage could be managed in Ireland. She had deliberately turned her mind away from that once she had custody of Henrietta. The little girl was now learning how to feed herself reasonably neatly. At least neatly enough so that a watchful adult could be reassured that she was getting adequate nourishment even if some of the food dropped on the tray or was distributed about her face.

It was easy to forget—for a few minutes at least—about Ethan's errand when she had Henrietta laughing while struggling to get her food into her mouth. Easy, too, to watch how determined the child was to learn to do it neatly. True, her efforts to keep her face clean sometimes meant that the cereal got entangled with her eyebrows from trying to wipe her mouth with her bib, as she had observed her mother or her nanny doing. But she had a wonderfully sunny disposition, and was quick to giggle.

Would her own daughter be as even-tempered, Melissa had wondered as she watched Henrietta. Was she? Was Ethan? Odd to think that she really knew so little of this man she was now about to marry. Yes, he was certainly quick to assume responsibilities he recognized as his own. He had come to Ireland to learn about the estate he would inherit, although she was sure he would have preferred to remain in England. He had been willing from the beginning to accept his accountability for their night of folly. So he was a good man, and that certainly should be enough to content her.

But was he even-tempered? She did not know. She suspected she herself was not. She was horribly afraid that her own moods swept up and down just as fingers sweep up and down the keys of the pianoforte. What if this child growing in her belly was like her?

"You look a thousand miles away." Caroline's eyes warmed as she watched Melissa over the cup of tea she had just been served. "Anything interesting there?"

"Is that tea fresh?" She reached for the teapot, but Caroline was closer and took it before Melissa could to refill her cup. "I am thinking how much I would love a nice sunny day, one warm and pleasant, and the two of us with Henrietta could take George for a long, lazy walk."

"Well, I have to agree that neither Dublin nor Ireland as a whole are doing their best to show off for you." Caroline turned so she could look out of the window as Melissa was doing. "When Martin left this morning he told me I was to let the footmen walk George both morning and afternoon because it was too cold for either of us to be out for long enough for George to burn off some energy. So I suppose that means both of us are housebound."

"Again." The word had no more than left her lips when it occurred to Melissa it was not polite to complain to one's hostess about anything she did not control.

"Oh, yes. Again." Caroline sighed and turned away from the window to poke at a piece of toast in the rack. "Still crisp, at least," she remarked, and pulled the jar of marmalade closer to her. "The only mercy I can think of is that by the time this poor baby is born, the sky will be blue, at least sometimes, and it will be warm and gloriously sunny."

"And you'll be able to take the baby out every day," Melissa murmured, her mind caught up by wondering where she and her own baby would be when spring was turning to summer. Here in Dublin? Most unlikely. At Kendall House—well, that seemed a possible location, unless Ethan decided they should return to England. He had a house in London, if she remembered aright, although possibly it was only rented. But there was a place in the country, too. Not a great estate, if she remembered what Anne had told her. She had been filling Melissa in about the people on her side of the family.

She found herself trying to remember—if indeed she had been told— where Ethan's mother lived. Was he close to his mother? If they did return to England, would he choose to live wherever she was, or to live wherever she did not?

There were times when she felt nearly overwhelmed by what she did not know.

"Well, ladies, still at breakfast?"

It was Ethan himself, suddenly breezing into the dining room. Both Melissa and Caroline looked up in surprise.

"I came down rather late, and Melissa has stayed to keep me company," Caroline explained.

Melissa concentrated on his face, trying to decide if his call at the church had gone well or badly. From what she could tell, he looked cheerful, so perhaps the arrangements were already made. Perhaps by the end of the week she would be a married woman.

Or perhaps not.

"Is there any coffee available?" Ethan sat down at the table, taking a seat about halfway between them.

"Of course there can be coffee available," Caroline rang the small silver bell. "You must be chilled straight through."

"Actually, it's not as bad as it has been. Calling it warm would be off the mark, but I did not feel I was frozen to the core."

"Did you have to walk far?" Melissa ventured to ask.

"Not that far." He brightened as a footman came in with a pot carrying with it the comforting scent of hot coffee. "Ah. Now that's just what is required." He watched the coffee as it was poured in his cup. As soon as the footman began to move away, he picked it up and took a long, clearly enjoyable draft.

Caroline watched him with amused curiosity. "What is your throat lined with? I would be screaming with pain if I drank coffee—or anything else—that hot."

Ethan grinned. "Practice. I went to Cambridge for a bit." He took another great swallow.

"Forgive me, but I thought Cambridge was for an education."

"That, too." He looked at them both for a long minute. "Can I persuade either one of you to have a great drink of coffee or whatever you prefer and then take a bit of a walk with me? It's the middle of the day, as warm as it's going to become, and it might do you some good to have some fresh air."

"Martin would kill me," Caroline answered promptly.

"So that is 'no'?" Ethan was the picture of innocence.

"I'll come," Melissa said, thinking how clever he was. This was one certain way to have enough time alone for him to report how his visit to the church had gone, and Caroline would never suspect any prearrangement.

"Are you sure?" Caroline's voice was anxious.

"We're not going to walk all around town, are we?" Melissa hoped she had put just enough anxiety in her tone.

"Not at all. But we are not going to stroll through St. Stephen's Green either. You and George must have explored that thoroughly by now."

"All right, then. I'll get my outdoor things."

"No coffee to start with?"

She looked at the pot, still steaming. "No, thank you. I don't know what material your throat is made of, but mine is the same stuff as Caroline's."

Ethan sighed pointedly, murmured, "Ah, well," and poured himself another cup.

He finished it just as Melissa appeared, bundled up as if the proposed expedition were to the North Pole. She worried she had overdone it when she saw his huge grin.

"It's cold outside," she muttered.

"Indeed." He was still grinning.

"Better be too wrapped up than not enough," Caroline pointed out.

Melissa looked over at her. "Do you think I look ridiculous?"

"Not at all," Ethan put in quickly. "And you have relieved my mind. I have absolutely no anxiety about taking you out into the wind and weather."

Caroline shook her head at him. "Ethan, you are being a nuisance. Melissa, I think you could relieve yourself of one of those scarves without getting too cold, but I haven't been allowed to go out forever, so I really don't know how cold it is. Maybe you could start with it in Ethan's pocket and then add it if you need it?"

"How do you know I have a pocket?" He cocked an eyebrow.

"All men have pockets. It's one of the few useful things about them." Caroline beamed at him as Melissa unwound the outside scarf—Caroline was quite right; there were two others underneath it—and handed it to him.

He stuffed it in his pocket. "Just a moment, ladies, while I get my winter apparel. It's not nearly so decorative as yours, Melissa."

Reassured by Caroline, who reached out to pat her hand, Melissa followed him into the entrance hall, where the butler was helping him into his heavy winter coat.

"Men get to wear practical heavy clothing," she grumbled.

"But we don't look so fashionable as you do." He wrapped one scarf around his neck, pulled on his thick outdoor gloves and added his hat on the top.

Melissa surveyed his well-cut and well-shined tall leather boots. "You don't do all that badly."

His eyes warmed as he looked at her. "Kind words, my dear. Kind words," as they went out the door and the brisk icy wind hit them.

"I don't think I have one more piece of outside clothing than I need." Melissa sunk her chin into her pile of scarves mounted all the way up the back of her neck to her bonnet.

As they moved away from the house Ethan took her arm, pulling her close to him. It was indeed warmer so.

"I had an interesting conversation with the rector at St. Anne's this morning," he said, almost into her ear. "He has agreed to marry us."

"At St. Ann's?" Melissa looked at him with wonder.

"Yes, indeed. In fact, I think I must make a greater point of Sunday attendance there. He is a remarkable fellow." They were moving smartly along, and although it was harder to see where they were going with her scarves pulled so high and her bonnet so low, the unmistakable silhouette of St. Ann's Church was directly ahead.

"Are we going there now?"

"Yes, I thought it would be appropriate for you to meet him before the ceremony. I gather the main irregularity will be that he will not supply the official notification he is bound to produce until some weeks later. He believes it could be misplaced for a time, so we will be able to inform the family ourselves, rather than have them stumble on public information."

"Oh." Melissa's word was more like a breath. "How kind of him." She had not considered that eventuality. Thank goodness Ethan had.

"I hope this is a good time for him," he said, holding her more firmly as they turned and climbed the few steps to the entrance. "I told him I would bring you by, but we made no specific arrangement as to time. He did ask when we wished to be married, and I said as soon as possible. If it will fit into his schedule, would tomorrow do?"

"Oh," she said again, this time more of a gasp. "So soon?"

"Is there any reason to wait?"

They had just stepped inside the great door, and she hesitated for a moment, trying to take the information in. Tomorrow? Had that not occurred to her, too, as a possibility? But to have it be real rather took her breath away. She felt as if she were being tumbled by an overwhelming burst of wind. One minute she had been herself, an ordinary girl whose most adventurous act had been to cut her hair short. Now, what seemed like only a moment later, she was a fallen woman, about to be saved from a lifetime of scorn and shame. She was carrying a babe conceived by accident and by luck the father was willing to marry her, even though she knew hardly more than that about him. Oh yes. And someday she would be a countess.

Then suddenly he was there, his fingers tenderly lifting her chin.

"Melissa? This is what you want, is it not?"

She focused on his eyes. He looked as if he were trying to see into her heart. And what would he see there?

She had no idea.

MELISSA LOOKED STRAIGHT AT ETHAN and spoke carefully.

"Yes. I will be a good wife to you."

He felt the smile lurking at the corners of his mouth. "That I was not worried about. And I can promise you I'll take care of you and the baby—and any others we may have."

So. He had not offered love, but she had never promised it either, nor appeared to welcome the idea that love would come. However, it was unquestionably better than it could have been, although he had never felt as remote from her as he did now.

She lifted her chin and smiled, deliberately. "Where is this rector, then?"

Her response broke the fragile moment between them. He looked around the vestibule inside the entrance. "I'm not quite sure. When I came before, I believe I came this far and then he was there."

"Which I am again." With a faint rustle of his clerical garments, the little rector came through one of the doors opening into the vestibule. "Mr. Hawthorne." He nodded politely.

"And would this be your betrothed?"

He had not expected her to be described so, Ethan thought, but she stepped forward and curtseyed.

"This is Melissa Preston," he said. "Melissa, the Reverend Bewley, the rector here at St. Anne's."

She nodded. "I know. I have been here with Caroline. Caroline Gallagher," she explained to the rector.

Odd. The little rector was only marginally shorter than Melissa. So he was not a midget or abnormally small, just very small for a man. The image of the rector and enormous Martin meeting (or worse, bowing to one another) crossed his mind and he looked away for a moment to control his expression.

"Ah, yes," the rector was saying. "Have you chosen the day you wish to be married?"

Melissa and Ethan looked at each other in some confusion. Melissa opened her lips as if she were about to speak, and then closed them, her eyes now cast down. Apparently she felt it was his place to make these decisions.

One day, another day—what would the difference be? Were any other important events impending? He thought not.

"Would one day be better for you than another?" He turned to the rector.

The rector's glance shifted from one of them to the other and back again. "What about today?"

Ethan would have sworn he could feel Melissa turning to him, but did not dare look to see her face. Today? Well, they had spoken about tomorrow…

"I can see some advantages to the present." The rector's tone was as calm and matter-of-fact as ever. "First of all, I would assume that, given our bitterly cold weather recently and her condition, Miss—Miss Preston, is it?—does not go out frequently, so that arranging excuses for her absences is difficult."

He heard her faint sigh of relief. He assumed it expressed her appreciation that the rector understood her situation.

"Mmmm," she said, with a bare single nod.

"There is also the question of witnesses. As it happens, the clerk who helps me is here at the church at present, and the cleaning woman is, I believe, doing the floors in the sanctuary. If that would suit—I'm taking it for granted you had not arranged witnesses yourself, Mr. Hawthorne?"

"I have not."

"Then should we rely on the adage there is no time like the present?"

Ethan and Melissa looked at each other for a moment. It seemed to him that her lips trembled just a little and then she firmed them and gave him a smile that was close to her usual smile. He reached out and took her hand.

"That would work best, I believe," he said, tightening his fingers around the hand that felt especially small in his.

The rector's glance switched to Melissa.

"Yes, please." Ethan was proud her voice was firm and determined.

"Well," the rector said and immediately swung into action. Within fifteen or twenty minutes all was organized. The clerk (a painfully thin, embarrassed young man who kept swallowing nervously) was collected, and as it turned out the curate was at the church as well. The cleaning woman, not being required, was excused from her duties temporarily while the rector, the witnesses, and the bride and groom assembled in the sanctuary.

The atmosphere held a strange muddle of scents. There was wood polish—well, of course. The cleaning woman had obviously stopped partway. Wood polish, and wax candles (that was a faint smell, compared to the polish), and the vague leftover hint of flowers that had been there until they were cleared away. Was that one of the tasks the cleaning woman had been doing before she was interrupted?

The rector, the Book of Common Prayer in his hands, took his position in front of them all.

"Dearly beloved," he began, and Ethan's mind threw up memories of other weddings he had attended. This was an extraordinarily simple one by contrast. There were no flowers, no music, but the little rector's words were spoken with genuine conviction, as if this were the grandest of weddings, the church packed with loving relatives and guests. When the clerk and the curate were asked "to speak now" of any objections, they both held their peace. The rector had written down Melissa and Ethan's names beforehand and apparently memorized them, because he spoke them with as much ease as if he'd known them from childhood. Ethan gave his responses firmly; Melissa whispered hers. To Melissa's embarrassingly obvious surprise, Ethan pulled a gold band out of his pocket when the time came for him to place it on her finger, and for the rest of the service he was aware and amused she was glancing down at it again and again.

At the end they were pronounced man and wife, and it was done.

For a minute or two after the ceremony was completed, the witnesses and the newly married couple stood where they had been standing, uncertainly.

"When did you get the ring?" Melissa whispered to Ethan, as soon as the clerk said something to the curate, who answered. Presumably their voices would mask her question so that it would not be heard by all.

"On my way back after I saw the rector this morning." He was curiously exhilarated by her obvious pleasure. For some reason he had not foreseen it would be important to her. He had simply remembered a ring was part of the marriage service and he would need to have one. But

Melissa was glowing, as she had not been until now, and he had to smile at the frequency with which her right hand wandered over to touch the ring. His intention had been to get a plain one, as he did not know her taste, but this one, with flowers and vines etched into the gold, had struck him as pretty, and so he had chosen it.

The rector, who had temporarily disappeared, popped his head through the door. "I have the register in my office. Would you all join me there?"

Ethan took her hand, the left one with the ring, and led her in the direction the rector had indicated. He lifted her hand with the ring and smiled down at it. Behind him he could hear the footsteps of the curate and the clerk, oddly hesitant. Surely they knew where they were going.

The rector's office was not a large one, and with five people it felt crowded. Was it like this for every wedding? Perhaps under normal circumstances they would go into the vestry. In the office, the registry book was laid out on the desk, with a quill pen and inkpot conveniently placed beside it.

Ethan dipped the pen in the ink and wrote more carefully than he did during the course of the day in Martin's office. With his line completed, he dipped the pen again, and handed it to Melissa.

She took it in her left hand. He was conscious of his own surprise. So she was left-handed, was she? He had never noticed before, but now, as she wrote and her hand moved across the page, the golden ring gleamed and glittered in the light coming through the window behind the desk.

Then it was the turn of the witnesses. They both signed—the curate left a tiny blot, which the rector sprinkled sand over and then shook the sand off the book into the waste bin. Somewhat embarrassed, the curate bowed to both Ethan and Melissa, congratulating them, followed by the clerk. Glancing around, first at the room in general and then at each other, they offered their best wishes and shuffled out of the office. Ethan could almost sense their relief when they were back on their way to whatever they had been doing before this odd interruption to a normal day's business.

He wished he had thought to ask the rector what the fee for the service would be, but pulled out his pocketbook and saw to his relief a five pound note was easily accessible. He pulled it out and handed it to the rector.

"With great thanks for your kindness," he said, handing it over.

It was clearly more than the rector had expected. His eyes widened slightly and he looked up at Ethan with a certain curiosity. "You are very generous, Mr. Hawthorne," he murmured.

"We are very grateful." Ethan still had hold of Melissa's hand, and had been fully aware of her quickly indrawn breath when she saw the bill. He had to admit to himself the small stir it had created made him feel like an earl-to-be. He was glad on this day of his marriage he could be extravagantly generous.

After that it was a quick business of farewells and good wishes, and an expression of hope on the part of the rector that he would see them in church this Sunday. They both nodded in agreement, although if it was still so very cold Ethan was unsure how Martin and Caroline would take a sudden passion for churchgoing.

Melissa had left her hand ungloved—mostly so that she could admire the ring, Ethan thought with a wash of affection surprising him—but as they opened the door to the outside she was scrambling to get the glove back on her hand.

It had snowed outside while they were being married.

Melissa looked around with wonder. "Snow," she murmured. "I didn't think it snowed in Dublin."

"I don't think it does, ordinarily." Ethan slipped his hand around her arm to hold her securely next to him. "I've wondered it has not snowed before now, with it as cold as it has been."

She lifted her face and suddenly, improbably, stuck out her tongue to catch a flake or two on it. Ethan laughed, and she giggled, just a little. He looked down at her uplifted grin and to his surprise found himself feeling truly hopeful. It was not that this had not been the marriage he might have thought he would have. In all honesty he had never given much thought to the possibility of this or any other marriage before the circumstances had changed so greatly. But now he was surprised to feel this rush of optimism. Before he had always joked with his friends about the horrors of a leg shackle and the vast empty wasteland of being committed to a single woman—in theory, at least.

But now, standing on the steps of St. Ann's Church in the snow that was just beginning to coat the ground, he knew somewhere deep in his gut this was not only the right thing to have done, but an arrangement that promised a good deal of happiness.

For better or worse, as he had just promised, it was done.

He looked down at his brand new wife, at the snowflakes falling on her curly head. She had pulled one of her scarves up over her bonnet, partly covering the hair over her forehead when they had stepped out and seen the snow, but now he felt the stirring of an idea. He had passed a shop the other day, and in the window...

"Come with me," he said briskly. "I have one more errand."

Melissa did not protest. She simply nodded, and when he tugged at her hand, followed him down the street. "We should not be gone for too long," she reminded him.

"If what I want is still in the window, it will not take more than a few minutes."

She nodded obligingly.

He hoped he was on the right cross street cutting over to Grafton Street. Still holding her hand, he peered into each shop window as they passed. Then he smiled with relief. He was reasonably sure this was the right one—yes.

He pulled open the shop door, setting the bell on top to ringing, and shepherded her through ahead of him, pulling the door shut behind. A small brisk woman—smaller even than the rector, he thought, amused—came out of a back room to meet them.

"May I help you?"

It seemed to be primarily a millinery shop, and the woman addressed her query to Melissa. Puzzled, Melissa turned to Ethan.

"That muff and bonnet in the window," he said easily. "Would it be possible for my wife to try them on?"

Although he did not look down, he was fully aware of Melissa's surprise as she looked up at him.

"Of course," the shop woman said. She went directly to the window and reached in past the other hats on display to pull out the one placed in the most prominent position: an elegant white fur-trimmed bonnet with a large, puffy white fur muff to match. She smiled at Melissa and beckoned her closer so that she could push back Melissa's scarf and remove the smaller, less fashionable bonnet under it.

Setting the scarf and the bonnet on the top of a cabinet, she placed the elegant white bonnet on Melissa's head and carefully tied the wide white ribbons in a bow to one side. Then she handed her the muff, and turned her to face a looking glass.

"Ohhh, they are so beautiful!" Melissa's murmur was rapturous.

"And so are you, my dear," Ethan said, hoping he sounded like a husband. He beamed at her. "Do you like them, then?"

"Oh, yes," she breathed. Her eyes sparkled. "They are wonderfully warm."

"In that case, we will take them," he told the shopkeeper. "Could you wrap the scarf and the other bonnet in a parcel I can carry?"

"Certainly, sir," she said, and pulled out some sturdy brown paper. While she was wrapping, Melissa tried once or twice to walk away from the mirror in a matter-of-fact way, and each time turned back to inspect herself in the bonnet. Although it was larger than the more ordinary bonnet she had been wearing, it was crafted so that the red-gold curls around her face still showed, shining against the white fur.

When Melissa at last turned from the looking glass, it was only to bury one hand in the muff and run the other over the top. "It is so soft," she marveled. She turned to Ethan. "Have you felt how wonderfully soft it feels?"

"Let me take care of this first," he said, drawing some bills out of his pocketbook. He handed them to the shopkeeper, then pulled off one glove and sank his fingers into the fur. "I thought it would feel like that from the look of it."

As they walked out onto the street, Melissa clung to his arm with one hand, leaving the other in the glorious muff. "This is so wonderful! I don't know how to thank you!"

"I thought we needed something to mark the day. After all, for the time being it would be better, I suppose, if you do not wear the ring."

As it was her left hand buried in the muff, she stopped on the road to fish out her hand, then take off her glove so she could look at the wedding ring again.

"You're right, of course, but I'm sorry to have to take it off. It's a lovely ring, Ethan."

"I liked it, which is why I thought of this." He reached into his pocket, juggling the parcel slightly as he pulled out a velvet envelope, and from that, a delicate gold chain. "I got a long one, so that it will enable the ring to hang down under your clothes, so you may still wear it even if no one else can see it."

She reached for the gold chain, and he handed it to her. After another momentary pause, she tugged off the ring, and started to thread the chain through it. But the chain fastening was closed, and Ethan, watching what she was doing, took back the chain and opened it for her. When she looked up at him with a faint smile of appreciation, he realized there were tears in her eyes.

"Melly?" he said, touching her cheek.

"Silly, isn't it?" she asked. "Maybe it's because—because I'm carrying a child. Women are supposed to get emotional. That's what Caroline says."

"You haven't done that so far." Ethan wondered if that came out sounding like an argument. He hadn't meant it that way. It had been intended simply as a comment, maybe praise for keeping such control of herself.

"Give me a minute and I'll be over it," she whispered. By now she had the ring on the chain and was trying to fasten it around her neck, hampered by the muff she was still holding.

"Here, let me do that." He took the chain from her hand, and clasped it in place. Her neck was soft under his fingers. The chain was long enough so the ring would hang below her bosom, far enough down so it would certainly be invisible to anyone who did not know it was there.

"Thank you." While it was being fastened, Melissa groped for her handkerchief and wiped her eyes.

"There," she said. "We can go back to the house now. But how will I explain the bonnet and the muff?"

"I saw them in the window and thought of you. That's even the truth," Ethan pointed out.

"But I don't have anything for you."

"I would hope not. That would make it even harder to explain. I'll tell them. You be still and listen." He took her elbow, she pushed her left hand back into the muff, her glove clutched in her fingers, and they turned in the direction of what was, for this time and place, home.

Their feet slowed as they came to the turn that would take them down the side of the Green leading to the Gallaghers' house.

"I didn't expect today to turn out like this," Melissa whispered.

"But it's done. No more debating and worrying."

"Yes, it's done." Her voice was low.

They didn't speak the rest of the way to the now-familiar front door.

28

MARTIN CAME OUT TO THE landing just outside the drawing room when he heard the front door opening and closing.

"We were about to blow the whistle for lost children," he called down to them. "You must both be frozen solid by now."

The butler took their outside clothes, but Melissa held onto the bonnet and muff. They were so beautiful she had to show them to Caroline. Besides, it would be infinitely easier for Ethan to explain them now than for her to suddenly produce them tomorrow or the day after and attempt some explanation then.

The ring was an unfamiliar lump against her chest, but fortunately she was fairly confident that unless a person knew that a ring was there, it would not be noticed. Her hand started to wander up to touch it through her clothes, and she disciplined herself to keep her hand where it would normally be. Hanging at her side? At waist level?

Of course not. What a silly goose she was being. Her hands should be firmly inside the muff, and she promptly slid them inside. After all, was she not taking that and the bonnet up to show Caroline?

She was preceding Ethan up the stairs, and as they reached the top, she lifted her chin and tossed a smile back over her shoulder at him. Martin, still awaiting them outside the drawing room, fell back in pretended shock and surprise at her elegance.

"My lady!" he said, and bowed.

Melissa swept a proper curtsey. "Sir."

She straightened up and turned into the room where Caroline was sitting, a light blanket over her lap.

"Melissa! What a wonderful bonnet and muff! Where did you get them?"

"I got them," Ethan pronounced and did a fair imitation of being insulted he had not been given credit immediately. "Does she not look ravishing? I had seen them in the window of what was, I suppose, a millinery shop. Wouldn't you agree?" He turned to Melissa.

"Mostly. I suppose they do have other things, like scarves and handkerchiefs and that sort of thing, but mostly hats," Melissa said obligingly. She looked at Ethan, one brow slightly lifted as if she were challenging him to finish his version of the afternoon's events.

"Be that as it may, I had seen these in the window a day or two since, and it occurred to me how well Melissa would look in the bonnet with her amazing hair. Of course, once I thought of purchasing the bonnet for her, I had to get the muff as well. They do go well together, I believe."

"Melissa, if you are training him for the wife he will sometime have, I must say you are doing a magnificent job." Caroline was beaming at both of them.

"I am insulted you think I need training," Ethan responded as smoothly as if they were discussing the weather. Melissa studied her muff and did not look up.

"Now, don't go all prickly," Caroline teased. "I think the bonnet and the muff are splendid, and this is certainly the winter when they will be useful. It was snowing today, Martin told me. Papa has written me they have had snow there for a week or two, but that is more usual. I don't know when they last had snow in Dublin, but I do know it was not recent."

"Yes, we saw the snow," Melissa said, pressing her nails into her palm to remind herself not to add "when we came out of the church." She smiled. "I don't believe it snowed for long, though, because I don't remember noticing it after we came out of the milliner's shop."

Martin, who was still standing, went over to the triangular cabinet in the corner where the glasses and brandy was kept. "I admit I don't know when it started snowing, nor when it stopped, but I do know that it is bitterly cold out there. Melissa, Ethan, could I pour you a bit of restorative brandy?"

Melissa was shaking her head before he had finished speaking, but Ethan, who had just sat down in the chair across from Caroline, got up again and joined Martin at the cabinet.

"Some white wine, Melissa?" Martin asked.

Again she shook her head. "No, thank you."

Caroline was about halfway through saying, "Then would you like a blanket instead?" when the footman appeared to announce dinner, so they all trooped down the stairs. Martin and Ethan carried their glasses, and Caroline helped Melissa take off the bonnet and hand it with the muff to the footman to take care of.

Melissa watched him, the muff large and furry in his hands, to be taken to some cupboard for storage with the bonnet and thought, a little wistfully, she would keep them forever to remember this extraordinary wedding day.

But of course she could say no such thing, and so she lifted her chin, tried on a smile, and followed the others into the dining room.

But her wedding ring bumped ever so slightly against her chest as she walked.

Later on, she was not entirely surprised to hear Ethan's knock at her bedchamber door. He had only met her eyes two or three times over dinner, but the conversation had been lively, and they had all remained at the table, still talking and laughing, instead of Caroline rising to take Melissa up to the drawing room to wait for the men. In fact, the four of them stayed there long enough so when Caroline finally did get to her feet, it was to announce she was still getting tired too easily, and if none of them minded, she thought she would make her way up to bed.

None of them did, of course, and in fact Martin remained with them until it occurred to Melissa he was taking his chaperonage duties seriously, and so she excused herself as well, pleading that she was looking forward to climbing into bed with a hot brick at her feet. Martin summoned one of the maids to arrange the hot brick for her, and sent her upstairs with the admonition that she should not allow Ethan to drag her around the city long enough to become chilled.

"It feels as if this miserable weather is getting set in for the winter," he said. "I can only assure you it is not always like this, but that does little good now. Go climb into bed and the brick should be there already or on its way." He turned to Ethan. "Do you wish to have one as well?"

Ethan, announcing he was tough and hardy, declined.

So the three of them went up the stairways together, Martin leaving them to join Caroline, and Ethan and Melissa continuing another floor up. They made a point of wishing each other a good night in somewhat more carrying voices than they might have done otherwise, and then Ethan waited for Melissa to close her door before closing his own, firmly, so that there were two distinct sounds.

Still, Melissa half expected his knock. When he came in, she was sitting up in the bed, still wearing the ring and chain she had, for the moment, pulled out from under her nightclothes, so that the ring gleamed in the candlelight.

"You like it?" A hint of surprise colored his tone.

She stared at him. "Of course I do. Did you think I would not?"

"I didn't know." He came over and took the ring in his fingers. "I am not always good at choosing, judging my sister's response to some of my gifts."

"Your sister must be extraordinarily hard to please."

He grinned ruefully. "No, I think it's more a problem of me picking out things for her she thinks are suitable for a child, not the grown belle she takes herself to be."

"Well, *I* did not think this ring appropriate for a child," she said, taking it from his fingers and capturing it in her hand. "If it did not mean telling Caroline and Martin the whole story, I would never take it off."

"But it does." Ethan sat down on the end of the bed, as he had done before, and looked at her. "Even so, it will have to be done."

"When?"

He shrugged his shoulders wearily. "I am no more enthusiastic about the prospect than you are." He turned away to look around the room. "Where are the muff and the bonnet? I was much surer about them."

She smiled at his back. "They're wherever the footman took them. I love them, too, so you were right about that as well." Her smile turned into a frown. "Which footman was it? I have a hard time telling them apart."

"They're brothers, all three of them." He spoke absently, and she nodded her head in comprehension. No wonder they looked so alike. If this child she was carrying would have brothers, or sisters, would they have so strong a family resemblance? It was very odd to think someday she and Ethan might be parents of a family rather than just a single child, but the ceremony that day had made it more than likely. His back was still towards her: she looked at it appraisingly. What would the combination of the two of them look like?

Of course, some children looked nothing like either of their parents. So there was no sure way of peering into the future.

"I wanted you to have something beautiful and extravagant." He turned and looked at her as if he were somehow embarrassed.

"Why?"

"I suppose I was thinking Caroline has so many beautiful things."

Melissa was on the point of snapping "And you think I do not?" when she swallowed the words and bit her lower lip. Surely he was not measuring himself against Martin and his wealth.

Fortunately he did not seem to be thinking in that direction. He huffed a sort of laugh. "You and I have only the clothes we brought with us when it was still the end of summer, edging into the fall. Neither of us had clothes suitable for winter, much less this winter. From all I hear, it is as bad in London. But I have been more fortunate than you. I am out and about frequently and can drop into a shop to buy what I need. You are moored here at home with Caroline, which is probably as well for our babe"—his voice softened a bit as he spoke the words—"but not so good for you. I wanted something special for you."

She reached out to run her hand over his cheek. It was slightly scratchy at this time of day. Had it been so on that not-to-be-forgotten night when the courses of both of their lives were irrevocably changed? She could not remember.

He turned his face to kiss her hand. "I have been worrying. When will you need different clothes? I wanted to get you a woolen dress, but I did not know your size, nor how to arrange such a purchase. I have seen at least two places that offer dressmaking, but they did not seem to have finished dresses available. How are we to cope with that?"

Melissa had wondered the same thing. But having just given her the muff and hat, it would be strange if he suddenly bought a dress as well. So far the high-waisted gowns that were in fashion managed to mask whatever roundness her belly was showing. Very little at present, but she did not know how long that would continue to last. A heavier fabric would not follow the contours of her body so faithfully. In the meantime, she could go on using shawls and scarves.

"I'll have to think of something," she said. "Is it not a pity that I cannot just ask Caroline? But you must not worry. I am sure I will think of something. I can be quite ingenious, you know."

He stared at her for a moment as if trying to read her mind, and then shook his head. "Time for bed." His voice was matter-of-fact. "Good night, my secret bride."

She had worried about this moment, and now she was nonplussed. So this was to be her wedding night? Well. Probably it would be better this way. Would she bleed again if it happened a second time? She had had enough difficulty then sounding convincing to Moira, asking for rags as if her courses had come upon her in the night. She had burned them bit by bit in her fireplace, which had taken a couple of weeks. She hoped the maid assumed she had saved them and was using them as needed, dealing with them herself. Whether she had convinced anyone, she did not know and could not ask. In her experience, servants seemed to know everything there was to know about the people in the house under any circumstances. But as long as there was no talk about it, and there had been none she was aware of, she hoped any speculation was long dead.

"Good night," she said, and found a smile for him.

He was on his feet now, and came to her, cupping her face between this hands. "I am not sorry." His voice was firm. "I just wish I could claim you publicly."

Suddenly his mouth was on hers, his hands had moved to her elbows and lifted her so that she was pressed against his strength. For long moments they were locked together, his tongue exploring the soft depths of her mouth, and her heart pounding with the onset of the passion she had felt before. Her arms struggled free so she could embrace him as she longed to do, and he held her in place with his, supporting her bottom as each attempted to get closer to the other.

"It is not wrong," Ethan breathed into her ear. "It must be secret for the time, but it is not wrong. You are my wife. We belong together now."

She had told herself she remembered little of that other night, but the urgency and passion were familiar already, and she pulled him down to the bed with her. She was as hungry as he was, and it was strangely familiar for both of them, now that they knew each other somewhat better, to repeat what they remembered and explore new varieties of sensuality.

In the end, she began the explosion and he hastily caught up so that they lay in each other's arms, breathing heavily and gradually letting their awareness of the room around them ease back into consciousness.

"Mmmm," she finally murmured.

His hand moved into her hair, stroking through the curly tendrils. "I wonder if that bothers the babe."

"Hope not," she said sleepily, and curled up closer to him.

He chuckled, and tried to pull himself halfway to sitting. "I have to creep back into my own bed, which will be cold and not nearly so friendly."

She tried to burrow into him again. "Don't go."

Ethan pulled himself loose. "I have to. Dream of me, little Melly." He pulled his clothes back on, haphazardly, and looked back at her, still smiling where she lay on the bed.

She watched him through half-open eyes as he opened and then shut the door behind him as silently as possible. As soon as she heard the faint sound of his door click shut, she scrambled up to look at the sheet on her bed.

This time there was no blood.

She sighed in relief, and blew out the candle—it would have guttered out shortly, anyway—and curled up again in the warm place under the covers. At least they both knew now the passion was still there.

But there had been no word of love.

TIME CONTINUED TO SLIP PAST the house on the north side of St. Stephen's Green. Dublin was semi-permanently covered with snow, and Dubliners, who were not used to such a phenomenon, complained about it vigorously. The only consolation—if it *was* a consolation—was that it was just as miserable in the south of England. In London, as the Irish papers reported, the Thames froze over to the extent that it was possible to hold a great Ice Fair on the frozen surface. The River Liffey was just as frozen, but since it was far narrower, it was less remarkable. Since both rivers were used for routine commerce, the blockage produced serious difficulties on both sides of the Irish Sea. The Sea itself was ferociously unnavigable, and the post was delayed again and again as mail boats too often were blown back into the port they had just succeeded in leaving, and one was lost with all hands.

Christmas came and went, and so did January. Using her shawls carefully, Melissa was able to mask most of the changes in her body, and of course neither Caroline nor Martin were expecting any.

Her pregnancy, however, moved forward regardless. It was in January that Melissa felt the baby move. At first she took the sensation to be gas bubbles in her stomach, but there was no accompanying sharp twinge. Later that day she felt the bubbles again and abruptly realized what it had to be. It was very strange, but the frustrating part was that she could not ask Caroline if she was feeling what she thought she was.

That night she excused herself early, claiming she was going to take a book upstairs with her and read herself to sleep. Instead, she sat on the bed, fully dressed, waiting for Ethan to reach his bedchamber.

The wait was longer than she would have chosen, but eventually she heard footsteps passing her door and going on to his room. She was almost sure she only heard one person, but she waited, just in case the manservant had come upstairs with him.

It was strange, sitting there in the quiet house listening intently for sounds. She could hear nothing from the floor below, and when she opened her curtains enough to see outside there was still some traffic—an isolated carriage now and again; a lone pedestrian wrapped up against the cold, scurrying down the footpath—but from within the house they seemed to be passing silently.

When she pulled the curtains shut again, she decided it had been quiet long enough to tiptoe over to Ethan's room.

She knocked as quietly as she could, wondering if he had gone straight to bed and to sleep. Would he be indignant at the idea of her waking him?

"Yes?" His voice from within was quiet, too.

She turned the door handle, and the door eased open.

Ethan was sitting on the bed clad only in his shirt and pantaloons with stockings on his feet. He looked at her not so much with surprise as with curiosity.

"Is there something wrong?" His voice was almost low enough to be a whisper.

She shook her head. "I had an odd sensation, and you are the only person I could tell about it." She tried to keep her own voice as quiet as possible.

His look sharpened. "Odd sensation? Are you worried about it?"

She shook her head again, more slowly this time. "I think I felt the babe move."

His face lit up. "Did you really?" He reached out his hand for her. "Come over here. Do you suppose I could feel it as well?"

"I don't know. It isn't doing it all the while—just now and then. But try." She took his hand and put it against the curve of her belly. She was definitely more curved than she used to be now, although the change had happened so slowly she wasn't sure she remembered exactly how she had been shaped before.

They stood there, both of them, his hand warm against her.

Please, baby, she thought. *This is your father.*

"I can't feel anything," he said after what seemed like a long silence.

"Nor can I." The disappointment bit into her. She had wanted so much to share this, to have him know. She started to straighten her shoulders and to move away when there it was again. That strange sensation, as if a fish wiggled in her belly.

"Did you feel that?" She realized her voice had risen, and clapped one hand over her mouth.

"Was that the baby?" His face was full of wonder.

"I think so. I mean, what else could it be?"

He was beaming at her. "There—I could feel our baby," he said, his voice marveling. "Just think. That little flutter is our baby moving around."

"He must still be very small."

"But growing." Melissa moved away a little, and Ethan's hand fell back against his thigh.

"Do you want to—to stay?" he asked.

She shook her head. "No, not now. I just came to tell you because it seemed so—well, so strange and miraculous and there was no one else I could tell. Poor Caroline. She told me once that when Henrietta first moved the only creature she could share it with was George, the dog, and he didn't seem to notice!"

They laughed cautiously and quietly together.

"Just a kiss then," he said, and lifted her face with his hands. His mouth was warm and gentle against hers.

She looked up him, and for a moment wished she could creep into his arms and stay there. But it would be wiser not to. She disliked sneaking about, but this was not yet the time to confess all. Wasn't that what they had decided the last time they had had a moment of privacy to debate it?

She turned deliberately, away from his hands, and very quietly eased the door open.

Neither of them said good night.

She shut the door behind her and went to her own room and set about getting ready for bed. The babe must have had its evening exercise, because all was quiet in her belly. Would it be sleeping now? Once in her nightclothes, she perched on the edge of her bed, remembering how simple her life had been when she first came to sleep in this room. Was she forevermore to live in a morass of complications?

It was too much to think about when her mind was dull with the need for sleep. Melissa crawled under the blankets, her feet seeking the heated brick wrapped in toweling under the covers at the foot of the bed.

In February the cold grew worse. Snow was now a constant presence, and slipping on ice a constant danger. Business and government froze in place. Even the oldest inhabitants mumbled miserably they did not remember a time so cold and forbidding. There was a week when Martin decreed that simply getting to the office was too much to ask of his staff, and so everyone stayed at home and did what was possible to be done. Unfortunately the difficulties of communication and reporting what was accomplished meant most everything came to a halt, just as it had in the streets outside.

The result of course was that both Martin and Ethan were at home. Martin could keep himself busy fussing over Caroline, who was beginning to look more and more expectant, even in her woolen dresses. She complained about it, of course, saying that with Henrietta she had not begun to show much change until she was close to six months, but this time she was puffing out like the mother of ten.

It was a new thing to worry about. Caroline had a doctor now, a friend of Martin's called Dr. Malloy. He had told Caroline, who told Melissa, she was still within the normal range, and most women grew larger with subsequent pregnancies. Melissa watched her uneasily, wondering if that was what accounted for the great differences in their sizes. So far, it was only Ethan who knew Melissa's belly was curving outward now.

She had two new woolen dresses, which helped. Her need for warm woolen clothing had become acute. It must have been in late January on a sudden impulse at the dinner table she had asked Martin and Ethan if it would be possible for one of them to arrange with a dressmaker to make a woolen dress for her. She wrote down her measurements, allowing for extra inches in the bust, waist, and hips. Given the cold weather, she said, it was worth the experiment to see if a dress made from those measurements without going for a fitting would be satisfactory. Ethan offered to see what he could do. He said if he remembered correctly there were a couple of dressmakers along the same street where he had purchased the hat and muff.

Whether he had paid extra for speed Melissa did not know, but two days later he brought her the dress, made up in pretty shades of blue. It fit reasonably well. Actually it was just a bit on the large side, but that was much more acceptable than being too small. Melissa was so encouraged that she asked Ethan to order another, this time in a golden brown tweed. With the green dress Caroline had loaned her at Christmas (which would soon be too tight), she was outfitted for the time being.

Their decision regarding when to admit to Caroline or Martin they were also expecting a birth (hopefully ameliorated by the fact of their marriage) wobbled from day to day. Some days Melissa could see no point in continuing to hide her pregnancy. Unfortunately those seemed to be the days when Ethan was convinced the revelation of his faulty judgment would hopelessly compromise his hoped-for cooperation with Martin once the weather finally moderated, when he must go north. Only then would he be able to discuss with his uncle the proposed split in authority between the man on the land (who would presumably be the steward) and himself in Dublin at least part of the time. He did not see how to go about arranging it without Martin's assistance.

Just as bad, the days when Ethan was eager to end the charade were the days when Melissa and Caroline had had a particularly intimate conversation about life in general. On those days Melissa was convinced Caroline would be stunned and appalled once she discovered what had been deliberately concealed. Their friendship would be destroyed, leaving behind a tattered ruin of painful politeness.

On any given day it seemed easier to continue with the deception. It was at night Melissa was sick at heart. Was Ethan also fighting with the issue at night, alone in his room? She did not ask.

She was indoors consistently in any case. The responsibility of walking George was handed over to the footmen, and she and Caroline knew only what of Dublin life they could see looking out the windows. Martin was determined that Caroline and her baby-to-be stay inside, and Ethan, as if it were a matter of little importance, suggested Melissa should keep her company.

It was rather like being a child again herself. Henrietta was delighted to have the two of them as well as her nanny to entertain her, and they often played in her nursery. The servants' bedrooms were in the attic, the men's rooms divided by a locked door from the women's. Henrietta knew better than to invade either of those areas, but the rest of the house and the stairs were open for exploration and the wonderful games of hiding she enjoyed with bursts of rolling giggles when she discovered either her mother or Melissa or was discovered by one of them.

The floor with Melissa's and Ethan's bedrooms was not so interesting, being taken up largely with guest bedrooms and, tucked away, useful rooms that in a country house with more space might be relegated to the lowest floor. There was a room for ironing and mending, a couple of box rooms for storage of whatever didn't belong anywhere else, and the housekeeper's room at the back of the house. Henrietta was most assuredly not allowed there, but she loved to investigate Melissa's room, to try to brush her own hair with Melissa's brush, and to peer into the small looking glass set on the dressing table.

Below that level was less adapted to a small girl's games. There was the floor with the suite for Caroline and Martin, originally planned with separate bedrooms for husband and wife, each with a dressing room attached. One of the bedrooms now served as a sitting room for Caroline, and it was there that she and Melissa most often retreated for needlework or just to sit talking by the large fireplace during this coldest of winters. Most of the most delicate pieces of decorative china and glass had been moved to higher shelves, but when Henrietta was there with them, as she sometimes was, a certain level of vigilance was necessary.

The floor below that, the *piano nobile*, was the level of the most important rooms—the drawing room, the library, and the grand guest room that must have been planned with the visits of people of importance in mind, overlooking the trees and flowers of the back garden. Caroline told Melissa with a sheepish smile she had been given that bedroom when she first came to the house. Martin had brought her there along with Henrietta and George the dog as well as their nursemaid, who had been desperately sick during the rough crossing from Wales. He was determined they should have a quiet night with proper beds before starting the journey up north to Kendall House.

"Of course I had no idea the room was anything special," Caroline confided. "And I was too exhausted to appreciate it in any case."

Henrietta was *not* allowed to play in that bedroom.

But the open space between the doors to the drawing room, the library, and the grand guest room was the largest clear space in the house, and in Henrietta's opinion was clearly the space that offered the greatest opportunity for unhampered play.

She and George were running around playing George's favorite game of chase, which he was just as enthusiastic whether he was chasing or being chased. The game had been going on for some time, with whoever was chasing alternated, and Henrietta's cheeks were glowing with exertion. George looked as happy as it was possible for a small, undistinguished dog with no celebrated ancestry to look.

Caroline, greatly enjoying the frolic, stood with her back against the railing that protected the edge of the open space that overlooked the entrance hall and rooms below. Melissa, at the double doors that were open to the drawing room, was keeping an eye on the direction of play so that neither Henrietta nor George would be so excited by the chase that they went too far and inadvertently tumbled down the staircase.

Downstairs the front door opened, and Martin and Ethan came in, stamping on the mats the butler had laid down to keep the tile floor from becoming dangerously slippery.

"Hello up there!" Martin called up to Caroline. "Watch your step, Melissa."

"Hello!" she called back cheerfully, and took a step sideways to push Henrietta closer to her mother so that Caroline could grab her before she tried to take the stairs by herself to greet her father.

At that moment she realized her own foot was half-on, half-off the top step, and before she could catch her balance she came crashing down the stairs, unable to grab onto anything, unable to stop herself from tumbling like a rag doll dropped from above.

She had time for only one thought as she fell.

"My baby!" she screamed.

30

FOR A MOMENT ETHAN WAS paralyzed by horror.

Then, as if propelled by a cannon, he was shoving Martin out of his way and running like a madman down the entrance hall to the stairway where Melissa lay crumpled, her fall finally ended halfway down the next-to-last step. He scooped her up in his arms and held her cautiously close to him. Was she still alive?

He thought he saw her eyelids flicker and pressed his hand gently against her chest. Miracle of miracles—he could feel a faint but steady thump. Her heart still beat.

The world around him began to take some shape again. There was Caroline, who had come a few steps down the staircase, Henrietta in her arms. There was Martin, who had grabbed a footman, wrapping a hand around his arm and giving urgent instructions, then taking off the overcoat he was wearing himself, and wrapping it around the footman, forcing his arms into the sleeves. The footman, a tall but slender man, looked drowned in the overcoat, peering over the collar, but presumably would be warm. Martin threw the door open for the man to leave at speed, and shut it immediately behind him.

The only thing Ethan could see in three dimensions and color was the woman in his arms. "Melly," he crooned to her, his head bent close to hers, "Melly, you can't leave me. Stay with me. I love you, my darling. Stay with me." The words came with such ease. How long had he known the truth of them? He prayed she could hear.

Martin, having dealt with the footman, came up behind him. "Are there any broken bones? I've sent for the doctor."

His words were a buzz in Ethan's ears. All he could see was Melissa.

All he could feel was her warmth in his arms. "Melly," he whispered over and over again. "Melly, stay."

Her eyelids fluttered and opened, and for a moment they simply stared into each other's eyes.

Martin leaned over both of them. "Where does it hurt?" His voice was gentle but unyielding. "The doctor is coming. Where does it hurt?"

For a moment Melissa's eyes moved over to look at Martin and she shifted her head slightly, but her gaze returned to Ethan. "The baby," she whispered.

"A doctor is coming," he told her. "Don't worry. Are you in pain anywhere in particular?"

A fugitive smile danced over her lips. "All over," she whispered again.

"Poor Melly," Ethan crooned. He shifted her very slightly in his arms and to his incredulous delight she moved just a little, settling herself against him with no cry of pain.

Caroline came a few steps more down the staircase. "Is she all right?"

"Malloy will be here shortly," Martin told her. "We'll know more then."

"Is the baby all right?" Melissa breathed. Ethan glanced up over her head and saw Caroline and Martin exchange glances.

"Baby?" Caroline asked faintly.

Melissa turned her head into Ethan's shoulder.

"There was a baby," Ethan told them. "Pray God there still is. We were married two weeks ago." He forced his lips to stop trembling, but could do nothing about his death-like pallor.

The door knocker banged loudly and repeatedly in the stunned silence that followed. Mr. O'Malley came from the direction of the dining room, hesitated—clearly shocked to see the scene on the stairs— and then moved swiftly to the door.

"Great heavens." For once Martin looked less than completely in charge of a situation. "Let this be Malloy."

"Oh, poor Melissa, poor you." Caroline came down the rest of the stairs and sat down, Henrietta in her arms, just above where Melissa still lay, supported by Ethan.

The front door opened, and entering quickly, frosted slightly by falling snow, came a youngish man, with a face full of freckles. "Somebody fell?"

Martin went to him at once. "Yes. Malloy, I'm glad you're here. She fell all the way down the staircase." He pointed over his shoulder.

The doctor glanced back at the stairs and nodded. He shook off his heavy coat into the butler's waiting hands and without a moment's delay went straight to Melissa's side, his snowy hat still on his head.

"Can you speak?" he asked her, kneeling next to her.

"Yes," she whispered.

"Let me just touch you to see—is there any part that hurts in particular?" His hands started to glide over her, just skimming the surface.

Melissa shook her head feebly. "I hurt—I hurt all over."

He nodded. "Whatever else you have done, I'll wager you will have some nasty bruises." When his hands slid over her abdomen he looked sharply at her for a moment and then continued with his examination. He finished with checking out her legs and feet, and then stood up again.

He turned to Martin. "By some miracle I can't feel that anything is broken. Is there somewhere a bed where we could put her so I might examine her more thoroughly?"

Caroline got to her feet, Henrietta still in her arms. "The bedroom by the drawing room is the closest and most convenient." She looked at Ethan. "Can you carry her there?"

Ethan, the color only gradually returning to his face, nodded. Martin came to his side, steadying his elbow as Ethan gradually rose to standing, Melissa still in his arms. Together they climbed up the stairs, Martin remaining just behind him to make sure he remained balanced. At the top Martin went past him to open the door of the bedroom and throw back the elaborate bedcovering so that Ethan could set her on the bed. The doctor was just behind him.

Dr. Malloy looked at the two men and hesitated, obviously waiting to examine her privately. Martin nodded, and went to the door.

Ethan spoke, finding his voice was scratchier than normal. "I will stay. She is my wife."

Martin surveyed both men and nodded, closing the door behind him.

"Can you help me get this dress off her?" the doctor asked. He rolled her gently to her side, and her eyes fluttered open and then closed again.

Ethan reached down to help. The buttons down the back were fortunately not small decorative ones, but it still seemed it took forever to undo them all and carefully pull her arms out of the long sleeves. When they managed that, and the doctor again with careful hands rolled her to her back, her wedding ring was on the chain, lying against her shift. Ethan felt a sharp stab of pain at the sight. What he wanted desperately to do was put the ring back on her finger where it belonged, but that was of the least importance to take care of at the moment. He let her hand slide out of his to fall limply to her side and straightened up. Grown men do not cry, he reminded himself, no matter how terrified they may be.

The doctor was already bent over her, checking her more carefully, more slowly and with undivided attention. His hands ran down her sides while he watched her face intently, presumably to catch any indication that a touch caused her pain.

As his hands moved lower, Ethan spoke, his voice still rougher than usual. "She is with child."

The doctor nodded without surprise. "How far along is she?"

"Five or six months? I am not sure."

"Too early," the doctor murmured.

Suddenly her eyes opened and she whispered, looking into Dr. Malloy's face. "Is my child all right?"

His hands took hers, cradling them. "I don't yet know. Have you felt the babe quicken yet?"

She nodded, her hair making a rustling sound against the stiff pillowcase. "Yes. Perhaps two weeks since."

"Has the child moved since the fall?"

Melissa shook her head, once, and her lips trembled. Ethan reached over to cup her cheek in his hand, and she lifted her own to take hold of his.

"Then we do not know yet," the doctor told her. "We will wait and see." He reached his hands back to her belly and felt about it, his look taking on an unusual intensity as he concentrated on whatever it was his hands were telling him.

"The womb is enlarged, but I cannot tell you much more than that." He lifted her shift for a moment and then lowered it again. "I do not see signs of bleeding. At this point we will hope the babe is well, and wait."

He smiled down at her. "So we can be hopeful."

He patted her legs, as if to reassure her, and untied her garters above her knees, unrolling her stockings to inspect her legs and feet. He made an odd clicking sound with his tongue, and said, "I think we will have bruises on your legs, all right, and possibly elsewhere as well. Is there any part of your body that gives you greater pain than the rest?"

She moved slightly, as if she were testing parts of her body. "My shoulder?" Her voice was still faint.

"This one?" When she nodded, his hands moved there and again his eyes were intent. She flinched once, and he circled around the spot.

She seemed to have great trust in the doctor already, Ethan observed. He watched them both, wishing he could immediately understand what the doctor was searching for, wishing that she could tell him what she was most afraid of. He hoped that the baby was alive and well, but as long as there were the two of them, there could always be another babe. What was critical—and why had it taken this for him to fully understand it?—was that she was all right and the two of them were together.

The doctor was lifting her arm up and down, and she was watching him trustfully.

"Does that hurt?"

"A little."

"More when I move it?"

She shook her head.

"I think that will be another bruise. You will be a splendid picture in a day or so, my dear. Beautiful colors all over you."

Her mouth curved in a small smile.

Ethan told himself it was ridiculous to be jealous of the man. He was a doctor, and doctors examined people. If he was kind and gentle, they came to rely on him, which was as it should be. He shifted his position, staying close to the bed, close to her.

At last Dr. Malloy straightened up and looked straight at Ethan.

"You are very fortunate. Your wife is fortunate as well—she must have fallen without trying to catch herself, and so she fell loosely like a rag doll, which causes the least damage. I am not sure about your child. At the moment there is no bleeding, although it may start at any time. I would suggest your wife remain in bed for the remainder of the pregnancy. The child has sustained tremendous shaking about, and it is my opinion the safest course of action now is to reduce your wife's movement as much as possible. We do not know how much more moving about will catapult her into labor, and at this time the babe is not mature enough to survive."

Ethan reached down and took Melissa's hand, which curled around his.

"I understand." He tightened his grip, and felt her hand squeeze his in return, just a bit. "I will talk to Mr. and Mrs. Gallagher, since this would mean that we remain here into the spring, but I am sure there will be no difficulties and we will make sure that my wife has no need to move from this room. Will you be able to come to check her from time to time?"

Dr. Malloy smiled. "That presents no problem. I live just along the western side of the Green, and can come every week or so to keep an eye on her. It is possible the babe may be born before the usual nine months, but we want to keep it where it is as long as possible. The longer before its birth, the stronger it will be after birth."

The doctor turned to smile down at Melissa. "You are a wonderful miracle," he told her. "At the moment we have every reason to be optimistic. It will require patience from you, because I'm sure it will be difficult to remain lying down for as long as we will ask it of you, but it is my opinion that for this child to survive it is absolutely necessary."

She looked up at him and nodded. "I will be good."

He laughed. "You're already good, my dear. You certainly made the best possible business of that fall."

So when he went out, Melissa was smiling her first genuine smile since she had fallen.

Ethan could not help the twinge of jealousy that it was the doctor who had provoked it. Now that they were alone, he sat down on the edge of the bed carefully, keeping far enough away from her so she would not be jolted.

"How do you feel?" It was a silly thing to ask when the doctor had just been there and he had heard every word they had exchanged, but he could not think of anything else to say.

She turned her head slowly to look at him. "Sore all over, mainly. There's no one thing that hurts more than anything else, so I hope he's right that nothing was broken." Her eyes, though, were worried.

"Is there something that feels wrong?" He leaned toward her anxiously.

Now there were tears welling in her eyes. "The baby doesn't move. Why doesn't it move?"

To say "I don't know" would sound cold, although it was the only truthful thing he could say. He reached for her hand, instead, his eyes fixed on her face, and kissed it gently. "Maybe he was surprised by the fall." Could an unborn child have emotions? Ethan had no idea. "Maybe he's waiting to see what happens next."

She smiled again, an odd crooked smile this time. "Maybe so." A short pause. "Where are Caroline and Martin?"

He shrugged. "Probably in the drawing room? I don't know. I would think the doctor might stop to have a word with them—he knows Martin, does he not?" He was not sure if Martin knew him in any capacity other than being one of his patients. "Do you want me to find out if they want to come in?"

She nodded carefully.

"Does your head hurt?"

Again that faint smile. "No worse than everything else." She moved carefully and closed her eyes for a moment. "I hate this. It is hard to feel that at any moment you might do something that would make it worse for the babe. Why does he not move?"

If only he were not so miserably helpless. Ethan picked up her hand again, and held it against his cheek. It was not cold, but hardly warm, either. If only it were half an hour ago or whatever it had been. If only they had not come through the door at just that instant—had that been what startled her? If only...if only...the words reverberated in his skull.

"I'll go ask them to come in."

She nodded again, just once. Still so carefully—it tugged at his heart. He carefully laid her hand down and stood up, his feet reluctant to move. When he stepped out of the room, he left the door partly open so that if she should call out for him, he would hear.

Clearly Dr. Malloy had left. Martin and Caroline were perched on the edges of their chairs, rather than sitting.

"How is she?" Caroline asked at once.

Martin had come to his feet.

"She says she is still sore," Ethan said. He considered mentioning her anxiety about the babe remaining motionless—at least as far as she was aware—and decided it would be better to wait. "But she is a bit brighter than she was," he added, feeling he should give them something to be hopeful about.

"Would it be all right if I went in for a bit?" Caroline stood as she asked, looking very small and frail beside the great bulk of Martin.

"I think she would be glad to see you."

"I'll step in for a minute as well," Martin said, taking Caroline's hand and setting it on his arm, as if they were about to take their positions at a dance.

Ethan preceded them to the door of the elegant bedchamber, feeling oddly as if he were the host here.

Caroline peered cautiously around him. "Melissa?"

"Please come in." Her voice was still faint.

The three of them trooped in, all of them looking uncertain and ill-at-ease. They arranged themselves around the bed, Ethan resuming the position he had had, at her side, and Martin and Caroline standing at the end.

"I am so sorry," Melissa whispered.

"Sorry?" Caroline stepped past Martin, coming to Melissa's other side. "What on earth are you sorry for?"

"All of it." Melissa gestured weakly with one hand. "I'm so ashamed, and now here I am and the doctor says here I have to stay, even when the weather warms. I have to stay until the babe is born or he'll be born too soon, and here I am in the middle of your house. It's all a mess and I can't do anything to change it." Towards the end, her voice sounded as if it were gradually failing.

"Don't be silly." In contrast, Caroline's voice was firm and determined. "There is nothing to make you ashamed with us. But what I need now are details: when in the world did you get married? Why didn't you tell us? We would have loved to rejoice with you. And don't fuss about staying here. I am absolutely delighted. Do they know when your babe will be born? Just think—they might be close to the same age, your baby and mine. Wouldn't that be wonderful?"

Martin grinned. "Caro, you've given her enough to talk about for an hour, and I doubt very much if she is up to that right now."

Caroline looked over her shoulder at him, her expression slightly irritated. "Well, all right." She turned back to Melissa. "Just answer one of them. Any one."

"We were married at St. Ann's." It was Ethan who answered. "A couple of weeks ago."

He had taken Melissa's hand again, but she pulled loose to feel around her throat for the chain. When she had it, she pulled it out steadily until the ring lay on her neck. "See? Isn't it pretty?"

The chain was long enough so that if she bent over just a bit Caroline could pick the ring up to look at it herself. "It is lovely, Melissa. What a splendid thing!"

"Now I can wear it on my hand." Even Ethan chuckled with the others at the satisfaction in Melissa's voice.

"Why didn't you tell us?" Caroline sounded more puzzled than indignant.

"I was so ashamed." Melissa whispered again. "And we were afraid— I was afraid that you would blame yourselves that we had gone off together, unchaperoned, and I couldn't bear you to feel it was your responsibility, when it was just—well, we were the only ones to blame."

"Pish," Caroline said.

Martin laughed out loud. "It is not the happiest situation in which to find yourselves, I can well imagine, but we are all family of a sort, and there is no reason for you to feel we are horrified or any of the other dreadful reactions you may have imagined. And we both feel privileged you will be with us, so we can share part of the anguish of waiting to see if this babe will choose to rest until he is strong enough to be born."

"Or she," Caroline put in, raising one eyebrow.

Ethan could hardly speak through the intensity of his relief. He had not really imagined the Gallaghers would in fact turf them out to the street, but the depth of their understanding was more than he had hoped for. He looked anxiously at Melissa. What was she feeling? Anything akin to his gratitude?

She was lying very still, an odd expression in her eyes, almost as if she was focused intently on something he could not see.

She reached out so suddenly to grasp his hand that he jerked with surprise.

"He moved!" Her voice was almost normal again. "Ethan, the baby moved!"

It was Caroline who saw the meaning first. "Thank God." It was her turn to whisper. "The babe is still alive."

EVER AFTER, MELISSA REMEMBERED IT as the waiting time.

In a way, as Caroline pointed out almost daily, it was certainly convenient that Melissa had been moved into the splendor of the grand bedroom in the rush to get her somewhere for Dr. Malloy to examine her, because it meant she was not two floors above the rest of the life of the house. A couple of elegant chairs were removed and relegated to storage somewhere and some of the most comfortable chairs were brought in from the drawing room so that coffee or tea after dinner became a regular social event for all of them to gather and discuss what had happened during the day.

Ethan, with Caroline's help, found her a personal maid, who helped with sponge baths in bed and did innumerable errands during the day, running up and down the stairs to fetch meals and to clear away whatever needed to be taken elsewhere. Bridget was a reliable Irish girl—the daughter of one of Martin's sister's neighbors—who also had a fund of wonderful Irish tales and legends to amuse Melissa during the long hours when Caroline was busy elsewhere, usually with Henrietta, who would otherwise have loved to spend the entire day crawling all over Melissa's bed while Caroline or Melissa tried to read her a story.

Somehow, as Caroline pointed out with mock indignation, the room where Melissa was had turned into the heart of the house.

Dr. Malloy took to arriving either in the afternoon—discovering that delicious biscuits were often served with tea then—or in the evening, when he could join the group of them and tell stories, shorn of identifying details, about his more bizarre patients. One of them, a woman who was supposed to be bed-bound like Melissa, would peer through her lace curtains when he was approaching, then run rapidly to her bedroom and sigh heavily when he was let in and came to her bedside, looking at him with pathetic Irish eyes.

"The most frustrating part," he told them, "is that the infant seems to be as great a fool as his mother, and clings on for dear life where he is. I now fully expect him to emerge as a nine pound wonder who will be walking at six months."

"Do you suppose there really is such a woman?" Caroline asked the next day when she was sitting with Melissa, doing some embroidery as the nanny had Henrietta elsewhere.

"Maybe he's invented her to terrify me," Melissa suggested, shifting a little in bed. The doctor had threatened her with having the foot of her bed elevated if she tried any such nonsense.

"Put gravity on our side," he had suggested.

"He might do that," Caroline admitted. "He's quite a lot like Martin. No wonder the two of them get along so well." She lowered her embroidery hoop to look at Melissa directly. "I will long remember how the two of them laughed when it turned out that rather being on the point of death, Henrietta was teething."

"How am I going to manage to get along without you if this baby manages to get born and keeps on living?" Melissa could hear the wail in her own voice and immediately shook her head. "Why am I asking such a ridiculous question? You are going to be busy enough with your babe. There's no way I can remain dependent on you forever."

"Well, you'll either be here where I can organize your life or up north where Anne can do it. She's twice as experienced as I am, you know. She has two children. Or of course there's my mother up there. She was reasonably good at it."

"Reasonably?" Melissa snorted, or came as close to it as a lady was allowed. "I do know your mother, if you recall."

Caroline got to her feet and walked to the window overlooking the back garden. "I think it must be getting warmer. The snow has melted enough so that here and there you can see the grass. Maybe I can now take Henrietta out to the Green—surely Martin would not take great exception to that."

"Surely he would." Melissa eyed Caroline with close attention. She was visibly with child now—Martin might well object on the grounds that she was past the point where she should be appearing in public, whatever the temperature. Her own hands strayed to her belly, feeling the increasingly prominent curve. She was still half-frozen with terror when her babe slept or was otherwise still for an hour or two, and felt the warm rush of relief when he or she—whatever—roused, and stretched an arm or leg in one direction or the other.

"The babe still seems to be a small one," Dr. Malloy had said yesterday when he had been there. He had come in the afternoon so that he could do a thorough examination without having to ask the gentlemen to take themselves elsewhere. "Although I have to say that estimating a babe's size before birth is a fool's performance. I cannot tell you how many times I have been embarrassed when I have predicted a small one, and a great sturdy babe emerges, or assured a mother she has a big baby, most probably a boy, and out pops a dainty little girl." He laughed at his own mistakes. "So all I will tell you is there is a baby there, and the longer he or she stays there the better it will be for all of us."

Melissa looked in the direction of the window, through which she could only see a slice of life outside from her bed. "How long do you think it will be?"

The doctor was in the process of gathering himself together ready to leave. He paused, and looked thoughtful. "Let's see. It's April now, although you would never know it from walking outside. We should be covered with spring flowers by now, and winter is just barely fading away. So, April. Well, I have no great hope of us getting all the way to the end of June, which is what I think would be the normal term, but my guess is we need the babe to stay put through May. The end of May? The end of May, even if I have to do as I threatened before and get the bottom of your bed hiked up so that you will look up at your feet." He smiled at her and took her hand to give it a friendly rub. "So you will be a good girl, and keep that babe where he belongs until the end of May, all right?"

Melissa nodded her head and smiled. He was such a kind and cheerful man that it was impossible not to smile at him when he was standing there. She watched him out of the room, pulling the door shut as he left, and sighed. Pleasant as he was, it seemed to her as if she had been in this bed—howsoever elegant it might be—forever already, and he was talking about another two months of it. As a minimum.

The baby, who had quieted when the doctor was examining her, poked an elbow (or a knee?) out and she ran her fingers gently over the bulge. It was pulled back in, and she let her hand rest on her belly. Even lying down, it was obviously rounded now. Not so much as Caroline, true, but enough so that she could tell the baby was getting at least a bit larger.

She turned just a bit on her side. What she needed to remember was that if she had been told that dreadful day when she had fallen that a month from then the baby would still be moving inside her she would have been ecstatic with joy. Not feeling morosely sorry for herself in spite of Caroline coming in to visit and Bridget's careful ministrations and all the kind things that Ethan continued to do for her. She knew it was important that her child grow as big and as strong as possible before he, or she, emerged to try independent life.

She must *not* be impatient. It would be wonderful if she could just close her eyes and sleep away some of the time, but sleep was elusive even at night.

She sighed a deep shuddering sigh, and felt the baby move again. In response? She patted her belly lightly, just in case the babe was paying attention, and reached for the book she had been trying to read.

She opened it, and began again at the top of the page.

Ethan did not like thinking it, and did his best to avoid doing so, but from time to time during the long waiting days he found the phrase "it's all very well for *her*" floating through his consciousness. She was lying peacefully in bed. He was expected to keep up with ordinary life no matter how much he wished he could remain at her bedside.

If only she had not fallen.

He had thought his heart would break when he'd seen her tumbling limply down the stairs, and the good Lord knew he was grateful that the babe appeared to have lived on, but living these months in a state of neither here nor there was enough to drive a sane man into hysteria.

She was his wife. She had his ring on her finger, now, and the delight on her face when he slipped it back into place was a memory he was afraid he would wear out by summoning it up too frequently. But it was as if she existed now in some kind of protective bubble. He could hold her hand or give her a chaste kiss if they were alone (which happened too infrequently for his taste) but God forbid their contact should go any further.

He was married, but he was not.

The person he spent the most time with was Martin, of course, and whereas Martin was as worthy and undemanding a person as existed, their association—which they had initially assumed would be two or three weeks at most—had now lingered on for close to eight months. Ethan had come to his office to learn principles of management, as well as how to be a successful employer of men, and he had certainly been given the opportunity to learn those.

He was now, in fact, operating almost as an extension of Martin's authority, overseeing Martin's business during this frustrating winter when the regular travel Martin normally maintained across the Irish Sea was of necessity suspended. There were great long letters to be composed by clerks, read and then rewritten to express subtleties that the first versions may not have included.

The bitter winter had created personal difficulties for some of the younger members of the staff, who had family responsibilities but not necessarily enough savings to maintain themselves when heating and food costs rose like balloons in the inevitable scarcities. Ethan had been Martin's lieutenant in working out what could be done to meet the needs of each while being fair to all.

Learning all this had undoubtedly been very useful for sometime in the future, but Ethan was not in the investment business himself. He was not in business at all, except peripherally. As a gentleman, he was expected to maintain himself on the proceeds of his land, and the whole reason he had come here in the first place was to learn how to do that most efficiently, so that he did not have to spend his life riding around in the fields, his days filled with keeping track of what his tenants and farm workers were doing. What he needed to learn from Martin's office he had learned months before.

But was he to go north to join his uncle and leave Melissa in Dublin? Of course he could not. Exactly how jolted his uncle and aunt had been—or Melissa's brother, of course, at Ballymuir—at the news that he and Melissa were not only married, but with a child expected far too soon, he would never know. Their response to his letters had been quick and on the surface level at least, congratulatory. Even Melissa's mother (and that was the one she had fretted most over) sounded genuinely pleased. No one was suggesting he should do anything but what he was doing: continuing to toil with Martin in the office and keeping watch over Melissa, although she had the whole string of Caroline and Martin and Bridget and the other servants at Martin's house and Dr. Malloy keeping watch as well. Most days there was virtually nothing for him to do.

He kicked peevishly at the bollard along Essex Quay. He had wandered there after he found himself more than usually restless.

Abruptly, he had risen from his desk in the half lobby outside Martin's office and walked away, leaving with the vague promise that he probably would be back later that afternoon but might not. Martin was otherwise engaged, so Ethan did not bother to explain anything to anybody.

What he should have done, of course, is try to find something interesting for Melissa in one of the shops on the way home. Instead he had turned in the opposite direction, heading vaguely for the River Liffey, where the life of commerce was stirring again after the difficult winter. There were craft of all sizes docked along the quays, and a reasonable number under sail, going in both directions.

"Hawthorne!"

He turned at the sound of the cheerful voice and recognized Halleck. He had seen some of him since that fateful dinner at his house that he and Melissa had attended, but in the time since her fall he had not made any personal arrangements at all, feeling that the least he could do was to be there whenever he was able to be.

"Halleck." They shook hands with vigorous good cheer.

"I would have expected you would be up in County Meath by now, or back in England," Halleck said jovially. "Had I known you were still in Dublin I would have called on you when I came back."

"Have you been to England then?"

"I suppose I was homesick," the man said with a slightly sheepish look. "It must have been late March when I risked the voyage back. A rotten voyage it was, I must say, but the mail boat did reach Wales, which is what it was supposed to do, and from there I went home as rapidly as possible. They have had as bad a winter there as we have here, and everything is as behind in season as it is here, but it was good to be there, notwithstanding."

Ethan remembered that at one point Halleck had sheepishly admitted he missed his wife, and was unsurprised that he had taken the first available opportunity to get home.

"How is that you are still in Dublin?" Halleck asked.

Ethan wondered how to explain the complications of his life here and decided to give as brief a summary as possible. "Several interesting events. For one thing, I married Miss Preston, and then of course with the severity of the winter the family felt it would be unwise of us to try to return north, even for Christmas, until the spring. Unfortunately, in a freakish accident, she fell down the stairs, and she was with child at the time. She was bruised but otherwise unharmed, and by a miracle the babe survived, so she is now remaining abed in the hopes of delaying delivery until the babe is developed enough to live."

"Oh, my God!" Halleck's face went blank with shock. "What a winter you have had."

Ethan nodded. "It has been difficult. We are still hoping she will be able to hang on for another month or two. Unfortunately, of course, the longer it goes on, the more heartbreaking it will be for her if in the end we are not successful."

"And for you."

Ethan shrugged. "Well, of course." He forced a smile, and tried to sound matter-of-fact. "And you are back in Dublin yourself."

"So I am. The complications, I fear, are not all resolved. But do not let me prevent you from returning to see how your wife is. There is a flower stand not far from here, and although not much is yet available, I would very much like to send you home with a bouquet for her, with my very best wishes."

They went off together, and found the stand. The selection was certainly not what one would expect in a normal April, but there were some spring flowers—daffodills and hyacinths—which were combined to make an attractive bouquet wrapped in green paper. Somebody must have had a glass house for the plants to survive, although how anyone had managed to keep a glass house warm enough in the winter they had just survived was more than Ethan could imagine.

"I forgot to give you my congratulations," Halleck said, as they turned away from the flower stand. "Here are the flowers for your wife, and my most sincere congratulations to both of you. Please give her my best, and tell her that every day, boring as I'm sure it must be, makes it more likely the babe may survive." He hesitated for a moment. "Here, take my card. I don't know which side of the Irish Sea I shall be on when the child is born, but please let me know what happens, and what your plans after that will be."

Ethan took the card, and although the bunch of flowers was large and awkward, managed to slip it into a pocket. The two men shook hands, and Ethan found himself on his way home, away from the river, traveling toward the house on the Green with a much lighter heart.

Had it been talking to Halleck, who was a family man himself and understood the difficult situation Ethan was in himself, although not a word about it directly had been spoken? He had no idea, but was immensely grateful that the fit of self-pity was bothering him no longer.

He arrived at the front door apparently just a minute or so behind

Martin, who was shedding his other clothing, handing his coat and hat to O'Malley, who thus opened the door with one hand but contrived to help Ethan out of his coat nonetheless.

"Flowers for me?" Martin asked with a great grin.

"No, unfortunately. Perhaps I should go to obtain some more?"

They both laughed, and Ethan explained that he had seen his friend Halleck, who had sent the bouquet to Melissa.

"That's kind of him," Martin said. "It's a difficult position to be in, is it not? I do not care for this condition of suspended animation. One would not wish it to end too soon, and at the same time it feels as if it has gone on forever. Melissa has my compassion—and so do you, by the way. Your position at present is not an easy one."

The two men looked at each other with greater truth between them than two men usually allowed. For Ethan, it seemed impossible to express in words what he was feeling, and he had the sense that much the same was true for Martin. But he appreciated that Martin had some understanding that he was struggling, too, dealing with the uncertainties.

In any case, it would be futile to try to discuss the situation further.

"I'll take the flowers to Melissa," Ethan said, and Martin nodded.

He went up the grand staircase quickly, but taking some care—the last thing they needed was for him to fall down the stairs and wreak some permanent injury. The door to what was now known as Melissa's room was slightly open, and he pushed it just enough so he could peep around the edge to see if she was asleep.

She was not. She was simply lying there, looking at the ceiling, and she looked more forlorn than he had ever seen her look.

"Melly?" His heart went out to her. "Melly, sweetheart, are you all right?"

She blinked, surprised. "Ethan? What's that you have?"

"These?" He lifted the bouquet. "Flowers. Flowers for you."

"Flowers?" The word was more of a squeak.

"Yes, you know. Flowers. They grow in gardens," he said, coming to the bedside and opening the paper the flowers were wrapped in so she could see them.

"Oh, they're beautiful." She reached out a tentative finger to touch one of the daffodils. "They look like spring. Is it really going to be spring soon?"

"Looks like it. I can't take full credit for the flowers. I did bring them home, but they're from Mr. Halleck, with his very best wishes. We came across each other down by the river, and as soon as he heard about you, he was resolved to send you flowers. Made me wish I'd thought about it first."

"I'm surprised there were flowers," she murmured. "It feels as if it has been winter forever."

"It does, but if you could see more out of that window, you'd see that the snow is almost all melted, and early bulbs are beginning to pop out. It is nowhere near as cold as it has been, but it's hard to believe that. Martin and I still go off in the morning swaddled with wool—coats, scarfs, hats—and then come home, like as not, carrying part of it because it's no longer that cold."

"'Like as not'?" Melissa's face was animated again, her eyes no longer dull. "Ethan, you begin to sound like an Irishman."

He shrugged sheepishly. It was all right to feel a bit of a fool if it made her laugh. He hadn't realized how much he had missed the person she had been before these last weeks. And from April to the end of May was not forever. All that was needed was to hold on and not give up. Not only Melly and the babe, but he had to hang on as well. Feeling sorry for himself would get them nowhere.

Had he been creeping close to that? He did not like to think so.

He sat down on the edge of the bed and allowed himself to touch her—how had he grown so wary of doing that? Certainly logic should have told him that running his fingers through her soft curls could do neither her or the baby any harm.

She almost purred like a cat, moving her head under his fingers as if his touch was exactly what she needed to feel. "Can you tell we cut it? Caroline and I—well, Bridget helped some, mainly getting all the loose hairs out of the bed. But I was feeling so plain and boring that I wanted to do something."

"You don't look plain and boring to me," he said.

She tipped her head back so that she could look into his face. "Really? It just seemed to me we haven't had much time together. Of course, I know that you've been busy…"

"Not that busy." He interrupted her. "Part of it is my fault. I have the feeling I have learned all I need to learn in Martin's office, and I don't see any way to stop attending with him. I mean, I believe I am useful to him in a way, but it's not necessary, and I have learned what I need to know. I suppose I'm impatient, and coming back here is a constant reminder that we live in his house. I suppose in a way what I do for his business is one way of repaying some of it, but I've had days of feeling sorry for myself, I guess."

Her smile was a genuine one. Had they ever talked together like this? "Well, if anyone gets a prize for feeling sorry for herself, I think I have to claim it."

"No." Ethan cut her off. "Yes, it's hard. You know that, and I know it. As long as you stay in this bed, you are doing everything you can. Please, Melly. Believe that. Believe me."

She leaned over so that her head rested against his arm. "Oh, Ethan. You don't know what that means to me. You don't know what you mean to me."

Just then, Bridget came in through the door with Melissa's dinner on a tray.

"I think they're just about ready to eat downstairs, Mr. Hawthorne."

Ethan started to get to his feet, and then settled back, next to Melissa on the bed. "Could you ask Mrs. Gallagher if I might have dinner brought up here tonight? I think I'd prefer to eat with my wife."

He did not need to look at Melissa to feel the warmth of her smile.

THE BABE DID WAIT UNTIL May. Not the very end of May, as Dr. Malloy had hoped, but the week before.

"How will I know?" Melissa would ask Caroline, as the weeks of May slid slowly past.

Caroline would shrug, and tell her when she had had Henrietta, it had begun when the bag of waters gave way. The first time she said that Melissa looked at her with round horrified eyes and asked what the bag of waters was. Caroline told her to talk to Dr. Malloy about it, and Dr. Malloy had made her a little drawing to show her how the process worked. At the same time he had asked if she would prefer to have a midwife. After consultation with Caroline first, and then with Ethan, she had decided since she knew and trusted Dr. Malloy and there was the possibility it might be a more complicated delivery (that was Ethan's suggestion), it would be better to have Dr. Malloy deliver the babe.

By then, Dr. Malloy was stopping by to check on her every day, or every other day, and when Melissa told him her back had begun to hurt, he looked at her warily, and checked her over particularly closely. Nothing else happened for two or three days, although the doctor came around every day after that until one afternoon Melissa felt a sharp cramping sensation.

"Get Mrs. Gallagher," she told Bridget, feeling her heart begin to pound. It was still too early. How could she stop it?

Bridget ran out of the room and in a minute or two Caroline came running, Henrietta's stuffed rabbit in her hand.

"What's happening?"

Melissa, who had started to lie down, came back up to a sitting position. "I had a pain—does that mean it's started?"

Caroline hesitated. "Not necessarily, I wouldn't think. I've been told some women have pains every now and then towards the end but it doesn't mean proper labor has begun."

"Oh." Melissa settled back against her pillows. So she would have to wait to know. "My back still hurts, if that means anything."

Caroline plopped herself into one of the chairs by the bed. "I don't know. Would another pillow help?"

Melissa shook her head. It wasn't that kind of backache.

"I could bring Henrietta in here to read her a story I started. Would you mind?"

Melissa shook her head again. Henrietta would be a distraction, which might help.

It did for a time, but then suddenly there was another of those cramps—she did not know how else to describe it.

Her gasp attracted Caroline's attention instantly. She looked over, half closing the book she had been showing Henrietta—she and Melissa had earlier made it up together of nursery rhymes and sketches, since Melissa had a good hand at sketching—and Henrietta immediately protested.

"Not right now," Caroline told her and continued to watch Melissa closely. "I think we should be keeping track of how far apart these pains are."

Melissa's eyes were wide again. "Pains? Do you think—could this be the beginning?"

Caroline was able to smile at her. "It might be."

Melissa stiffened with fear. "Must we call Dr. Malloy?"

"Oh, not for some time yet. Sometimes the pains start and then they stop, I've been told."

Melissa fingered the edge of the sheet. "But it's too early. It's not much past the middle of May. The babe may not—this might be too early."

Caroline leaned over Henrietta and the book to take the closest of Melissa's hands. "We don't know yet. We shall have to wait and see— and I know you have waited so long already."

Melissa shut her eyes and tried to make her body limp. Tried to tell her womb to let the babe stay there, not push it out into the world if it was too early. Little by little she felt the muscles relax. If she could only stay that way…

As she lay there, she could hear Caroline's voice again, reading the rhymes and showing Henrietta the pictures. Caroline had gone through this, and was facing it again, she told herself. Of course Caroline had not been trying to hang on to Henrietta for months already. As far as she knew when it began, Henrietta was ready to be born, and in fact she had been. So, presumably, was this new baby. Her worry would not help anyone.

"When do we send for Ethan?" She hoped Caroline did not hear the fear in her voice.

Caroline looked at her over the top of Henrietta's head. "Not for a while yet. We need to see what is going to happen, whether it is happening all at once or slowly."

Melissa nodded. Her heart felt like lead within her chest.

It must have been ten or fifteen minutes before there was another pain. It came just after the great clock in the hallway had chimed, as it did on the hour and quarter hour. Was that the second chime she heard now, or just the first?

Caroline's voice halted briefly when she heard the involuntary noise Melissa had made—was is a gasp or a cry?—but she carried on serenely until she came to the end of the book. Then she looked over at Melissa. "I think I will return Henrietta to her nanny. I'll be back in just a minute. Bridget is close if you need her."

"I'm fine," Melissa said, although she was not at all certain she was. She wished she had Ethan's pocket watch with her, but the pocket watch was presumably in Ethan's pocket at Martin's office now. She would feel a fool if she sent a footman to the office to borrow the watch—it would come home when Ethan did.

She wished he were coming home now. But why? So they could sit looking anxiously at each other? Men were not supposed to be around during this womanly business. But Dr. Malloy would be. If Dr. Malloy was to be there, should not Ethan be there as well?

She rolled over slightly, mostly just to change position. Childbirth was a very strange process, if this is what it was like. She felt completely normal, then a shocking cramp, then back to normal again. What must it feel like to the baby? If what they called labor was starting, was the baby strong enough to stand it?

And who was the baby? Was she on the edge of finding out?

While she was wishing, she wished she were the sort of person who could read or even find needlework a soothing mental distraction. It would be nice to be able to reach for something to do, instead of watching the ceiling and waiting for whatever came next.

The door opened, and Caroline slipped in.

"How are you doing?" Caroline asked, but instead of it just being a friendly remark, she seemed to want an answer.

"Nothing since just before you left."

Caroline nodded. "Everyone has told me it is a hard process to predict. It may be it will fade away and nothing come of it until a day or two later."

"That would be better for the baby." Melissa's voice was flat.

"Mmmm."

"I can't help wishing I could know. Waiting is horrid."

"Mmmm," Caroline said again, her needle dipping into the fabric and emerging again with another neat stitch accomplished.

"Ohhhh," Melissa gasped.

Caroline set down her needlework. "I think it might be as well to send to Dr. Malloy to ask when he feels it would be appropriate for him to come."

Melissa lay quiet, letting the tight sensation melt away.

"Please send for Ethan, then," she said when she could speak again.

"I will." Caroline disappeared through the door.

By the time she came back, Melissa had had another cramp, which she reported.

"I do think it is beginning," Caroline said, her voice calm and quiet. "At least the babe should be small, which is a blessing in a way."

"And a worry in another," Melissa said. What if the baby was born dead? She had not felt it move recently, at least as far as she remembered. Her attention had been on the cramps. Did it take as long to birth a dead baby? She did not want to ask.

Caroline picked up the needlework again, and Melissa watched her needle poke in, and come back out, in again—the silk thread was a lovely golden color, the needle leaving a bright row of stitches behind.

When would Ethan get here?

She closed her eyes and listened for a movement. Well, not listen precisely, but that was the closest word she could think of. There was none. No cramp and no movement of the baby. Had both stopped? That would be unfortunate, with both Dr. Malloy and Ethan summoned.

Then just as she was adjusting her mind to the belief it had stopped, the cramp seized her again, harder this time.

Not meaning to, she cried out.

At that precise moment, the door opened and Ethan rushed in.

"Melly! Are you all right?"

She was still breathing hard, letting the tail of the cramp ease away.

Caroline, who had kept her needle still while the cramp lasted, looked up at him and smiled. "I think we have started."

"It's too early."

"Apparently the babe does not think so."

"Is Malloy coming?" He ran his hand through his hair, looking anxiously at Melissa.

"Yes." Caroline's voice remained even and pleasant.

Melissa took a deep breath. "I'm glad you're here."

He set his jaw. "I am going to stay." He looked at Caroline as if he expected her to object. She continued to smile at him.

Melissa's voice was closer to normal. "We can ask Dr. Malloy."

"I am not going to ask him." Ethan sat on the edge of the bed and took Melissa's hand. "If he, being a man, is going to be here, so am I. That is the way it is going to be."

"I would have wanted to have Henry with me, had he still been alive," Caroline said quietly, her needle still creating even stitches. "I think it would have helped."

The three of them kept silent, then, Ethan's thumb moving easily back and forth over the back of Melissa's hand.

It must have been five minutes or so before Bridget opened the door and announced that Dr. Malloy was there. Ethan had been keeping track with his pocket watch, and was able to tell the doctor that the last pain had been three minutes before.

Dr. Malloy nodded, and turned to Caroline. "I think it would be best to make the bed ready now."

"Of course." Caroline rose to her feet, setting her needlework down on the bedside table, and went to fetch the extra sheets that would be needed.

"I need to examine her," the doctor told Ethan.

Ethan nodded, laid Melissa's hand gently on the covers, and stood. "I will come back when you are finished. I intend to remain with her."

The doctor looked at him for a moment, and then said, "Fine. It might be a difficult time."

"If she must be here, I will be."

The doctor's eyebrows lifted and his smile was slightly crooked. "That is fine with me."

"It has started, then?" Melissa asked in a small voice.

Dr. Malloy's attention switched entirely to her as Ethan walked toward the door. He hesitated slightly. Waiting for an answer?

"I believe so," the doctor said, leaning over her.

"Will the babe be alive?"

"I cannot promise anything at this time, but it was moving earlier in the day, was it not?"

She closed her eyes. "Yes, I think so." Her face stiffened, as if she were listening. "I thought I felt something just now."

"The hardest part for the babe will be the breathing. That will tell the tale, but we will only know how his breathing will be after he is born. It is encouraging to know he is still with us now, but do not fear if you do not feel much during the birth—all babies quiet during the process, perhaps because so much else is going on. But we will know soon." He reached down and took her hand as Ethan had done. "The important thing is you have done everything within your power to make sure this babe has every chance. I know it has not been easy, but you have done all you could do. I want you to remember that, whatever happens."

Melissa's lips trembled, but she took a deep breath, and nodded.

So it began.

For Melissa, and presumably Ethan, the whole business was not proceeding anywhere as rapidly as Caroline and Dr. Malloy seemed to think. Apparently the sharp cramps would better be described as labor pains. She had had no idea what to expect. Had she been married in a more orthodox fashion would her mother or Aunt Elizabeth have told her anything? She doubted it. From what she had always gathered, the conversation on a girl's wedding eve was taken up preparing the bride for the adventure of the wedding night. Would her mother have explained anything during her pregnancy, had they been in the same place?

The pains were now coming so close together that they were more of a blur of feeling rather than distinct sensations. Ethan was with her all the time, miraculously knowing when she needed to feel his hands on her shoulders and when she needed to separate, battling the experience on her own.

Dr. Malloy was sometimes silent and sometimes oddly conversational, talking with Ethan and Caroline and even Melissa as if all four of them were at some extraordinary dinner party, having an interesting discussion over the dinner table. At one point when Melissa thought she could stand it no more, Dr. Malloy talked about some strange gas called ether. Some people were using it to enjoy its extraordinary effects, but he wondered about its potential in medicine. Another time he was discussing dogs he had known, with Caroline chiming in eagerly to tell him about George and his exploits.

All of a sudden everything changed, and Dr. Malloy's intensity was obvious to each of them. Instead of the terrible cramping she was now too familiar with she felt an overwhelming urge to push. Push? Here, in front of everyone? Because now there were not only Ethan and Caroline in the room with her alongside the doctor, but Bridget and other maids were scurrying in and out, bringing in hot water and chips of ice, so good on her throat, towels and more sheets as necessary, and carrying out armfuls of things Melissa made no attempt to identify.

"Gentle, now," Dr. Malloy said suddenly, and Melissa felt Ethan's hold on her change. Suddenly he was cradling her shoulders, leaning against her, his eyes fixed below.

Later she could not remember whether she had felt the baby slip from her body. There was a breathless silence in the room as all movement stopped, and everyone watched the small pale creature in Dr. Malloy's hands.

"Breathe, little man," he whispered. "Now—breathe."

To Melissa's shock, he turned the thin little body over and slapped his back. And again.

Then there was a choke, a gasp, and the diminutive body discovered he had a huge voice. He roared, choking and gasping, absolutely furious. As if to make matters worse, the doctor clamped off the cord and cut it.

The babe took strong exception to everything. His small arms and legs churned with fury, and he continued to scream. He was going rapidly from pink to red in the face.

"He breathes," Dr. Malloy said quietly.

He wrapped the newborn in the soft blanket Caroline handed him, the end of it dangling down as he passed him over for Melissa to hold.

"Your son, I believe," he said.

Ethan bent over her shoulder. Melissa glanced at his face, and suddenly, unbelievably, it was there. He was looking at her, and in his eyes was the look of love and adoration that she had seen on Martin's face, and so hungered for herself. It was there, and it was for her.

"You did it," he murmured, only loud enough for her to hear. "And you are still here, my love. I was so frightened I would lose both of you. I love you, you know. Most of me would die if you were no longer here."

"Don't die," she whispered back. "Stay with us. I need you, because I love you, too. Never forget that."

His hand nestled around her neck, and the sweetness overwhelmed her. Ethan loved her, and their baby was alive. It was too incredible to be true, but the last of her fear drained gradually out of her body.

The baby, still objecting to his new life, wriggled and choked a bit, which seemed to make him even more furious. He managed a deep breath and went back to yelling.

Together they inspected this brand new person squirming in her arms. Ten toes, ten fingers. Two tiny but perfect ears. A snubbed little nose. He abruptly stopped crying and stared at them with what looked like as much fascination as they felt looking at him.

"Is he still breathing?" Caroline asked anxiously.

Melissa nodded without speaking. He was small, as they had said he would be, but his miniature chest was rising and falling regularly, as if he already knew that was what he needed to do. His skin was pink and healthy-looking and he gazed at them with wide-open eyes.

"He has blue eyes," Ethan said, touching the baby's cheek with a tentative finger. "Like yours, my love."

"That may not last," Dr. Malloy said. "It sometimes takes awhile for the eye color to settle. Maybe even several months." He leaned over the baby. "He's a sturdy little thing, for all that he is small."

"He doesn't have much hair," Melissa said, running a hand over the bit of his head not covered by the blanket.

"Nothing unusual." This time the doctor did not even glance over. He was writing in a notebook. "Some do and some don't. Usually grows in for a few years at least, and then we get back to some do and some don't." He ruffled his own reddish hair, which was beginning to thin.

Melissa and Ethan were still close together, admiring their son.

"He's still breathing," Melissa marveled. "Almost from the very beginning."

Their voices were low, but the doctor overheard. "As long as he's that nice pink color, he's getting air into his lungs, and he turned pink almost at once. We are lucky he is such a sturdy young one, considering the fall you took."

Melissa breathed a heavy sigh of relief.

"May I get up now?"

All of them laughed, even Dr. Malloy. "Yes, but your legs will be very shaky for a while. Better to take it slowly until you are used to being up and around again."

She nodded, letting her head sag back against the pillow. No wonder they called the whole process labor. Her eyes followed Ethan out of the room, as Caroline cleared the room of the men so that she and Bridget could clean her up. She would welcome that now.

Tomorrow. Tomorrow would be the first day when she would not have the fear rising up to catch in her throat. He was safe. Her baby was safe.

Dr. Malloy turned at the door. "Good work," he said, and walked out.

Melissa shot to a sitting position. Where was the baby? He had been there a minute ago—what could have happened to him? "The baby?" she squeaked.

Caroline looked at her with a broad smile. "You have to keep track of him now he's separate. Don't worry. Bridget has him and is giving him his first bath."

"Oh." She settled back. "We have to name him. I did not dare to think of names before."

"Never mind." Caroline pulled the covers away and tugged Melissa's soiled nightdress over her head. "You have plenty of time now."

Melissa smelled the delicate fragrance of the soap, coming from the basin of warm water Caroline was balancing, a cloth in her hands.

"That's right," Melissa murmured with content. "Now we have all the time in the world."

ETHAN SAID HE SHOULD BE named Randolph. Randolph Ethan Hugh Hawthorne.

"Randolph?" Melissa looked dubious. "That seems like a great deal of name for such a small baby."

The new Randolph, now three days old, was taking to life on his own with greater enthusiasm than he had shown at first. His mother discovered he liked best to eat. If he had eaten, his next favorite activity was sleep. In between, but preferably just after he had eaten, he was content (but for a definitely limited period of time) to lie and look around, presumably taking the measure of this world into which he had been thrust.

This was one of those times.

He lay on a blanket in the grand bedroom, which had become the Hawthorne bedroom, accommodating all three of them. Melissa and Ethan shared the great ceremonial bed, which she had inhabited alone for so long and found much more inviting now Ethan slept there as well. The baby was trying out the cradle chosen for the Gallaghers' expected baby.

Ethan's attention seemed to be still fixed on the name.

"Well, he's going to be the Earl of Kendall someday, and my father's father was the Earl of Kendall, and he was Randolph. So this is the new one."

"Oh." Melissa looked at Ethan thoughtfully. "It still seems a lot of name."

"And then Ethan for me and Hugh for your brother."

The new Randolph stretched, as if trying to demonstrate he would be big enough for all his names soon.

His father, who would be the Earl of Kendall first, reached out to run his finger over the baby's head. "I think he's growing already."

"The eyes of love." Melissa stood up, still relishing that she could. "But he's still breathing. After what Dr. Malloy said, that's all I worry about."

"He turns red when he cries hard," Ethan pointed out with considerable pride.

"I think it's the pink he is the rest of the time that matters." Melissa leaned over and picked the baby up. "He's still limp," she remarked, kissing his head so he would not think she was complaining.

There was a faint tap on the door. Melissa, Randolph up against her shoulder, went to open it.

Caroline was there. "I don't want to bother you, but I'm curious about the baby. How is he today?"

"Fine," Melissa said, turning slightly so that Caroline could see the baby's face. "I've just fed him and he is being obliging. The next step is falling asleep."

"You forget how tiny they are," Caroline said reminiscently.

"Well, of course he's smaller than the average. Smaller than your baby will be, most likely. I asked Dr. Malloy about that when he came over yesterday, and he said that early babies generally grow up to whatever size they were going to be anyway. Although how do you know what that size is?"

Caroline shrugged and bent over to look the baby directly in the face.

"He has a name now," Ethan said with some pride. He had quickly changed from the lounging position on the bed cover he had been enjoying to a more suitable one of sitting upright on the edge. "He is going to be Randolph Ethan Hugh Hawthorne."

Caroline looked thoughtful. "Where did the Randolph come from? I know I've heard that name before."

"It's from our grandfather. Our fathers' father, the Earl of Kendall, as little Randolph here one day will be."

She nodded. "That's right. That's where I've heard it." She reached over to pat the back of the baby, who was sliding contentedly back into sleep.

"Have you decided what to name your babe?" Melissa asked.

Caroline shook her head. "We've talked a bit—Martin wants an Irish name so it will match with Gallagher, but until we know whether it's a boy or a girl, there's not much point in choosing. Whatever it is seems as if it will be as big as Randolph here is small. Look at me! When the doctor was here yesterday he shook his head and said he hoped the babe would come soon, looking at the size of me. Of course, since Martin is the father, who knows how enormous his child might be!"

She was laughing, but Melissa could hear an edge of worry in her voice. She knew from what Caroline had said about the birth of Henrietta—and more importantly, had not said—she had had a far more difficult time than Melissa had. It was might not be the size of their babies alone making the difference, but it must be easier for a small baby to slide out than a big one.

"Oh, you are not as big as all that," she said cheerfully, patting Caroline on her shoulder.

"He has gone to sleep again." Ethan spoke up. "He does a lot of that."

"Randolph is very new," Caroline said defensively, as if the babe were being criticized. "They do sleep a lot at the beginning, which is a good thing. Gives their mothers a rest."

"Randolph's mother has me," Ethan pointed out, and in fact he had not been back to Martin's office since the baby had been born. June was approaching, and the roads were fully clear. They had been for some time. He and Melissa had even been discussing whether it was not almost time for them to go north again.

It would be soon. Ethan had learned what he had come to learn, Randolph was safely here, and it was surely time for the Gallaghers to have their house to themselves. Still, it was true that Randolph was very new, and Melissa hoped to be there when Caroline's baby was born. To help, of course, but mainly just to be there. She knew what Caroline's presence had meant to her.

So not now. But soon.

May slid into June, and it began to seem that there might be a spring and summer after all. Dublin, the bleak city Ethan and Melissa had known only in the autumn and winter, turned out to enjoy a spring as well. Spring bulbs bloomed everywhere. The fragrance of hyacinths lifted the spirits of passersby. Dutch tulips exhibited a wonderful range of colors. When three weeks had passed, Melissa wrapped Randolph up warmly in a nest of blankets and took him for a walk in the Green. Caroline came with her part of the way, before deciding that she was simply too big to exhibit herself in public.

"It all would have been very well for you," she told Melissa, "You were perfectly presentable all the way to the end."

"Probably not. Remember I was lying down all the time, so there was never a chance for anyone to be embarrassed by my size."

"Be that as it may, I feel like a pregnant elephant." Caroline tried to wrap her pelisse firmly around herself, but there was plainly more of Caroline than there was of the pelisse. "It's nice enough for you to walk a bit farther. I am going back to the house while we are still close."

With which she turned around firmly and retreated.

Melissa took Randolph for a long, luxurious walk in the warmth, all around the perimeter of the Green. Almost everyone glanced at the baby, but only three older motherly women were bold enough to stop her and admire him. Melissa showed him off proudly, but as she walked away she thought how odd it was. She would never think to stop and talk to people she did not know before now. All the rules had changed. She was no longer an anonymous young woman. She was a mother, and the whole world—well, at least a reasonable part of it—took a proprietary sort of interest in new babies being born.

She came back to the house to find Randolph was to have infant company sooner than anyone had planned.

O'Malley let her in, and Ethan appeared from Martin's office immediately.

"It's begun," he said, and seeing Melissa's blank face, elaborated somewhat. "Caroline has started."

"What do you mean?" Melissa asked.

Ethan turned around and seemed relieved to see Bridget coming down the stairs. "Leave Randolph with Bridget, and you go see Caroline. Martin has sent for Dr. Malloy but he is nervous as a cat. I'm staying with him; you stay with Caroline until the doctor is there—or as long as she needs you."

Melissa handed the baby over. Providentially he had been fed just before they went on their walk, and had fallen asleep on the way home, so she could run up the staircase with a free mind for a little at least.

It seemed odd to go to the second staircase—she had not done that since Dr. Malloy had put her to bed after her fall—and run up those stairs as well to the bedroom suite overlooking the street and the Green.

"Caroline?" she asked tentatively, pushing the door already open a crack a little farther.

"Oh, Melissa." She hardly recognized Caroline's voice. She sounded as if she were on the edge of tears. "It started just like before—the waters broke and there's a terrible mess all over by the drawing room."

"Not now," Melissa reassured her. "I just came past there myself. They have cleaned it all up, so you must not worry about it. Have the pains started yet?"

Caroline nodded gloomily. "Where is Martin? I was so alone last time."

"Well, this time you will not be alone. I will be here except when Randolph needs feeding. Bridget has him and can bring him to me here. Martin is fluttering all over his office, from what Ethan told me, waiting for Dr. Malloy to come so he can escort him upstairs himself. You see? The maids know what to do and this time we are both experienced women, so there is nothing to worry about." She pulled over the closest chair and plumped herself firmly down into it. Thank goodness, she thought. Thank goodness we are still here.

And indeed this time the house and all its inhabitants were comfortably familiar with the process of childbirth. All, that is, except Martin, who had not been present during any part of Randolph's birth. Martin was plainly terrified now it was his wife suffering. He brought Dr. Malloy up to the bedroom, and then began on a series of lamentations mainly arising from his size and her size and the probability that the baby would be enormous and it would all be his fault and…

At which point Dr. Malloy asked Melissa to fetch Ethan, who could take Martin back downstairs and pour him some brandy or something, so that his woe would not be increasing Caroline's distress. Melissa did so, and came back to her chair by Caroline's side, all too plainly hearing Martin's distraught voice all the way down the stairs, until Ethan must have steered him into his office, and he was too far away to hear.

Caroline had mentioned casually that her experience of labor had been much more difficult than it seemed Melissa's had been, and watching it unfold again, Melissa saw with aching pity that it was apparently the same a second time.

"It should be easier, since she has already had one child," Dr. Malloy murmured to Melissa, "but there is something odd about this pregnancy. I'm not sure exactly what it is, but it feels different. Perhaps—Mrs. Hawthorne, would you be good enough to send one of the footmen to my house? I will give him a note to deliver to my butler. He can summon a wise old midwife I have worked with from time to time. I would like to have the benefit of her experience."

Caroline's eyes were closed and she seemed to be enduring another pain, so whether she heard or not Melissa was not sure. She looked at Caroline and tried not to speculate what might have persuaded the doctor to ask for assistance. He had made no such request when he was attending her, at least as far as she remembered. Was it an enormous baby? Caroline had certainly begun to look rounder before Melissa had. At the time Melissa had thought it probably had something to do with the circumstance that Caroline was married and the fact of her increasing was a positive delight to both of them. The situation had been entirely different for herself and Ethan, and she had done everything possible to mask what was happening to her body. Then, too, at the end of her pregnancy it was hard to determine how round her belly had become because she was always lying down, wearing loose-fitting nightclothes.

Time went on. There were intervals when Caroline lay back against the pillows, breathing hard and apparently recuperating, and then it would sweep over her again and she would be crushing Melissa's hand. How long could she bear watching Caroline's torture, Melissa wondered desperately, changing hands when she could so Caroline could hang on, but not squeeze the same hand each time.

The old midwife arrived in the middle of one of the spasms. She stood by the door, a hood over her head, and a crisp white apron that enveloped her dress. There were wrinkles all around her eyes, but her eyes themselves were keen and watchful. As Caroline's breathing gave some indication that she might be through that pain, the midwife approached the bed, and laid her hands on Caroline's belly. Her touch was so light that Caroline did not appear to notice it, but she ran her hands over both sides and around.

She looked over at Dr. Malloy. "Yes. You are right. There are two."

He nodded slowly. "I thought so. She is a twin herself."

"How long has it been?" the midwife asked.

He pulled out his pocket watch and consulted it. "Seven hours. I think I came here very close to when the waters broke."

Melissa, her eyes grown wide as saucers, said, "Yes. You were here within maybe half an hour." Her mind reeled. Caroline was having twins?

"How is the position?" the doctor asked. "I was not sure enough to investigate too closely. Her husband is a very large man, and I did not want to do a single large infant any injury."

The midwife nodded and smiled, her mouth full of crooked teeth. "Martin Gallagher," she said. "He is a good man, but large." She returned her hands to Caroline's belly. "Let me see," she murmured.

Caroline tossed her head. She seemed only partly aware of what was going on around her. The midwife leaned over her, and the midwife's body blocked Melissa's view of what she was doing but suddenly Caroline gave a great prolonged groan, and the midwife stepped away, nodding with some satisfaction.

"There," she said. "It should go swiftly now."

Dr. Malloy nodded sharply, and moved back to Caroline's side. Caroline groaned again, and he said, "Yes. The babe is moving now."

The midwife stepped away. "Both were trying to be born first," she said. "I would wager two sons. They will race each other from this time forward."

From that point everything happened at once. Caroline's eyes opened and her face took on a wholly absorbed concentration. "I must push," she choked out, and the doctor nodded and murmured something to her and with a sudden rush, a babe, coated with blood and mucus, slithered out into the doctor's hands.

It was indeed a boy.

Dr. Malloy glanced over at Melissa and smiled. "Go tell poor frightened Martin Gallagher that one son has been born, and there will be another child shortly."

The midwife was wiping off the babe and wrapping him in a soft blanket—could it be the same blanket that Randolph was wrapped in just a few weeks ago? The wrapped baby was handed to Caroline, who still looked dazed but with the start of joy lighting her face.

"Mrs. Gallagher, your son," the doctor said, as Caroline dropped Melissa's hand to reach for her baby.

"And another to come," the midwife told her as Melissa rose.

"Another?" She heard Caroline's bewildered voice as she shut the door behind her and darted to the stairway, across the great landing and past the drawing room, and to the grand staircase.

"Be careful!" Ethan roared up the steps at her.

Melissa, totally absorbed by her mission, stopped dead and looked at him as if she had never seen him before. "Caroline has had a son!" she cried out. "And there is another babe still to be born."

Ethan's face went blank. "Two?" he asked.

She had slowed her steps, and continued down the stairs. "Two. Where is Martin?"

Ethan ran up the last two or three steps, took her elbow firmly in his hand, and walked with her, slowly, down the same steps. "He's in his study."

They turned the corner together and walked to the study door.

"He's been suffering the torments of the damned," Ethan told her. "He's well past making sense. I hope it is more the panic than the whiskey, but he's had plenty of both."

He opened the door, and peered in, then opened it all the way.

Martin, looking much like an owl, was sitting at his desk, a glass and a bottle in front of him. Melissa had no idea how much had been in the bottle to start with, but there was considerably less than half there now.

"Have you been drinking as well?" she whispered.

"One to start with," Ethan muttered. "Say, Martin! You are the father of a son."

Martin blinked and straightened up carefully. "A son?"

"And another coming," Melissa put in.

Martin did not appear to know what to do with his face. A great grin had started until Melissa spoke, after which a curious blankness took over. "It's still happening?" he asked, his voice puzzled.

"Twins," Melissa said. "Caroline is giving birth to twins."

Martin made an incoherent noise and stumbled to his feet. "Twins." He started to march toward the wall rather than the door, and Ethan caught his elbow and managed to steer him to the opening. "Twins!" Martin shouted.

He continued to shout all the way up the stairs. Ethan pushed Melissa forward to grab his arm, and he stayed a step behind them, making sure that no one stumbled and the triumphant progress up the stairs be interrupted by a spectacular fall. The shouting and Ethan's watchful guidance continued up the next staircase, ending only when Martin, now leading the other two, exploded into the bedroom where Caroline was sitting against the pillows, a blanket wrapped infant in each arm.

"Caro, the magnificent!" Martin bellowed, and threw his arms around all three of them.

"Was it another boy?" Melissa whispered to the doctor.

"Mrs. McHaffey said it would be, and so it was," Dr. Malloy admitted.

The midwife, whose name only now did Melissa know, was no longer pristinely clean, but she smiled at the assembled crowd.

"Two great boys," she said. "Well done, Martin Gallagher."

34

FOR THE NEXT TWO WEEKS, Martin and Ethan amused each other greatly (although their wives took to rolling their eyes) by demanding every morning, "Anyone else born today?"

The newest residents of the house on the Green were promptly equipped with two new cradles.

"Well, of course Randolph can keep that one. We need two that match," Martin announced grandly.

In addition to the cradles, they acquired names: the firstborn son was Maghnus Benedict Gallagher, and the second, Niall Charles Gallagher, because Maghnus meant great or large, which he was bound to be, and Niall meant a champion, and both of them were names of Martin's two brothers. Then they each carried the name of a grandfather in the middle. Benedict was Martin's father and Charles was Caroline's.

With three practically brand new infants, life in the house on the Green seemed to function on a 24 hour clock, with light brightening the windows at any hour of the night or day. There were also new faces. It had not taken more than a day or so for Caroline to grasp the point that more washerwomen were needed considering the volume of clean laundry now required. Then, too, even with Henrietta being a single child Caroline had had a nursemaid to help cope, and now that there were two...well, it seemed obvious. Two new fresh-faced young Irish girls, both the oldest daughter in large families and thus accustomed to dealing with infants, joined the household. Agnes took possession of Maghnus because when being introduced he punched her in the eye with a wandering fist, and Clare wanted Niall because he had just been fed and when presented burped, producing a milky white mouth that curved into what would be a smile when he got older.

As the Gallaghers groped with the ramifications of suddenly becoming a family of five rather than three, the Hawthornes were beginning to sort out their possessions. The volume seemed to have multiplied out of all reason. Even so, it was time to return north with their new son to present him to the family and the place that would sometime in the very distant future be his to care for. He was continuing to grow larger rapidly. Since the Gallagher infants were in fact twins, neither was as large as each might have been had his been a single birth. So although Randolph was three weeks older (a fact he would almost certainly use to his advantage when in later years the boys came together), the three of them were very close to the same size. Sorting out which garments belonged to which therefore was a major challenge, even with the best will in the world.

"I'm sure some of these must be yours," Melissa fussed as she surveyed the pile of nappies she had been presented with. Ethan, who had listened to her lament about the problem of dividing up the infant clothes, came up with the brilliant suggestion that a spot of ink on a hidden corner would distinguish Randolph clothes from Maghnus and Niall clothes.

So Melissa was sitting, quill pen in hand, ready to mark, but she could not believe the height of the pile.

"Oh, for heaven's sake, Melissa, don't worry about it," Caroline said comfortably. She was nursing Niall at the time—she was almost always nursing one or the other—and Henrietta was playing at her feet. "It's not as if nappies are the price of rubies. If we need more, we can send out Agnes or Clare to get some more. I promise you, it will be much easier for me to do that in Dublin than for you to do it at Kendall House. I've lived there, I will remind you, and Drogheda, which is the closest town, is not up to what we expect after the conveniences of Dublin."

"I shall miss Dublin." Melissa was almost surprised to hear herself say that, because of course although she had lived there nearly a year, almost all of the time it had been either too cold to go out pleasurably or she had been confined to bed.

Which Caroline pointed out to her.

"I know," Melissa admitted. "But I felt the city had much more available."

Of course it did. They had been taking advantages of Dublin's variety recently. Bridget would take care of Randolph while she and Ethan went out for the evening, sometimes to a concert, sometimes to the theater. It was odd, but unlike the average pair, most of what would normally be considered courtship activities were taking place when they were not only already married but parents. But the warmth and joy she had seen in Ethan's face when Randolph was born was still there, in delicious flashes. Added to that, the pleasure of being alone together was wonderfully new.

"Is Bridget still quite determined to go with you?" Caroline asked. She now had Niall over her shoulder, patting his back with experienced ease.

"Yes, and I'm more glad than I can say you agreed to let her go with us. I hope she will not mind being so far from Dublin and her family, but it is a positive blessing to have someone who knows us and knows Randolph. I don't know if you could say yet that Randolph knows her, but she must be part of his familiar world. Oh, for goodness sakes," she exclaimed suddenly, realizing that she had managed to get an identifying ink mark not only on the nappy but on her own finger. "And I picked this ink because Ethan promised me it was long lasting."

She laid down the nappy on her knee, set the quill pen on the blotter, and looked around for something to wipe it off with. They were in Caroline's sitting room, where the two of them had spent so many hours over the course of this year.

Caroline handed her a somewhat stained burp cloth.

"I shall miss your house, and you, of course," Melissa said wistfully, wiping absent-mindedly. "I will miss the sounds of traffic around the Green, and the cozy evenings when Ethan and Martin came home. It is strange now Ethan no longer goes to the office, but works in Martin's study. I suppose it will be like that at Kendall House."

"Probably," Caroline said. Niall had fallen asleep, and she held him cradled in her elbow. "Remember, you will be living the life both of us were brought up to lead. Martin is the one who has the odd pattern of life, compared to our families. Your father did not go out to work any more than mine did. I think one of the great things having you here has done for me is to help me get used to this different pattern, because I had always had Anne. I am so glad Martin gave me that cottage not far from Kendall House so I can go up with the children—just think of that, Melissa, me with three children!—and spend time with you and Anne in the old way."

Yes, Anne, Melissa thought. She would enjoy Anne so much more now their lives would be so similar.

"Hugh and Martin get along well together, do they not?" she asked Caroline.

"To the extent that they have spent time together," Caroline said. "It will be interesting to watch as time goes on and we see more of each other. I know Martin will want to go north if only to have the chance to visit with Ethan and find out how he is doing and share all of his own news with him."

"I am going to make more of an effort to spend time with Hugh." Melissa heard the sincerity in her own voice, and smiled. "When I stayed with them first I'm afraid I was young and self-centered and most of all indignant I had been shipped off to Ireland."

"That's right. You were, were you not?" Caroline laughed. "I had forgotten all about that. How comical to remember it now when I see you sitting here marking nappies and looking so content. And that pretty ring on your finger. I suppose it is just as well you came here!"

She stood with the baby in her arms, looking down at him fondly. "Do I dare to take him to the nursery myself, or will that rouse Maghnus instantly and I'll be back sitting here feeding him? Perhaps I should just summon Clare and wait until Agnes comes with Maghnus a little later." She reached for her little silver bell, and then dropped her hand.

"It's not fair to make Maghnus wait because I just fed Niall," she decided. "Besides, what I really need is a fresh pot of tea. Everybody— Dr. Malloy and both Clare and Agnes keep saying I need to drink a lot to have milk for both of them. I certainly am eating all the time. Would you like me to run down to the kitchen after I've given Niall back and get tea and biscuits for both of us? After all, you're feeding Randolph, too."

Melissa nodded enthusiastically, and as Caroline left the room, thought with a sudden pang, I shall miss this. I shall miss this.

But when they were finally all bundled into the elegant coach Ethan had hired for the trip home, she found the prospect of things to come more exciting than it had been during the busy days of preparation for the journey. The nappies were marked; Randolph's clothes laundered and packed, the miscellaneous treasures she and Ethan had acquired during the momentous year were in boxes or trunks. Ethan had had a single small trunk when he had arrived, he pointed out, and how that one trunk had multiplied itself into three he could not quite calculate. Besides the three there was a pile of boxes, in one of them the white fur bonnet and muff. Not to be left out, Bridget had her case, her eyes bright with excitement at the prospect of a journey.

It was the final goodbye. Melissa had climbed into the carriage once, and then remembered she was going to take some of the bulbs from the back garden to plant at Kendall House—Caroline had helped her wrap them in brown paper—and here she was coming so close to forgetting them! They were restored to her, and handed to Ethan to find some place for them. Bridget was already seated, Randolph mercifully asleep in her arms. Would he remember this house? Well, not from this time, but as the adults were all making plans for the next time they would see each other, it certainly seemed that down the years…

"Come *along*, Melly dear," Ethan was saying, standing not quite as patiently as he had been by the carriage door, waiting to hand her in.

Melissa, giving Caroline what had to be the second or third final hug, detached herself reluctantly and gave Ethan her gloved hand. He helped her to her place, climbed in himself, and then quickly, as if he feared she might pop out of the carriage again, shut the door firmly.

"Goodbye! Goodbye!" The voices called back and forth, becoming merged into a single sound of farewell. Passers-by looked at the loaded carriage gradually easing into motion and at Caroline and Martin, O'Malley behind them in the door, all three waving, and smiled themselves, taking pleasure in the warmth of friendship.

"Oh my, it is going to be quiet with only the three of us." Melissa sighed, leaning back against the well-upholstered seat.

"Remember Aunt Elizabeth and Uncle Charles will be there."

She smiled at him. "I know. But I shall miss Henrietta running about."

Ethan looked at Randolph, still sleeping in Bridget's arms. "It will not be long before our own son is running about, making a racket."

"It's hard to imagine." She looked around, running a hand over the richly upholstered seat. "This is a lovely carriage. It must cost the earth."

"I have become a man of means, my love," Ethan said. "You do remember me going to work like a real business man?"

Melissa looked at him warily. "Yes," she admitted.

"Well, it seems Martin has banked for us my portion of what has been earned while I was there. I am going to be bringing Uncle Charles some peace of mind and resources we can fall back on if at any time it seems the estate needs building up. More than that, Martin has taught me how money makes money, so until it is needed, my gold will be making more gold for us."

"Gold makes more gold?" Melissa beamed at him. "The way people make more people?"

"Not quite the same method." Her husband grinned at her. "But I am certainly prepared to undertake both. Do you think Randolph may be in need of another Randolph?"

Melissa blushed and looked over at Bridget, but her maid seemed to be nodding off already with the movement of the carriage. The baby slept in her arms.

"Well, perhaps. A girl this time would be a nice change," she murmured.

"A sister? If she looks anything like her mother, she will be a gift to the next generation of young men." He ran his fingers through her curls, as he so much liked to do. "Is there any way to guarantee that she will have her mother's hair? You have the most beautiful hair, dear heart. I think that is what I fell in love with first. A pretty face, looking out from under a mass of red gold curls."

"Ethan, my love." Melissa felt like a cat, purring. "I don't know what she would look like, but I do think a girl might be nice."

"We will have to see what can be done, Melly mine," her husband said, and taking no notice of who might see him, kissed her firmly in his own particularly delightful way as the carriage crossed the river, going north.

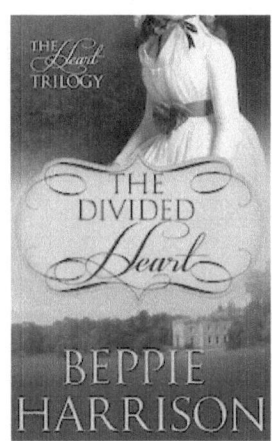

THE DIVIDED HEART

Lady Anne Hawthorne, the daughter of an Anglo-Irish earl whose family has been established in Ireland for many generations, finds herself torn between two warring communities: green and lovely Ireland and its rebellious Irish people, and the English who have prospered there during centuries of domination. She meets two men, one a reckless Irishman and the other a handsome Englishman, come to Ireland to take up his inherited title and estate. Before she makes up her mind on what to do, Anne has to decide where her heart belongs. Is she to be English or Irish?

– Available Now –

THE BROKEN HEART

It is 1811, the wondrous year when Lady Caroline Hawthorne will at last leave provincial Ireland and make her way to the elegance and excitement of London—the center of her dreams for years past. Indeed, Caroline sails across the Irish Sea to make her debut in all the splendor of the Season, and it seems all of her dreams are coming true. She falls in love with the Earl of Linnell, the heir to his father, the Duke of Apthorp, and he is enchanted by her. They marry that summer, and happily ever after begins.

But happily ever after is transformed into aching heartbreak, and Caroline stumbles from the heights of romance to the emptiness of despair. Forced into starting again by the unexpected cruelty of events spinning out of her control, Caroline must find the path back to an endurable pattern of life, trying not to hope, learning to deal with life as it is. And, should love come again, will she dare open her heart again to meet it?

– Available Now –

THE GRANDEST CHRISTMAS

Back in Ireland of 1815, everyone knew of the enormous gulf between ordinary people and the Anglo-Irish aristocracy. Elleanor Maguire of County Clare is as conscious of it as anyone else, and yet for this Christmas she is being tugged over the boundary to celebrate the holiday with her magnificent Uncle Martin, who has married into as grand a family as exists. Elleanor's heart has been broken and Uncle Martin is convinced a touch of luxury will help. But when Elleanor flounders in unfamiliar territory, there is the steward of the estate, John Bowyer, to reach out a hand of understanding. Given the differences of age and experience between them, can understanding turn into more under the mistletoe?

– Available Soon –

ABOUT THE AUTHOR

Beppie Harrison has hopscotched across the world during her life. She spent her childhood in Hawaii, then first moved to California, and later New York. She married an Englishman and lived in London for the first ten years of her marriage, and spent considerable time in Ireland since. She has four children, two home-grown, one adopted from Thailand and another from Chile. She has published eight non-fiction books before she switched to fiction. She now lives in Michigan with her husband and two indignant cats.

Visit her online at www.beppieharrison.com.

www.ingramcontent.com/pod-product-compliance
Lightning Source LLC
Chambersburg PA
CBHW050019180626
46810CB00002B/489